FILTHY HOT

THE FIVE POINTS' MOB COLLECTION: FIVE

SERENA AKEROYD

Created with Vellum

WARNING

THE FOLLOWING story contains scenes that allude to:

- Violence/Graphic Torture
- Child Sexual Abuse
- Rape
- Suicide

Take this trigger warning to heart.
Please.
<3

AUTHOR NOTE

DEAR READER,

Light of my life.

Accepter of my craziness.

(Hopefully) adorer of my Feckers.

There are some scenes in this one... Trust in the trigger warning. Back away. Please. <3 But you can have faith that I never write anything with the view to being gratuitous.

And know this, I'm angry on your behalf. If you're a survivor, feel each hit and know I'd make them bleed for you.

With that being said...

Welcome back to Hell's Kitchen.

May you fall for this Fecker as much as you've *tumbled* for his brothers.

Much love,

Serena

xoxo

O
O'DONNELLY

THE CROSSOVER READING ORDER WITH THE FIVE POINTS

FILTHY
NYX
LINK
FILTHY RICH
SIN
STEEL
FILTHY DARK
CRUZ
MAVERICK
FILTHY SEX
HAWK
FILTHY HOT
STORM
THE DON (Coming Soon)
THE LADY (Coming Soon)
FILTHY SECRET (Coming Soon)

PLAYLIST

If you'd like to hear a curated soundtrack, with songs that are featured in the book, as well as songs that inspired it, then here's the link:

https://open.spotify.com/playlist/3S0xW7QBs5ileBs0QHSjNk

ONE

FINN

TWENTY-SEVEN YEARS AGO

"DID you think Conor was being weird?"

I frowned at Aidan Jr. "Huh?"

"You really need me to repeat myself?"

"Not my fault you mumble," I groused. "But Conor's weird all the time. How can you tell the difference?"

"This was more different than normal."

I rolled my eyes but, still, I'd bite. "How do you judge between regular weird and different weird?"

"I don't know," he mused as he threw his hacky sack against the ceiling, the rhythmic bang-bang-bang was almost enough to make me zone out.

Aidan Sr. said that Junior had hand-eye coordination issues, ones that meant he could never hit a target no matter how many hours they spent at the gun range.

Of course, Junior didn't have diddly-squat wrong with his eyes, he just didn't have his father's hunger for blood.

But how the hell did you explain that to one of the most feared men on the East Coast?

It was a surprisingly easy question to answer—you didn't.

As a result, Aidan had gone to no less than three eye specialists, with each one telling his father that Aidan's eyesight wasn't just twenty-twenty—he could have flown a fucking jet plane if he wanted.

When the eye tests hadn't worked, then had come therapeutic techniques—throwing the hacky sack against the ceiling with one eye closed, and catching it with the opposite hand.

It wasn't working.

Junior had the mafia equivalent of the yips.

"He looked like he was going to puke."

I frowned, thinking about Aidan's words, and trying to judge if he was overreacting or not. Trouble was, Aidan wasn't that kind of guy. Just because he hadn't killed someone yet didn't mean his instincts weren't spot on.

"I guess he looked a little shaky," I murmured, rolling onto my side to peer at him.

Aidan's bedroom was the size of my old apartment. I'd always loved hanging out here, and not just because he had cool shit, like that Super Mario Bros. game and the Nintendo console that I'd been dying to get my hands on for ages, but because Lena was nice and always had plenty of food on the table for us to eat, and though Aidan Sr. was certifiable, he was really cool with me.

Junior had a TV of his own, as well as cable, and a mini fridge—why the hell wouldn't I want to live here?

More than that though, *he* was here.

Was it whacked to think of him as more than a friend?

I wasn't a guy he'd picked to be on his crew when he grew up. That first day of school all those years back, we'd gravitated toward each other and had stuck together ever since. It wasn't like we were gay or anything. It was... Well, I guessed it was odd. He felt like he was my brother.

Which meant his kid brothers were mine too.

He and I had always been close, but since I'd moved in, it cemented things.

The O'Donnellys might be crazy, they might be more infamous

than Capone in the area, might terrify most people, but they were family. They'd taken me in when I was at my lowest and they'd saved my ass. I really fucking wished that wasn't literally.

"He's going to choir practice, right?" I asked, trying to think back to what Conor had said when he'd come to Aidan's room earlier.

"Yeah," Aidan confirmed.

An uneasy feeling settled in my gut and though I knew it might open a can of worms, I muttered, "I don't like that priest."

"Father McKenna? What's not to like? He gives us fewer Hail Marys than Father Doyle. Plus, his sermons don't drone on for-fucking-ever.

"Shit, I almost wish he'd take over full time. Does Father Doyle really need to come back from the Vatican?"

There was no denying the sermons were shorter, and the confessional 'punishments' weren't as taxing, but some guys just gave off a vibe, didn't they? A creep factor. I knew how that worked. My dad had that in fucking spades.

Nerves hit me, even though it was stupid to feel anything other than stuffed full after Lena had crammed roast pork down my stomach like it was going out of fashion. It wasn't like Mom hadn't fed me, but food just tasted better here.

Maybe because I was safe?

Because I knew nothing could touch me inside these walls?

I knew how it felt to feel vulnerable inside your own home, even worse I knew how it felt to see a man look at me like *that*.

Like I wasn't some kid, a nuisance, but as if I were tasty.

Conor was a weirdo, and he definitely did unusual shit but if Aidan said he looked like he could puke, then there had to be a reason for it.

Cautiously, I asked, "Do you think he's one of them? That's why Conor's scared?"

The pounding of the hacky sack against the ceiling slowed. "One of them, what?"

"A perv."

"Who?" His eyes bugged as he gaped at me, and I knew then and there he'd never thought anything about the new guy other than the fact that he was better than Father Doyle because his sermons were shorter. "The priest?" he rasped. "A fucking pervert?"

I growled, and it was stupid to be pissed but I couldn't help it. I was glad he'd never been a target of a sick fuck but his disbelief grated on me—in my short life, I hadn't been so lucky. "Yeah, Aidan, the fucking priest. Not Conor. Jesus."

He rolled onto his side. "A kiddy diddler?"

"Yeah," I said gruffly.

"Shit, I just thought Conor was being picked on at choir practice or something. That's a big leap, Finn. Anyway, Da wouldn't just castrate anyone who touched his kids, he'd—"

Butting in, I countered, "Haven't you noticed?"

"Noticed what?"

"How McKenna is?" I grumbled. "He's always touching."

"He's Irish," Aidan said slowly. "You know it's their way. Da hugs and kisses me. He ain't a pedo."

"He's usually drunk when he does too," I retorted.

"True." Aidan scowled. "You've given me a bad feeling, Finn."

"You're the one who started it."

"Being bullied and being messed with are totally different things."

I just shrugged.

He wasn't wrong.

Maybe I was projecting my own experiences on this. Hunting for shadows where there were none to be found.

I didn't look at men the same anymore. I knew what they were, what they could do. What they were capable of. But just because someone was creepy didn't mean they were sick too.

Hoping Aidan didn't think my leap was too large, that he didn't piece shit together, I didn't say anything, just waited for the hacky sack to start being tossed again because that meant Aidan thought I was overreacting.

Only, it didn't.

I really wished it would.

"What if you're right?" Aidan questioned after a couple minutes.

"I'm not. I was just thinking worst case—"

"Conor's not afraid of anyone. You know that. He's a headcase."

My lips twitched but I couldn't deny he was right. Conor was either going to turn into his father or Ted Bundy. I wasn't sure which yet. Or maybe he'd be neither. He was a cool kid, just had more energy than someone hopped up on coke, but had the ability to focus on inane shit which meant he'd have been skipping grades like they were hurdles and he was at the Olympics if his dad had allowed it.

I'd seen the little nut complete a two-thousand piece jigsaw in less than ninety minutes, and the way he could talk back to Aidan Sr. without getting slapped upside the head was genius in and of itself.

"Do you think we should check?"

"The community center is only around the corner," he pointed out.

Unease and, though I didn't like to think it—*instinct*—had me jumping to my feet. "Come on. It won't do any harm to check."

Aidan scampered to a standing position too, and he shoved me in the side, muttering, "You got me freaked out for no reason at all."

"I'll bet. He'll just be looking green because Brennan was talking about how pork is the closest meat to human flesh over dinner."

We shared a glance, and I had no idea why, but that look had both of us taking off at a run.

Aidan Sr. believed in living close to his territory, but also, in living near his church. Only in this part of Hell's Kitchen, Five Points, was a regular priest like the Pope. Aidan Sr. treated them as if they were the fucking second coming but everyone knew that was because he was obsessed with heaven.

Either heaven or just not going to hell, I wasn't sure which and I wasn't about to ask him.

In all honesty, as Aidan and I raced out of the apartment building, down the street to St. Patrick's and onward to the community center, I wasn't sure if I wanted to think that heaven could house people like Sr. If it did, well, that was fucked up. We all knew the shit he'd done. Whispers of it were a constant serenade in this part of the city...

Heaven needed harsher entry requirements if Aidan Sr. was in line for a penthouse overlooking St. Peter's pearly gates was all I'd say.

We made it to the center, with me reaching the entranceway first. I wasn't sure why, but I raised a finger to my lips, telling Aidan to be quiet, and slowly opened the door.

I heard no sounds.

No singing.

Conor was a soprano. His voice was so high, Sr. said the angels could hear him when he sang. Brennan said that was why Conor was his favorite, but I didn't really think their da *had* favorites. He treated them all the same—like toy soldiers.

Aidan and I shared another look as we walked in and found an empty hall.

"They meet here, don't they?"

Aidan shrugged. "They do when Father Doyle isn't living it up large with the Pope."

"Conor wouldn't lie about choir practice," I said uneasily. Normally, I'd have laughed but I just felt so on edge that even dissing our least favorite person couldn't knock me out of this frame of mind.

"Only if he woke up this morning and decided he wanted to lose a finger. You know what Da's like. No lying or else."

Though he was being serious, Aidan punctuated that by rolling his eyes.

After a while, the constant threats, the dire warnings, and the promises of retribution were like water rolling off a duck's back—I got it. I'd reached that point too.

"Should we check the church?"

"The door was closed. It was padlocked."

My brows rose. "That's strange. It's never locked."

"It *is* strange. You're right." It was Aidan who was looking green around the edges now. "Fuck, Finn, what's going on?"

"We could get in through the basement window. The lock on it is faulty," I said, thinking fast. "We could check it out?"

"Yeah, I think we should. How do you know it's faulty?"

"They keep getting it fixed but it never works. Anyway you weren't the one who had to spend the summer there with Father O'Brian."

Aidan's lips twitched. "I remember. For stink bombing the confessional."

My nose crinkled—not my finest hour.

As we ran out of the empty community center, we raced down the street toward the church that was like the beacon of light in this part of our territory. Whenever I stepped foot on holy ground, I expected angels to either start singing or for demons to try and grab me because I was sullied, a sinner, and I was entering God's home.

Maybe my imagination was too wild but I always sucked in a breath whenever I crossed the gates, awaiting that first response from Upstairs or Downstairs.

Because this wasn't a fucking movie, I didn't get either, and though relief hit me, I didn't stop, racing across the small patch of grass we weren't supposed to walk on never mind run on, then veering around the side of the church to the basement window I knew we could break open.

Once we made it there, I dropped to my knees, looked at the lock and found myself relieved that the idiots hadn't replaced the window yet. Jimmying it up, I rolled through the window because it was about six feet wide but only two feet or so deep, and barely managed to stop myself from colliding with the ground face first.

Aidan's descent was a lot more graceful, but that was him. Light on his feet.

"It's creepy down here," Aidan muttered as we maneuvered around the boiler, a lot of shit they stored down here—shit I'd put here which was one of the reasons I knew about the window—and toward the doorway.

We exited into the hallway that housed a couple of offices and which led to the south transept where, over the sounds of our breathing, it was whisper-quiet.

I was used to it humming with life because to be a Five Pointer was to be at ease with this place. The church was a home away from goddamn home.

The air itself seemed to throb though, like it was quiet but charged. Whether that was from our tension or not, I didn't know.

"Where are they holding practice if it isn't here or in the community center?" I grumbled.

"I don't know. But I've got a weird feeling. You were right before. Conor wouldn't lie to Da."

No. He wouldn't.

I moved over to the altar, tipping my head back to stare at the murals that had terrified me as a kid. They'd seemed to soar upwards back then, like they were reaching for heaven itself.

With my eyes on *Heaven on Earth*, I often asked why God had forsaken me whenever I made my way to take the sacrament, and I asked again here, now, when the church was quieter than it had ever been and the very noiselessness made my ears ring.

My relationship with God was a weird one, and in my world, questioning my faith, any doubts at all weren't acceptable.

Aidan popped up at my side and I watched him heft one of the candlesticks from the altar in his hand, murmuring, "Any other parish, these probably would have been stolen by now."

Grateful for the interruption, I snorted. "Aidan Sr.'s wrath is too Old Testament for anyone's stomach. He's better than ADT at keeping thieves away."

"True," he agreed. "Can you imagine him stuffing three thousand locusts down someone's throat?"

"Yeah." I shuddered. "The hard part would be finding three thousand locusts."

Both of us snickered at that, then we heard it.

A sob.

Followed by a hushed whisper.

Everything inside me stilled. Freezing solid.

Another whisper. A choked gasp.

Aidan's hand tightened about the candlestick, and I reached back, grabbing the nearest thing to me and, hefting it, we stalked forward.

Both of us knew to be quiet without even looking at one another, and we whispered down the aisle like ghosts.

"Confessional," I murmured on a breath, veering toward the booth, him at my back.

I reached for the door to the priest's section, and I was glad—glad because it meant I could spare Aidan this. No brother should have to see what I was witnessing, and I'd already been through much worse.

The priest had his hands on Conor's head—

No.

Just, no.

Hatred bloomed inside me.

I didn't just see the priest and Conor, I saw me and my father. I saw the shit that fuckers on the streets had done to other homeless kids who were just trying to fill their stomachs. Things that I might have had to endure if Aidan hadn't figured out I'd run from home and that I needed somewhere to live.

The second the door opened, the priest jumped, and though it took me a second to process everything, it took him longer. By the time his hands had stopped holding Conor down, mine were working.

I reached forward and slammed the altar ornament into the priest's head, only then realizing it was a plate. A fucking plate.

Christ.

With him dazed after my hit, more from my brute force than the shape of my weapon, I grabbed Conor's shoulder and pulled him away. His face was tear sore, pink, his eyes drenched. Terror and hope and hatred and wrath blurred into one in his gaze, and while I thought he'd be down for it, I growled, "You don't want to see this, Conor."

He snarled, wiping his hands over his wet cheeks, as I dragged him away. "I do!" Bloodthirsty little shit.

Ignoring him now I'd shoved him out of the way, I reached into the confessional and went to grab the priest by the throat, but he was on his knees now, sobbing, his hands in the prayer pose as he pleaded with God for forgiveness.

He hadn't tried to run so that meant he knew what was about to go down.

"You'll need more than God to forgive you," I rasped. "When Aidan Sr. finds out—"

"No!" Conor wailed. "Da can never find out!" He snatched the plate from me and made to hurl it at the priest, but Aidan was there, the heavy gold candlestick held high as he commanded grimly, "Conor, move back."

"Leave this to your da," I urged. "He'll make the bastard pay."

But Aidan wasn't here anymore.

The kid who found it hard to shoot targets even though he had twenty-ten vision had left the building.

The kid who played Super Mario and howled whenever Freddie Krueger got busy with it was no more.

In that moment, I saw Aidan Jr. ascend to his place as his father's heir, and all for the love of his baby brother.

The candlestick swung high before he brought it down, lodging it in McKenna's shoulder as blood sprayed, bone shattered. The gold ornament stuck fast, making the priest howl as Aidan dragged him out of the booth by it, with him flailing around like a dead fish. The way it was wedged into his shoulder would have made another person gag, but we weren't just 'any' people—we were Five Pointers.

Aidan and me might be fifteen, Conor might only be seven, but violence was in our veins.

Seeing that Jr. wasn't about to stop, I shoved Conor over to a pew and said, "Stay."

"You're not the boss of me, Finn," he growled, but for all his ferocity now his big brother was here to protect him, I couldn't stop overlaying what I'd seen mere minutes before.

His mouth—

My stomach churned. "You don't want blood on your hands, Conor. You're not made for that."

He frowned at me as McKenna's wails to God turned into an endless chant now Aidan was bashing him to fucking pieces with one of the altarpieces.

Conor swiped at his snotty nose, mumbling, "What am I made for?"

"I don't know," I told him, meaning it. Not in a bad way, I just knew Conor was special. Somehow, what I'd thought earlier about him either being like his da or Ted Bundy had shifted. Not because of what I'd seen, just what I'd realized. "I don't think blood is your path." He was way too fucking smart to be wasted on the streets.

"Grab his feet, Finn," Aidan growled, and I jerked my attention back to the scene, grimacing when I saw the state of the priest.

Blood had pooled beneath him, spattering around the pews, getting into the cracks in the tiles. His groin was a matted mess of torn flesh, and through it all, with every strike of that fucking candlestick to his body, McKenna prayed.

He begged for forgiveness.

He prayed for absolution.

Not once did he apologize to Conor.

Not once did he say he was sorry for what he did, just that he was sorry for falling into temptation.

Like a seven-year-old boy could ever be that.

As if he could fall into the same category as eating too many fucking cookies.

Aidan wanted me to hold him down, but I couldn't bear to hear him pray any longer so I turned to Conor and asked, "Do you have your Swiss Army Knife?"

His bottom lip wobbled as he nodded. I saw shame flicker over his face, crisscrossing his features and I knew he was thinking that I thought bad of him for not using the weapon.

But he was seven.

A kid.

Forced by a man who held our eternal souls in his hands to do something heinous.

Forced by a man who his father revered.

In our parish, a priest was not just next to God, he might as well have been God himself.

I clapped him on the shoulder as he passed me the pen knife, and I raced over to the bastard's side and smacked my fist into his jaw. That shut him up, thank Christ, but his head rocked back and forth, his eyelashes fluttering as I pressed my now-aching hand to his nose, squeezing the nostrils until his lips parted. After he gasped for breath, I let my fingers dart inside his mouth and pulled on his tongue.

"There's no forgiveness for you, you fucker," I growled as I hacked at it with the pen knife.

The second the blade was lodged deep, I grabbed his hair and dragged his head back as I sawed off the muscle that would let him talk with God.

Not anymore.

Let the motherfucker try to worm his way out of this without the ability to speak anymore.

He wailed and writhed, choking and sputtering, screaming and shaking as he gulped down blood, but Aidan did me a solid and held him down.

"May you burn in hell," I ground out, and it was eerie as fuck because Aidan said that at the exact same time as I did.

"May you burn in hell."

Blood gushed from his mouth, spurting all over us, and as the copious wounds on his body began to take effect, we watched as the mashed up flesh that had once been a son of Christ left this mortal coil and was slowly accepted into Satan's embrace.

As the light flickered in his eyes, I gave him the only last rites he deserved: "I hope demons fuck you in the ass with hot pokers for the rest of eternity."

And he died.

Which solved one problem, but triggered a whole host of others.

Aidan, panting from the brute force he'd used, stared down at the corpse like he was just waking up, like he was just starting to register what he'd done.

"Call Uncle Paddy," Conor ordered, his voice clearer now, satisfaction lacing it but also, authority.

I turned to look at him while Aidan stayed staring at the bloody mass on the church floor—his first kill.

Seeing the change in Conor lessened my nerves. His lips wobbled a little and his eyes were still wet, but they were burning with relief now that they were pinned on McKenna's corpse. His trauma was slowly coming under lock and key as his brain whirred to life.

"You sure?" I questioned.

"Paddy isn't reliable," Aidan argued shakily, wiping his sweaty forehead with the back of his hand and smearing blood everywhere. His voice was definitely home to a quiver, but he seemed to take strength in the change in Conor too. "He's my godfather as well, Conor, but you know what he's like. Grandda used to say he's got less use to the Firm than a chocolate teapot, and you know Da agrees."

His younger brother dipped his chin, and for the first time since the priest had perished, stared right at me. "Uncle Paddy will know what to do," he declared, sounding more confident than a seven-year-old should. Never mind one who'd just been raped.

I knew he wanted me to convince Aidan, but shit, there was no convincing him. Like his da, he did what he wanted, *when* he wanted.

"He's good at avoiding Da's wrath," Aidan admitted begrudgingly.

"Uncle Paddy's smarter than he lets people think," Conor retorted, his tone firming.

"We should just tell Da," Aidan argued.

But Conor's confidence crumbled. Like a house of cards going up in smoke, the vulnerable kid of before made an abrupt reappearance. "No!"

"He won't judge you," Aidan said softly, his shoulders slumping when Conor started to cry again. "He'll be glad we—"

"No! Please, Aidan. Please! I don't want him to know." His tears morphed into sobs, his small frame shaking and trembling as he stood there, arms wrapped around his stomach, pleading with us.

Aidan and I shared a look, and the change in Conor, so abrupt and sharp, made me want to do as he urged. It did the same with Aidan too. I just hoped Conor's faith in Paddy O'Donnelly wasn't wasted. Because if he didn't help, we were fucked. Maybe not as badly as McKenna, but still screwed.

The second Aidan Sr. learned we'd killed a priest, without being told what that fucker was doing to his son, was a day *we'd* have to endure an eternity of being fucked with hot pokers too.

While I knew my place was in hell, dying at fifteen wasn't on my bucket list.

Especially when this wasn't something I could confess to, not in this church, anyway...

TWO

AIDAN

PRESENT DAY - JULY

"I HAVEN'T DONE ANYTHING, Mr. O'Donnelly! I swear!" Wintersen screamed at me.

Ignoring him as well as that gnawing ache in my belly for another tablet, I asked, "You looked where you shouldn't have looked. You touched what you shouldn't have touched. And you dared desire something that will never, ever belong to scum like you."

I picked up the bottle of caustic soda, and approached the bench I had him tied to. His head was duct-taped in place, his hands and that barrel-like stomach were secured as well.

"I'm the last face you'll ever see, Wintersen. But don't worry, you won't be blind for long."

I upended the bottle over his face, making sure the full flood went into his eyes, which I'd taped open.

His screams were a sweet serenade.

"This is what you get," I shouted, louder than his cries as the chemicals corroded soft tissue and turned it into mulch, "when you even think about touching something that belongs to an O'Donnelly."

THREE

LODESTAR

PRESENT DAY - NOVEMBER

"YOU KNOW WHAT A SUPER RECOGNIZER IS?"

I cast the leader of the Satan's Sinners' MC, West Orange Chapter, a dismissive look. "Of course, I do, Rex. They're very rare—" My words waned as I figured out where he was going with this.

A super recognizer was someone who had the ability to always remember a face down to every last detail.

Scotland Yard had a team of them monitoring CCTV footage, and they'd been proven to be more accurate than computers at scanning a face, registering it, and then finding it amid a crowd.

"You're one?" I shot a look at the ex-sex slave who'd been rescued by the MC. She was sitting opposite me at the kitchen table I'd staked out as my work surface.

Amara dipped her chin, her gaze on the table.

A part of me wondered if that was a sign of her nerves, or proof she was lying, but maybe it was neither. Maybe it was a force of habit, and not just submissiveness or anxiety or bullshit.

We'd shared a similar life path, unfortunately for us, but that was about as much as we had in common. It didn't make me trust her. Quite the opposite, in fact.

"She says that some of the people who owned her were New World Sparrows."

Eagerness filled me as I leaned forward. Suddenly, Amara had become very interesting. "You telling the truth?" If she wasn't, then I'd have to rip her a new one for trying to mess with me.

I didn't have the luxury of time that I could waste.

She nodded, but remained quiet, allowing a brother in the MC to defend her.

I batted his words away and chose to focus on her.

"So, what gives? What do you want, Amara? You tell me, as well, not these guys. You got a mouth on you, don't you?"

Her gaze darted to mine, and her eyes were loaded with a wildness I didn't necessarily understand but could empathize with.

"Every man who ever raped me, who owned me, who tortured and abused me, I can describe them in great detail," she whispered. "They haunt my every waking moment. I know they were important men. I know they were Sparrows. I know I can help."

"I figured you could put them through a facial recognition program, Lodestar. We'd be able to put the faces to names, and we'd finally be able to start taking those Sparrow sons of bitches down."

I didn't bother looking at Rex, just kept my eyes trained on her. "And what's in it for you, Amara?"

I didn't trust selflessness.

Everyone was selfish.

To be human was to be selfish.

Her smile, when it came, was soft. So soft that it made me think she was going to say something completely different than what she actually uttered:

"I get to kill them."

Now *that* was logic I understood—she was finally talking my language.

And I had just the way of getting those faces that were haunting Amara out there.

Savannah Daniels.

I just had to make miracles happen and get her to stop ghosting me.

FOUR

AIDAN

PRESENT DAY - NOVEMBER

"DIPSHIT."

Finn's voice rumbled over me, but I didn't look up from the sofa, from the blanket fort my forty-two-year old ass had made this morning. Instead, I remained in my little cocoon, trying to avoid the aches and pains and the general misery that was detoxing.

People said junkies were weak, that addicts were no-hopers. If they knew what it took to come down from Oxy, never mind heroin, then they'd understand that this was a level of agony few could endure.

Few *would* endure.

And to those people, in the future, I'd tell them to go fuck themselves.

Da included.

In fact, I'd get in his fucking face, and I'd ram my fist into his—

"Oy, fucker," Finn snapped, kicking my foot. "Why the fucking fuck didn't you fucking tell me your motherfucking ass was at Conor's?"

"Wasn't that pure poetry?" Conor questioned, ambling over from a part of the room I couldn't see within the confines of my blanket fort.

He had that stupid cat in his arms, the one with diamantés and now frozen custard covering it.

I didn't think he took the creepy ass thing to bed, but Conor rarely surprised me.

Everyone thought he was batshit because he was a genius. That was because they didn't know the truth. Would never know it either.

A shiver whipped its way down my spine making me feel like one of those eggs in the scramblers I'd been watching on TV—

"Jesus, is he having a seizure?" Finn rasped, his concern clear even if it wasn't my priority right now.

If I looked like I was having a seizure, then that was nothing to how this personal earthquake felt.

"Nah, he's getting better now. Just a little longer and he'll stop looking like Stig of the Dump."

"Who's that?"

"A character in a novel."

"Never heard of him."

"He's by Clive King, a British author."

"Clive King?" Finn queried. "Are you being irritating on purpose?"

"No," Conor said slowly. "I don't think I am. I mean, it's not my fault that all you read is *Playboy*."

"Feck off, and don't you dare tell Aoife that," he groused. "I read one fucking copy when I was sixteen and it was *yours*—"

"Semantics," Conor disregarded, before he plunked himself down on the sofa.

Right on top of me.

"What are you doing?" Finn spluttered.

"It stops the tremors," Conor replied easily. "Pass me the marshmallows."

I heard bags rattling, paper crinkling. The sweet sugary scent of candy combined with Finn's lemongrass aftershave almost made me want to puke, then I felt more pressure, and realized Finn had sat on top of me too.

Brothers.

Fucking pains in my ass.

God love ‘em.

"Why are you here anyway? Aside from critiquing my cat?"

"It’s weird, Conor. You’re like some Bond villain. Except, at least, Blofeld’s cat was alive."

"This one doesn’t shit or piss or need feeding. Which part of my lifestyle makes you think me having something alive in here would be a smart move?"

"Do you think it’s wise that Aidan’s staying with you? I don’t want him to become something ‘dead’ because you’re incapable of keeping something alive."

Conor grunted. "He’s autonomous. Mostly."

Finn snorted. "Good to know."

Paper rattled some more, a bag creaked. "Why are you here anyway? Thought it was your day off?"

"Yeah, and I should be dick deep in Aoife right now but that fucking friend of hers—"

"Which one?"

"Jen." He huffed. "She showed up. Some guy screwed her over."

"She’s hot. Can’t blame him for the screwing."

"She’s insane. The guy dumped her so she took a key to his Ferrari."

Conor snickered. "Sounds like fun."

"Well, it might have been at the time but now the guy’s suing."

"For how much?"

"Forty grand for the paint job and thirty for emotional distress."

Conor guffawed. "Emotional distress? For the paint job?"

"Probably after being in a relationship with Jen." Finn grunted. "Anyways, she’s there, snotting all over my fucking furniture and Aoife being Aoife is way too goddamn soft where that shark’s concerned."

"Which is why you're here? And why we're being graced with your charmingly miserable company?" Conor queried.

Finn lived just across the way. You could see his building from every angle in the room we were currently sitting in.

"Well, that, and did you hear?"

"I mean, I might have. I have ears. What in particular?"

"Such a pain in my ass," Finn muttered under his breath. "Davidson's making a speech about the Sparrows."

Conor cackled. "So, Mr. Oval Office has decided to fly his yellow belly into the nest, huh?"

"More like out of it. It's on Channel Four. Took him long enough."

Through my misery, I saw the infomercials I'd been watching flick over to Channel Four. I didn't complain, because what the fuck did I care what we were watching? What the fuck did I care about the Sparrows or the President or—

"My fellow Americans, the stain on our democracy from these so-called New World Sparrows need only be as deep as we allow it. If we can stop that taint from spreading further," the President declared, "then their toxicity can be cut off at the source.

"After a brief investigation by the FBI, several Congressmen and -women, Senators, even staff within my household have been uncovered as being a part of this body of people who, right here right now, I'm declaring as enemies of the state.

"I will not allow such a presence to undermine this republic in which we all live, for which millions have fought and died to protect...

"As of this moment, I can assure you, whether you voted for me or against me, the Davidson Presidency has your back. We will purge this presence from American soil and restore it to its former glory!"

"Puke alert," Conor mumbled.

Finn hummed. "He's good though. You can't deny it. That's how he reels them in."

"Like suckers." Conor made a gagging sound. "I don't mind his politics, just how he does his speeches."

"He'll get in again. You know that, right? Especially if he gets the exterminators in for the NWS like he's promising."

"You don't think he is one?" Conor queried. "It'd fit. Why wouldn't they have Sparrows in both parties?"

Even in this state, a state that made 'death warmed over' seem like a walk in the fucking park, I knew what he was talking about.

As he sat back, his weight settling on my legs in a way that was seriously uncomfortable, the TV flickered off of Davidson and switched to scenes from a few days back.

City Hall surrounded by cop cars, an active shooter alert ongoing, and then scenes that I was sure most would find harrowing. Except, my brothers and I weren't exactly the norm.

A dirty cop was squatting in a corner of the New York City Mayor's office, squealing like the pig he was, about how he'd been given the job of killing Mayor Coullson by a Republican politician.

Jason Young had, only a couple years ago, been the running mate of Davidson's opposition. That he was a Sparrow and that he'd been arrested in conjunction with Coullson's death was all over the news still.

"My name is Detective Craig Lacey of the 42nd Precinct," the squealing pig declared to the world in a video that had since gone viral after his death and the Mayor's murder. "Yesterday evening, I received a call on my burner cell from Congressman Jason Young." He grabbed something from the table, turned it around to display Jason Young's Caller ID on the log. "At nine-twenty-four, he made the request that I dispose of Mayor Coullson as he had broken ranks and was in talks with someone who was working against the organization.

"When I speak of an organization, I'm talking about the New World Sparrows, a body of people for whom I have worked since my first year at the NYPD Police Academy.

"Congressman Jason Young is also a member of this group, and I have been in contact with him for some years."

He switched onto an app, and there was a soft hushed voice,

faintly masculine but androgynous that whispered, "*Coullson can no longer be trusted. Those on high say he needs to be silenced. The usual payment will be made once the job is done.*"

When the recording was complete, Lacey muttered, "This morning, I realized this was a trap. I was never meant to make it out of this room alive. If they think they can take me down for knowing too much, then they can think again.

"The Sparrows are everywhere—"

There was the sound of a faint explosion, as if a glass door or a window had been smashed, and he jerked like he'd been hit. But his head twisted to the side as he looked for the source of the bullet's entry, then he snarled, "Those bastards—"

Someone promptly shut him the fuck up by shooting him.

Because of this Young, however, the entire world knew about the New World Sparrows; a threat to everyone's personal liberties and a group that was affecting my da's bottom line.

We were involved in the extermination process. Not because they were the 'toxicity' the President declared them to be, or because they were infiltrating the very mores upon which this nation was founded, but because they were business rivals.

"He's a prick but I don't think the President's a Sparrow," Finn mused, but he sounded like he was chewing.

"Why not? Davidson's smarmy as fuck."

Finn shrugged—the motion made me want to hurl. "I just don't."

Silence fell a second, but even I knew Conor was like a dog with a bone. Something Finn had said had triggered him, and where Kid was concerned, silence wasn't a good thing.

"Have you spoken with him?"

"Maybe at a gala or something. You know the shit your da makes us attend."

"So he's a prick because of his policies." Somehow that was both a statement and a question.

Con would have made a great CIA interrogator. Sometimes, he

came across as naive, but beneath it all, a brain ticked away that someday, scientists and colleges would fight over to dissect.

Finn grumbled under his breath, "Yes, Conor. He's a prick because of his policies."

"Shay would agree with you. He hates him."

"Most kids his age who are as woke as him probably do," Finn replied absently.

"You're not getting laid, are you?"

"What the fuck does that have to do with you?"

Conor sniffed. "You're miserable. All the time."

"I'm not."

"You are. I just assumed it's because you're not getting any."

"I'm getting plenty. It's—" He sighed. "Never mind. You wouldn't get it."

"Why wouldn't I? Because I'm not married?"

Finn fell silent. "You never know what goes on behind closed doors."

"Is Aoife whipping you with a roll of pastry? I'm sure there's porn out there for that. Get a live stream going, earn some bucks at the same time."

"This isn't a joke, Conor," Finn rumbled. "Nothing about this is funny—"

I groaned. "Can you fuck off and leave me to my infomercials?"

"Conor says sitting on you is good for you," Finn pointed out, no remorse to his tone. Even in my state, however, I picked up on the fact he was relieved to change the subject. "And you deserve to be sat on for going off grid, you asshole. Why the hell didn't you call me or text me?"

"Didn't realize we were—" Pain knifed through my head. "—dating," I finished with a gasp.

"Was that supposed to make me want to get off you? I don't think so." Finn sniffed. "Fucker."

"You're going to have a problem with Jake when he starts talking properly, not just Dada stuff," Conor said calmly. "You say 'fuck' a lot."

"And you don't?"

"Yeah, but I don't have a toddler, do I? It doesn't matter if I swear."

Finn paused. "You sound sad about that."

"Maybe I am. My cat doesn't care if I swear."

"It's not a cat. It's an ornament. An ugly one at that." To me, he groused, "Aidan, tell your brother that that cat isn't fucking real."

"He's right. You swear a lot," I rumbled.

"Fuck off. I have a lot of stress to deal with. A lot of fucking stress. If saying the word 'fuck' makes me feel better—"

"That's just the placebo effect," Conor chimed in. "And my cat is as real as I want it to be. He's *my* placebo. You swear, I have a cat who doesn't talk back."

"That's weird," Finn grumbled. "You're getting weirder, Con. We need to either get you laid or get your da to arrange a marriage for you."

I groaned again. "Can we have this conversation—" Nausea churned in my stomach. "—another time? When I'm not dying?"

"We're all dying," Conor muttered. "All of us. All the time."

"Now's not the moment to get existential on us, Con," Finn pointed out. "Anyway, can detoxing off Oxy be that bad? I mean, it's not heroin. They say it's harder to quit smoking and he did that when he was in his twenties. All those centuries ago."

"You're three months younger than me," I rasped. "Remind me to stab you—" I gasped out in pain before I could finish threatening him.

"I will when you're not in a blanket fort," Finn retorted snidely. "Why is he having withdrawals?"

"Because dumbfuck had started having some heroin here and there."

"Jesus," Finn boomed.

"He says it wasn't enough to get addicted, but we both know that's bullshit. That's why he's acting like Mount Rushmore is erupting."

"Once," I muttered. "Just once." After that last NA meeting, I'd fucked up.

Royally.

Waking up from that high, though, had put the pain I suffered because of my knee into perspective.

"Thank God for that," Finn muttered. "Aidan, what the hell were you thinking?"

I didn't have the chance to answer before agony sucked me under, not that I even had a reason for why I'd been so fucking stupid other than an excuse they wouldn't accept—that chronic pain was like an abyss. One you could never escape from. One that made drowning seem like a fun time. One that made me feel as if waves of spiders, their eight legs tipped in hydrochloric acid, were crawling up and down my spinal cord, sending chaos throughout my nervous system.

Heroin had seemed like an easy escape. A paradise few would ever understand because release and relief went hand in hand and, in this society, we were just supposed to man up. Suffer in silence, to the point where narcotics were the only freedom we could ever feel.

Because neither of them wanted to hear that, I didn't bother interrupting Conor when he stated, "I've been reading some books about it, so the situation is under control."

"Does that mean you're an expert now?" Because Finn knew my brother, he wasn't even joking.

Conor hummed. "He's progressing at the right pace."

"Did the books tell you to sit on him?"

"Nah, but I have to get him back for all the shit he did to me when I was a kid, don't I?"

Finn snorted out a laugh. "True. How long's he been here?"

"Just under a week. Showed up on my doorstep after I was dealing with that little problem Eoghan had."

"You mean the decapitated head on his doorstep? Con, bro, that's more than a 'little' problem."

"Not really," Conor mused. "Bodies are a lot heavier and more cumbersome. That was quite easy to dispose of."

"Knowing your da, he put it on a spike and has it in his office," Finn said with a grunt.

"Maybe. He's very medieval, you know that."

"Yeah, figured as much over the years," was Finn's dry comment. "Aoife told me Victoria's sleeping better though."

"Huh. I guess you can take the girl out of the Bratva but you can't take the Bratva out of the girl. Not sure MaryCat would be A-Okay with finding a bleeding head on her doorstep, and she's Irish Mob."

"She's technically a Satan's Sinner now," Finn said wryly. "Just don't tell her ma that."

"Did you hear what that cunt's next game is? It's not right, I'm telling you."

"What?" Finn queried. "I ain't heard nothing. Not since she gave birth to a boy, anyway."

"She went to Da and asked him for help in having the baby taken away from MaryCat because she's crying all the time and has post-partum depression."

"No fucking way," Finn snapped. "Jesus, what did your da say?"

"He asked me to look into it," was Conor's grim retort.

Finn's disbelief was clear. "You're helping them take her baby away from her? MaryCat will make an epic mom. You know that as much as I do."

"I'm not helping," was Conor's reply.

Finn made an 'ah' sound. "You're sowing seeds?"

"Yes. I've asked her to come around tomorrow."

"Digger's coming too?"

"I suppose. I don't imagine he'll be letting her go anywhere in the city without his protection. She's safe physically, but clearly he knows what her mother's like."

"A fucking cunt?" Finn grunted. "Wait until I tell Aoife this."

"Be careful she doesn't spread it to the other women. I need this on the downlow."

Finn heaved a sigh. "You're right. They're getting to be as thick as thieves."

"Safety in numbers," Conor pointed out.

"I need to vomit," I moaned.

"You've needed to puke for days," Conor replied, his lack of sympathy clear. "You'll get used to it soon."

"Shouldn't we do something?" Finn asked, fidgeting on top of me.

"No. He's going cold turkey."

"You sure we shouldn't take him somewhere?"

"We can't exactly take him upstate to a rehab center, can we?" Conor snorted. "Da would really love that. His eldest declared a junkie in the eyes of the world."

Finn hummed his agreement. "You sure you know what you're doing?"

"As much as I ever know what I'm doing."

"Is that supposed to be reassuring?"

"No. So, why do you think Davidson is a prick?"

"Fuck off, Conor."

"No, really. Tell me."

"I already did. His policies—"

"No, tell me the truth."

Finn fidgeted on top of me again, and if my brain had been working, if I hadn't been in survival mode, I might have recognized that for the tell it was.

All I knew was that the motion was enough to have me surging off the sofa, rolling out of my blanket fort, shoving them to the floor like I was a banana boat and they were frat brothers in Cozumel on Spring Break, then falling on my face on the floor where I promptly puked out my entire digestive system.

Going cold turkey?

Only for the brave.

FIVE

SAVANNAH

SIX WEEKS LATER

Four days before Christmas

THERE WAS a noise on my terrace.

Now, that might not have freaked out a lot of people, but I wasn't a lot of people.

Plus, I lived seventy-four stories up. It wasn't like Spider-Man could get onto my patio. But neither was it accessible to squirrels or opossum. I was also pretty sure that birds didn't fly this high after midnight. Weren't they supposed to be asleep? Preparing their little voices for their morning choir?

Did I mention that birdsong drove me nuts?

Goddamn noisy fuckers.

Still, I'd take an orchestral movement from a thousand of them if it meant that noise was a skyrat.

Sitting up, I stared around my bedroom, and tried not to be freaked out.

"You shouldn't have watched *IT*, Savannah. What a stupid thing to do," I muttered to myself.

Horror movies were my biggest weakness.

I didn't have the stomach for them, but I was oddly addicted to the sheer insanity of their stories.

As a journalist, I'd learned over the years that the truth was stranger than fiction so horror movies were a weird comfort to me.

But last night's choice was definitely an idiotic move on my part. I'd been jumpy ever since, to the point where a soft noise on my terrace was waking me up.

I sighed. "You really are a dumbass."

My ears strained in the silence of my place, half expecting Pennywise to mutter back, "Your ass is definitely dumb but oh, so tasty."

To which, of course, I had to reply, "Thanks, I spend a lot of time in the gym working on it."

Grinning to myself at my ridiculousness, I picked up my phone to look at the time, grunted at the number of notifications, then as I rolled out of bed so I could go check things out, slipped my cellphone into the pocket of my sweats.

The joy of living alone was the ability to have open doors. No privacy needed when you had three-thousand square feet to yourself. Of course, that was all well and good most days and nights, but I'd admit to getting a bit spooked as of late.

It wasn't every day you were helping to crack open a conspiracy.

The New World Sparrows were a secret society that functioned within the boundaries of the justice and political arena. It sounded hokey as hell to me, but I'd learned the truth when an old friend had asked me to help get the story out there.

At first, I hadn't believed in any of that. Star had always been weird, and so prone to coming up with stories that she made the students in my Creative Writing class in college look unimaginative, so I'd come close to ignoring her.

Because my career had stagnated ever since I'd become a whistleblower at TVGM, and with very little rep left, I didn't feel like damaging it over Star's nonsense until, of course, I'd come to realize that all her 'stories' were fact.

Not fiction.

Jesus, I felt so bad about that.

An old family friend told you she'd been a sex slave, and you went and blocked her?

"Man, I'm such a bitch," I grumbled to myself as I tripped over a couple of pillows that had taken up too much room on the bed so I'd tossed them onto the floor while I slept.

Of course, I'd been conceited and arrogant for years. It was only since I'd been knocked off my pedestal that I'd come to realize any of that.

A reformed bitch trying to shrug off her 'mean girl' crown wasn't breaking news, but it sure as hell felt like it to me.

So, when Star had come to me with this whole NWS shit, telling me about a woman who recognized every face she'd ever seen, including the men who had trafficked her overseas, who'd raped her, sold her, owned her, and that Star had figured out a way for her to get those faces down on paper so she could run them through a facial recognition scanner, my ears had pricked up.

When some massive names from the political sphere had popped out of that scanner, and I was talking names from the upper echelons of the government here, well, that had me creaming all over it. Not just because I wanted to apologize to Star either. But because, hell, what a chance to make a difference, to right some wrongs.

"And, if I'm lucky, earn back Star's friendship," I whispered to myself on a sigh.

Stepping out of the bedroom, I ambled over to the wall of glass that had pre-programmed drapes. From nightfall to daybreak, the curtains were open. From daybreak to nightfall, they were closed. That meant I had a panoramic view of the city as well as my terrace.

Spider-Man wasn't there.

I mean, that was a pity, but I was kind of glad. Especially as, who the fuck knew? Spider-Man could be a Sparrow too.

Shivering at the thought, I stopped a foot away from the glass and looked out onto the world.

New York really was how they said it was—it never slept. Not really. The thousands upon thousands of glittering lights had, once upon a time, given me the heebie-jeebies.

Before I'd morphed into *the* Savannah Daniels, global warming and climate change had been my pet cause. Seeing all these lights was a reminder of how much energy we consumed even when we were supposed to be at rest.

Then, of course, it had led to me thinking about how many lights were on in Tucson, Dallas, Chicago, LA, and Atlanta too. Major cities all of them, but what about the minor? What about the towns? And hell, that was just the US.

How many other lights were on in Madrid, Paris, Tokyo, and Brazil?

See?

Just thinking about it made me shiver again, but I'd grown up since then.

Sort of.

From my position on the front line of the news, I'd come to learn that nobody really gave a damn about the climate. About the planet either. They just said they did but they still didn't recycle, still had sex in the shower even though that wasted a gazillion gallons of water, and it didn't stop them from picking up discounted meat at the store even if that beef came from a super farm where bacteria was treated better than the cattle.

Aware I sounded judgmental from my position of privilege, I gnawed on my bottom lip, and decided that *IT* was the least of my worries. We were living in a horror movie, one that was just slow burn.

Wincing, I made to twist around when my foot knocked against something. It rattled against the glass, then clattered to the floor. It scared the heck out of me until I remembered I'd spilled coffee out on the patio earlier and had cleaned it up, then left the mop here.

"Lights on," I declared to the room at large, swooping down to grab it.

With it in hand, I cast a final look at the view ahead, only, with the light on, I saw more of my reflection than before.

Movement shifted behind me as I caught a face in the window and I screamed.

Holy fuck, I screamed so loud that I scared myself as I jerked around, catching the intruder as he swarmed toward me like some kind of fucking ninja.

His face was mean, nasty, and that I saw it period told me he didn't intend on my surviving tonight. He had a massive scar slicing down from his right eye all along to the curve of his lips. I'd heard about those clown grins before. Someone—I'd assume they weren't friends—placed the tip of a knife to the corner of his mouth then sliced up.

His presence here told me he wasn't the kind of guy I wanted to be friends with, so even with the curiosity that really would be the death of me, I had no desire to know why he had a one-sided, scarred grin.

"Who the fuck are you?"

No answer.

Armed with a mop, I was pretty sure I wasn't going to survive.

He had a knife. Not a gun. Did that give me more of a chance?

No one else lived on this floor so I knew I had to rescue myself.

Dad insisted on security, but I dismissed them when I was at home.

Who was going to get to me in a secured building that was owned by the O'Donnellys?

No fucking one.

Or so I thought.

Famous last words.

I had to save myself.

Jesus.

I hadn't done that. Ever.

I felt like he had wings as he flew toward me, so fast, so fucking sure of what he was doing, so I did the only thing I could. I stuck out the mop and waved it from left to right.

Sure, I looked like I belonged in a Groucho Marx movie, but I'd played field hockey in school. I had a mean arm when I chose to use it.

The mop, still wet, sent a tiny shower of coffee beads spraying all over my crushed gray velvet sofa but I decided not to worry about that as my blood could, very likely, be decorating it next.

"What do you want?" I screamed at him, still waggling the mop.

No reply.

Silent motherfucker but he grinned at me, laughing at my weapon.

That made me want to prove exactly what I could do with a stick.

I prodded the mop in the air then quickly twisted it around. Because Dad was who he was, I'd been trained to defend myself. Of course, my instructors had never imagined I'd be armed only with a piece of cleaning equipment.

Knowing I needed something heavier, I tried to think about what the room contained, all while I stabbed the air as he finally got into my personal space.

His arm went high, arcing upward as he started to bring the knife down, so I shoved the wet, slimy mop head in his face.

He darted to the side, ducking down, but I followed, smushing the mop like I was wiping the floor with it, then I pushed hard. He yelled in surprise as I carried on pushing forward. I tried to find his mouth, to find the depressed cavern that came now he'd parted his lips but to no avail.

"I'm gonna make you deep throat this, fucker," I snarled even though it was bullshit. His hands wafted in front of him, grabbing the mop and shoving it aside but I was ready for that.

Giving it one final push, I let go and leaped over the sofa, scuttling along the cushions like I'd done as a kid, then I made it to the coffee table. The glass was cold beneath my feet as I dipped down and reached for the remote lying there. I sent it soaring at him and laughed, crazily pleased with myself, when I scored a hit.

I wasn't going to die today.

I just had to get out of here.

I had to go one floor up.

I had to.

In that place, safety lay.

"You fucking bitch," the guy snapped.

"What was I supposed to do?" I panted, staring at the coffee-grounds that mingled with his scar. "Just let you kill me?"

Yeah, not going to happen.

I grabbed a coffee table book, one that was full of artsy pictures that made no sense but had the advantage of being a hardback and with over four hundred pages in it, and I swooped that from left to right as he approached me.

If I hit him, in just the right spot, he might stagger back—

Any plans screeched to a halt when he jabbed forward with the knife, and when he missed, pretty much did as I did, began swaying back and forth like he was a snake charmer who was attempting to lull me into a false sense of security.

Not gonna happen.

I had two sisters and a brother. I was used to sneaky little shits distracting me.

Panting, I focused on trying to kick him in the balls, going for the soft stuff first. When I scored a hit, he yelped, then I went for his nose with the book, but my hit glanced off his temple instead.

He surprised me by darting around the coffee table. I jerked back and out of the way, then as he swiped at me, he managed to slash me.

"OW!"

That bastard.

He'd gotten my thigh.

Nothing deep, just enough to fucking sting and I knew it was gonna bleed like an SOB because it ran all the way around the outer edge of my leg to the inner side.

Goddammit.

Pissed, aware that I was running out of time, energy, and now blood, and that I needed to get out of here fast, I swung the book hard. He batted it out of the way with the knife, and only dumb luck let me keep a firm hold on it.

I reacted faster though.

I brought the book around before he could jab at me with his weapon, and when the hardback collided with his skull, the thud was more than satisfying.

His eyes turned dazed and his head rocked like I'd spun it on its axis.

With him distracted, I brought the book back again, swinging wide with it like Dad had taught me to when playing golf—one of his coping mechanisms—twisting with all of my body and putting every ounce of strength into my hit.

It collided with him, the corner hitting him on the temple.

He fell to his knees, going down like a house of cards, yelling when they knocked into the edge of the glass coffee table. It smashed under his weight and I screamed as my support buckled out from under me. I had a millisecond to react and I dove forward, squealing with pain when I face-planted on the floor.

Groggily, I rolled onto my back, aware time wasn't a luxury in my possession, and breathing hard, I scrambled onto my knees.

When I said that every bone in my body hurt, it wasn't an understatement. In fact, it was being generous. My legs felt like cooked noodles, but that was nothing to the way my head, neck, and shoulders seemed as if I'd knocked all the joints out of alignment. And my hands? Sweet lord.

How could falling such a tiny distance hurt so fucking much?

My knees wobbled as I pushed onto my feet, and the lightheadedness that had spots dancing in my vision almost had me falling back down again. Gasping, I stared blindly at the coffee table, at the man lying face first amid the glass, not really registering it as I tried not to pass out.

I had to move.

I had to hurry.

Who knew when he'd wake up?

Who the fuck knew?

With him unconscious, I had more choices, but my brain was still stuck in survivor mode.

I had a phone, I even had a panic button, but I was bleeding and whatever I did, the blood from the cut on my thigh would follow me wherever I went, leading the bastard to me like a trail of nuts with a horde of carnivorous squirrels after them.

Staring down at the blood-stained carpet when I was finally standing, I grabbed a throw pillow from the sofa, swiped my foot against it to get it as clean as physically possible—news flash, it barely worked—then I did the only thing I could do—plucked at the fabric of my sweats beneath where he'd slashed through them and held it taut, so much so that I whimpered with pain. Hoping that would catch the blood so it wouldn't just drip down my leg, I wobbled out of the room with one thought in mind—get to the penthouse.

Get to the O'Donnellys.

You know in movies, whenever you saw St. Peter's gates, there was a song, with harps, I thought. Gold angel dust—not the PCP kind —glittered around them, and the openings were lodged into pearly white clouds?

That was the front door at that moment.

A choir of angels serenaded me as I made it there, hands scrabbling with the doorknob. It came as no surprise it was unlocked. After all, the bastard had gotten in somehow, but I still wasted precious seconds as I tried to figure out how to turn the goddamn handle.

Pissed at myself, I finally managed the simplest task in existence, and opened the door just as I heard him groan.

That sound sent shivers down my already weak spine, and I accepted that my time was more than just running out.

I could hear the ticking clock in my ear as much as I sensed how jarring that fall had been. My brain felt foggy but I had to act. It was either move it or lose it.

Literally.

Gritting my teeth, I darted out into the hall as quickly as I could, fear giving my knees the strength I needed to move faster.

There was technically only one way to reach the penthouse—a private elevator. But one time, I'd gained access to the helicopter pad up there.

I'd never know how my dad had pulled that particular string but he'd done it because Mom was rushed to the hospital with a punctured lung of all things, and I'd had to go through the emergency fire exit, up the stairs, and to the helicopter pad where my winged carriage had awaited me.

There, I'd learned about another set of stairs that would take me down to the penthouse's terrace, and gave the owner easy access to that exit.

I didn't know which O'Donnelly lived up there, but I was praying it was Aidan. He'd help me. He would. I knew it. He'd helped me before when I was young and stupid.

"Jesus, let it be Aidan," I rasped to myself.

I darted over to the elevator first, then summoned it. The doors immediately opened because the upper floors accessed a different elevator, one that only served a handful of people. Rushing in, I pressed the button that'd take me to the ground, then jumped out as the doors started to close.

Thanking Christ that the way I was holding my sweats meant blood wasn't dripping onto the floor, I peered down at the blood-soaked fabric and knew it wasn't going to hold for long.

Praying the intruder would take my actions with the elevator to mean I'd gone downstairs, which would have been the smart thing to do—the move that every blonde bimbette in a horror movie would *never* do—I stayed on course and headed for the fire exit.

I needed an O'Donnelly.

Someone had managed to break into a secured apartment building that required four different access codes to breach.

Someone had managed to do all that and then get into my apartment itself.

I knew who.

The Sparrows.

Because I'd been the one to break the news about them, because I'd been the one to write that initial exposé, to reveal the first round of faces and their purported crimes, they were gunning for me.

When you had a secret society coming after you, who were you gonna call?

Well, the Ghostbusters were out, but the Irish fucking Mob sure as hell felt like a safety net when the cops themselves had been infiltrated by the NWS too.

So, up it was.

I just never imagined that I'd be trying to find safety in a group of people who, once upon a time, had wanted me dead too.

SIX

AIDAN

"EIGHTY-EIGHT, eighty-nine—" I chanted the numbers under my breath, breathing hard through my HIIT workout.

As I curled up, my abs bunched, and sweat dripped down my pecs and along my torso. It also beaded on my forehead, slipping into my eyes and making them sting.

Once I hit a hundred, I moved over to the elliptical, the only cardio machine in Conor's home gym that didn't fuck with my knee.

Conor's building didn't have an indoor pool, whereas I had one at my place. Over the many years of physio, I'd come to learn that the elliptical and swimming were my only options.

The second the withdrawals had begun to fade, instead of drowning in misery, I'd decided to burn off my frustrations in the gym.

Was I saying it was easy?

Hell, no.

I didn't want to be in here. I wanted to be back in my goddamn blanket fort, but I didn't have that option.

On the outside, and to the rest of the world, I might be one of New York's most eligible bachelors, but I was the heir to a crime family. Nothing about that kind of life allowed a man to rest on his laurels.

I was lucky that my brothers were solid gold and that they'd pulled rank to save my ass from myself—and Da.

Six weeks of avoiding the office, Sunday dinner, *and* Thanksgiving?

Unheard of.

Da had blown up my phone from time to time, but Conor would answer and he'd do what he did best—confound our father with facts, figures, and information. Pertinent and otherwise. By the time Da was done with those calls, he'd forgotten he had an heir and probably needed a whiskey.

But in three days' time, we'd be heading over to the family estate for Christmas Eve, and wouldn't be leaving until Boxing Day.

Few in the States recognized the 26th as a holiday, but Aidan Sr. was a king of his own sovereign borough and did whatever the fuck he wanted, when he wanted.

Three days at home.

Three days without Oxy with my father in the vicinity.

Three days with him bitching at me for missing Thanksgiving all while driving me crazy.

Jesus Christ.

I upped the intensity level on the elliptical, seriously needing not to think about that.

The problem with living so high up?

Working out was boring.

You couldn't people-watch, and I wasn't the kind of guy who liked having the news on the TV while exercising. Workouts were depressing enough without having current events force fed into your fucking ears too. Audiobooks had lost their appeal since the Oxy as well.

Bored, I looked over the terrace ahead. There was a small dipping pool but it was too cold right now to use, and a nice seating area that I knew Con had probably never even noticed, never mind sat on.

As I stared, trying to focus on anything other than the goddamn excruciating agony in my knee and the gnawing ache in my gut, I saw a woman rushing down the staircase that led to the helipad above us.

Blinking, pretty fucking sure I was tripping, I stopped moving the elliptical pedals and carefully climbed off.

Moving over to the sliding door, unconcerned because the glass was bulletproof, I was more bewildered about what the hell was happening here.

Of course, just as my bewilderment grew, she went flying down the stairs, falling flat on her face in the process.

If I were a jackass, I'd have laughed. Before the drive-by shooting that had made mincemeat out of my knee, I'd been a jackass, but now? I winced because when she dropped, it was like a belly flop without a pool to break her fall.

I opened the door, and hobbled out with lights flaring into being as the motion sensors were triggered.

The cold hit me, the harsh chill of the December night colliding with my overheated flesh, making the perspiration feel like icicles that were clinging to my skin. I shoved those pansy ass thoughts away as I limped over to the stranger's side, and looming above her, I managed to roll her onto her back.

She had a cut on her hairline that was already bleeding, scrapes on her chin and nose, a bad cut on her thigh, but as much as I noticed all her injuries, the one thing that resonated was her identity.

Savannah Daniels.

The one I'd pushed away.

While I knew she lived on the floor below the goddamn penthouse, seeing her flying down the stairs from the helipad was as much of a surprise as St. Nick tripping down them.

I tried to crouch lower to reach her but my fucking knee wouldn't let me.

Concerned for her, I hobbled back to the gym, toward the door and hollered, "Conor? Get your ass out here right now!"

Eoghan was the best medic, thanks to his training, but I knew

Conor was good at a lot of shit he kept from Da. He'd know what to do more than I would.

As I moved over to the box of fresh towels, I grabbed a couple, then retreated to her side once more.

Carefully covering her up with the terry cloth, I was about to lose my patience with my brother when, finally, I heard his, "What the hell's wrong with you now? If you want to puke on me again to get back at me for—" He paused. "Who the fuck is that?"

I twisted around. "She came down from the helipad."

He peered up at the sky. "I really didn't need to know that angels exist tonight, God."

Despite my concern, I snickered. "She's no angel." More like a demon. A fucking menace to my dick. "She's a journalist."

Conor's frown eased. "A journalist? Should we throw her off the helipad?"

My lips curved. "Maybe another time."

He hummed. "I've always wanted to throw someone off there."

"Jesus," I muttered, recognizing his earnestness. "Why?"

"I want to see if they're like toast."

"Why the fuck would you think there could be a similarity?"

"The science is there." He scowled at me. "Would they land face up or down from a building of this height?"

"I don't want to know why that's even a question, Con, but no, I don't want her dead. I know her."

He stepped closer. "How do you know a reporter?"

"Remember that pain in the ass Da asked me to handle about five years ago?"

His frown puckered. "I don't remember much about last week, Aid."

I heaved a sigh. "She was digging her heels in, talking to a lot of our associates, somehow managing to wheedle her way into conversations with people she wasn't supposed to. Started sniffing around Paddy's place in the Hole."

"Where those bodies are buried?"

I nodded grimly. "Exactly." Of course, that hadn't been what she was looking for.

Conor didn't need to know that, however.

"Oops." He clicked his fingers. "I remember. Da wanted you to shut her up."

I grimaced.

"What's she doing here? Why isn't she 'shut up?'"

"I don't know." I peered over at the helipad, answering the first question while ignoring the second. "How do you gain access to that?"

"Those stairs."

"There has to be another way. Unless she flew in, which we know she didn't, or if she was waiting there since the last helicopter flight."

"I doubt it. The last time it was used, it was—" He paused. "Oh."

"Oh?"

"Savannah Daniels. That's her, right?"

"It is. How do you know?"

"She recently moved in beneath me."

"Unlike you to know that," I pointed out. I mean, *I* knew that but it was unusual for Conor to know too.

"Her dad got in touch with me. Asked for a favor."

"What kind of favor?"

"His wife was rushed to the hospital in Philly. He needed his daughter there, stat. I obliged and that was how I learned about Savannah."

"Very philanthropic of you," I murmured.

"Not really. He promised to send me tickets to a concert. It was the week before you darkened my door." Conor beamed. "That was an awesome show."

"Of course, her dad's Dagger Daniels." I snorted. "*noxxious*. How could I forget?"

His chin jutted out. "You could have tried to score me some tickets from her before."

"What? While I was trying to convince her not to write that

exposé? While also not killing her like I was supposed to? Yeah, Conor, you meeting her folks was my priority.

"Anyway, stop fucking talking. Look at her."

"I *am* looking at her."

"I mean, check her out."

"I did. She has nice tits."

I growled under my breath. "Conor, my patience is wearing thin."

"You're not Da, you know?" He peered at me. "I'm not scared of you."

"Fucking should be."

His lips curved but he crouched down at her side, then pulled out his phone from his pocket. He turned the screen on, then pressed it to her mouth.

"She's breathing, Conor. We don't need to do that test," I said wryly.

"Just checking."

Okay, maybe he didn't know anything about field medicine.

When he put the flashlight on, I watched as he shone that in her face, then he lifted her eyelids. Her pupils puckered, retreating into tight circles.

"I think that's a good sign."

He turned the phone around then tapped the screen. When I heard a ringing sound, I folded my arms, waiting to find out who he'd called.

"Conor, there'd better be a good reason you're waking me up at two AM."

"You wake up early, don't you?"

"Not this fucking early. Each moment is precious, dick, and the first voice I want to hear when I wake up isn't yours." Eoghan yawned. "What do you want?"

"Someone just fell down the stairs. Face-planted." I cleared my throat. "She knocked herself out."

Eoghan grunted. "Sounds like a dipshit move to me." He paused.

"Wait. *She*? Hang on, where are you? I thought you were at Conor's? There aren't any steps there."

Ignoring his other questions, I replied, "There are from the helipad."

"Oh, yeah. I forgot you had one of those on your building. Conor, you weren't trying to throw someone over the side, were you? Finn told me you asked about that."

Hell, this wasn't the first time he'd verbalized it?

"Conor, we need to get you to a shrink," I muttered.

"It's only for enemies. Jesus. You'd think you hadn't killed anyone before." He huffed and folded his arms across his chest.

Ignoring his petulance, I told Eoghan, "She tripped, has some cuts and scrapes, but she's unconscious."

"You don't want her to be? "

"No."

"You're not torturing her?"

"*No*." Torturing women was Da's thing anyway. "She's just unconscious from the fall."

"I'd hope she is, considering Conor just threw you under the 'Murder One' bus," he said wryly.

"I'm not worried about that."

Silence fell at my declaration.

Until they both decided to speak at the same time.

"Why the hell not?" Eoghan burst out.

"Did you want to kill her anyway?" Conor queried, calmer but no less confused.

"No," I groused, "I don't want her dead. But she knows how things work in this world. She was well aware she flew too close to the sun last time. No way she'd throw us under the bus now."

Maybe that was wishful thinking, naïveté or stupidity, but I knew she wouldn't.

Back in the day, she'd had every reason, every goddamn right to be scared of me, to go to the cops to try to evade the Firm's reach, but she hadn't.

She was too smart for that.

"There's a hell of a lot of information to unravel there, Aidan. How do you know her?" Eoghan demanded. "It sounds like you fucked her or something."

"I wish," I muttered, reaching up to rub the back of my neck.

It was freezing out here, but I needed the cold to stop me from getting overheated. Just thinking about the few times we'd met up was enough to give me a hard-on.

"You wish? You mean..." Conor paused. "You didn't?"

"No."

"Holy fuck," Conor breathed. "She's like your penguin."

"My penguin?"

"Yeah. They mate for life."

"Or in this instance, they don't mate throughout life," Eoghan said with a cackle. "How can his soul mate be someone he hasn't fucked?"

"Could you have said anything less romantic?"

Inessa's comment should have been jarring, but I wasn't surprised he was having this conversation in front of his wife, wasn't shocked that he hadn't left the room.

As one by one, my brothers all started getting hitched, I'd admit, seeing the differences between their marriages and our parents' was refreshing. A bit of a relief as well.

My time was coming.

Da would expect it soon enough.

I could already feel the shackles closing around me.

Not because a wife was a ball and chain, but because of what that marriage would represent.

We might only be criminals to some people, but we were a dynasty too, and the heir to it was expected to wed and make little heirs of his own.

I was surprised I'd made it to forty-two without being forced down the aisle.

"Of course I could be less romantic if I tried," Eoghan pointed out, utterly without shame. "But I try for you. That has to give me some bonus points, surely?"

Inessa just snorted, but I heard shuffling, as if she were getting out of bed.

"That reminds me, we're going on our honeymoon in the new year. Aidan, I'm covering your tracks, I'll expect you to cover mine while I'm gone."

I blinked. "Da knows, right?"

"He does."

"Then what's the problem? Even he doesn't begrudge a honeymoon. Especially one that's taking place months after the wedding," I said dryly.

"Who knows where he's concerned. What I *do* know is that we're getting our asses on that plane and not a fucking war with the Bratva or the Sparrows is going to stop our honeymoon. Ya got me?"

"I do," I agreed, because it wasn't much to ask, was it? Every man and wife deserved a goddamn honeymoon. "I'll cover you as much as I can."

"Thanks. Okay, so back to your penguin."

"Her name's Savannah," I grumbled.

"Savannah Daniels," Conor pointed out with glee. "Her dad's Dagger Daniels. Fuck, I wonder if we save her life if she'll get him to meet with me again. This time alone."

"Why? So you can jack off in front of him instead of just thinking about him?" Eoghan questioned with a laugh.

"Fuck off, Eoghan. You're the one who joined the Army. Overcompensating, much?"

"You have seen my wife, haven't you?" Eoghan bickered back. "I don't have to compensate for shit— Wait. Did you say Savannah Daniels? Didn't she just break the Sparrows' story?"

Conor and I shared a look.

"I don't know," I admitted. "I haven't been watching the news."

"I've been busy," Conor agreed. "Lodestar said that news was breaking about the NWS, but I didn't bother keeping track, not when I've got bigger fish to fry."

Though I arched a brow at what, clearly, was an admission that he was friends with an ally's hacker, I stayed silent as Eoghan said, "You know she lost her job after she told everyone there was a toxic work environment at TVGM? Apparently, the series' runners and producers had a casting couch."

This wasn't news to me.

"How do you know that?" Conor questioned.

"Inessa told me."

He hummed. "She lost her job for telling people that her bosses had furniture that they used to cast people with?"

Eoghan started snickering. "Okay, now I know that crap about you starting PornLandia is bullshit. How the fuck do you not know what a casting couch is?"

I eyed him carefully. Conor's relationship with sex was strange to say the least so it wouldn't surprise me if he was joking, or if he was being serious about not understanding what a casting couch was.

"It's basically when a producer who can choose between four new members of staff will pick the one who fucks him," I explained quietly.

Conor winked at me. "Ohhhhh." I shook my head at him, wondering why he pulled these moves sometimes. "That makes more sense."

"You mean other than the network being concerned about their staff's taste in interior decor?" Eoghan laughed again. "Kid, gotta love the way your brain works. Anyway, yeah, she blew the whistle on that, then got fired for it."

"How's that fair?" Conor demanded, while I stayed silent.

"It isn't. That's the point. Anyway, Inessa told me she lost a lot of credibility, but yesterday, she shared some links on her personal social media and they went viral."

"Of course they did. She's Dagger Daniels' daughter." Conor huffed.

"Not everyone still gets boners for ancient rock bands," Eoghan sniped. "It hit the news last night. She revealed names tied to crimes and evidence to back it all up. The whole nine yards."

I whistled under my breath. "You didn't know about this, Con? Lodestar really didn't give you any details? Just told you she was working on something?"

"I knew she had something planned." He cast me a look. "The day you arrived and asked for help going cold turkey?"

"What about it?" I replied, wondering if that was even a question.

"Do you remember anything about it? Or the run up to it?"

I just remembered visiting an NA meeting at the end of the week, and making a promise to myself that I'd quit Oxy.

Then, I'd made shit a thousand times worse before the weekend was out.

I wasn't about to tell my younger brothers that though.

"Not much."

Conor frowned, but explained, "The Mayor was a Sparrow. Remember?"

"Vaguely," I said grimly, reaching up to rub my forehead where I was sure my perspiration had turned into icicles now.

"Well, we tried to turn him. We got some leverage over him, then the Sparrows sent a dirty cop in to kill him when they figured out he was compromised.

"But the Sparrows had set a trap for the fucker. He killed the Mayor but the NYPD showed up at City Hall and had the place surrounded. They had snipers and everything on patrol. Fucker got shot and toddled off to hell with a bang.

"Before he died, though, he made a video and had his wife send it to all the news channels. He explained what the Sparrows were and declared that Jason Young was the guy who'd told him to take Coullson out. He's that dick Republican who wears suits that are a size too small."

I almost laughed at the description.

I remembered Young. He'd been the presidential running mate in the last election.

"You really don't remember any of that?" Eoghan asked warily.

"No." My retort was grim, but I figured that was understandable.

"Either way, ever since then, I know Lodestar's been working on a way to keep on spreading the news."

So, the night following Savannah's breaking news, she ended up here? Unconscious?

That couldn't be a coincidence, could it?

Slowly, I verbalized my train of thought: "So, somehow, the neighbor on the floor below you, who also happens to be the journalist who broke a story on the Sparrows, sneaked up onto the helipad after cracking Conor's security system, and descended to this level… Do we think there's a reason for that?"

"Whatever it is, it can't mean anything good," Eoghan muttered.

And even though it was my brotherly duty to disagree with him on principle, this time, I couldn't.

SEVEN

SAVANNAH

I WOKE up in a living room I didn't recognize, surrounded by men I didn't know. At least, not in my dazed state.

Screaming, I jerked upright, arms flailing as I tried to figure out where the hell I was and who the fuck I was with.

There were five of them.

Looming over me.

But...

Christ.

They were hot.

And when I said hot, I didn't just mean like regular hot. I was talking Chris Evans' hot. Henry Cavill smokin'.

Of course, that didn't diminish my panic.

Rapists could be cute.

Then, I saw him. Immediately, my heart slowed and I began to calm down, even as my head started to throb with the makings of a migraine.

He wasn't standing in the circle around me, he was just off to the side, sitting on an armchair, shoulders hunched as he leaned forward, one elbow propped on a knee while he had the other leg resting outstretched in front of him.

When recognition hit so did relief.

As did want. Need. Regret.

Those tangled emotions did more than hit me. They sank inside me like the ocean flooding holes kids dug in the sand to make sandcastles.

"Aidan?" I whispered rawly.

"Savannah." He rubbed his thumb along his bottom lip. "How are you feeling?"

"I'm okay." Total lie. But I was surrounded by the O'Donnelly brothers. You didn't jump into shark-infested waters and willingly slice your wrist open, did you? "What's going on?"

I peered at his brothers.

I'd never met them before, but they were as notorious as Aidan.

You didn't *not* know the O'Donnellys in New York.

"You fell down the stairs—"

Ouch. That was why everything hurt more than it had before.

My hands dropped to my lap and I winced, saw that my leg had a massive bandage on it, which was a reminder of that bastard who'd slashed me there.

Blood peeped through the folds of the gauze, and I winced again at the solid punch to the gut that was the realization I'd almost died tonight. Because it had to be tonight still, right? It was dark out. Not even dawn.

Someone clicked their fingers in front of my face, making me jolt in surprise.

"How did you even access my helipad?"

I darted a look at Conor. So, he was the one who lived here. *His* helipad, huh. I'd tried to find out the legal owner of the penthouse when I'd started the motions of buying my place downstairs, but had run up against a dummy corp.

"I called someone..." I winced. "A hacker friend. She helped me."

"The hacker was Lodestar, right?"

"I can't tell you that. I don't want you to retaliate against her. She saved my ass. I promise you, I wouldn't have done it if I didn't need to be here. I'd never have called her and asked her to do what she did if I wasn't desperate."

Conor tensed. Nothing about the man was mild, meek. If anything, he wore his strength in the lean ropes of muscles that twined about his limbs, but at that moment, with how his shoulders bunched up, he appeared even bigger than before.

His mouth tightened. "Okay, let's cut the BS. We both know you're friends with Star." When I just gulped, he soothed, "We're allies."

Surprised, my lips parted which appeared to be all the answer he needed. Dammit to hell.

Your first attempt at subterfuge against the Irish Mob and you fuck up, Savannah. Way to go. Not.

Still, allies?

God, that verbiage alone told me they were friends.

Hadn't I recently informed Star that she was the only person I knew who had nemeses?

Looked like she had allies too. *Go figure.*

"We used to be as close as sisters," I answered. My smile was sad. "Until things changed and she went away."

Conor tipped his head to the side. "She was the one who helped you break in, right?"

"She did." In less than ninety seconds. It was kind of worrying that she'd been able to break through something I'd assumed would be tighter than Fort Knox with that much ease.

I'd also been surprised at her lack of gloating.

Star was a gloater. She liked to win.

If anything, when the code to the security door had flashed green as it opened, she'd muttered, "Sorry, aCooooig."

"Wait, are you aCooooig?"

Conor grunted. "I am."

"She beat your security again, Conor," one of the men, Eoghan, mocked.

"She said it was hard, if that's any consolation," I said with a politely apologetic smile, pinning it in place as I lied to him to spare him from the ribbing of his brothers. I had siblings too. They were fucking brutal when they wanted to be.

The guys snickered, well, all except for two of them—the eldest of the bunch.

At one point or another, I knew I'd run across them at galas, had seen them with their wives, even if we hadn't been formally introduced, but having them all together in a circle around me? Intimidating.

"Enough," Aidan rumbled, casting glares his brothers' way.

"How does she keep doing that?" Conor groused.

"I'm not sure," I replied meekly, all while I was wondering when the last time was that Star had hacked into a Five Points' building.

It wasn't a lie, though. I truly didn't know. I had long since stopped asking Star how she could do the things that she did. I knew my godfather, her dad, had started to wash his hands of her, but his death had stopped that in its tracks.

Part of me wondered if Star was aware of how close she'd come to being cut off from her dad, but I knew she wouldn't have changed her behavior anyway. Why would she? She was always so certain that she was right.

Until recently, I'd been the same too.

No wonder we'd gotten along so well as kids.

Both of us were pains in the ass, bullheaded, without the good sense to know when to quit when we were ahead...

Which was why the next words to fall from my lips were:

"Is there a reason you're all standing around me like this? It's kind of creepy."

"You're the one who managed to sneak into my penthouse, and breached my security. Just because Star is an ally doesn't mean your actions are consequence-free."

I was ready to deal with the consequences, especially after what I'd come close to handling downstairs. I just didn't need them standing around me like this. It was giving me ideas.

Ideas I really didn't need to be having, not when I'd just fended off a murder attempt in my apartment.

Okay, enough time spent wasted by thinking with my ovaries; I began to process exactly how badly I was hurt instead.

I knew there were no broken bones, but that didn't diminish how every part of me felt as if I'd been run over by a Mack truck and my shredded sweats, the hole in them even bigger as they'd torn it wider to bandage me up without stripping me down, were soaked through with blood, which was really gross.

Damn, I needed a shower.

Gnawing on my bottom lip, I decided to blank out the other brothers, and focused on the one who had gotten me out of trouble all those years ago.

I had no reason to think he would help me now, not after everything that had happened at TVGM. I'd been lucky that he'd bothered with me in the past, but as we looked at one another, our gazes tangling much as atoms might before nuclear fusion, I had a feeling he'd be my only hope.

With the Sparrows gunning for me, it hit home just how worthy my cause was. They wanted to silence me. Aidan could be my one true chance at getting out of this alive while exposing the bastards.

I just wished that my brain wasn't still foggy. To the world, I presented a ditzy façade, because that was what people expected from Dagger Daniels' daughter. They didn't realize I was a shark who'd do anything for a story. But right this second, I felt like the airhead I usually projected.

"Talk to me."

With those three words, it was as if the rest of the room's occupants faded without me having to pretend the brothers weren't there.

The discordant decor that was anything but comforting, the weird diamanté-studded cat that was wearing a red-and-white

'Where's Waldo?' scarf which was propped on the sofa by my feet, the men who were crazy handsome and all dressed as if they belonged in a Quentin Tarantino movie, and the myriad pains in my body seemed to disintegrate into dust.

It was just me and Aidan.

I'd ask where we went wrong, but there'd never been anything right about us.

I'd never even kissed him, and he'd never tried to cop a feel.

We'd eaten a meal together, he'd held my hand, had pressed one of his to the small of my back. The tips of his fingers had trailed over my nape when he'd helped me put on my coat before we headed out for dinner.

That was the sum of the physical interactions we'd shared.

But in the here and now, as I looked at him and he looked at me, my body remembered him. It was hardwired to never forget him.

Which was way more terrifying than Pennywise.

"Savannah." There was a rumble to his tone, a warning, something that hit me in so many ways that I was hard pressed not to shiver.

There was little point in lying to him. Men like these had heard far worse stories than the one I was about to tell. I just had to pray that they weren't involved with the Sparrows. I had to pray that my faith in Aidan wasn't wasted, and considering I was still alive and that he hadn't had me killed as promised, I didn't think it was ridiculous to have faith in him.

"Have you heard about my exposé?" I whispered.

"Yes, my sister-in-law has apparently been keeping Eoghan well-informed on the situation."

I studied him, noticing that his cheeks were a little gaunter than before. The strain around his eyes deeper, the bridge of his nose had thicker creases, and he was markedly thinner than before, while still muscled. None of that took away from his appeal.

Those life lines, proof of his pain, were like a story that his features silently told the world. Stories were my jam. My lifeblood.

So his not only filled me with questions, but made me concerned for him.

Aidan wasn't just one of New York City's most eligible bachelors. He was the heir to the O'Donnelly throne. An emperor in the making. At least, of the underworld.

With the salt and pepper flecks, his tangled dark waves made my palms itch with the need to tame them. Either that, or to make them a thousand times worse.

His bright green eyes were muted somehow, as if the feeling behind them was disconnected. Like he felt too much or as if he experienced it through a fog. His lips were thinner from the pressure he exerted on them too.

Considering his position, that didn't come as a shock, but still, it actually hurt to behold. How had the years we'd spent apart affected him? Changed him?

I knew who he was. I knew what he was.

That was how we'd met, after all.

When I'd tried to learn his family's dirty little secrets, and they'd sent him in to 'handle' me...

I had no rights to this man. Just as he had no rights to me. But that didn't take away that gnawing sensation inside me. Something told me—

"Savannah? Is your head still hurting from the fall? You really cracked it when you went down."

Oops. Apparently I had been lost to my contemplation of him for longer than I realized if he thought I was acting concussed. I didn't think his brothers would accept my drooling over their eldest sibling as a legitimate reason for hesitating over what I told him, either.

And 'cracked it' was an understatement. My chin felt like it had come up close and personal with Mike Tyson's fist.

"No. I'm fine. I promise," I assured him with a soft smile.

He dipped his chin, that sternness still there. A sternness I didn't remember. One that made something inside me squirm.

"Want to tell us what the hell's going on?"

I figured I owed them the truth. Plus, if Conor was allied with Star then that meant I'd been right to come to them. Surely they'd help keep me safe once they knew how important my work was?

God, I hoped so.

"I guess I need to start at the beginning."

"That would be helpful," Aidan confirmed, his tone deep.

His scowl made a reappearance a few seconds later. Reminding me to get a move on but also of how he'd yet to smile.

Aidan had been quick to laugh when I'd met him. A devilish twinkle in his eye at all times despite the reason behind our meeting.

What the hell was going on with him?

His mouth pursed.

Yes, I was looking.

Clearing my throat, I muttered, "You heard about what happened at TVGM?"

For the first time, I knew I sounded wary. He technically should know, but I had no way of measuring if he did or not.

Truth be told, the second I'd learned we had a casting couch at TVGM, the second I found out what the producers were doing, one bastard in particular—Derick Wintersen—I'd had to speak out.

My daddy, his reputation, who he was and our family status, had protected me. Dagger Daniels was American rock royalty. Whether I liked it or not, I was famous. As a kid, every part of mine and my siblings' childhoods had been documented in the press. That came with plenty of disadvantages, but many perks too.

Ironically enough, my dad had nothing to do with my getting a job on TV. That was down to a certain someone in this room.

Having been reared in a way I could only classify as traditional, especially considering O'Donnelly Sr.'s reputed obsession with the church, I half expected them to cast me disapproving looks for what I'd done. But the youngest, Eoghan, grunted, "That was bullshit. Why they fired you? No wonder they lost millions of viewers."

Yeah, TVGM, a morning show that aired nationally, hadn't

expected to lose a good chunk of its audience when they kicked me to the curb. Ha.

Though the loss hadn't earned me my job back, I was still pretty damn pleased that the American public had sided with my family, if not me, over the TV show.

"Yeah," Aidan rumbled, "you did good, Savannah."

My throat tightened at that, flooding with emotions I really didn't want to be feeling right now.

His praise sank into me though, like water into parched skin. Public reaction to what I'd done had been polarizing; that he supported me meant more than he could know.

"I've met Poliski, the network controller, and his cronies," Declan said, breaking into my thoughts. "That 'Help The Elders' gala last year in Tribeca? He was such an asshole.

"There was an auction, and they had women walking through the groups of tables holding the lots. If he could have super glued them to his side, he would have. Even so, his hands rarely left those poor women's asses." His mouth tugged up in a snarl. "Kneed him in the nuts when I caught him trying to force himself on one of them in a restroom."

My brows rose.

Were the O'Donnelly brothers feminists?

I was pretty sure I'd not just fallen into a safe haven, but into a parallel universe.

I stared at them, feeling a little like the proverbial deer in headlights.

What was happening here?

"Oh, yeah? What were you doing in a quiet restroom, huh?" Finn jibed.

Declan smirked. "My waitress wanted to be with me."

"Remind me to tell Aela that when you don't listen to me," Conor chimed in, uncaring that his brother practically seared him in two with a stare worthy of a death ray.

"Carry on, Savannah," Aidan advised gruffly when I just carried on gaping at them. Both touched and amused by their rapport. "This is a tough crowd to keep focused."

His brothers grunted and huffed, but only one of them, Brennan —rumor had it that fine piece of man meat was off the shelf—snarked, "Like your focus ain't shot, Aidan."

The others snickered, at what I had no idea, but Aidan's mouth just tightened a little more, before he gestured at me with his hand, indicating I should continue.

Shame.

These guys should consider starting their own reality TV show.

Manhattanite Mobsters... I knew I'd tune in.

"Ever since I got fired," I stated, before my brain could veer even further off course. "I've been trying to find ways to make a difference. I know it sounds hokey but it's true.

"They took my social media profiles away from me, but they were tied to the show anyway, and I already had my personal ones, so I've been using them as a platform. Trying to trigger change."

Sure, I sounded like every other Manhattan socialite at that moment, but when the chips were down, you had a choice to stand up and be counted or to lie down and die.

Which, surprise surprise, wasn't something I was ready to do just yet.

"Star, I mean you called her Lodestar, and I grew up together on the road..."

"What do you mean? Grew up together?" Aidan queried, frowning at me. He cast a glance at Conor. "Star is related to somebody from *noxxious*?"

I snorted. "Her dad was Gerard Sullivan. As much as I love my dad, everybody knows Gerry was *noxxious*. That's why they changed their name after he died. Dad says the world is a shittier place for having lost him, so the group has to be as well."

"Why didn't they just split up then?" Brennan asked, his brows high.

"They love the road too much. Love the life." I shrugged. "It's not for everybody, but it's all they know. All they've really done their whole lives. Anyway, the fans still want them. Dad played to a packed out crowd in the Hard Rock Stadium last Wednesday. Ninety thousand fans were there." I shrugged again. "They're still big."

Conor whistled under his breath. "Shit, I wish I'd been able to get tickets."

"I think if you help me, Dad will set up in that corner over there and play you any song you want if you ask him to."

The brothers chuckled when Conor staggered back and plunked himself down in an armchair opposite me. I had to smile, because he looked both shell-shocked and exhilarated. It was a bizarrely childlike expression on such a handsome mobster's face.

"I'm surprised your dad didn't go apeshit at TVGM for firing you," Finn commented.

"He wanted to, but I stopped him." I sighed. "There have been rumors about him for years, how he treated groupies and things like that. I'm not defending him, and I'm certain he wouldn't want me to. I think he knows there was a long time, when he was younger, that he was a jackass. Things changed after he met Mom. Had kids." I hitched a shoulder. "The second he says something, that's the second one of his old groupies comes out and calls him a hypocrite.

"There is no advantage to him getting involved, especially as it wouldn't have saved my job. Anyway, I'm a grown woman. I can handle these things on my own."

Brennan grunted as he folded his arms across his chest. "Yeah, it really looks like you're handling things so well."

I squinted at him, and because I was feeling woozy, that was the only reason I didn't jump to my feet, stalk toward him, finger proudly prostrate as I prodded him in the chest.

"I saved myself tonight. Nobody else. An intruder not only managed to get into my secured building, but all the way into my apartment. I'm standing here, buddy. Maybe bruised and with a few cuts and sprains and a headache sent from hell, but I'm alive. Because I thought fast, because I can handle myself."

"Then what are you doing here?" Brennan retorted, wearing a smirk that I wanted to slap away.

Jackass.

"Brennan," Aidan growled, and even though it was ridiculous, I smirked at Brennan, oddly secure now that Aidan was sticking up for me.

Jesus, I guess I could've just blown a raspberry at him.

It wasn't that Brennan was visibly affected by Aidan's comment, just that he was sticking up for me.

"I can handle my shit, but I know when things are over my head," I retorted. "Dealing with misogyny in the workplace is a little different than exposing a secret society to the world and fending off a murder attempt from a ninja assassin with a scar from here to here–" I pointed at the corner of my mouth and let my finger drift up to my eye.

Brennan scowled. "What did you say?" he demanded, his tone borderline angry.

What the hell?

Maybe another person would have been intimidated but I'd been raised on the road. Had seen rockstars blowing coke as well as each other before I hit the age of ten, and had been around a bunch of high motherfuckers who'd made Ozzy Osborne look tame.

That in mind, and headache as well as body aches be damned, I scowled at him, and as aggressively as him, snarked, "Are you hard of hearing?"

The brother beside him, Declan, snickered. "Yeah, Brennan, are you deaf?"

Brennan flipped him the bird, then to me, reiterated, "A scar from the corner of his mouth to his eyes. As in, a knife traveled the entire distance?"

I thought about the thick ridging and scars along my attacker's jawline, and slowly nodded. Now that I thought about it, I had no idea how that was even possible unless the knife was curved or something.

I'd seen crazier shit in my years, though. Had reported it too.

People were capable of horrendous things. Seemed like every year, the world just grew worse.

Because Brennan expected an answer, I told him, "Oddly specific, but, yes. I think so."

"What is it, Brennan?"

It was only when Aidan looked at his brother that I realized it was the first time he'd taken his eyes off me.

I felt the loss of his focus as if it were a whisper-like caress along the back of my neck.

"I'm coming across that more and more. Not scarred, though. They're fresh. They've never brushed up against our territory so I've kept an eye on them. To me, it was a case of 'Not my monkey, not my circus.' Plus, I knew they weren't in cahoots with the *Famiglia* so any dissent among the Italians was a bonus."

"Who are you talking about?" Conor sniped.

Brennan cast me a glance. "Should we talk in front of her?"

I almost scoffed at the derogatory way he said, 'her,' but Aidan replied before I could, "She knows far worse shit than you can imagine and has never gone to the cops. Have you, Savannah?"

It sounded like there was a smidgen of pride to his declaration, but if anything, it was a source of shame to me that I'd caved in to his demands.

I liked my legs attached and my brain not in a coma though... That was why I'd never gone to the cops.

"I haven't said dick to anyone."

Aidan tipped up his chin and when we stared at each other, I recognized something else.

Apology.

In the soft, rueful slant to his mouth.

Regret.

In the way he rubbed his forehead.

He'd used something I was ashamed of to instill a sense of trust in his brothers...

And he was sorry for it.

That shouldn't have impressed me as much as it did.

"You've met before?"

"Jesus, Declan, how fucking slow are you?" Eoghan groused. "Of course they know each other."

Declan gritted his teeth. "Fuck off, Eoghan. Can't you tell? They ain't—" His brow puckered. "Were you friends?"

Because that was so alien a concept?

Then, of course, I looked at Aidan and had to sigh.

Of course, it was.

Men like Aidan didn't befriend women.

They fucked them. Sneaked out in the middle of the night. Never called them again.

Men like Aidan were pricks.

Why did God have to make them so pretty?

Talk about the real crime against humanity. My belief, however, was confirmed when all of the brothers looked horrified.

Jeez.

If their gaping mouths were anything to go by, he'd fucked a lot more broads than I could begin to guestimate.

"I don't know what we were," Aidan admitted softly, "but it doesn't matter right now. What matters is what happened downstairs. Brennan, you'll handle him later?"

I wanted to feel uneasy, wanted to be discomfited by the hidden meaning behind Aidan's words, but I didn't have it in me to emote that way. Not when I might never have been able to get away. Not when I might be dead now.

Torture was for the ages of the Spanish Inquisition, but ever since I'd been dealing with the injustices of the patriarchal society in which we lived, I'd admit to being more bloodthirsty than before.

"I'll have some answers before midday."

Aidan nodded. "Good. Now, explain about the scar."

Brennan reached up and scrubbed the back of his neck. "You guys heard of the Valentinis?"

My eyes flared wide. "I have."

Eoghan, Declan, and Aidan shook their heads. "No," they murmured, confirming they had no idea who the family was.

"Seriously?" I muttered. "Call yourself mobsters? Don't you know who the enemy is?"

"While you're completely correct, Savannah, my brothers aren't complete dimwits. The Valentinis were extinct by the sixties.

"As far as I know, they retreated to Sicily to lick their wounds after the Fieris came close to wiping them out when they took over New York."

"Jesus," Conor murmured. "That was way back in time. But I remember Da and Grandda used to bitch about them. Said they were sons of bitches. But it was kind of nostalgic? Like, those were the good old days, kind of thing. By comparison, while they were enemies and Italian, they were angels." To me, he said, "Da hates the Fieris."

"Not that there are many left now," Declan said with some satisfaction.

I snorted. "Not sure anybody ever liked them. But are you supposed to like a Mafia family?"

Conor snickered. "Remember who you're talking to."

I shot him a sheepish smile. "Oops."

Conor grinned, his humor morphing and transforming his entire face once more. "I like her."

Declan nudged him in the side. "You don't like anyone."

"That's not true. I'm just very particular. Is it my fault that people are sons of bitches?"

Eoghan shook his head. "Your intolerance is showing."

"I didn't realize I had to be tolerant," Conor said with a frown, his confusion clear.

"Don't feel like you have to be tolerant for my benefit," I said, amused at how perplexed he was. He grinned at me again, erasing at least five years off his face with that one small gesture. "See? I knew I was right to like you."

Hiding a smile of my own and deciding to get the subject back on track, I turned to Brennan and queried, "I've never heard of a Valentini who did half a Cheshire cat grin."

"What do you know about the Valentinis?" he countered.

"Everything. I'm a mafia/mob aficionado." I shrugged, unashamed to admit to such a pastime. "I've always been fascinated by the underworld. I'm pretty much an encyclopedia on the topic," I boasted.

"Let me guess, that's how you got into trouble with the family," Declan said wryly.

"You'd be right. But let's face it, if I hadn't met Aidan, I might not be here today. So I figure everything happens for a reason."

"You'll have to explain that logic," Eoghan countered. "As far as I can tell, there's no correlation between the two.

"Whether or not you knew us, that attacker would still have come after you. You exposed a lot of powerful men yesterday, that was always going to have repercussions."

"I'm only in this building because I know it's owned by an O'Donnelly." I cast Aidan a look. "That's why I moved underneath the penthouse. Everybody knows the O'Donnelly boys live in their father's apartment buildings." Because I was nosy, I asked, "I know that he doesn't hand them out eldest first. So... what do you have to do to earn an apartment?"

"That's enough family history for one day," Aidan argued.

"I've barely heard any family history at all," I complained.

Conor snickered. "Some shit you really just don't want to know. Anyway, Miss Encyclopedia, tell us about the Valentinis."

"It's a little off topic, isn't it? From, you know, the murderer downstairs..."

"You're alive," Conor reasoned. "That means he's not a murderer. Yet."

I squinted at him. "Attempted murderer, then."

"Better. Now, explain."

"If you insist," I groused. "Back in the fifties, the Valentinis ran New York City. Then Fieri came in and turned everyone's heads. He wanted to stop small-town prostitution rings, get involved with more trafficking operations, drugs and humans so the Italians would control the largest share of the sex industry in Manhattan.

"The world was opening up after the war, transport links evolved, and as a result, it meant it was a lot easier to smuggle people into the country.

"The family's predominant source of income over the last ten or so years has been their major prostitution rackets. The *Padrino's* vision morphed into their current market.

"Regardless, the few Valentinis who survived retreated to Sicily. As far as I know, they're still there."

Brennan shook his head. "That's just it, they're not. I've heard rumors. Granted, rumors are nothing concrete. But..." He scrubbed a hand across his jaw. "I've been talking to the few old boys who are still alive and they say that back in the day, there was one Valentini who used to cut up the faces of his enemies.

"He even scalped a couple."

My nose crinkled at the bridge. "That's so gross," I huffed. "Anyway, this guy's face... It was an old scar. Definitely no less than eighteen months. Two years, max. I'm not the best at math but I doubt the dude who collected scalps for a living is still living and breathing."

"That's my concern," Brennan said gruffly. "They've been underground for a while. I just don't know why." He pursed his lips. "Around the Italian patch, more and more guys are showing up looking like lopsided clowns."

"Why have you never mentioned them?" Aidan questioned.

"Because they've never tampered with our business. Do you know how many players are out there? Two bit pieces of shit that not even the cops are really interested in?

"Da knows about them because it's my job to keep him in the loop, but I didn't think the rest of you guys would be interested as you're not out on the streets like me."

"Hey, I am," Declan complained.

Brennan rolled his eyes. "Not like me."

"Who knew this was a competition?" Conor chirped at me, and I smiled, oddly at ease with him.

Hell, oddly at ease with them all.

That was weird, right?

Here I was, surrounded by guys who weren't exactly idols but the stars of an obsession that went back as far as childhood—well, maybe not them, but their family—and I was enjoying myself.

I'd almost been killed!

That I needed the reminder was very concerning.

I cleared my throat and asked, "Before you guys get into this even further, ya know, who works more and shit like that—" Brennan arched a brow at me but I just smirked back. "—will you guys help me? I've barely started with the exposés, and I have dozens more articles to write."

"Who's your source?" Finn asked. "Where are you getting all this information from? I read the one you released today—it was in-depth stuff. You needed help with it."

Conor grunted. "Ain't that obvious? Lodestar, of course."

I wasn't about to agree or disagree. Star *was* my source, but she had one of her own we both wanted to protect.

Deciding it was wise to change the subject, I informed them, "Yesterday, my phone started blowing up. If this Valentini is after me—"

"He isn't," Brennan said immediately.

I scowled. "Then why did you bring them up?"

"Because the fucker who tried to knife you had been injured by him. That sound like the work of a friend or foe?"

I pulled a face because apparently my brain wasn't firing on all cylinders. "Huh."

"Yeah. You and whoever did that to him are on the same side." Brennan shot Aidan a look. "You willing to vouch for her with Da?"

Aidan firmed his mouth. "Yes."

He straightened up, getting to his feet, but the second he did, his eyes fluttered closed, his nostrils flared while his jaw tensed. His skin blanched, and every part of him tensed up.

I watched the transformation and hurt for him. Hurt on his behalf.

My gaze dropped down the lean length of his form and found the brace around his knee.

Biting my bottom lip, I fought the urge to do something, to flutter around him, to help him take the pain away when there was nothing any of us could do to stop that.

Though he sucked up all my attention, I had to see what his brothers' reactions were, and as one, I saw they felt his pain too. They hated it and sympathized.

Though not a brother, Finn's regret was the deepest. I got it, even though it wasn't exactly his fault. Everyone knew his wife had been knocked down in that same drive-by on their wedding day of all days.

A sharp exhalation escaped Aidan as he opened his eyes and rasped, "We're working against the Sparrows too, Savannah. Mutual enemies mean you've befriended the Five Points, I hope you're ready for what that means."

And with that cryptic comment, he limped off, leaving me on the sofa, with his brothers.

Mobsters.

On any other day, I'd think that I'd died and gone to heaven.

Today?

I just wanted to head after him and do something, *anything,* to make him feel better.

That, I'd recognize later, was the moment I should have known everything changed...

EIGHT

AIDAN

THE PAIN WAS EXCRUCIATING, radiating up and down my leg, almost hitting my hip, making every part of my lower body throb.

What was worse?

The need for relief.

I wanted an Oxy like a thirsty man needed water.

I wanted the escape.

I wanted the blurred lines—shit, I didn't just want it. I fucking needed it.

No one should have to live with this.

No fucking one.

I snapped the second I entered the bedroom Conor had given me, slamming my hand into the wall, uncaring that the drywall crumbled, uncaring that it added to what I was already feeling.

The rage was new.

Normally, I just popped a pill. Swallowed relief, taking comfort in the chemicals that fucked with my system. But I couldn't do that anymore.

I couldn't.

I'd had the taste of heroin once. I knew why we were wealthy now. I knew how we were filthy fucking rich because one dose of that wicked tincture, and that was it. You had the taste. It wouldn't leave you. It was with you forever. Haunting you.

Chasing after you, relentlessly. Endlessly. Worse than the pain. Because that triggered more of it, just of a different nature, while you carried on hunting that first high. Nothing, and I mean, *nothing*, was ever as pure as that original hit.

I'd been clean for forty-one days, and each of those was hard won. The pain, right now, felt all the more acute because Savannah was here.

I remembered the last time we were together. I'd been whole. Normal in myself. Tonight? I felt like I was missing a limb. I felt weak. Hobbling around while she sat there, like a goddamn angel sent to torment me, to remind me of what I'd lost.

I snarled under my breath as a small wave of crumbling plaster fell from the wall, decorating the black marble floor with dust.

As I twisted around, hobbling away from the door, a knock sounded.

My breath froze in my chest, because I knew if that was one of my brothers, they wouldn't have knocked.

That meant it was Savannah.

Savannah who was more trouble than she was worth.

Savannah who, even bloodied, bruised, was never down for long, and who looked like sin sitting on Conor's sofa. A sofa that had housed me and my blanket fort. That had seen me sweat into the leather, shuddering and jittering with tremors as I detoxed.

Why did she have to handle my brothers so well?

She'd sat there, somehow regal even though they were acting out. Brennan being a douche, his usual self when he was in front of people, when he wanted to act the big, bad O'Donnelly Fixer. Conor smiling at her, saying he even fucking liked her. I knew why too. She hadn't doled out any BS to us. He liked the truth. So did I.

What I also knew? From watching her every goddamn morning on TVGM?

She wasn't always so truthful.

She was, in fact, a liar.

The ditzy airhead she showed the world was a façade. I'd met the shark. I knew what went on behind those pretty brown eyes, and her analytical mind was hot as fuck.

"Aidan?" she called out softly.

I gritted my teeth. "Come in." Would she call my name like that if we were fucking?

Nobody said my name like her.

I wasn't sure why. It wasn't like she had an accent or anything. But she said it differently, and it made my ear drums shudder with delight.

I sucked in a breath, my mind veering away from the pain for a second as she opened the door.

In a pair of sweats and a tee, both of them dirty, with her looking disheveled after her escapades tonight, she had no right to be so beautiful.

No fucking right.

Still, the memory of her being attacked had a tic twitching in my jaw. I'd seen the state of her apartment after Baggy and Forrest had come and helped retrieve the SOB who thought he could hurt Savannah.

"I'm proud of you for tonight."

She blinked. "For defending myself?"

Her squirming had me arching a brow at her. "What is it?"

A huff escaped her lips. "Nothing. It's nothing."

I smiled a little. "What is it, Savannah?" I repeated, my tone just a touch sterner.

I'd noticed that about her before. She was hard to pin down sometimes, but with a little authority, she usually caved in.

Her nose crinkled. "I'm a modern woman."

"I know you are." Had I said she wasn't?

"Well, good. I'm glad you know that." Her nose crinkled some more. "I shouldn't want you to be proud of me. Shouldn't need that."

She cleared her throat. "But I like it." For a second, disgust laced her features, and I knew it was aimed inwardly.

I wasn't sure why I was so careful with my words, I just was. "Shouldn't we always want people to think we've done well?"

"We shouldn't," she disagreed with a small shrug. "But it is what it is."

I frowned. "What does that mean?"

"It means..." She heaved a sigh. "Never mind. Is everything okay?"

Unappreciative of her answer, I limped forward, not even thinking of my fucking leg, just needing to cage her in. To get her answer. To know where her mind was at.

As I approached, her eyes flared wide. Not in fear. The pupils dilated, swallowing up the pretty brown irises that reminded me of mahogany.

With that one involuntary gesture, I found myself at the limits of my control. Her beauty did that to me. She wasn't the girl-next-door kind of hot, wasn't a supermodel. Savannah had curves on top of curves, but her face was exquisite. Porcelain skin, arched brows that framed her features, a delicate nose and lips that were a dusky pink I wanted to lick.

Everything about her was tactile.

Which was why she was so fucking dangerous to me.

On the outside, she looked harmless. On the inside, she possessed a rapier sharp intelligence that'd slice me in two if I didn't watch out.

"What, Savannah? What does it mean?" I demanded.

"This isn't fair," she groused. "I'm not firing on all cylinders!"

I smirked at her. "That puts me at an advantage then. I'll take that considering I know how much of a shark you are regularly."

Something flashed in her eyes. "I'm not a shark."

"Yes, you are," I countered. "Don't think because you fool every other dumb fuck out there, you ever fooled me. I can scent a predator when I'm near one." I reached up and tapped her nose. "Now, what does 'it is what it is' mean?"

She rolled her lips inward, like she was trying to watch her words before she blurted out, "I'm weird with you."

"Weird?" I scowled. "You're not weird."

"That's sweet of you to say but you're not inside my head."

"No. I'm not." I tipped my chin. "Care to share what's going on inside it?"

"Not particularly." She pulled a face. "Not tonight. Tomorrow. Yeah, tomorrow I'll tell you everything."

I couldn't stop myself from laughing. "What? When you're less shaken?" A kinder man would have backed off. *I wasn't kind.* I hummed. "That wasn't a request, Savannah."

"No? Well, it sure as hell sounded like one. One I choose to refuse."

"What if I won't let you refuse to answer, hmm?" When did I get so close? So close that I could smell her perfume, one that reminded me of peaches, so close that I could see the individual lines of the grazes on her chin and jaw.

She squirmed again. "Stop it."

"Stop what?" I rumbled.

Her hand wafted in the very minute amount of space between us. Less than two feet? "This. Stop it. Back up."

"I don't think you want me to," I rasped, leaning forward.

All of a sudden, she had her back to the wall and I had my forearms on either side of her head. The relief was immediate on my knee, the pressure shifting, but I wasn't thinking about that. Just about pinning her in place.

Savannah needed that.

Otherwise she'd squirm free.

A growl escaped her. "What's going on with you?" she attempted to deflect. "Why are you so angry?"

I scowled. "I'm not angry with you."

Her expression cleared in an instant, and I noticed the tiniest corner of her bottom lip was sucked between her teeth. "I didn't—" She heaved a sigh. "Okay, not with me. What, then?"

"I don't matter," I rasped. "What you went through tonight—that's why I'm mad. You shouldn't have had to deal with that on your own. Where the fuck were your security, Savannah? I know your father insists you have them."

She scowled. "What use would they have been? He got into my apartment, Aidan. How were my guards supposed to get to me before that bastard slit my throat?"

Rage throttled me, filling me with a tension that was unlike my usual temper. It was selfless, not selfish. Revolving around her because she was right.

She was fucking right.

As her truth resonated, I rasped, "Okay, that settles it. You're going to stay with us. No one apart from Lodestar would fucking dare creep into our penthouses. At least that way you'll be safe."

Her eyes measured mine. "Fine."

I blinked. "Fine. *Fine?*" Jesus, that meant she was terrified and just not showing it. I'd never known a woman reply that fucking fast without even bitching about independence and all that other shit.

My hands dropped down, sliding along her arms until I reached her wrists which I cupped. "I'll keep you safe. You don't have to be scared."

Her gaze darted to my chest. "I have a lot of exposés left to reveal," she murmured softly. "It could take weeks."

Weeks with Savannah?

Christ, she'd drive me insane.

Absolutely fucking insane.

She was chaotic and invasive. Always asking questions. Relentless when she was on the hunt for answers. She was so fucking beautiful it hurt.

This rehab shit was hard enough without that sweet kind of torture hovering around me too.

So why the fuck did I say: "You'll stay for however long it takes, Savannah. Do you hear me?"

NINE

SAVANNAH

I SHOULD HAVE ARGUED.

I knew I should.

I should have said, 'Hey, motherfucker, I'm a big girl. I managed to stop some assassin dude with a mop and a coffee table book. I can do it again.'

Not only did I not want to risk it, but I really didn't want to.

Did you want to guess how many times I'd seen the bastard since the last meeting we'd had together?

Zero.

Zero times.

Nought.

0.

Nil.

ZERO.

That should have been impossible in New York when we ran in the same circles, when I'd seen his brothers and his family several times at boring galas and fundraisers...

Which told me he'd actively avoided me.

Which told me I got under his skin.

Not in the whole parasitic kind of way. In a 'I have to avoid her because if I don't, things will deteriorate fast.'

And when I said deteriorate, I totally meant 'we'd end up fucking so hard that no mattress in the city would be safe.'

No mattresses *would* be safe. Not in a ten-mile vicinity, that was for damn sure.

Have you ever just looked at someone and thought about their dick sliding inside you?

That was what Aidan did to me.

To this day, when I jilled off, I used him as inspiration.

I used his face to get me off because that and his hands were the only things I'd ever really seen.

Until today.

I'd seen one knee and a calf; the other was covered in a brace. I also got to see some yummy forearms, with lovely veins wrapped around them. Just like veins would wrap around his dick—

Goddammit. This was what he did to me. Took innocent musings and made them all dirty!

It was totally his fault.

I had nothing to do with it. *Whatsoever*.

It was all on him for being so fucking delicious. That tic in his jaw made my clit pulse at the same beat, and the way he smelled? A little salty and sweaty from the gym, well, wouldn't you know it, it just made me want to lick him. Even if he was skinnier than before, he was still muscled and through his gym shirt, I saw how his pecs pushed against the fabric.

I wanted to bite him.

Sooo badly.

I didn't think that had anything to do with the fog taking over my brain either, nor the migraine from hell that was starting to make itself known.

I wanted to dig my nails into his back, to scrape the hell out of it, to claw and scratch just so when he put a shirt on the next day, he remembered exactly who he'd been to bed with.

For all of these reasons, I'd said 'fine.'

Of course, men being men, of which Aidan still was one, even if he was definitely special, he couldn't just roll with it.

Instead, he frowned down at me like he'd have preferred an argument, then uttered fighting words, "You'll stay for however long it takes, Savannah. Do you hear me?"

Well, look at me just adding an extra *three* weeks to every exposé I needed to write.

Hell, maybe I could tie him up with me for the next thirty frickin' years.

Because I figured he wanted me to argue, I scowled at him. "If you insist."

"Oh, I do." He growled as he pushed back and away from the wall. Away from me. I missed his heat. Damn, did I miss it. I missed his smell and the way the air around us seemed to tingle. Didn't he feel that? "I'll take you to a bedroom. You can get some rest—"

"Rest?" I snorted. "Not going to happen." I flexed my sore hands as I thought about how he'd just answered my question.

He apparently didn't feel 'that' because if he did, there was a perfectly great bed right behind him.

I didn't even take up that much room on the mattress.

"You've been through a trying ordeal, Savannah," he grumbled.

"I'm not eighty-nine, Aidan," I retorted.

His eyes narrowed. "If I have to put you to bed myself, you'll get some sleep."

I perked up. "Okay."

He frowned. "Okay? What the hell's going on with you tonight?"

Shit. "Like you said, it's been a trying ordeal." Shit. I might have backpedaled a little too far because he no longer looked suspicious, just amused at how damn perky I was at the prospect of him hustling me between the sheets. "I guess I *am* more tired than I thought," I said, faking a yawn that I kind of ruined because as I faked it, a real one popped out. You know the kind. A jaw-popping, face-cracking, lion's roar of a yawn.

Aidan snorted. "Thought as much. Come on. I'll take you to a spare room."

"Thank you," I said sheepishly, trudging after him as he pulled the door open and limped into the hallway.

Carefully reducing my pace to match his, I peeped over at him. When he sensed my focus, he cast me a glance and his lips curved.

He smiled!

He only fucking smiled!

A real one. A *genuine* one. Not a twitch of his mouth at the corners or a smirk. But a beautiful one.

And it packed as much of a punch as ever.

Holy shit. Be still my heart and my ovaries because things were setting in for a bumpy ride.

Every part of me pulsing—yes, even my bones—I smiled back. His eyes darkened, and he quickly looked away.

Why did he do that?

Grrr.

I remembered how it'd been back when we'd first met, and whenever things could have evolved, or at least moved forward a few steps, he'd always backed off.

He wasn't just the one who got away, he was more the phantom of the fucking opera.

Shaking my head at the analogy, then wincing when the migraine had lights dancing at the periphery of my vision, I muttered, "Are you going to set a guard on me?"

"Why would I? You'll be staying here. With Conor and I."

"Until my exposés are all published?" I asked carefully, trying not to get excited.

"Yes." His mouth firmed. "He might not like it. None of us have lived together for a long time. If that's the case, we'll go to my house."

Well, I wasn't about to complain.

"Okay, well, whatever's easiest for you."

Me.

I was easiest for him.

Seriously.

Bend me over and spank me, Aidan.

I'd take it.

He grunted. "What is your family doing for the holidays?"

"They're going to Hawaii." I pursed my lips. "I wasn't going to go."

"Why not?" He frowned at me. "Aren't you as close to them as you used to be?"

My nose crinkled. "Do we really have to get into it?"

His frown hardened and, in response, my lady bits softened.

"We had a falling out over Thanksgiving."

"Over the holiday itself or because of it?"

I mumbled, "Umm, during Thanksgiving weekend."

"What about?"

"Camden, you know, my brother—"

He laughed a little. "Yes, Savannah, I know the singer who's won more Grammy awards than Adele."

I grimaced, because everyone knew my goddamn brother. They just didn't realize what a prick he was. "Well, he and I got into a little spat, and I've decided not to forgive him."

Aidan was quiet a few seconds, and as he guided me into a spare room that was as eclectically designed as the rest of the place—why was there a fountain beside the bed? Wouldn't that make anyone who stayed here need to pee all the time?—he eventually asked, "About your career?"

Humming, I said, "He told me I was stupid to risk it all when I should have known nothing would change."

Aidan frowned. "Nothing would ever change if people didn't try to make a difference."

"Exactly!" I stopped peering at the fountain that was somehow like a waterfall running down exposed brickwork, and twisted around to stare at him. "He said I was an idealistic no hope and that—"

He arched a brow at me when I stopped, too mad, still fuming enough that it made the words hard to get out. Of course, he then proceeded to stun the fuck out of me by drifting toward me, not stopping until we were standing in front of one another again, and his hand moved up to cup my chin. As his thumb stroked along my bottom lip, I was pretty sure I'd died and gone to heaven.

"And that...?" he asked softly.

"I'd have been better off being like Aspen and Paris."

"I'm not sure what that means? Snowy in winter and rainy in spring?"

I had to grin. "I meant, my siblings." Despite how goddamn mad I was at Camden, I laughed. "Although they do both those things too."

"Snow and rain? Seems like they're more active than your brother realizes."

Sniggering, and pleased because this was the Aidan I remembered, *playful,* I murmured, "Well, I can't deny they're lazy. They want to get into reality TV so they can consider that a job. Daddy's trying, but he can only do so much. They're boring. All they do is shop." My brow puckered. "Who'd want to watch people do that?"

"I think the Kardashians have made a pretty good living out of it," he said wryly.

"You know who they are?"

"I'm a mobster, Savannah, not dead," he retorted with a short laugh.

"True."

He stopped rubbing my lip. I wanted him to carry on. Damn.

"I'm surprised the cameras don't just want to follow your dad around."

"They do. That's the problem. Dad's not interested in that shit anymore. He just wants to play his concerts and live as much of a quiet life as he possibly can." I shrugged. "I was in a position to make change. I'm Dagger Daniels' daughter. I had standing with the station, and a platform in which to disseminate the truth. What should I have done? Let countless innocent women be hurt?"

Slowly, he shook his head, his eyes darkening as he murmured, "No. You did the right thing. Sometimes doing that isn't enough.

Sometimes, not even that will instigate change, but if you didn't try, you'd never know, would you?"

"No, I wouldn't know," I confirmed softly, uncertain what his response would be. "As it stands, at least they lost a lot of ad revenue."

His grin was like quicksilver. "That's the best way to hurt anyone —their pocket." I hummed, then stifled a disappointed sigh when he pulled back, rasping, "I have to go out, Savannah. But you'll be safe here while I'm gone. Conor will have changed the access code to the helipad by now, and will probably be shoring it up like it's the Pentagon."

I snagged my fingers around his wrist. "Where are you going?"

"I want answers about who's targeting you. Just a vague belief that it's the Sparrows isn't enough."

I bit my lip.

Now he was trying to keep me safe.

Funny how this hero was about to go and help torture someone, no?

Not exactly what romance was made of, but I'd take it.

"I want you to get your ass into bed and rest. If I find out you didn't sleep, well, there'll be consequences."

"Consequences?" I tipped my head to the side. Conor had already threatened me with those, but it sounded far more interesting coming from Aidan. "What kind of consequences?"

"You don't want to find out."

With that, he began limping away, but I couldn't let him go, not without saying, "Be safe, Aidan."

It was either say that or tell him I really, really, really, *really* wanted to find out.

A journalist's most fatal flaw was their incessant need to understand. To find answers to the questions that few dared ask.

Well, I dared. I dared, all right.

Even if Aidan had gotten that rumbly vibration in his throat, that soft snag that made a shiver rush down my spine.

When had he become so masterful? Before, he'd dominated. There was a distinct difference.

Had the years apart strengthened him? Changed him and made him adapt to the current situation in the city?

I had to figure it did.

Had to figure that I'd changed just as much as he had. The years apart had forged us into the people standing here today.

And Aidan?

Well, he'd been forged into an even sexier bastard than before.

God help me and my ovaries. Especially where *consequences* were concerned.

TEN

SAVANNAH

FIVE YEARS EARLIER

EVERY DAY, I followed the same routine.

I got up at six, did yoga, showered and changed, headed downstairs for poached egg on toast and a chai latte, watched the world go by at the corner table which overlooked a corner of the street and then a good chunk of a pathway into Central Park, then got on with my work for a few hours.

In between jobs thanks to the last position I'd had at the *Record* falling through when I'd called my boss out for being a misogynistic jerk who spent more time trying to look down my blouse than read my editorials, I was dedicating my newly freed up schedule to my passion project—New York City's crime families.

I wasn't an idiot. I'd expected that my rummaging around the ancient history of NYC's various groups of mobsters would ruffle some feathers.

I just never expected when I went down for my breakfast that particular morning that Aidan O'Donnelly Jr. would be sitting there, at my table, evidently waiting on me.

I wasn't even looking at anything that recent. When I said ancient history, I meant it. I was looking back in the late eighties, early nineties. Stuff that should no longer be of interest to the O'Donnellys, yet the heir's presence here told me otherwise. It informed me that where I'd been digging, I'd touched a nerve.

The thought thrilled me.

"Good morning, Ms. Daniels."

Christ, what a voice.

Deep. The smallest hint of a growl.

I arched a brow at him as I approached the table. "You're in my seat."

"I think we both know I wouldn't be here if someone hadn't gone hunting in all the wrong places."

Hunting.

That was the word for it.

I knew his presence was a warning, and I knew I should be scared, but this kind of thing was in my blood. I loved the chase. Loved the *hunt* for a story, and when my instincts were triggered, I was worse than Dracula scouting for blood after a week-long fast.

I sank into the chair opposite the man I knew the family called 'Junior.'

He wasn't just a junior because he shared the same name as his psychotic father. In looks? They were like mirror images.

Rumor had it that before he'd wed Magdalena O'Shea, Aidan had been one of the city's most eligible bachelors. Back then, there'd been no hiding from his mobster ties, and still the women had *allegedly* flocked to him.

His sons and their links to the mob were a little different. A little more evolved.

I knew they were as dirty as their daddy, but that didn't mean shit without proof. They hid behind dummy corps and all kinds of legitimate fronts that prevented people as good as me from finding them.

Damn their hides.

I knew I could play this one of two ways.

Be truthful. Show him I was no fool. Get nowhere fast because he'd stonewall me.

Or...

Play the fool, and lie, and maybe get a chance to dig deeper into his family history.

Well, when I put it like that—there was no choice, was there?

"I don't know what you mean." I blinked at him. "Who are you?"

A hard glint appeared in his eyes. "Is that the way you want to play this?"

Oh, man, I loved that his verbiage tied up to my thought processes.

Not that I was supposed to love it, of course.

"Play, what?" I countered. "I reserve this table every day." Twisting around, I pretended to look for a server. "Maybe I'll just call the management over here so they can be the ones to clear things up."

"There's nothing to clear up. I'm at the right table. I'm here to speak with you."

"I have no idea who you are," I lied. "And my mother told me never to speak to strangers."

"You listened to her?"

"Didn't you listen to your mother?" Rumor had it the O'Donnelly brothers were under their mom's thumbs. Total, complete, *utter* Momma's boys.

Although, looking at just how much of a man Aidan Jr. was, his mother couldn't be the pint-sized mafia princess she was rumored as being.

Junior hummed under his breath. "I read your piece on the Suez Canal. The one you posted last year in the *Record*? Discussing how trade wars and political instabilities were going to make for trouble down the line...? I'm not sure an airhead would be able to dissect the probability of container ships wedging it shut."

"Airheads are capable of quite a lot of things. We can even breathe without life support," I told him without blinking.

"Aren't you smart? Breathing autonomously? I truly am impressed." He said that without blinking too. "However, when I'm sent on a task, I don't just leave it down to fate. You're acquainted with who my father is. I'm also sure from the research I know you've been doing, that you're well aware of the fact that he doesn't appreciate mistakes. Mistakes equal failure in his mind, and he isn't the kind of man who anyone would like to fail." He smirked at me as he leaned over the table. "I researched you quite thoroughly. Even spoke with a few previous editors of yours. You pissed most of them off."

Christ, he really had done his homework on me.

"Not my fault they have fragile egos."

"Fragile egos?" A laugh escaped him. "They said you were insubordinate and unruly. That you routinely went ahead on assignments that were given to someone else—"

"Because they insisted on sending me on fluff assignments. Anything with any meat went to the people with penises." My mouth tightened with irritation at my blurting that out, but he merely carried on as if I hadn't spoken at all.

"Your editors were more than willing to give me a heads-up about what kind of writer you are. I read a mixture of the fluff and the grittier, meatier articles. Especially the pieces you wrote in college." He tilted his head to the side. "You can pretend to be an airhead with men who don't listen and who think with their dicks but I'm no fool, Ms. Daniels.

"I think, in fact, you'd be the fool if you underestimated how much it would piss me off for you to carry on with this ridiculous charade."

My brow furrowed. "Are you seriously autopsying my personality?"

"Are you dead? You look alive to me."

"You just slayed my character." I glared at him. "How dare you?"

"Oh, I dare worse." He leaned in, somehow looming over me even though that wasn't physically possible when we were both on the same level. "You're not an idiot. You know who I am. You know why I'm here so cease with the petty messing around and maybe I can save your ass before someone decides to take you out first."

I jolted back. "*What?*" Shock had me complying and I dropped my charade. He wasn't wrong about that—I did wear a mask. Sometimes, it was the only way to get people to do what I wanted. And when I said people, I meant men.

Put on a vacant look, dress in a low-cut blouse and a short skirt, wear a vapid smile, and suddenly, they heard you. They even sometimes forgave you when you 'misunderstood' the assignment and went ahead and did what you wanted anyway.

Those three editors he'd spoken with had only fired me, not because I was unruly, but because they'd each come onto me and I'd spurned their advances.

Fucking men.

Toxic pieces of shit.

"You heard me." His eyes narrowed. "I'm telling you to stop with this—"

I raised a hand. "You mean 'someone' will put a hit out on me if I don't stop what I'm doing?"

The only person I knew who was higher than him in the Five Points was his father. As the heir, I knew he was pretty much Sr.'s right hand man as his father groomed him for the job of leading the Irish Mob.

He tipped his chin to the side in assent.

My brow puckered. "I don't understand. I'm not looking at current events. I'm not even investigating things that will take your family down. Why would that be—" Despite myself, I swallowed, nerves fluttering in my stomach like a hive of bees had overtaken it.

It wasn't the first time I'd put myself in danger for a story. As a journalist, a good one at that, I pissed off a lot of people. But there was a difference between being threatened, between getting mugged and having my bag with my research stolen, and having a hit put out on me by the head of the Irish Mob.

Jesus.

Aidan Jr. just blinked at me. "I think we should start back at the beginning."

"What? Why? Just answer me!" I barked.

"See? Only a stupid person would maintain that act when there's a death threat on the line. I'm relieved to see that you're not an idiot."

I frowned. "Is this a joke?"

"I rarely joke about business." His nostrils flared and a glimmer of irritation sparked into being in his beautiful green eyes. Yeah, did I mention this guy was hot? "My name's Aidan O'Donnelly."

"I know who you are," I muttered impatiently. "Just as you know I'm Savannah Daniels."

He hummed. "Funny how you're the only one of your father's kids to go into an actual line of work rather than just riding on his coattails."

"Not sure you can judge anyone on that considering you're going to sit on the Five Points' throne one day." I arched a brow at him. "Nepotism at its best, no?"

He smirked a little. "Nepotism or maybe I'm just the right person for the job?"

"Is there ever a right person for that kind of job?" I leaned forward, but before I could say another word, Suzy popped up with my chai latte and a set of silverware wrapped up in a napkin.

"Five minutes, Savannah. That okay with you?"

After clearing my throat, I broke my heated stare with Aidan and shot her a look. "That'll be great, Suzy. Thank you."

She smiled at me, then to Aidan, asked, "You sure you don't want anything to eat?"

He shook his head. "I'll have one of those chai lattes and some water, please."

Of course, when he smiled at her, she blushed.

I wasn't sure if I could blame her or not.

Suzy was barely nineteen and had the palest skin. Even her freckles stood out in stark relief on her cheeks. They were pretty much the skin-version of exclamation points.

At nineteen, I was sure that I'd have just melted into the ground if an older guy like Aidan even deigned to look at me, never mind order from me with a politeness that I didn't think he'd be capable of.

Let's face it.

He was the heir to a criminal empire.

Did he have to smile at nervous waitresses?

Or did that just mean he wasn't an asshole?

Gnawing on the inside of my cheek as Suzy stuttered out her understanding, I reverted my attention to him and stared straight at him, so that he'd feel my glance.

When she headed off to get his order, he turned back to me and I murmured, "Didn't think chai latte would be your thing."

"I'm a big fan of cardamom."

A laugh escaped me. "Seriously?"

He quirked a brow. "Seriously. Not all..." His lips twitched. "*Irishmen* are 'meat and potatoes' kind of guys."

"No? Just most of them?"

"I feel stereotyped," he retorted.

I frowned at him, because I'd been about to say that men in his position couldn't be anything other than stereotyped, but he was here to help me, wasn't he? Not to kill me. Like he said would happen if I didn't listen?

Any amusement at a mobster appreciating chai having died, I rasped, "What are you doing here?"

"You've come to my father's attention, Ms. Daniels... May I call you Savannah?"

Unease unfurled inside me. "If you want."

He hummed. "Well, Savannah, no one wants to come to Aidan Sr.'s attention, do they? As I'm sure you'll know from your research."

Slowly, I shook my head.

I was a bulldog where a story was concerned, had known I might piss people off, but could never have anticipated that the Five Points' heir would be the one to come to threaten me.

That was taking things up to so high of a notch, I couldn't even see it overhead.

"How have I?" I rasped, my hand tightening about my cup. "I

don't understand. I also don't understand what you're doing here? You're trying to help me?"

He rubbed his chin. "My brother's a massive fan of your father. I'm not altogether sure he'd be happy if Dagger's daughter were to end up on life support because of something that happened in our family's history."

I tensed. "You're doing this because of your brother?"

"That, and..." He shrugged. "My father's very annoyed at what you're doing."

"Isn't that more reason to comply?"

"I'm not a yes-man," he countered softly. "I don't jump when he tells me to—"

"But do you ask how high?" I retorted.

He smirked. "No. When he told me about you, and I did my research, I learned a few things. You're not a person who wastes time. You go after a story with all the zeal of a bloodhound who's caught the scent of blood.

"I read the fluff and the heavy-hitting stories and came across a strong voice. One who doesn't dissemble. Who cuts through the bull-shit." He wafted a hand at me. "That was how I knew you were all act when you came in. I saw you calculating the odds of what would let you manipulate me the easiest the second our eyes met." His smirk deepened. "You might be accustomed to dealing with morons, but we raise them smart in my line of work."

"Kill or be killed," I rasped.

"Pretty much." His gaze darted from me to Suzy, and I saw she'd brought a tray over. My small plate of toast was on there as well as Aidan's order.

Jesus, I wasn't hungry.

I was nervous.

Nerves made the gnawing ache in my belly have different conno-tations.

How, in less than five minutes with me, had he managed to figure out that I tended to play a role?

Was it just dumb luck or had he really read through the many and varied editorials and articles I'd written over the years? Not even my mom had that level of dedication.

The second Suzy darted away, her cheeks just as pink as before, I questioned, "Exactly how much of my editorial portfolio have you read?"

He raised his cup to his lips and with a measured glance at me, took a deep sip. After he swallowed, he murmured, "Every piece I could get my hands on. Including the articles you wrote in college." He hitched a shoulder. "I'm thorough."

"Why?" I muttered, aghast and bewildered at the extent of his research into me.

That level of investigation would have taken weeks. Surely? I'd written a lot of pieces in my time. So much that I probably couldn't even remember half of them.

"Because I wanted to understand you," he stated calmly.

My brow furrowed as I shoved my toast away and leaned deeper into the table. The marble surface dug into my belly, but the cold seeped through my shirt and actually made me feel better because I was burning up as if I had a fever.

"What's to understand?" I whispered, trying to figure out his true game here. "I'm so confused," I admitted. "I don't understand why what I'm researching has led to this."

"If you're going to darken the mafia's door, then you should be prepared for the fallout," was all he said.

"I'm looking into your family ties. That's it," I spat. "Nothing about your business."

"I spoke with a friend of yours from college too," he mused, his finger moving around the rim of his cup. "She said you were obsessed with the mafia in the city."

I blinked. "Everyone has a hobby. Which friend?"

"It doesn't matter. What matters is if you have the mafia as a hobby, then it's bullshit that you don't know the repercussions of messing with things you should leave well alone." He arched a brow.

"You know the Five Points' rep, and I'm sure you know what family means to my old man. Family is all," he intoned grimly. "You mess with the family, you mess with the Firm."

My stomach twisted into knots as I cut through the bullshit entirely. "Your uncle's dead." Padraig O'Donnelly had purportedly died at the hands of an Albanian mobster. "How is that a threat? I was trying to figure out what happened to him. That's all."

"And that, as you can imagine, is incredibly delicate ground," Aidan pointed out. "My father loved his brothers. To the point where he barely talks about them with us, never mind in public. You start messing with their memories, then that's just inviting a ton of bricks to fall down on you."

I flinched at the imagery, and as much as I hated to admit it, I was scared.

Scared.

Me.

Something about Aidan O'Donnelly Jr. set my nerves on edge.

Maybe it was his calmness? His acceptance of the situation? His ease with discussing death and an in-depth stalking into my past? I didn't know, but this was serious.

So serious that, fangirling aside, I could feel the ticking of a clock in my head that was warning me my time on this planet was running out...

"If I tell you something, will you listen?"

A furrow appeared between his eyebrows. "If I wasn't here to listen, Savannah, then I wouldn't be sitting opposite you. I'd just have ordered—" His lips twisted. "Well, I'm sure you understand."

I knew he'd paused on purpose, deliberately evading those two words that my heart heard regardless of whether or not he'd uttered them.

The hit.

Jesus.

"My intention wasn't to piss off your father," I admitted. "It was to curry favor with him."

That shocked him.

His reaction was stark. He sat back, his eyes wide, his mouth slack. Flummoxed was the word, one my mother would use and which few Americans would ever understand. Stunned, bewildered... that pretty much defined flummoxed.

"Curry favor?" he repeated softly. "He'd like that. Sounds like what a commoner does with a king."

As much as he could be deliberate with his words, I could be too.

"Yes. I intended to *please* him. Not agitate him."

"Explain," he commanded, his tone stern.

"You're right. Your... research into me was right as well." Although, I'd like to know which so-called friend would tell a fucking mobster that I was obsessed with the mafia. Talk about a frenemy. "People in your line of work have always fascinated me."

"Why?"

"I don't know why. They just have."

"That's a lie."

His stark words hit me like they were a bullet. Each one to the shoulder and then to the gut. I might as well have jerked back in response to them, but managed, barely, to stand my ground.

"I beg your pardon?"

"There's no begging for anything. Certainly not a pardon if you goddamn lie to me again, Savannah." His mouth tightened and a clammy sweat made my back stick to my shirt. "I thought we'd already established that I can see through your lies. You might pull the wool over some fat fuck editor's eyes, but you can't do the same to me.

"Now, we started things off so well," he rumbled, making the hairs at my nape stand on end. "You were being honest. I believe you about not wanting to annoy my father. Let's not take things down another path."

Outraged, I glowered at him, but my fear for the situation which had begun spiraling out of control, was going to win.

For the first time, I knew what death looked like.

It was this man here.

He'd sign my death warrant with a disinterested arch of his brow as he made the call or sent the email.

This beautiful face shielded the heart of a murderer, even if those deaths were by proxy and not with his own hands... Although everyone knew that to enter the Five Points, you had to spill blood, so Junior wasn't so innocent after all.

He looked like a businessman. His suit was sharp, elegant. A fine pinstripe that was so delicate, it was almost nonexistent. His shirt was white and the Oxford knot of his tie was pristine. The rich scarlet and gold contrasted perfectly with his dark navy sport coat. From across the table, I could scent his aftershave. Clean, citrusy undertones with the faint hint of something deeper, lighter. A fresh tone that was as elegant as the man himself.

He was a shark. But he could have been seated on any board of directors in Manhattan. Well, to be fair, he *was*, I just meant he could do that without having the part-time gig of being a mobster as well.

"Now, less of the bullshit," he rumbled. "Why have men in my line of work always fascinated you?"

Fear hit me, fear worse than the one memory that drove me to this day. That guided me down all the wrong paths and took me along for the ride when a story intrigued me to the point of not eating, drinking little, and barely sleeping. Fascination was an understatement.

My heart started pounding as I stared at him, blasted by his resolve, seared by the nasty twist to his lips... Was this the expression his enemies saw before they were tortured to death by him?

Feeling nauseated, heart throbbing in my ears now like there was a string orchestra in my head, I whispered a truth that had haunted me since the day it had happened: "I saw Jerry Isardo being stabbed when I was twelve."

He frowned, but he evidently believed me because it didn't morph into a scowl. "That was unfortunate." Jerry Isardo's stabbing had been big news back in the day. In some circles, it was still talked about.

Despite myself, I had to snort. "Unfortunate isn't the word. It was a..." I hesitated, "...trying time."

"I'll bet." He scraped a hand over his jaw. "What happened?"

"I was being driven home from school." I swallowed. "The car braked to a halt when Jerry ran out in front of us. We clipped him. I can still remember the sound of the metal colliding with his bones." Thousands of hours of therapy made it so that I didn't need to flinch at the memory. "Then another guy came running behind him, dragged him off the fender and stabbed him." I blew out a breath. "Right in the stomach."

"He gutted him. I remember."

I pursed my lips. "There was blood everywhere. The car, the windshield. It sprayed."

"Must have hit an artery." His tone was as clinical as mine. His came from a lifetime in that world, mine came from time with expensive psychotherapists.

"He must have, yes. At the time, I didn't register any of that, of course. I was just blindsided."

"I can imagine."

"Not sure you can, not being raised the way you were."

Silence fell at that, and just when I thought I'd pissed him off, he agreed, "You wouldn't be wrong, but I wouldn't want a daughter of mine to see that. Whether she was a part of the life or not."

"Do they have a choice?" I asked bitterly, surprised by my tone, especially when Aidan's ability to scare me hadn't abated.

I'd never been scared of a man in my adult life.

Until today.

With barely any words, with only a few inferences, he'd managed to...

God, I didn't know what.

My throat was dry as he replied, "No, none of us have a choice. I'm sure your research would have shown that too."

I dipped my chin, because I did know that. A little like a bar mitzvah, the various mafia families all had their own ways of introducing kids into their world. From boys, they turned them into men with their various hazing methods.

It was disturbing.

Even to someone who was acclimated to the way they worked, it was difficult to process.

Kids were meant to be protected. Shielded. Not inserted into the path their fathers and brothers and uncles had been forced to take too. It was wrong on so many levels.

My mouth twisted as I murmured, "It begins and ends with blood."

"That's almost poetic."

"There's a twisted kind of poetry to the way you all lead your lives, don't you think?"

He stunned me by snickering. "If you told my da that, then he'd say there's nothing poetic about our life. He'd say we weren't fairies." He tipped his chin to the side. "Yes, he's a politically incorrect old bastard. What would you like me to do? Make him woke? I'd like to survive my thirties if at all possible. The old fucker can't live forever, after all."

Well, wasn't that a lot of information to process?

"I never imagined he'd be woke. Everyone knows you're expected to follow the Catholic way if you're in the Five Points."

Aidan hummed. "And God help you if you're different."

I frowned. "Are you... *different*?" I wasn't even asking for a scoop. As much as he made my skin crawl with nerves, he was hot. The level of hot that made a woman sigh when she found out that the man in question was gay.

He snorted again. "Savannah, my dubious reputation is hard-earned. No, I'm not gay. But I can appreciate things my father doesn't. We're not cut from the same cloth." He pursed his lips. "That was a hard way to be introduced to adulthood."

Recognizing that he was talking about Isardo, I dipped my chin. "It took me a long time to get over it." Lie. I wasn't over it. I had just adapted to knowing that society wasn't as clean cut as it appeared.

"I can imagine. What I can't imagine, however, is a therapist telling you to research the deadly wars between factions in the city as a means of helping you process what you saw." He grunted. "So what made you take that leap?"

"I wanted answers that no one would give me. I wanted to understand, and no one was willing to help me do that."

"So you took matters into your own hands?"

"Yes. I found out that the Fieri *Famiglia* was at war with a small group of Dominicans." I shrugged. "That was why Isardo was targeted."

"He was a *capo*," Aidan agreed. "One of the thirteen Fieri had back then. Did it help? You knowing the reason for his death?"

"Not really, but I found that I was interested. It read like a story to me." I hitched a shoulder. "It might be your life, but to the average, everyday person, it's pretty insane to think you guys spend your days as if you belong in a Tarantino movie."

"Trust me, it isn't just insane from the outside looking in." He heaved a sigh and surprised me by reaching out. Tension hit me, of a different variety however. The way the tips of his fingers looped around my wrist, gently squeezing had me gulping in surprise. "Now that I understand where the obsession stemmed from, I'll stop prodding that particular wound."

I straightened my spine. "I got over that years ago." His touch still burned me when he let go.

I could tell you *exactly* where each fingertip had seared my skin.

"That kind of violence leaves stains on your soul," he countered, and that he disagreed with me was clear. "If you're an adult, then it's hard to process. As a child? Impossible." He shook his head. "I regret that you had to see that."

He meant it.

For a second, I thought he was being funny, then, much as he read my expression, I read his.

Remorse.

God, my heart started pounding in my ears again.

"It isn't your fault," I whispered, touched because he meant it. He didn't know me from Adam, but he genuinely felt bad for me.

His remorse resonated on a different level too.

One survivor speaking to another survivor.

I felt it without him even having to utter another word.

Everyone who knew about that day in my life thought I was over it... The nightmares had stopped, sure, but that didn't mean I hadn't found coping mechanisms to deal with something I should never have had to see. He got it where few ever could.

"No, it isn't, but I understand more than you can imagine." He dipped his chin. "Why did you want to get on my father's good side?"

His kindness made me answer truthfully. "Because I want to write his biography."

He stared at me.

Then he stared some more.

Then his lips twitched. "Have you ever had the misfortune of meeting my father?"

"I've seen him at galas, much as I've seen most of your family at political events and charity fundraisers, but I've never made an effort to be introduced to you."

"Why not?"

I squirmed a little, but admitted, "You're not supposed to meet your idols, are you?"

His brow puckered. "Idols? That's a strong word."

"I used it for a reason. As you've already ascertained, I have quite a developed lexicon," I rumbled, eying him with annoyance.

"What's to idolize?"

"I don't worship you. It's more like you're my version of Justin Bieber or a K-Pop band." I wafted a hand at him. "Don't think anything of it. I know you all put your pants on the same way and use the bathroom much as I do."

"Funny that the daughter of a rockstar doesn't mention her father in that explanation."

"I've no need to. Because of him, as much as I love him, I know more than most that there's no need to worship a singer or a musician.

"They're more flawed than most because they have access to things few people should have at their disposal."

He pondered that, but didn't comment on it. Instead, he said, "My father's ego is as big as Manhattan Island. You stroke it by telling him you want to write his biography, he'd bite your hand off."

"Is that supposed to be a good thing?" I asked wryly. "In your world..."

As my words waned, he smiled. "True. I just meant he'd be very happy with that offer. That was before, however. Not anymore." His smile waned. "You've pissed him off by rubbing salt in wounds that are very much open still. It might seem like decades to you, but to him? Paddy's death in particular might as well have been yesterday."

"I wanted to give him closure."

"We have closure."

"I don't believe the Albanians killed him," I argued, but he raised a hand to stop me.

Before I could get angry at him thinking he could shut me up by raising his damn hand, Suzy murmured, "Is everything okay, Savannah? You haven't touched your toast."

I tensed, then darted a look at my forgotten breakfast. I heaved a sigh. "I'm sorry, Suzy, everything's fine. I just lost my appetite."

"Would you like me to take it away?"

I winced at the waste, but I couldn't eat it now. "Thanks."

"Would you like something else?"

While I appreciated her solicitousness, mostly I just wanted her to go. Quickly shaking my head, I murmured, "No. Everything's great. Thank you."

"You're a very bad liar, do you know that?" Aidan murmured the second she'd gone.

Gritting my teeth, I snapped, "I'll have you know I'm a great liar." I winced at how loud that had been, and cast a quick glance around me to see if anyone was listening.

Great.

They were.

Receiving a few funny looks from the tables on either side of me, I muttered, "You did that on purpose."

"No, I didn't actually. I'm just surprised at how poorly your old editors read you that's all."

"You met with every one of them?"

"I told you. I'm thorough."

Shaking my head, I snapped, "None of this makes sense. Why would you investigate me this deeply? I'm nobody to you."

"Not to my father. You touched upon an old wound, remember? But I'll admit, he didn't want me to come to you. He just wanted me to deal with you."

I gulped.

"Yes. Pretty much like that," he confirmed. "However, the fact that you were researching Paddy's death made me curious."

"Enough to go digging through my past, I can see."

"Well, you've been digging through mine, haven't you?" His smile made another reappearance when I winced. Seeing he'd scored a hit, he murmured, "I don't think you're in a position to judge."

Because he wasn't wrong, I just bowed my head in acceptance, but it didn't stop me from muttering, "I would never have tried to hurt you or anything."

"Neither would I. I was curious, don't forget. It was my father who meant you harm. I'm the one who'll save your ass if you do as I say."

"You want me to stop what I'm doing even though I'm telling you, here and now, that your uncle wasn't killed by the Albanians?"

My declaration had his jaw tightening. "I'd like to read the files you have on him."

"No 'please' or 'thank you?'" I sniped.

"I don't think they're required in a life or death situation, Savannah."

He surprised me by getting to his feet. The chair scraped against the tiled floor, jolting my nerves, and I tipped my head back to look at him looming over me. Christ, he was impressive. I felt like a mere acolyte peering up at a god, pleading for his attention.

Which, after this conversation, was the last thing I wanted, but he was...

I didn't know how to describe it.

Awe-inspiring made him sound like a piece of architecture.

Aidan was far too tactile for that. Far too close to hand to be anything that was cordoned off from the public reach.

I bit my lip, trying to wonder why my belly pulsed with heat as he pulled together the two halves of his jacket, and as he buttoned them, looking nothing more dangerous than the usual sociopaths that were CEOs on various boards around the city, I almost swallowed my tongue.

"I expect you to give me everything you've discovered without argument. I'll be by your place around eight this evening. I don't want to be kept waiting."

For a second, I knew he'd done the impossible.

He'd made me speechless.

As I sat there, sputtering, he strode away without another word. Without even a backward's glance.

His arrogance knew no bounds, but I guessed it was forged in fire.

He knew I'd comply. Knew I had no alternative if I didn't want my next address to be in the city morgue. Still... he'd given me until this evening, hadn't he?

I was pretty sure I was close to cracking exactly who was behind Paddy O'Donnelly's death, and like any journalist worth their salt—a deadline wasn't something to fear, but something to embrace.

Switching on my phone, I glanced at the clock and then whispered to myself, "Eleven hours. Plenty of time."

To solve a murderless murder.

ELEVEN

AIDAN

FIVE YEARS EARLIER

"WHERE'S YOUR HEAD AT, AIDAN?"

I cast a glance at Finn. "Nowhere."

"Not even on top of your shoulders?"

Smirking at him, I rolled my eyes. "If you say so."

He grinned at me, then cuffed my ear in a move that was classic Magdalena O'Donnelly. In a move we'd also patented over the years, I ducked just before his hand collided with the side of my head and swung out of the way.

"Think I've lost my edge?" I jeered.

"I know it," he retorted, slumping down opposite me in the visitor's chair in my office. "I saw your focus disintegrating over the course of that meeting. That's normally your jam. What's going on?"

I pulled a face. "Nothing."

"Really looks like it," he retorted, arching a brow at me. "You can bullshit your brothers and your father, but you forget, I know you too well."

My nose crinkled. "Fuck off."

I'd pulled this move on Savannah earlier today, so I didn't need him trying to get into my head. I was too accustomed to the power plays that rocked our world. The corporate version was watered down and it was why, though she had balls as big as Finn, I'd eaten Savannah up and spat her out to dry.

Of course, I'd have just preferred to eat her.

Fuck, she was banging.

Mahogany silk bobbed around her shoulders, shielding a stubborn jaw that housed lips that were made for blowjobs. Her eyes gleamed amber-brown that were topped by thick lashes. Her nose was dainty with a thin bridge, her cheeks like sharp ice picks that made her face heart-shaped.

In a word, she was gorgeous.

Every fucking thing about that face was enough to launch ten thousand ships to me, never mind a thousand.

And those yoga pants? Good God. They'd left nothing to the fucking imagination. I'd tried to see if she had a cameltoe but as much of a prick as I was, my level of asshole didn't sink that low.

Gaping at a woman's pussy as she moved toward the table I was sitting at wasn't one of my regular moves.

Drumming my fingers on the desk, though, I recognized that Finn was uniquely placed to help me. While a part of the core O'Donnelly brother unit, he and I tended to drift together, leaving the others behind. The perks of being the eldest, but also, the ones who shouldered more than the rest realized. They'd never fucking know the shit we did to keep Da off their backs, and I didn't want them to figure it out either. I didn't do it for glory or for their appreciation, I did it so they could have more of a life than either of us did.

"Come on," Finn jibed. "You know you're going to tell me."

"What the fuck are you doing here, anyway? Don't you have your own office to go to?" I sniped.

His lips curved. "Oh, now I know we're getting somewhere. Come on, tell me." He made a 'come here' motion with his fingers. "What's got Junior's panties in a bunch?"

"Fuck off," I groused again.

"Never," he declared, his smile widening.

"True dat." I grunted. "You know that little problem Da had me handle?"

"Which one?" Finn countered. "Ain't there about ten million we have to deal with on the regular? I wouldn't be fucking surprised if one day he sends us out on a coffee run."

I snorted. "Yeah, I wouldn't put it past him. Especially if that shit with the Tongs happens again."

"The poisoning?" He shuddered. "Yeah. He'd probably get me to taste everything first."

"Nah, more like Declan," I joked. "You're the money man, I'm the heir, Bren's the Fixer, and Kid's way too useful behind a computer."

"And anyone can shoot a gun?" Finn retorted, laughing as we discounted Eoghan's talents with a sniper rifle.

Grinning, I nodded. "Well, this task in particular was to find that journalist who'd been digging around into the circumstances of Uncle Paddy's death."

Finn frowned. "Thought that was an easy one? Just get one of the runners on it?"

I grimaced at what he *wasn't* saying. "It should have been that easy." The cops would just think it was a mugging gone wrong... we'd done it way more times than was smart, but why fix what wasn't broken?

"Why wasn't it?"

"I did a background check on her." Not altogether unusual, but I'd pulled one of the Firm's contacts inside the NYPD to get a complete run down on her and had discovered who her father was.

While Conor's appreciation for her father's shitty music had been a compelling argument over why I shouldn't automatically have her killed because she was pissing Da off, mostly, it was the fact that Dagger Daniels was notoriously protective of his family.

Everyone remembered what had happened to one of his youngest. He'd gone apeshit when she'd been kidnapped. His private security had found her first, the cops lagging way behind as per goddamn usual, and as miracles would have it, not a single kidnapper had survived the encounter...

Right.

Like miracles were ever that kind.

While I wasn't afraid of a rockstar, I was concerned about the publicity. We had a rep in Manhattan, but Daniels' was worldwide. The last thing I wanted was Acuig shares taking a nosedive because of *noxxious* fans deciding to fuck with the stock market to get back at us.

Because I knew Finn would tell me that nobody would connect the dots between the Five Points and Acuig Corp, I didn't bother telling him any of that. Instead, I just said, "She's hot."

Finn shook his head. "You always think with your dick, man."

"Like you fucking don't," I groused. "I looked into her—"

"I bet you goddamn did."

"You make that sound like I was jacking off outside her bedroom window," I grumbled. "I just looked into who and what she is."

With a mocking glint to his smirk, he murmured, "And who and what is she?"

I rubbed my chin. "Smart."

"So?"

"I read a lot of her articles—"

"Jesus, how fucking banging is she?"

I glowered at him. "I read." Sort of.

"You read reports," he corrected. "I don't think I've ever seen you pick up a newspaper. Or a book." He frowned, like he was deep in thought. He wasn't doing it to be irritating either, just genuinely trying to think back to a time when he'd seen me with a book. Which was probably school.

"This was research."

"Research," he repeated with a nod. "Okay. So, what did you uncover?"

"Da's not happy with her because she's asking about Paddy."

"You told me that already."

"She's not the kind of person who'd waste her time on a story that wasn't there."

"The inference being that there's more to his death than your father thought?"

"I think so." I rubbed my chin. "All we know is that an Albanian shot him." I shook my head. "That, and how he killed Jurkavic in retaliation, is all he'll tell us."

"True. But why would he lie?" His brow puckered. "Are you just looking for conspiracies where there aren't any?"

"No, she is. I'm telling you, though, she wouldn't waste her time if she didn't think there was something to the story."

He kicked up his leg and let his ankle come rest on the opposite knee. Settling back in the seat, he murmured, "Exactly how hot is she?"

I snorted. "I'm not just thinking with my dick."

"You sure?"

"Positive. Anyway, Jemima made sure my balls were drained for a good two weeks."

Finn snickered. "Jemima—the human Dyson."

"Exactly." I wasn't about to tell him that I'd called my *sometimes* girlfriend over for a quickie because I'd met with Savannah Daniels.

"Why do you think it matters to her?"

"I asked her."

"You've met with her?" he sputtered.

"This morning," I confirmed. "She says she wants to write Da's biography, and thought this would be a way of getting in his good books."

Finn coughed out a laugh. "Are you shitting me?"

"No. I wish I was."

"She'd have been better off just approaching him with a biography in mind."

I grimaced. "Trust me, I know. I told her that."

His eyes widened. "She really wants to write his biography?" he muttered to himself. "Who the fuck would read that?"

"No one?" I retorted dryly. "It couldn't be published until we were all in our graves."

"True. What the fuck? Does she have daddy issues or something? Have a crush on him?"

"Something happened to her when she was a kid. The mafia has fascinated her ever since. At least, as far as I've managed to uncover."

Finn narrowed his eyes at me. "Sounds as if you'd like to uncover a whole hell of a lot more than that."

"Yeah," I agreed simply. "The truth."

"About Paddy? Why? Why dig up the past? She was doing it to get access to your da, but now that's out of the window, what's the point?"

I growled. "Why aren't you listening to me? Because she wouldn't waste her time if there wasn't something to uncover. Doesn't that make you question shit? Make you wonder what the fuck happened that day?"

He blinked. "We were, what? Sixteen?"

I nodded. "Paddy helped us. He deserved more than to die that way."

Finn pursed his lips. "I don't disagree, Aidan, but I don't see how raking up the past is going to help."

"I've never felt right about him going the way he did." I shook my head, then I told him something I hadn't told anyone. "He called me. The night he was shot. I was with Harriet Crossley."

"You didn't pick up?" Finn queried quietly.

"When I was with the high school mattress?" I snorted. "Course I fucking didn't."

I had so many goddamn regrets from a life led astray at an early age, and not picking up that call was one of them.

"What do you think he wanted?"

"I'll never know, will I? But maybe he knew he was being

followed? Maybe there was something shady going on? You know that triggered that spat with the Albanians." I reached up and rubbed the bridge of my nose. "I just have a feeling."

Finn sobered up. "Really?"

I hummed.

Gut instincts and me didn't get along well. Hadn't done since I'd listened to Finn that day and found my brother being raped by a priest. Now, when I got the stirrings of one, it always set me on edge.

I grimaced. "I just think I need to see this out."

"What's your game plan? I assume your da thinks you're going to have her killed?"

"He's dumped it on my desk," I confirmed. "He won't check up on things as long as she stops digging around. She doesn't write under her full name so he doesn't even know she's a woman."

"It is weird that he's trying to silence someone who could give him closure on Paddy's death," Finn agreed, his brow furrowed. "Okay, so, you're going to have her continue her investigation on the downlow?"

I shook my head. "No. I asked her to have all her material ready for eight PM tonight."

"You're going to finish the investigation yourself?"

Slowly, my smile grew. "No. It was enough of a challenge to light a fire under her ass. I spoke with a lot of her past bosses. She's not the kind of woman who likes to have something taken away from her, and she'll carry on working regardless.

"I scared her today though."

I knew for a fact that wasn't something that happened often.

Finn mocked, "Your ma would be proud."

I rolled my eyes. "I don't get my rocks off by scaring women, Finn, you know that. She just had to understand the severity of the situation. If I hadn't taken an interest in what she was investigating, she'd be dead by now. She needed to realize that sniffing around, in situations like these, leads to repercussions."

Repercussions that a woman, who'd been shielded and cosseted all her life, would never understand.

Even when her family had been targeted, her father had paid to make sure their enemies were taken down.

While Dagger Daniels wasn't in the mob, he definitely had a 'kill first, ask questions later,' policy.

"And she's learned that lesson?"

I shrugged. "For now. I'm sure she'll find a way to get into the faces of the wrong people along the way."

"You want to bang her?"

"Got a dick, don't I?" I picked up my phone, scrolled through the gallery, found a couple of pictures of her, then showed her to him. When he whistled, I hummed. "Exactly."

"You want to keep her alive to have her as a side piece?"

"Not sure a woman like her could ever be a side piece," I admitted with a low voice.

"What's that supposed to mean?" Finn sputtered.

I didn't have a clue, didn't even know why I'd said it, just knew that I meant it.

She wasn't a Harriet Crossley, wasn't the two-buck whore of Manhattan. And God love those kinds of women. I had no issue with them spreading their legs for me whenever I clicked my fingers, but they weren't the marrying kind.

Savannah Daniels wasn't a slut, nor was she the marrying kind. I didn't have a goddamn clue what she was, but fuck, when Jemima had deep-throated me this morning, it hadn't been her mouth I'd imagined doing the swallowing, but Savannah's.

Six hours later, I found myself outside her apartment building.

I half expected that I'd have to break into it, or, at least, get Conor to help me out by corrupting the security or whatever the hell it was he did, but when I pressed on her button, she let me in.

As I strolled into the foyer, I discovered that Savannah's father was definitely paying her bills because she'd been unemployed for a good two months now, and this place was not cheap.

Whistling under my breath, I nodded at the doorman, then strode to the bank of elevators and summoned one. As it arrived, I thought about what I'd said to Finn earlier.

I fully expected for her to have made leaps and bounds in her investigation, but once that was done, I didn't think she'd quietly leave things behind.

Not when this was all she was working on.

My mouth pursed at the thought, because if she carried on digging, I'd have no choice but to kill her. I really didn't want to have to do that. But she'd give me no alternative if she didn't leave well enough alone.

Everything that her editors had told me, indicated that she was incapable of backing off and backing down.

That'd lead to more shit along the way, however.

I'd told Da I'd deal with the problem, and there was no avoiding that we both knew what that meant. I wasn't a troubleshooter, for God's sake. Dealing with problems typically meant that someone's blood got spilled. Rarely, if ever, mine, and most definitely the problem's.

With that in mind, I turned over the situation in my head.

Acuig Corp. had recently been buying up a ton of companies under Finn and Kid's new strategy to spread the net as far as we could over Manhattan's skyline. The companies didn't matter, the real estate did, but that meant we had interest in a lot of diverse industries.

I knew, for example, that we'd recently taken over the building where TVGM's studio was housed.

As I stepped out of the elevator, my Brioni shoes sinking into the deep scarlet plush of the carpet, I headed over to 0789 as I contemplated whether or not Savannah would accept my gift with grace. I doubted it. Grace wasn't something I'd associate with her.

She was, I thought, pretty similar to her name.

Hot, steamy, but capable of enduring the worst hurricanes and coming out on top.

The door was open when I approached, which was indicative of the building's safety, and when I stepped inside, I found chaos.

Even better, I found Savannah, leaning over her computer, notes everywhere, pads everywhere, a white board out in front of her, laden down with faces of pretty much everyone I knew.

As I closed the door behind me, I decided not to disrupt her. I'd come to collect all of this, whatever the hell it was I had my eyes on, but she was definitely in the middle of something.

Something that might make this problem go away.

The apartment was light, breezy. Not what I expected from her. She wasn't a pallid kind of woman. No wishy washy blues or pinks for her. But that was what I got.

I'd expected something as rich as the hallway—scarlets and golds. Instead, I'd have said it was the opposite. The place was lived in though. Comfortable.

The white sofa was massive and, the only word I could use to describe it, was squishy. There was a huge bump in the corner unit of the sectional, where she evidently spent a lot of time. A large knitted blanket was artfully draped over it, and there was a coffee table beside it too, with a stack of books and a coffee mug resting on top of that.

The sofa was the centerpiece of the entire room. Though it was neither opulent nor elegant, I could easily see her sitting there. In fact...

I twisted around, trying to see if she had a cat.

I could see her with a cat.

Curled up on that sofa with it, reading and plotting some story. Some revenge or whatever.

When I found one, tightly packed into a small ball, I smirked to myself, glad that I'd read that right at least. The Siamese blended in with all the other colors in here, very tonal and neutral. Which was, I thought, why I was so surprised.

Savannah wasn't either of those things.

Barely twenty-five minutes in her company and I knew that.

Stepping over more sheets of paper, I headed for the white board and looked at what, essentially, was a crime board.

What looked like Paddy's autopsy report was tacked on here—how the fuck she'd gained access to that I had no idea—then there were the major players of the Albanian mob back then as well as our family.

A lot of the guys on our side were dead. That's why we had the Old Wives' Club. Lots of widows left behind as their men were buried six feet under thanks to the Firm and the many wars my father had engaged in back when he was my age.

"Is it true?"

I jolted a little, the blast with the past taking me back in time. "Is what true?"

"That your father ran a sword through Milao Jurkavic because of what he did to Paddy?"

Grimacing, I muttered, "Is that story still going around?"

She hummed without looking up. "It is, and I highly doubt it's a story."

"Urban legend, then."

Now, she looked up, and her eyes glinted with humor. "I'm sure there are many urban legends floating around the city because of your people, but I don't think this is one such occasion."

If someone had told me that a semi-smile was capable of triggering a semi-boner, I'd have told them to fuck off and take some more laughing gas because that was the level of ridiculousness from that likelihood.

Yet, here I was, my dick hardening as I saw the faint curve of her lips twitch higher, and that knowing gleam in her eyes... She wasn't trying to turn me on, was just calling me out on my bullshit.

Fuck.

I almost growled under my breath, but though I could easily have turned this into something else, could have coerced her into bed, could even have fucking seduced her if I wanted, I did none of those things.

Twisting away, I reached up to rub the back of my neck.

I wasn't a good guy.

I wasn't.

And maybe, this morning, before I'd met her, I'd have done every single fucking one of those things so long as I ended up between her goddamn legs.

But one thing had saved her from me.

One goddamn thing.

Isardo.

Not because he'd died. The bastard had deserved that. All fucking Italians deserved to end up skewered at some point. But that she'd seen that? That she'd witnessed it and at twelve?

Even now, my jaw clenched down at the thought.

No little girl should have to see that.

For that matter, no little boy should have to either.

I'd done worse at twelve than see someone getting gutted, and I mourned for the kid I'd never had the chance to be as much as I mourned for Savannah.

Jesus, a mobster getting maudlin. Maybe someone should just hand me a Sig Sauer right now and I could end this fucking misery?

Grunting under my breath, I said, "You do know how foolish it would be to have this place stocked up with any recording equipment, don't you?"

She tipped her head to the side. "You seem to misunderstand my intent here, Aidan."

"What intent is that?"

"I have no desire for anyone in the Irish Mob to go to jail."

My brow puckered at that. "Why? It's not like we're the good guys."

"Maybe not." She smiled. "But the Five Points handled Isardo's killer for me. It was only when he died that I finally got any sleep at night." She blinked. "I suffered with night terrors for years after the incident."

I stared at her. "Are you being serious?"

"About the night terrors? Or the fact that I'm not against the Irish Mob?" She shrugged when I struggled to answer her. "There's no need for me to lie."

Well, that could be a half-truth, but she appeared earnest. The best lies were founded in the truth though. I actually knew who'd taken out Isardo's murderer—Eoghan. It had been one of his first kills. Even before he'd served in the Army, he'd been good with a rifle.

I could easily imagine how learning of the death of the guy wielding the knife that day would bring her peace. It was whether or not she wished to cause us shit that I doubted.

"Do you know who took him out?" she asked, her eagerness unfeigned.

I pursed my lips. "I do."

Her mouth parted and she betrayed her excitement with a slight shift in her position—she sat upright, jerking forward as if she needed to hear more. "He tried to kill my driver, do you know that? He started for the driver door when the cops arrived."

"Jesus," I rasped.

She didn't bow her head, but I could see how those memories still took their toll on her. "I was pretty sure I was going to die. Then, he got away, and the cops hunted him down, my dad even got our private security firm involved but they never found him." Her smile made another appearance. "The Five Points, however, did."

"How do you know that?"

"I made it my business to find out."

My mouth firmed. "It wasn't because of Isardo," I replied, needing to make sure she knew that.

"Why would I care? He was dead. He couldn't come after me."

Her nostrils flared a second, and I knew there was something she wasn't telling me about that day, but rather than prod an old wound, one that wasn't healed no matter how she might think it was, in a stern voice, I asked, "You're certain there's no recording equipment in the apartment, Savannah?"

She blinked, then shook her head quickly. Responding like a dream to that faintest hint of authority in my voice.

Fuck, it was hard not to start panting.

Would she bend over the sofa just as politely if I asked her to?

Maybe over my knee?

Clearing my throat to dislodge those unhelpful imaginings, I asked, "If you switch them off now, I won't be angry."

She swallowed. "I have voice recorders, but they're not on," she whispered. "I need them for work, but I'm not recording our conversations."

That, I believed.

I'd scared her again.

Because I went out of my way to scare people every day of the fucking week, both men and women alike, I shouldn't be as irritated with myself as I was.

How had Finn phrased it this afternoon?

That Ma would be proud of me?

Not.

There'd been a long while where Ma was scared of Da. Only as they got older, as we left adolescence behind, did she grow some balls. Even those were hard won, mostly through what she'd endured at the Aryans' hands.

In apology, I admitted, "Jurkavic deserved worse than being run through with a sword for what he did to Paddy."

Her shoulders relaxed the faintest amount, and I knew she was relieved by my response. Not because of what I was saying, but because it meant I believed her. It was a leap of faith, but we had so many fucking officials in our pocket, I was pretty sure not even God himself would be able to worm his way out of letting any Five Pointer into heaven.

"Maybe before, but Jurkavic was innocent of killing your uncle.

I'm pretty sure he was guilty of a whole lot of other stuff, but killing your Uncle Padraig, no."

Though she'd been as predictable as I'd anticipated, had strived to find the answers to this story before I took it away from her, I was mostly relieved that she'd figured this out so I didn't have to get involved. I'd have taken over if I'd had to... I was just glad that wouldn't be necessary.

Finn wasn't wrong. Me and the written word weren't the best of friends.

Audiobooks, sure. Just regular books? No.

Twisting around so I could stare at her, I asked, "What's your proof?"

Her face lit up at my question. Literally. As in, she suddenly beamed with energy. Like this was her life's blood. Like this was the reason she got up in the morning and went to bed way too late at night.

Her hair was a mess from running her hands through it too much, and I was pretty sure the toast she'd sent back this morning was smearing her mouth again, meaning she'd attempted another round of breakfast after I left the restaurant. Her clothes were no longer clean and wrinkle-free, but stained with coffee and rumpled, and she looked a thousand times hotter than this morning.

Bright-eyed and bushy-tailed could have described her at breakfast. Now she just looked like a wreck. A hot wreck. One I'd bend over the sofa, grab a handful of that thick hair just so I could make sure she never moved out of place.

"You have to be amenable to accepting the impossible."

Because my thoughts and hers were clearly on two different train tracks, one heading for Mexico and the other for Canada, I had to laugh.

Rubbing my chin, I moved closer to her, stepping around the various shit on the floor and perching my ass on the end of the 'L' part of the sectional.

Once I was seated, I murmured, "That sounds like you want me to suspend reality."

"That's pretty much a big part of it, but I do have proof. Of sorts."

I squinted at her. "Circumstantial?"

She nodded quickly.

"Well, I'm not a court of law. Make your arguments, councilor, make them good and I'll listen."

She beamed a beatific smile at me, and fuck if that didn't make me lean back so my dick wasn't trapped.

Christ.

"Okay, so the Albanians hated Milano as much as your father did. Did you know that?"

"I think everyone hated that SOB. Even his fucking mother. He was the type of bastard who'd turn his grandma in to the cops if he thought he could make a profit on her arrest."

She dipped her chin. "Right? That fits with everything I've found. He was cruel and abusive to his family, and to his men, he handed out severe punishments for light insubordination. Anyone who questioned him was whipped, for God's sake."

"He created an army of yes-men," I agreed. "Da used to bitch about them all the time. 'Like a bunch of robots,' he said."

"That's right. But even robots have a breaking point. When your father came calling for Jurkavic, no one even stopped their compound from being overturned."

I blinked. "I mean, I wasn't there so I don't know for sure, but that doesn't sound right."

She shrugged then showed me some pictures.

As I stared down at them, I frowned. "What am I looking at?"

"That's the gate to their compound. If you can see, the way it's been forced open... only one of the locks was engaged. Not all six."

Scowling at the image, I held it up to the light and squinted at the two sides of the damaged gate that, if memory served, Da had rammed with his customized Range Rover. The bull bars on there would take down a fucking Mack truck, never mind a gate.

I hummed though, when I saw the way the two sides of the gating had been ripped apart. "There would have been a lot more damage if more locks had been engaged."

"Correct. So, when I looked at that, I started to wonder what else was off about the narrative we've been fed."

"I can understand why you'd look deeper."

"Don't ask me how..." She peeped up at me. "...I managed to get access to some of Jurkavic's bank accounts—"

I arched a brow. "As easy as that, huh?"

Her smile nearly blew me off the sofa. "Not everyone sees through the airhead act."

Grunting, I muttered, "Men are fools."

"They are for a pair of tits and a short skirt," she agreed, which made my blood pressure surge some more. "Anyway, this was his personal account. Look at where I've marked."

She shoved some documents at me, and reaching out with my left hand, I drew them closer and found large red rings circling some dates.

"Are you a southpaw?"

The question jarred me from what I was looking at. "Yeah, I'm left-handed."

As she hummed, I read the documents, forcing myself to focus on the dates, times, numbers, and names, which were, to be frank, a nightmare.

Slowly, I stated, "These are flight receipts."

"They are," she said brightly. "He was in Italy when Paddy...died."

The repercussions of that rammed themselves home. As hard as if my dad's old Range Rover, a beast that was long since a burnt out shell in a scrapyard somewhere, had done the deed for me.

"No one ever said he was in Europe. I'd have heard."

"I know."

The Albanians didn't go for a crap without Jurkavic's approval, and if he was out of the country, that meant... Shit. That meant quite a few things weren't as cut and dry as we'd come to believe.

"That doesn't mean he wasn't behind Paddy's murder," I muttered.

She scoffed. "Your father didn't target another Albanian. Not saying others didn't die in his attempt to reach Jurkavic, but once he took him out, that was it."

"They instigated those little spats afterward," I mused, thinking back to the past. "Not him. But he went in hard and stomped them out." Reaching up to rub my forehead, I frowned. "His men didn't give him an alibi."

"And with a sword sticking through his belly, I don't think Jurkavic had much of an opportunity to explain what happened to him, do you?"

No.

He hadn't.

Da had told me the story.

Jaw working, I rasped, "Da said the compound was minimally guarded. They took out security, then infiltrated the house. He said it was easy, but he's a cocky piece of shit. He'd think it was easy because we were so well-trained, not because the Albanians were trying to get rid of their leader."

"Jurkavic was asleep, wasn't he?"

I nodded. "How did you know that?"

She shoved another piece of paper at me. I squinted at it, then heaved a sigh as I forced myself to focus once more. My brain, apparently picking up on the fact that she was going to keep doing this, shoving evidence at me for me to scan, decided not to obey.

If I ever told anyone that the letters danced and weaved around the page as if they were on mushrooms, I knew I'd never hear the end of it.

Forcing myself to focus helped sometimes, but I'd pay for it at the end of the day with a killer migraine. Thanking God for text-to-voice tools that let me keep up the charade of reading with ease, I stared down at what I came to realize was Jurkavic's autopsy report.

"You already knew about the sword," I accused, once I'd figured out what I was reading.

She smirked at me. "I just wanted to see if you'd be honest with me."

"Did I pass the test?"

"You didn't fail."

"Damn me with faint praise, why don't you?" I mocked, but I steadfastly ignored the way her cheeks blushed as she laughed. God, she was pretty. When I reached the Toxicology section, I frowned. "They doped him up with Rohypnol?"

"Fitting, don't you think? Considering, at that time, they were the biggest peddlers of date-rape drugs in the Tri-State area."

"Definitely fitting. So, Da skewered a drugged-up nemesis." My lips curved. "If only I could tell him that. He's rather proud of his abilities with a sword." Her cheeks blanched, and as I picked up on that, I decided to state the obvious. "You're scared of him? Probably a very smart thing to be. A lot smarter than trying to get into contact with him to write his biography," I pointed out.

She flushed. "It seemed like a smart idea at the time."

"If you don't mind bringing predators to your door, then sure it is."

I stared at her, long enough for her gaze to dart from mine and down to her notepad. It was a dickish move, but staring contests were a surprisingly painless way of establishing dominance.

We weren't dogs, but we still found ways to submit to those who were bigger, meaner, and nastier than us. For all that Savannah undoubtedly thought she was the top dog in her world, in mine? She was a gnat.

Pursing my lips, I murmured, "So, the Albanians sacrificed their leader the second they could?"

She nodded. "Pretty much."

"Interesting."

"That's not all."

Of course it wasn't.

I tipped my head to the side and made a motioning gesture with my hand for her to continue.

"Would you say your uncle was a fit man? Physically and mentally?"

Scowling in contemplation, I replied, "Well, yeah. He was younger than I am now, and he was always healthy. The O'Donnellys have strong genes." Go figure. And they said that only the good died young...

That last year, though, I remembered Paddy well. He'd hauled that fucker McKenna out of the church on his shoulders like he was carrying nothing more than a bag of potatoes.

"He was a big guy. No discernible health issues, but they wouldn't have told us boys if there'd been a problem."

She passed me another round of papers which made everything inside me cringe.

"What am I looking at? Specifically?"

"Firstly, just read the stats."

A squint at the sheets had me discerning that I was looking at yet another fucking autopsy report. "You've had a really cheerful day, haven't you?"

"I'm quite a morbid person. It didn't faze me."

No, I could tell it was quite the opposite. Savannah was clearly in her element.

Heaving a sigh, I struggled once more to focus on the words, but when I finally did, by piecing apart the numbers from the text, then shuffling around the individual letters to make up the word, I frowned at what I discovered.

"Uncle Paddy was over six foot."

"Exactly," she declared, her voice brimming with glee. "The body that went under the pathologist's knife was below six feet." She wafted a paper at me. "There's a picture of your father and uncle at a governor's fundraiser event about three weeks before he died. Like you said, he was a big guy. About two-hundred and twenty pounds, wouldn't you agree?"

As I glanced at a face I saw every day in the mirror, because all the O'Donnelly men looked alike, I sighed.

"You miss him?"

I shot her a look. "I do. He was my godfather."

"So?"

"You're not Catholic, I assume?"

"Lutheran." She shrugged. "Not practicing."

"Well, sadly, I do." My jaw cracked when I reached up and shoved it to the side. "Godparents represent a lot within the Catholic faith. They're literally a second parent. Padraig was more than just an uncle. He was the person I called on when I fucked up. When I didn't dare go to Da. He was mine and my brother Conor's godfather. We both depended on him."

Confusion filled me when I came across medical terms on the report that further didn't fit my uncle's state of health when he died.

Brow furrowing, I dared to phrase out loud what sounded way too insane to be real. "If the guy on the pathologist's table was too short and too small to be Paddy, plus had a pacemaker and a fucking stent in his arteries, then it's pretty damn obvious that it wasn't Paddy being sliced and diced." Heart both sinking and soaring, I rasped, "Does that mean he's alive then?"

"We have facts. One: he wasn't shot by the person he was supposedly taken down by. Two: the guy on the coroner's slab wasn't your uncle. That doesn't mean he's alive. It just means that what happened that day wasn't as cut and dry as we thought."

Mouth pursing, I rumbled, "Nothing ever is with my family." I cut her a look as I slipped my phone out of my jacket pocket. "This information never leaves this room, Savannah."

Her eyes flared wide. "What? Why the hell not?"

I wasn't surprised when she scuttled to her feet, her arms wide, her shoulders straight, spine perfectly erect as she exploded with a type of energy that few could ever contain, never mind exude.

She bristled.

Every part of her was engaged in the outright rejection of my words.

I'd have smiled if I didn't think she'd go for my jugular.

"This is good news! Your dad will be happy—"

"Happy to have been lied to? Happy that his younger brother pretended to get shot? Happy that that younger brother not only faked his death but triggered grievances between the Irish and the Albanians to get away?" I shook my head. "Nothing about that is going to go down well."

What fucking hurt the most as well was that Uncle Padraig was as much of a flight risk as I'd sensed. There was a reason I hadn't wanted to call on him that day in the church with McKenna.

I loved him. I always had. He'd been a great uncle, and an even better godfather—willing to do shit that few would ever dream of for their godchildren—but that didn't take away from what I'd instinctively known: he was unreliable.

Her shoulders slumped and I knew she'd not only listened to me, but she was well aware I was right. A sigh escaped her as she twisted around to stare at her Murder Board, and I knew she was thinking about all the hours she'd spent on this, not just today but in the run up to meeting me too.

Regret filled me once more, especially when she bent over and picked up something from the floor, giving me a perfect glimpse of an ass that'd make a Georgia peach look bad.

Sometimes, life had a way of handing you lemons that you just couldn't make lemonade out of.

Goddammit.

Heaving a sigh, I watched as she trod over to the board and started pulling pictures down, tugging forms and documents and God knew what else aside.

That she didn't argue with me told me she knew this was a lost cause. I found that I was disappointed. I'd quelled her rebellion, but I didn't want to put out her fire.

"Come to dinner with me?" I rasped, watching as she tensed up and expecting her rejection.

Then she peered over her shoulder, stared me square in the eye, before letting her gaze drop down over me. At that moment, I knew I'd never been checked out as thoroughly in all my life.

Fuck, she did a better job than a goddamn CT scan.

She eyed me up and down, then the peevish displeasure at my taking this find away from her disappeared, and though I didn't necessarily trust that, I trusted the gleam that appeared in her eye, the way her pulse skipped on her throat and knew before she verbalized it what her answer would be.

"Let me go and get changed."

TWELVE

CONOR

PRESENT DAY

"I CAN'T BELIEVE you did that. Again. Do you know what shit you cause every time you hack my fucking system, Star? Jesus Christ. You not only make me look bad, but I lose hundreds of thousands of dollars because Da fines the fuck out of me."

Silence fell at my opening greeting.

Some more came.

And some more.

Then, she groused, "You finished?"

"I think the silence indicated that, didn't it?" I snapped.

"I won't let you talk down to me, Conor," she warned, then she heaved a sigh. "I didn't want to have to do that, but what the hell was I supposed to do?

"Savannah needed help and I knew you could give it to her, knew that you'd keep her safe. I'm not going to apologize for protecting a friend from a mutual enemy."

Growling under my breath, I snarled, "You could have phoned me. I'd have opened the fucking front door for her!"

There was a throb of quiet that seemed to have a heartbeat of its very own, then, in a small voice, she muttered, "Oh."

Oh.

Yeah.

I took that to be an admission that I was right. That she was fucking wrong.

I blew out an annoyed breath, but before I could say another word, Star stunned the hell out of me by saying, "I'm sorry, Conor. Sometimes... Sometimes it's just hard to think normally."

Because I got that, because I couldn't *not* get that, I reached up and rubbed my eyes. I was pissed, wicked pissed, in fact, but her apology came as much of a surprise as the rest of her words.

"I understand, Star. I'm probably the only person who does, so maybe try to not piss me off?"

"I-I just didn't think. I reacted."

"I know. But where I'm concerned, you don't have to, do you? You just call me. You just say, my friend has a problem. Can you please help me? Christ, I'll even help without the 'please.' Just try not to cost me five hundred thou every time you need something, huh?"

"That's how much he'll fine you?" She sucked in a surprised breath. "Fuck, your dad's a real piece of work, isn't he?"

"You're only just figuring that out?" I questioned dryly.

"Well, no, but I didn't think he'd fine you for a fuck up."

"He does. It's a deterrent, and it usually works."

"Did he fine you the first time I hacked your system?"

I hummed. "He did." A ping sounded on my phone, and I frowned, pulling away to stare at the notification before gruffly telling her, "You didn't have to do that."

"No, but it's not fair for you to take the hit when it was my fuck up."

I grunted as I stared at the five-hundred large that were sitting pretty in my bank account, which was proof that she not only knew my account number, but that she'd known it for a while.

What was her game and why did it give me a boner?

Why did everything about this crazy fucking piece of work get me hard?

Heaving a sigh, I muttered, "It's not your fuck up if there was a way into my code, no?"

"No."

"Maybe instead of taking down my system, you can help shore it up?"

"It's one of the best systems I've come across," she offered.

"You don't need to boost my ego."

She snorted. "I'm not. Look, I said sorry and I paid you back for the fine that'll hit your pocket. I have no need to smother your ego in kisses."

I'd let her smother other parts of me in kisses though, that was for goddamn sure.

"It can't be that good if you keep on breaking through it."

"There's probably only a handful of people that could." I heard the shrug in her voice. "Truth be told, I only found my way in because I was working under pressure. I wouldn't have spotted the weakness otherwise. You know how it is when adrenaline is riding you hard."

I'd like to ride her hard.

"Nothing should be weak. I need it to be working perfectly. My brothers' lives depend on it, Star." And they were all that mattered. More than my parents, more than the men, my brothers were the ones I had to protect.

"We'll fix it," Star promised after a few seconds. "Together."

Warmth filled me. And it had no business sinking into that nice, ice-cold pit inside me either. But like most things where Star Sullivan was concerned, she didn't ask. She just did. "Thank you," I rasped, appreciating the offer, as well as knowing that I'd take any help she had to give if it meant perfecting my system.

"You're welcome." She hesitated. "I really am sorry, Conor. But thank you for helping Savannah."

"I think she'll need the help," I pointed out softly. "I don't think this will be the only time they target her."

She grunted. "I should have planned ahead for that."

"You should have told me. I'd have put guards on her."

"She's stupid," Star muttered. "She's one of those people who tries to avoid her guards because they cut into her privacy."

My lips curved. "Not sure that's stupid, or just a desire for autonomy. It's not like she's had much of that over the course of her life."

Star snorted. "You do know I was raised amid the same hype, don't you?"

"Yeah, but everyone handles that stuff differently. You decided to become a CIA agent," I said dryly. "You're probably more deadly than most assassins that people could send your way. Savannah decided that the truth would be her shield."

"Well, from where I'm standing, it ain't that much of a shield," she said with a sniff.

I smiled, because how was I supposed to argue with her after the night's events?

"She's safe now. She's under our guardianship."

"Sure she'll love that." Star laughed. "Guardianship? Be sure to use that specific word and that'll get her running."

"I don't know, she's pretty shaken up," I said softly. "She fell down the stairs, and has a lot of bruises. Nothing that some make-up shouldn't be able to cover, but they still look nasty."

"Christ, I should check in with her."

"No. Aidan's taken her to a bedroom. She's going to get some rest first. I'll have a doctor come by in the morning if need be."

"Do your brothers know you're this efficient?"

A smile curved my lips. "Now, where would the fun be in that?"

She cackled. "One way to keep them on their toes."

"Also one way for them to not give me more shit to do on top of the crap I'm already drowning in." I smirked. "Okay, you get going. We both need to rest."

"You think I'm going to sleep? Thirty-six hours into running down this code, Conor. I'm about four away from hitting the jackpot."

Intrigued, I propped my feet up on my cat's head, sank back into my desk chair and demanded, "Tell me more."

THIRTEEN

AIDAN

BY THE TIME I'd showered and changed, the pain hadn't abated all that much, but I knew this was my new normal. I was going to have to accept it and find a way to move past it.

Easier said than done, but the warmth from the shower made it a little easier on me.

As I'd cleaned up, I'd thought about how Savannah and I had first met, about the secrets only she and I knew regarding the family, and I had to admit that it felt like fate that we were crossing paths again when I'd gone out of my way to avoid her.

How crazy was it that of all the people Lodestar, Conor's hacker friend, knew, it was her.

I mean, if I'd known Lodestar was Star Sullivan, Gerard Sullivan's daughter, I'd have figured it out faster. But that was news to me. Not Conor though. He truly was a sneaky pain in the ass. As much as I knew his mind was a tangled Gordian knot, not unlike the code he lived in, I also knew that there was way more going on with him than my brothers realized.

Feeling like a fool, as I stepped by the bedroom I'd put Savannah in, I carefully opened the door.

It was a breach of privacy, but the urge to make sure she was okay was too strong to ignore.

The lights were off, but she'd kept the curtains open. Beyond her French doors, there was a soft, muted glow from an outdoor lamp that lit up the patio, and it enabled me to see the small hump she made in bed.

This was as close as I'd ever gotten her horizontal on a mattress and for the first time in what felt like forever, my dick actually twitched. Through the detoxing process, my sex drive had gone into hibernation. I'd been more focused on actually getting through the day and surviving than getting off.

Trust my dick to come back online for her.

I heaved a sigh as I closed the door.

To this day, I wasn't sure if that meal together had been wise or foolish. As we ate, I knew she was that rarest of gems—a woman with conversation. A woman with understanding of the world around her, with a voice and opinions and dreams and desires she wasn't afraid to discuss. With her knowing that I was well aware her airhead act was exactly that, it let down her barriers, made her open up in a way that I thought few ever accessed.

I liked that. I had at the time and to this day, I still did.

Our evening had been cut short by work. I'd gotten a call, and I'd had to leave before we could finish dessert.

When I'd arrived at Da's warehouse, the one where he did some of his nastier work, and had found him elbow-deep in corpses that he was hacking apart with a saw, as well as some other shit that had gone down that night, I'd decided that ghosting Savannah was the safest bet all round.

For me, but mostly for her.

I should have known that getting her a job at TVGM wouldn't be enough to stop her from popping into my world once more. Should have recognized that we were destin—

Christ.

I didn't need to go there.

I really fucking didn't.

I wasn't a nice man. I wasn't a good one either. She deserved better.

She didn't deserve this life.

Me.

Leaving her to rest—not running from desires I had no business having—I sucked in a breath as I passed Conor's office and peeped in through the door. His workspace took up the entire length of his penthouse because he had several desks, each with six or more monitors running at the same time.

Finding him with his feet propped up on one of his desks, a phone tucked between his shoulder and ear, I left him to it, then limped over to the elevators.

As I did, my cell buzzed. Peering down at it, spying Finn's name, I arched a brow and connected the call.

"What?"

"Crazy coincidence, don't you think?"

I pulled a face, then ducked my gaze away from my reflection in the elevator doors. "What are we? Bitches now? You really want to talk about this?"

He heaved a sigh. "No. I just saw the way you looked at her, Aidan. I ain't seen you that fired up in a long time."

My shoulders shuffled at his words. "I don't want to talk about this."

"Maybe you don't want to, but that doesn't mean you shouldn't. I mean it, bro. The way you looked at her? The way you responded to her? You were like the old Aidan."

"He's dead."

"No, he ain't," Finn snarled. "Don't be a dumbass. It's great that you've detoxed, and it's even better that you're staying clean, but what's your reason to get up in the morning, huh?

"The drugs drove you for so long, but this fucking business we're in, that's not going to get anyone fired up when that alarm blares at five goddamn AM and you have to slog away at a job that isn't exactly good for the soul."

"Has Aoife been making you watch Julia Roberts' movies again?"

"*Eat, Pray, Love* wasn't as shit as you think," he grumbled. "But there's no fulfillment in our line of work. The money's good, man, we both know that, but it's not like it's going anywhere. The other shit, it's just going to drag you down, back into that pit. You need something to keep you on the straight and narrow."

I frowned at his words because I knew he wasn't wrong.

That didn't mean he was right.

But still... I did feel different.

For the first time in six weeks, I wasn't thinking solely about my knee, about the pain I was in, about Oxy, or about working off my frustrations in the gym.

Instead, I was heading out. I was dressed, I was showered. For the first time in a while, I'd shaved, and not because I had puke in my beard but because Da expected us to look a certain way when we left the house on business.

Huh, Finn *wasn't* wrong.

I felt fired up inside, and knew that when I made it to the Hole, the place where Brennan did his best work, I'd be just as riled and tangled up inside with the need to find answers that would help me keep my personal temptress safe.

"I know this sounds crazy, man, but I'm pretty sure that after you met her, you fucking changed."

"Shut up," I thundered. "You're talking out of your ass," I groused as the doors to the elevator opened and spat me out on the garage level that was Conor's alone. While I limped over to my Bentley, I muttered, "She didn't fucking change me." I barely goddamn knew her.

"Maybe she didn't, but whatever you found out did." His tone told me he didn't believe that, but he fell silent a second. "You never did tell me what that was."

I grunted. "You're going to cut off when my Bluetooth shifts."

"You mean, you want me to cut off." Finn chuckled. "Go on, fuck off. Just be aware of what she does to you. Maybe if you're aware of it, you won't push her away like you did before."

Opening the door to the car, I purposely pressed the ignition button so that the dash would fire up and it would disconnect us. Unapologetically, I let the call fade away, but Finn's words didn't disappear so easily.

As I plunked my ass into the driver's seat, I thought about how I wouldn't be able to separate myself from her until she'd finished publishing all those exposés...

Because I knew for a fact that I wouldn't be comfortable leaving her with guards.

I just... *couldn't.*

I'd relied on them for years, but look at what had happened tonight—how could I trust them to keep her safe when, with the first real threat to her life, she'd had to defend herself with a fucking mop and a coffee table book?

I'd seen the carnage for myself, and rage continued to filter through me at what she'd had to do to survive. A mop and a coffee table book were all that had stood between her and death.

I might never have seen her again if she wasn't such a fighter.

My hands tightened around the steering wheel to the point where the leather creaked, but I ignored it. My palms burned, but I ignored it. Savannah was...

I blew out a breath.

I didn't fucking know what she was.

I really didn't. I just knew she was something, and that something routinely popped into my thoughts even though I hadn't seen her in a goddamn lifetime.

Hopped up on Oxy, I'd still thought about her. Thought about what she'd uncovered. The secrets in the family, the truths and lies that were burrowed within the O'Donnelly clan.

Filthy secrets and filthier lies.

She'd become tangled up in them in my mind, and it messed with my head. As much as I needed to protect those secrets and lies from ever seeing the light of day, I needed to protect her too. They all went hand in hand.

Mouth tightening with frustration, I got on my way.

At this time of the morning, the traffic wasn't as bad, but somehow, as I drove off the island and into Brooklyn, I got caught up in a traffic jam and it took me about twenty minutes longer than I'd have liked to make it to Brennan's territory.

As was often the way when I had the misfortune of coming into this part of our world, I waved my hand at the corpses Da had buried in one of the lots here. There were pigs and a politician or two buried within that ground, earth that would forever be untouched no matter how much the value of it soared. Not that I could imagine that happening in my lifetime. And when I was dead, and Da was gone, who the hell would care about some rotten old bodies that were secretly buried?

A guard visually tagged me and bagged me the second I showed up on the compound, so I drove in and parked with little to no fuss.

Wasn't it fitting that I was in Paddy's old stomping ground?

This had been his home away from home before Brennan had taken over it, and my brother hadn't done anything to improve the place.

It looked decrepit, derelict. Barely functioning, in fact. Inside, it was like a bordello, because Paddy's taste ran as deep as his flighty nature.

Grimacing at the thought, then grunting as my knee started to buckle when I was standing, I huffed out a breath, tried to inhale and exhale to get the pain back down to manageable levels, before I accepted that wasn't going to happen and that I needed to struggle through it.

As I pondered which would make me look weaker, a cane or walking like this, I forced myself into the mindset required for what was about to go down.

Mostly aware that I was being watched by the guards monitoring the area, I knew I couldn't stick around for long. They'd figure out something was wrong, and while I knew the family was aware of my addiction, my brothers, by some miracle, had managed to keep a tight lid on it. That was probably helped by the fact that my position in the Points was managerial rather than hands on like Brennan. I'd done my time, served on the frontlines, had handed many a man's ass to him. That was it for me.

I only got involved when it was personal.

Tonight was the definition of personal.

While I limped over to the warehouse, the door opened and I saw Forrest, one of Bren's right-hand-men, waiting for me.

His crew was unlike the one I had, most of my brothers' in fact. Brennan's were like secondary brothers or something. They were closer than close, whereas my crew were mostly autonomous. They knew when I called on them, they had to act, but I had a good Captain in charge, so Lucas handled most of the shit for me. That had been the way even before the accident.

Dipping my chin at Forrest, I asked, "He's expecting me?"

"Yep, told me to wait on you to guide you toward the main event."

I shook my head. "I don't want to go to the office."

"You want to get your hands dirty?" Forrest arched a brow, then scanned me. "You're not exactly dressed for the part."

"Aren't I?" I replied grimly as I stepped through the doorway, letting him close the door behind me.

"Not like you to get involved, Aidan," Forrest rumbled, frowning at me. "Everything okay?"

Because I knew how much he meant to Brennan, I cut him more slack than I would usually. "I'm fine, Forrest. Seriously."

He shrugged. "If you say so. You look wired."

I almost huffed out a laugh. I looked wired now? Christ, the only thing I was hopped up on was adrenaline and fury.

As I limped through the gaudy offices, following Forrest even though I knew the exact route to where Brennan tortured our enemies, I grimaced as the stench hit me.

"Jesus," I rumbled.

Forrest snickered. "He shat himself early on."

My brow furrowed as I recalled exactly why I loathed wet work.

For Savannah, however... well, I'd make an exception.

And it *was* for Savannah. It had nothing to do with the Five Points' need to get rid of the Sparrows. To eradicate them not only from our city but from the country, it was for her.

The thought had me gritting my teeth because I had enough weaknesses without adding some more to the list.

Coming face to face with the fucker who'd thought he could hurt her, *kill her*, I stepped between the crates that were scattered around the floor, and made my way to the area he was standing in.

"You work fast," I muttered at Brennan when I took in the state of the guy who was at the top of my shit list.

Hanging from a meat hook, he had duct tape over his mouth, but it wasn't enough that I couldn't see the thick scar running down one side of his face. His eyes were wild amid the bruises, and with every step I'd taken toward my brother, he'd wriggled and writhed like he could worm his way free.

Not a chance.

Still dressed all in black from his attempt at hiding in plain sight amid the shadows, I could nevertheless see the patches of wet where he'd pissed himself thanks to the spotlight that was focused on him.

"Baggy warmed him up for me first," Brennan discounted.

I eyed my younger brother, took note of the way he'd rolled his sleeves up, how the once-pristine white of his shirt was now spotted with blood, and murmured, "If you say so."

On top of the crate nearest to Bren, there was an array of tools that had me itching to touch them. Finding some shears, I picked them up, then drifted nearer to the fucker.

As I did, he tensed up, and though he carried on wriggling and writhing around, I prepared myself for him to kick out, for him to target my weak side.

Only, he didn't.

Maybe he saw my resolve, but whatever it was that had made him shit himself, made a reappearance. The fucker didn't fight. He engaged in flight. Only, pity for him, he was skewered in place.

As I plucked at the neckline of his tee, I dragged it away from his body then pressed the shears to the fabric. Cutting it, trying to touch him as little as possible, I managed to part his shirt in two. I cut along his shoulders as well, leaving him in rags. Then, I did the same with his belt, before starting on his jeans. Brennan headed over, well aware I was getting the fucker naked, and helped by taking the shears from me and going all the way to the floor.

When I stepped back, he was still covered. Barely.

I turned to Brennan. "You got a power washer?"

My brother laughed. "I do. Forrest!" he hollered.

"On it," his crew man declared, a giddy tone to his voice.

Within minutes, I had a Karcher in my hand and it was rumbling, the system working as I raised the nozzle and power washed the fucker clean.

As icy cold water pummeled his skin, the high pressure had him screeching as his clothes were ripped away. I moved all the way around too, cleaning up his shitty ass—clearing that up for my benefit not his—and I didn't stop until he was as pink as a shrimp.

By the time I was done, the water had made abrasions on his flesh. Not only that, but the cuts and tears that came from his original beating, had been torn wide open. His face was a spider's web of cuts that told me he'd gone head to head with some glass and had lost.

Eying those wounds, I turned to Brennan and asked, "Salt?"

He hummed, but Forrest was already scampering away. He returned with a bag of what looked like sand.

"This is all we got, Aid."

As he placed it on the crate in front of me, I used one of the knives laid out to tear the plastic apart. "You got any vinegar?" I asked as I picked up a handful of the gritty sand.

"Nah, but I can head out and get some."

"I think that would be a good idea." Then, I turned to the cocksucker, and I smiled as I began rubbing it all over his face, into the hundreds of tiny cuts.

Once he started screaming, Brennan cackled. "I forgot how good you were at this, Aid."

Because wet work really was like riding a bike, I shot him a look. "I just don't like getting my shirts dirty."

Both he and Forrest grinned, but I didn't stop until the fucker's entire body was covered in sand. Having copiously poured it into his open wounds, the salt within it had him howling in agony, and I made sure that I rubbed it in hard so the abrasion would triple his pain.

I stepped back when he looked like some kind of weird art project, then I reached up and pulled on the duct tape covering his mouth.

His screams came louder, as did his pleas, but I ignored them.

I just had one thing on my mind. "If you want me to wash the sand away, you'll tell me who sent you."

FOURTEEN

SAVANNAH

THROUGH THE MANY and varied hangovers I'd experienced in my life, I thought I'd understood what the term 'death warmed over' truly meant.

Waking up feeling like shit wasn't something that happened often, but I wasn't a saint and I really loved a glass or five of red after a long, shitty day. My brain didn't appreciate the tannins, however, and my bottle of Malbeck usually packed as much of a punch as a donkey's kick to the pussy.

That, however, was nothing in comparison to the level of *ouch* that hit me when I woke up.

"Jesus, Mary, and Joseph," I rasped out loud as I fell onto my back and starfished the space.

After a couple minutes, I groggily patted the nightstand, knowing I'd put my phone there after I'd showered and changed into a guest bathrobe. When I saw the date and time, my sleepy eyes bugged.

One AM on the 22nd?

Those were eighteen hours I'd never be getting back. Ugh.

There was no forgetting where I was or what was happening,

though, just the *when*. Especially as I felt every single hit from last night's attack.

Plus, my bed wasn't a waterbed, and didn't slosh every time I moved.

Neither was there a waterfall at my side, reminding me I needed to pee, nor did my room have such a perfect view of the terrace or let in this much light—although, why the hell the terrace lights were blaring at one AM was beyond me.

Was it weird for me to want to get up just to go and turn them off?

Then, of course, I thought about the owner of those lights and what his response would be to that.

Which led to thoughts on the brother of the owner of those lights...

As I peered up at the ceiling, gulping, trying not to feel like a girl about to ask a guy out for prom, I whispered to myself, "You're in the same apartment as Aidan O'Donnelly."

The only man who I'd never give him shit over light pollution.

The only man who'd ever ghosted me.

The only man who... I sighed.

"Soul mates don't exist," I told myself as I rolled onto my side, then edged off the bed. "And if they do, they shouldn't be asshole mobsters."

Desperately in need of both caffeine and ibuprofen, I tightened the knot of the belt around my waist, grimacing when my wrists protested the move. Peering down at my hands, I saw that one was a little swollen.

Feeling worse for wear and sorry for myself to boot, I used the bathroom then trudged out of the bedroom after fighting with the doorknob to get out—because apparently you needed a degree in engineering nowadays for that small feat—then I stepped down the hall in search of humanity. Humanity who'd be able to get me my two drugs of choice.

I found a really wide and long room first. There were a ton of computer monitors on several different desks, each of them switched on and making me cringe at how much electricity they were wasting. At least they weren't all showing screensavers, but appeared to be doing something. Only God knew what though.

There was a loud whining sound too, and I quickly sourced it as coming from Conor O'Donnelly. He had a pair of headphones on that was piping what I assumed was music into his ears. The volume was so loud that I could hear the whistling sound from over here.

Though I almost wanted to chide him for it, I left him alone, especially when I caught him digging deep into a pint of frozen custard.

A part of me wanted to ask him to split with the good stuff, but mostly, sugar wasn't what I needed right now. It might solve the ache in my soul, just not the one in my body and head.

Then, of course, that was when I saw it.

I peered at the screen he was focused on and flinched.

Like that, my myriad aches disappeared, proving that mind over matter worked when you were embarrassed AF.

Unable to help myself, I stepped closer. One thing that hadn't changed in all the years I'd been on TV was the strange compulsion to watch myself. That sounded super conceited, but it wasn't. It was like I was preparing to watch myself fuck up.

I never did.

Somehow, the only time I'd ever messed up on screen was purposely.

And this was the one time I'd never watched myself back.

I hadn't fucked up.

Everything I'd done had been with intent.

Every-damn-thing.

I wasn't sure how he knew I was there, but Conor spun his seat around and grinned at me a second before he shoved a massive spoonful of frozen custard into his mouth.

He pulled off his earphones, placed them on the table, and with that, the sound boomed around the room.

Wincing, I asked, "Why are you watching this?"

"Because I like to know who we're getting into bed with."

My lips curved. "You should be so lucky."

"Oh, I fear I'm taken," he declared, one hand flying wide in a grandiose gesture that was worthy of an actor in a Shakespearean play. "But I know someone who isn't." He squinted at me a second, then turned back to face the monitors in question.

Yep.

Monitors.

He pressed a button and, suddenly, there were six of me in front of him.

Six of me sitting behind the desk, a smile planted on my face that looked innocent as fuck. I'd been practicing for this moment all my life. I knew how to be an airhead. I knew how to sell a look, to let everyone think there was nothing going on between my ears.

How wrong they were.

How fucking wrong they were.

It took thirty-four years to forge a reputation, and thirty-three seconds to destroy it.

"Wasn't that fascinating?" I declared to the camera, just as it panned wide to Stewart Allsheim, my co-anchor. "Who knew a cat could knock on a door?"

"I can see why the video has gone viral," Stewart agreed, a smarmy smile fixed in place that he thought made him seem engaging. He was wrong. "But we're going to look at a video that's hit one hundred million views and its audience is already growing."

The screen cut off, and though it appeared to be a TikTok video fading into view, it wasn't.

I'd cut through a Chanel purse for this, making a slit in the lining so I could place two phones there and have them record both of us throughout the entire interview.

Having positioned it on the coffee table, between myself and Derick Wintersen, the studio VP who was capable of making or breaking a career at TVGM, at the time I'd had to hope that I'd get us both at the right angle.

God had been on my side.

Wintersen was a fat fuck, who looked like Jaba the Hut on a good day, and had *the* worst breath I'd ever smelled in my life.

He'd also left me alone.

From the first day I'd shown up there to that very moment. I knew why too. Aidan. It wasn't my daddy or my name, a standing in society that I'd always courted, it was Aidan.

The Five Points.

They'd protected me from this creep.

I didn't know how, just knew why he'd never come onto me before.

"I'm starting to feel left out," I crooned.

Wintersen leaned forward, the chair creaking under his weight as he asked, "In what way, my dear?"

"Well, I know the reason you gave Sally Livingston the anchor position was because she was nice to you."

"Nice?" His lips curved. "Nice sums it up. Do you want to be nicer to me?"

"It depends. What's in it for me?"

He grinned, a knowing cast overtaking his expression as if we were both speaking the same language. "It depends on what you want. Sally wanted the anchor position on Wednesday mornings."

"Maybe I want more than TVGM."

"You have aspirations. So good to hear," he crooned. "Well, you know my leverage is mostly over the TVGM studios, but..." He winked. "I do have friends on Channel Four."

Smiling, I leaned forward. "That sounds very interesting. No more early mornings." I laughed, and it was so natural that even now, I grimaced. How was I this good at faking?

Past Savannah let her hand trace the seam of the armchair I was sitting in, at the same moment as I crossed my legs. A deep split appeared in my skirt, one that drifted obscenely high, enough that he licked his fleshy lips.

"I think it's the first time I've seen you in a skirt, Savannah. You usually wear those boxy suits."

I just smiled at him and let my fingers fall to my thigh. "What would I have to do to get the position?"

"Well, you'd have to be...nice to me," he said softly, sinking back into his seat, his hand dropping to his crotch as he palmed himself. "But you'd have to be nicer than Sally." He smirked. "Can you do that, Savannah?"

In answer, I dropped to my knees and though the distance between us was short, and a little cramped, I crawled over to him. He swallowed, his Adam's apple bobbing. Once I was near, I placed my hands on his knees, and purred, "I can be very, very, very *nice*."

That was when my arm reared back and I punched him in the junk.

Conor hissed. "Ouch."

I grinned, despite myself. "You should have heard him whimper."

"I'm surprised he let you go on air after that happened."

"He'd set up an internal audit, basically looking to take me down, but I did that the evening before I went live the next morning, and I paid some of the runners to make sure the footage wasn't pulled before the video ended."

"Let me guess, women he'd creeped on over the years?"

I winked at him. "You got it." Releasing a shaky breath, I admitted, "That was the first time I watched it back."

"Really?" Conor twisted to look up at me. "Who edited it for you?"

"I did it myself."

He snorted. "Bullshit."

I squinted at him. "Are you trying to be an asshole?"

Best to deflect here.

I had no desire to get anyone in the studio into trouble, and I knew Acuig Corp. had a stake in TVGM so the O'Donnellys would be invested in knowing who'd helped me—this was definitely a dangerous topic. Getting me a job was one thing, but I had no idea how invested they were in the daily operations. Aidan hadn't given me shit about Wintersen, but Conor might be different.

"My brothers will confirm that I don't have to try to be an asshole." Conor laughed at his own joke. "I'll keep digging if you don't tell me," he warned, his tone shifting so abruptly from amused to dark that I glowered at him.

"Someone high up in the network helped me," I admitted begrudgingly. "I'm not going to name names."

"Why are you protecting her?"

"Because he was threatening to ruin her career if she didn't fuck him." I shrugged and attempted once more to deflect the topic of conversation, "Aidan got me the job at TVGM. Did you know that?"

"I figured it out when I looked into you. I've spent quite an interesting evening following up on your various exploits. Especially when it comes down to Aidan. I knew there was something between you, but I couldn't figure it out.

"At first, I thought you were his mistress but a woman like you isn't exactly mistress material."

I scowled. "Is that an insult or a compliment?"

He grinned. "Depends on your inclination. Not sure you should be scowling at me. I didn't mean it as an insult this time," he corrected, his grin fading. "I meant it as a truth. You wouldn't be a mistress. Mistresses don't usually wear suits." My wardrobe appeared illogical to him and he frowned. "I just can't understand from how you first met, why it would lead to you getting a job out of it. Are you blackmailing him?"

It was my turn to grin. "Would anyone dare blackmail a Five Pointer?"

That had him grunting. "You'd be surprised."

I blinked. "Seriously?"

He tipped his head to the side, his eyes both distant and penetrating—which was weird, trust me—as he scanned me over like he was an X-ray hunting broken bones. "Seriously." He hummed. "Anyway, are you?"

"No. I'm not."

"Then why did he give you a job?"

I pursed my lips. "You'll have to ask him."

"Oh, I will. I just thought I'd be likelier to get an answer out of you rather than him."

"At least you're honest."

"It's a failing of mine. I think you'll be sticking around long enough to learn that..." His gaze dropped down over my form once more, but it was oddly non-sexual. "You'll need clothes."

"Yes."

"Ask Aidan to take you down to your apartment."

"Why? It should be safe now, shouldn't it?"

"The intruder killed Thomas last night to get into the building. Whoever sent him obviously doesn't mind spilling blood to get to you. It's best not to go anywhere alone. Not just for your safety but for civilians too."

Shock hit me, as well as a deep regret. "Thomas, as in the doorman?" I staggered back until my ass collided with his desk. "Oh Jesus, his wife just had their third child."

His brows rose. "You knew that?"

I swallowed. "Of course. I sent her a bouquet of flowers." Chills whispered through my body. "Oh, my God. He's dead, and it's my fault."

Conor's brow puckered. "It isn't really. It's the people who sent the guy who came to kill you."

I shuddered. "I need to do something to help—"

"He's an employee of Acuig Corp., Savannah," he said softly, soothingly. "Don't worry. We take care of our own."

Blinking, I rasped, "If you do a *gofundme* or something, then tell me, okay? I want to contribute."

He blinked. "Okay, but we don't work like that."

They were the Five Points. Of course, they didn't, I thought woodenly.

His hand hovered over my knee like he wanted to comfort me but didn't want to impose. "Truly, Savannah, it wasn't your fault."

It was, though, wasn't it?

"There'll be a lot of blood shed before this whole farce is over," he intoned grimly, his eyes darkening as he glanced up at the screen once more. "You did good with that prick. When I was looking into you, I researched him.

"The network and the studio helped keep his behavior from the board. I don't think Aidan would have let that go on if he'd known. Especially not when you were at risk." His gaze turned curious once more. "Your security seems to be a priority of his."

"There's no point in fishing with me. I've got three siblings. I know how to keep a secret."

He snickered, but his eyes turned, in a word, googly. "Do you really think your dad will play for me?"

The question had me blinking a second, my brain whirring as I tried to process why he was asking me that exactly, and then I remembered. I'd told him Dad would set up in the corner and play any song Conor wanted.

"I don't see why not. Although he hates New York. That would probably be the hardest thing of all—getting him to come here."

Conor wafted a hand. "I have houses all over the States. I could go to him."

My lips twitched. "Houses or safe houses?"

He waggled his finger at me. "Houses."

Lifting my arms and cupping my elbows, I bit my lip as I tilted my head back to look at the screens.

"Before the exposés, this was the most useful thing I'd ever done in my life," I told him softly.

"Useful? That's a weird way of phrasing it."

"Is it? I'm a celebrity's daughter. I'm Dagger Daniels' spawn. Everyone knows me, at least, they think they do. Everything I've gotten, they think came from my connection to Dad. No matter how hard I work, no matter how much I try, everything will always be because I'm my father's daughter." I cut him a look. "Don't get me wrong, it comes in handy sometimes.

"I'm pretty sure the only reason the network didn't sue is because of Dad, well, and Aidan, but that wouldn't have stopped Wintersen I don't think. And I'm not saying that I feel sorry for myself, because I don't. I have a great life and a lot of that is because of my father, but it was just... *good* to be able to go in there and destroy that smirk.

"All these months later, it still triggers an adrenaline rush like no other."

"He quit soon after, didn't he?"

I nodded. "His wife petitioned for a divorce too. I regret hurting her, although having to be married to that bastard must have been a punishment in and of itself."

Conor asked, "You don't think he'd hate you enough to send someone after you?"

I snorted. "No."

"He lost everything," Conor pointed out. "Career, family, reputation, his whole life because of what you did."

"He deserved it. He ruined a whole host of lives before I came along and served him some justice." I scowled at him. "Are you on his side?"

Conor snickered. "Me? No. I'm just trying to figure out who'd want you dead. That's all."

"It's to do with the exposés, surely?"

He dug his spoon into his carton of frozen custard. "Yes, it's more than likely, but I'd be remiss if I didn't check out every avenue, wouldn't I?"

Begrudgingly, I admitted, "I guess."

"I'll admit I know it's a dead end. I'm just giving you shit."

I frowned at him. "How do you know that?"

"Because Wintersen's gone missing."

"What?" I sputtered.

"He's gone missing," Conor repeated.

Unease filled me at the way he was looking at me. Like he expected me to understand what was happening.

I swallowed. "Aidan?"

Conor winked. "I reckon, don't you?"

Jesus.

I turned to look at the screen, at Wintersen's puckered up face, trying to think that the bastard was dead because of me, trying to reconcile that Aidan had protected me more than I even knew, and my mind tripped on it. Stalling on the thought that two men had died because of me.

I wasn't sure why he would go to such lengths to protect me. Just as I couldn't understand why I'd never been able to forget him.

Nothing about us made sense, but that didn't stop the rightness that filled me at the thought of him. Never mind the inherent relief I'd felt at seeing him again.

Not just because he represented safety, but because it had been too long, and it made my heart happy to be in his presence once more.

Weird, for sure, but maybe I needed to start embracing that weirdness.

Weird kept me alive, after all.

"Did Thomas suffer?" I whispered, needing to know, needing to compound the guilt.

"Stab wound to the heart. The guy was a pro." Conor's tone was wooden, emotionless. Somehow, I knew that the colder he sounded, the more he actually felt.

He'd called Thomas by his first name. Not just by his job description.

He'd cared.

"His poor family." I bit my lip and with a final glance at what had been the cherry on the sundae, a video that had gone viral, a video that had taken down a whole host of execs on the TVGM board, that had triggered the #MeToo movement in my old place of work and that had single-handedly destroyed my TV career, I stepped back and away without another word.

Dipping out of the room as quickly as I'd dipped in, leaving Conor to his investigations, I moved further down the hallway.

Guilt and remorse entwined, powerful enough to almost steal my breath.

"Poor Thomas," I whispered to myself, unable to believe that my actions had led to an innocent man being murdered.

Was it wicked to hope that the O'Donnellys had made the bastard pay? That they'd hurt him? Badly? It wouldn't bring Thomas back, wouldn't make up for his widow's grief, wouldn't change the fact his kids would be raised without their father, but there had to be some justice, didn't there?

Some karmic, cosmic vengeance?

The need to see Aidan hit me harder than before.

There was no safety within these walls, not even within his embrace, but he made my brain stop overworking. If anything, I reverted to a giggling teenager when I was with him, and as bad as that was, as embarrassing, right now, with a man's blood on my hands, I needed that.

As I padded down the hall, trying to seek out Aidan's location, I had to admit the penthouse was massive. Big enough to make me jealous even though it was far too much real estate for one man.

Did Conor get lonely? Haunting these halls by himself?

He'd said that he was taken. By whom? I'd never heard anything in the gossip columns about him dating anyone, and the O'Donnellys were hot news in Manhattan.

On the hunt now, I opened a few doors, found some bedrooms, a really cool home theater that looked like it was never used with huge sofas planted in there, and another room that appeared to be some kind of aquarium. One wall of fish, that was pretty much all I saw.

Grimacing at the sight and wondering why he was obsessed with water, I ducked back into the hallway and carried on my way.

When I heard grunting, my body quickened. It really shouldn't have. I wasn't this dumb, wasn't so overly hormonal that they had control over my brain, but damn, that sounded like sex.

Curious by nature—hell, that was one of the reasons I was damn good at what I did—I continued onward, unsure if I wanted to see a show or not. Bypassing a stuffed bear in mid-roar—God, who had taxidermy anymore?—I found a gym, and swiftly realized I was about to get a free show anyway.

Aidan, who had two sets of massive dumbbells in his hands, was stacked.

I mean, he'd been stacked before. But he was thinner now, his body far leaner, so I could see every damn muscle.

Every.

Single.

Muscle.

They rippled and tensed, grew taut and hard as he tugged on one of the various torture devices that I hated and refused to use. Yoga was my thing. Pilates too when I was in the frame of mind for it. Gyms were Satan's way of trying to make humans miserable in my opinion. Still, having seen Aidan working out, I could say I was a convert.

Holy hell, how was he this ripped? And how did his clothes hide all his splendor?

I pressed my hand to my chest, the move stupid but reactive—almost like I was trying to calm my thundering heart—and that was when the pain reminded me that my hands were delicate right now. The gasp I uttered had Aidan casting me a glance in the mirror.

The ease in which he did that told me he'd known exactly where I was standing.

Had known I was watching.

Had been watching me.

Why was that hot?

"Good morning, Savannah," he rumbled in a voice that had me swallowing.

"Morning, Aidan. Do you have any ibuprofen?"

As he lowered the weight in his hand, he asked, "Where are you in pain?" His brow furrowed. "Do you need to see a doctor?" He limped over to me, reminding me that for as much as he looked strong and shredded, he was also injured.

I wasn't sure why that made him even more attractive. It wasn't like he needed the help, after all.

"I don't think so. I might just need a wrist support and a splint?" I raised my hand. "I might have sprained it."

His expression darkened at the sight of the slightly swollen joint, but he rumbled, "Take a seat on the pommel horse."

The pommel horse? My brain only really processed the word *horse.*

Because this apartment was full of animals, dead (the bear) and ornamental (the weird cat,) I half-expected to see a real life one, but instead, I found the gymnastic kind. It was too high off the ground, and my ankles were tender as well so I just leaned back against the oddly dense instrument which felt weird against my butt.

Uncomfortable, I took a look around and wandered off to the massage table in the corner.

With a wall of mirrors, four shelves of different weights, then an elliptical, a treadmill, and a rowing machine, as well as a kind of frame that had loops hanging from it that could have been a sex toy but was more than likely an all-in-one gym, I quickly grew bored. By the time Aidan was trudging in, I was eager to look at him just because he was way more interesting.

"Why aren't you by the pommel horse?"

"This is lower to the ground. It's easier for me to lean against."

My logic must have appeased him because he ordered, "Hold out your hands," before handing me a bottle of water as well as a couple of pills.

A part of me wanted to ask what type of pills they were. The O'Donnellys sold a lot of dubious chemicals, after all.

But this was Aidan.

He was... Hell, I didn't know what he was. I just knew he'd never hurt me.

"Are you this bossy with everyone?" I complained, even as I complied once I'd taken a sip of water and had downed the meds.

His lips twitched. "Mostly everyone."

I rolled my eyes. "Good to know," I grumbled as he began to unpack bandages, as well as a few other pieces from the first aid kit he propped on the massage table beside me.

Having seen him in action last night with his brothers, and comparing it with the few other occasions we'd been together, I wasn't surprised at how he sat back and listened, analyzing rather than diving face first into a situation. Wasn't surprised either that every movement he made as he patched me up was precise, oddly compacted as if he did everything with efficiency.

Last night, I'd also seen how he'd commanded his siblings without anyone being aware of it. As strange as that sounded, it was the truth.

I didn't think they were aware of how they were all angled toward him, how they all looked to him first for direction. Considering he was the heir, I guessed it made sense. Being oldest did have some perks, but... maybe not. Didn't brothers tend to resent the guy who'd inherit everything simply because he'd had the good fortune of being born first?

Or was that just in royalty?

Weren't the O'Donnellys the crime world's version of royalty though?

Or was this particular crown a burden that no one wanted to wear?

Distracted by my thoughts, he patched me up without me even really registering it. Not because it didn't hurt, as it did, but because he was careful and adept, telling me this wasn't the first time he'd carefully doctored cuts and scrapes, taped up a splint and bandaged a wrist for extra support.

I half hoped he'd ask to see my thigh, but no joy.

"I'll keep an eye on you over the next few days. If the bruising and swelling gets worse, then I'll have to arrange for them to be X-rayed."

I blinked. "I have insurance."

He cast me a glance, but his lips twitched again. "Savannah, your apartment is prime Manhattan real estate. You live in The Sharpe, for God's sake. It never occurred to me that you didn't have it. Whether or not you can use it is a different matter entirely."

I winced. "I think I rattled my brain."

At least, I hope that was what had happened. After that nasty fall off the coffee table, and then that dive down the stairs... maybe I should be grateful I hadn't done myself some lasting damage.

"Yeah, you keep coming out with some odd shit." He sighed. "Maybe I shouldn't have let you sleep. Not if you have a concussion."

Odd shit. Well, that was one way to put it.

"I'm all right," I groused, although being concussed would sure as hell explain the random crap that escaped my mouth and the way my body was more in charge than usual. As in, how it wasn't letting me forget that Aidan was fiiiine.

In fact, the more that I thought about it, the more that I was relieved he thought I was concussed. If I did something that was out of the ordinary, then he wouldn't think it was all that strange.

At least, I had to hope he wouldn't.

Surely people said strange things around him all the time?

Humming at the thought, I peered at my newly taped up wrist and murmured, "Thank you, Aidan. I appreciate it."

"You're welcome. Like I said, I'll monitor you. Make sure you don't need some medical intervention, but the worst of it looks to me as if it's just a regular sprain from your falls. Not compound fractures or anything. I'd be able to tell the difference."

"I think I would as well. Aren't compound fractures when bones pop out of the skin?"

He snorted. "Sometimes. You're gruesome, aren't you?"

Was I?

I didn't think so.

Morbid, sure.

"Maybe?" I peered at a bead of sweat that was swirling through the meager chest hair on his torso. "Do you think we could go downstairs so I could grab some things? I don't have anything to wear apart from this robe, and I'm not sure I can live in it all day."

Like that, without even meaning to, I changed the vibe between us.

A soft sound escaped him, one that had the air clutching in my lungs. I peered up at him, saw the strange gleam in his eyes and knew, from that one glance, he felt it.

This thing between us.

A livewire that bound us together.

It had been there since the beginning. Since that first moment our eyes had collided in my once favorite coffee spot. The place I'd gone every day for months after, hoping he'd be there, waiting on me again. Only, he never had, and I wasn't that desperate that I'd go and hunt down one of the eligible O'Donnellys—I wasn't about to make an ass of myself over a fool man who'd ghosted me.

Even as I accepted that he didn't deserve me after what he'd done, I also accepted that I knew why he had.

Without putting words in his mouth, I'd seen the second he'd had to take a business call at the end of our meal, and how a mask had come down over his features as a result.

Like any joy, any feeling, any sense of pleasure that was to be found in our time together had immediately disappeared.

Washed away like dirt in the rain.

It had hurt to behold. Even now, the memory of it was enough to make me cringe, because that level of control, that ability to shut everything off and become an automaton wasn't something to envy but to dissect.

After being ghosted though, it made a woman doubt herself. And as confident as I was, I wasn't *that* confident. Still, the way he looked at me now was a reminder of what arced between us.

Of the heat and the tangled whip of fire that lashed at us both.

It sounded like an exaggeration, but it wasn't. It was the whole-hearted truth.

My breath stuttered in my chest as I watched him watch me, his gaze dropping down to the knot of my bathrobe.

"If I tugged on that," he rasped, "what would I find underneath it?"

I swallowed. "Me and little else." A bandage didn't count as a covering, did it?

He growled under his breath, and then his hand dropped to the knot and he pulled on it.

Once.

Then he stopped.

My heart did too.

He kept his fingers there, around the loose tie, and I waited, heart in my throat now, as I wondered if he'd tug on it, carry on until it opened, revealing my bare body as I promised.

The ache in my head and wrists were memories of another time, another place.

They'd gone, whispered away by the non-existent breeze in the gym.

I was pretty sure the clock froze as well as the rest of the world, the universe itself contracting as he stared at me. As I stared at him. Our gazes tangling with the force of the atoms themselves in the Hadron particle collider.

Then, he did as we both wanted, but neither were willing to say.

He tugged.

The knot parted, the tie falling away, and a sliver of my body was revealed to him.

He groaned under his breath as that same hand slipped to my waist, parting the two halves of the robe and showing even more of my form to him. I didn't do anything, determined that he'd make this first move, seeing as he'd been the one to make the last.

At that moment, my brain was wired to focus on him and only

him, which, with the clusterfuck I'd made of my life, was exactly what I needed.

I felt the pressure of his fingertips against my skin as if each one were a burning brand. It was insane how deeply they seared me, as if he'd pressed them against a fire then pushed them into my skin. Crazier still that it felt so good.

He gripped me there, for a second, before he traced my ribs, soaring higher and higher until his hand cupped my breast.

All air stuttered out of my lungs, my lips parted noiselessly as I looked down at where his tan hand connected with my pale flesh.

Biting my lip, determined not to say anything or do anything that would enable or disable him from making a decision, I groaned too when his other hand moved to my hip, dropping down to shape the line where groin met thigh.

He brushed against the gauze bandage, muttering, "When I saw you bleeding, I nearly fucking lost it."

"You bandaged me up?"

His eyes met mine. "You think I'd let another man, even one of my brothers, touch you?"

His words, so possessive and sure, triggered a discordant reaction inside me. I loved that he sounded so insanely covetous. But I wanted to scream at him because he was the one who'd pushed me into other men's arms by disappearing the way he had.

He had no right to be all jealous now, and yet, tell that to my ovaries. Ovaries that really wanted him to claim what he was stating was his.

"Do you know how long I've dreamed about seeing you naked?"

Because I was both pissed off and horny, the truth wasn't far from hand, so I rasped, "You were the one who walked away."

Which was both the truth and bullshit. In his defense, there hadn't been that much to walk away from. Not really. We'd met three times. Two of which had been all business, and that evening supper hadn't exactly been a date, but it had been *one* meal together.

It just felt like a lot more because the chemistry between us seemed ancient.

Nothing this powerful was nascent. It was forged in that big soup the universe came from. Big talk but that was the power of the connection between us.

I'd spent thirty-four years on this planet and, not once, had I experienced even an eighth of this response to another human being.

His mouth tightened. "My world isn't something I'd wish on anyone."

"Your world is one I've studied for years."

"Then you should be smart enough to recognize that you should have backed the hell away from it."

"I did, didn't I?" I murmured. "I went to TVGM like a good little girl."

His jaw tensed. "You knew I set that up for you?"

I dipped my chin. "Of course. The leap was too sharp for it to be anything other than nepotism. My father's name helped, but it wouldn't have done anything if I hadn't been wedged into the position."

His mouth firmed. "I'd do it again."

"I know you would," I retorted. "I didn't say I resented it, did I? I just said that I did as I was told."

"Obedience never did sit well with you."

"Like you know me enough to recognize that," I snapped.

"I know enough. I've fucking watched you every goddamn morning, Savannah. Jacked off in the shower after watching you talk about that year's biggest fucking pumpkin, and tried not to wish you weren't on morning television so you could wear a short skirt so I could fantasize about tugging it higher and bending you over that desk so that I could fuck you until the only news you were interested in was how many orgasms a woman can have during one screw."

I pressed a hand to his chest and pushed. "You're the one who walked away," I repeated. "Not a single call, Aidan. Not a single text. I wasn't going to beg for your attention."

"I almost wished you did but I know that's not in your nature."

"Damn right it isn't." I gritted my teeth. "I'm telling you now, Aidan O'Donnelly, if you keep on touching instead of looking, I'm not going to let you walk away next time."

He stiffened up at that, tension invading his limbs. "Savannah—"

"Don't even think about trying to bullshit me." For as much as I'd thought my head was foggy, at that moment, I'd never thought clearer. "I'm telling you now. If you don't move your hands away, if you carry on with what you're doing, I will snap a ball and chain so tightly around your fucking ankle you'll wonder if it's going to cut off the circulation to your foot."

His lips twisted. "So brave for so early in the morning."

"Not brave, just pissed off with you hovering. Who knew the heir to the Five Points wouldn't be able to make a decision about a little woman?" I jeered.

"There's nothing little about you," he rumbled.

"Should I take that as a compliment?"

A laugh grated out from between his lips. "Your personality is bigger than your ass," he said wryly.

"I repeat, should I take that as a compliment?"

His hands dropped, and just when I thought he was going to pull away, to back off and disappointment started to strum through me, a shadow of grief too, he dropped them to my waist and, skin to skin at last, slid them around and down until he was cupping my ass.

I groaned when he squeezed my cheeks then tugged them apart. His fingertips did that searing thing again, so that I felt them in my sit spot and right between the crease where my pussy and ass almost met.

Biting my lip, I rasped, "Is that a declaration of intent?"

"You don't want to be in my world."

"I spent my whole life studying your world," I countered. "If anything, I know what I'm coming up against."

"You had a taste of it yesterday. Why the fuck couldn't you just stay out of trouble?" he snarled.

"You said you agreed with me blowing the whistle at TVGM," I retorted, not afraid to get in his face about that.

"I do, I did, but you didn't have to get wrapped up in this Sparrows' shit." He released a breath that gusted over my lips, and then stunned the hell out of me by leaning down and pressing his forehead against mine. "Why couldn't you just marry a TV executive and have kids and settle down and be safe?"

I knew it was a rhetorical question. The man had just told me he'd doctored my wounds because he couldn't stand his brothers' hands on me, for Christ's sake. But still, rhetorical or not, it made me freeze. Well, every part of me except for my tongue which, as usual, came to my aid.

"If that's how you feel," I ground out, "how you really goddamn feel, if you'd prefer another man to be touching me, to be fucking me, to be filling my pussy with his seed then—"

He snapped.

I felt the break in his control. Felt it, reveled in it, *luxuriated in it.*

His hands didn't just hold me now, didn't just squeeze, they bit into me.

Hard.

Nasty.

Tight.

Firm.

Fast.

He wasn't going to let me go.

Thank God for small mercies.

FIFTEEN

AIDAN

THE FIRST MOMENT we'd met, I'd learned she was a pusher.

She pressurized everything and everyone around her. I knew that. I just never thought she'd be able to do that to me.

But the thought of another guy fucking her, of him getting her pregnant—as much as I wanted the temptation out of the way, I couldn't stand it.

Whatever the fuck it was between us, something that acted like a massive, supercharged electro-goddamn-magnet, it couldn't handle her belonging to another.

I couldn't allow it. I wouldn't allow it.

I'd dealt with her hook-ups over the years, frightening them off when I thought they were getting too close after I ran background checks on them, all while I'd hoped she'd find someone better than me.

Instead, she'd confirmed what I already knew—she had shitty taste in men.

But her taunts made the beast inside me snap. The beast who'd pulled at the chains I'd looped around its neck whenever another man had approached her, tore free of the restraints, finally liberated from my desire to keep her safe from this world.

It had one thing in mind—a feral need to claim her.

I knew she felt it because she tensed, but curiously, she didn't pull away. That would have been smart. The intelligent thing to do, and as clever as she was, I knew she was too curious for her own good. Years of researching my family would have told her that, pre-Oxy, my control was legendary.

She wanted to see it break.

She wanted to be the one to rupture it.

I could read her with an ease that didn't come to me when I was reading a fucking book.

After the day's events with barely any sleep, I'd admit that now wasn't the right moment for her to be taunting me.

Adrenaline was riding me high, and bloodlust flew alongside it.

I hated what happened after I killed a man. I hated it because it was like a sickness in my blood, as addictive as fucking Oxy.

I felt like my da at those moments, felt as crazed as him, and that was good for no one. If I shared that same sickness...

God.

Just the thought made me want to push her away, but that image came to me again and the beast snapped its jaws in fury. I'd started it, I knew that, but she'd perpetuated it.

The thought of her round with child.

Another man's fucking child.

No.

Just no.

A snarl escaped me as I dropped my head, bowing it until our mouths were a hair's breadth from one another's. I could no more hide this from her than I could hide the boner I knew was pushing into her stomach.

"Last night's intruder... would you like to know his name?"

She tensed, her head rearing back with surprise. "W-What?"

"Would you like to know his name?" I taunted, even though I'd never tell her. Would never sully her that way. But I wanted her distracted. Wanted her scared. The beast wouldn't let her go, but if she was scared, she might run, and that was the only way I could save her from me.

The beast would never hurt her.

I could never hurt her.

She swallowed. "You know it?"

"I know everything. The first time he pissed his pants in kindergarten and how many goddamn brothers and sisters he has."

Her mouth quivered. "Y-You tortured him?"

"I did." Brennan's crew might have started it, but I'd fucking ended it. "Do you want to know what I'm capable of, Savannah? You think you know, you think you've read enough shit, but I don't think you have.

"Because as clinical as it can be on a piece of paper, written by a journalist whose job it is to note the facts down with ink not blood, it's never the same as knowing it firsthand."

Her throat bobbed. "I can handle it."

"Are you sure? Are you sure you want to know what I did in your name? How I sliced and fucking diced him to make him pay for daring to cut you?"

Her eyes flared, and her tits jiggled as she released a soft gasp. Her breathing came hard and fast. "Tell me," she demanded, her fingers digging into my pecs.

"Do you want to hear how I flayed him alive? How I made him beg for death? All so that I'd know who paid him to get to you?"

"Y-You skinned him?" she breathed, her eyes wider still.

"I did. Parts of him," I corrected. "Other parts I just cut. A thousand cuts to make him pay for that single one on your thigh." A sharp laugh escaped me. "Been a long time since I've gone to that much effort."

"You did for me though."

"I did." My mouth tightened as I saw her shiver, but not with revulsion like I'd hoped. Not with appreciation either. A complex mixture of desire and fear that was as intriguing as the woman herself.

"Did you find out who sent him?"

"Of course I did. It was the Sparrows. And we need to have a talk about that," I rumbled, "just not now."

"N-Not now." She blinked. "I-I don't know what to say."

"What is there to say? I told you, this world is cruel and filthy. It's not a nice place to be. The second I listened to your articles, I knew what you'd do to me. I knew that inquisitive mind, that opinionated bitch who brought experienced editors to their knees, would be like nectar to me. Someone with a voice, who wasn't afraid to use it. Who wouldn't be afraid of me." I jerked my head to the side. "I knew you'd be the one to flay *me*. Then I saw you, then I met you, and I knew it like you'd signed my death warrant yourself."

"Then why the fuck would you walk away?" she grated out, her hands smoothing over my chest to grab my shoulders. Her nails dug in, biting deep as she screamed in my face, "Why the fuck would you do that? Why would you ghost me?"

"Because you think you know my world but you don't. You saw one sliver of it in real life and it sent you into a spiral that triggered an unhealthy obsession with the mafia.

"Your therapist should be shot, because here you are. Yet again. You've waded headfirst into the fray and are a part of it whether you like it or not. The difference between here and now, Savannah, is that I'm not the man I once was.

"Back then, I was a conceited prick who thought I ruled the world because I was Da's heir. I had any pussy I wanted, could buy a fleet of Ferraris... most of humanity was at my feet, and I was more than okay with that. I had a rep for being a nasty piece of shit when things went south but that was it.

"Now, I know what pain is. I know what suffering is. I know that it's there, whether you're a part of this fucking life or not. This time, I'm not going to walk away. You won't be chaining yourself to me. I'll do that so you're the one who has to decide. Run, little girl, because that's the only way I'm going to let go of you now."

"You're giving me whiplash, Aidan," she rasped, and I saw exactly how unafraid she was. After my confession, she should have been cowering in front of me, but she wasn't. If anything she stood on tiptoes to get in my face. "One minute, you're pulling back, the next you're chaining me to your side? I think you're the one who needs to learn to be more decisive."

The way she prodded my chest with her finger had the beast gnashing its fangs.

"Don't play with monsters, Savannah," I warned, "not unless you're willing to get bitten."

And with that, I dropped my mouth to hers, pressed my teeth around her bottom lip, and did as I promised.

I bit.

SIXTEEN

SAVANNAH

THE SECOND HIS teeth pressed into the soft, tender flesh of my lip, I moaned. I had no choice.

It hurt.

It stung.

It was exquisite.

I needed that more than he could know, more than he could possibly recognize.

A growl escaped him as he pressed down harder, enough that my ass clenched and I popped up onto tiptoes once more as I moved into him to diminish the sting. As I did, I lowered my hands, pressing them to his pecs, touching him, softening him with my caresses, needing him to keep on biting, to never let go, but wanting the pain to fade.

A whimper escaped me when, finally, he released his hold, but not for long. Just enough time for him to slip his tongue between my lips, to thrust it against mine. To take my mouth. To claim it. To do as I'd known he always would—to possess me.

Own me.

God, how I needed him to own me.

My whimper morphed into a mewl as he ate into my mouth, teasing me and tearing into me, ripping me apart and building me back together.

I cried out as his hands finally moved, those long fingers and wide palms pressing into me, parting my ass wider until the tips dug into my labia.

I knew I was wet.

Shamefully so.

Ridiculously so.

My body was a patchwork quilt of bruises and aches after last night, but I didn't feel any of it. Didn't know it was there because my pussy had taken control. Just like it had been begging to for years.

As he fucked my mouth, I let him, head tipped back, taking everything he gave until he started to pull away. The second he did, I followed, not letting him stop, wanting him to carry on, needing this to never stop, to forever continue. To always happen.

A growl escaped him the longer I tangled my tongue with his, when I started to fight back, to fuck back, to savor and sample, to taste and to tease.

Soon, we weren't just sharing saliva, but air. I could feel his cock digging into me as much as I could feel the exertion that came from breathing with how heavily his torso rubbed up against mine. Then he lifted me. By my ass alone, and I squeaked, *squealed,* pulling back because I wasn't sure what he was doing until he raised me to the massage table.

The brute strength of the move, because I wasn't a small woman, and because of his injury had my heart skipping a beat. It wasn't like he'd carried me across the Brooklyn Bridge, but still, it was unanticipated.

No more so than when he dove for my throat and started sucking down on it, biting it and nibbling it before palpating his tongue against it, continuously raking his teeth down against the flesh so I knew I'd be wearing a hickey.

A groan escaped me as my head tipped back, giving him better access, needing that to be the biggest fucking hickey any woman had ever worn. Maybe, every time he saw it, he'd remember. Be reminded of what we had together—this insane chemistry that hadn't died with the years that separated us, that couldn't even, I believed, be killed through neglect. Something this powerful just couldn't fade away.

Then he froze, and just when I thought I'd lost him, when I felt sure he was going to walk away, he rasped, "I need to shut the door."

Dazed, I blinked at him. "What? Why?"

"Conor—" He growled. "I don't want him to see you like this."

Touched, I slipped my fingers through his hair, dragging my nails along his scalp, feeling his shudder as he bit me there, like he couldn't stop himself from touching me that way.

Good.

"He's busy," I rasped.

I had to pray that he was, because sweet lord, I didn't give a damn if his brothers waded in so long as they fucked off immediately.

I needed him.

I needed him so bad.

I arched against him, grinding into him, encouraging him to forget. It seemed to work, because when I brushed my tits into his chest, his mouth slid down, down, down to my nipple. His teeth caught the tip, and he pulled on it with a ferocity that had me yelping.

Every move he made spoke of the violence in him, and I knew that at this moment, I was feeling the raw Aidan. The man who'd killed. Who'd committed violence.

In my name.

But all I could think was that Thomas' killer had gotten what he deserved.

That wasn't a PC thought, and I knew I should have found Aidan's confession abhorrent, should have been repulsed but maybe he was right.

Maybe I *was* gruesome.

Maybe violence didn't scare me.

I'd seen it when I was young, had seen my dad be violent during situations that were out of his control. I'd seen him beat a paparazzo, watched as he destroyed rooms if any of his kids were ever injured or harmed. I didn't fear fists. They could hurt, but I'd never had them used against me.

Just for me.

In my defense.

To keep me safe.

Shivering at the thought, I clutched at him as he bit my nipple, tugging on it to the point of pain before he leaned forward, pushing me down against the massage table.

When he bowed over me, his lips pressing along the length of me, slipping down my torso, I knew what he was going to do and nearly died as he found that crease that had so fascinated his fingers. He kissed it, brushing it with his lips and tongue before he delved between my legs.

A shaky gasp escaped me as I stared up at the gym ceiling.

When I woke up, I hadn't expected this. Couldn't have expected this. And yet... it felt like I'd been waiting for this moment all my life.

For him to kiss me like this, to touch me, to hold me, to take me, to claim me.

To make me his.

I whimpered when his tongue found my clit, and in contrast to the violence of before, he didn't bite, but he was ferocious with each gesture he made. He didn't just flick his tongue against the tiny nub, he devoured me. Eating me up in a way that made me think he'd spent a lifetime ravenous.

A scream escaped me when two fingers were thrust inside me, spearing me wide open as he scissored them apart, filling a space that had needed him for so fucking long. I hadn't been celibate, but by God, I might as well have been. With his hand, he'd done more for me than some dudes had with their entire frickin' bodies.

Back arching, head falling against the densely packed leather, it felt like my entire being was vibrating as he sucked down on my clit with a hunger that made me want to explode.

I felt him shifting around, moving, but I didn't care, didn't give a damn so long as he didn't stop touching me.

As he sucked on my clit in tangent with thrusting those deliciously thick fingers inside me, I growled as he raked up against the front wall of my pussy. A vibrator was the nearest anyone had ever gotten to my G-Spot, and I pretty much howled when he found it, then metaphorically clutched it and didn't let go.

"Ohmigod, Ohmigod, Ohmigod, Ohmigod, Ohmigod, Ohmigod," I howled, and my heels dug into his shoulders, which had me whimpering because I'd forgotten about my sore ankle, but the pain entwined with the pleasure because, holy fuck, what kind of magic was this?

Energy reverberated around my insides like someone had dropped an atomic bomb in my womb, and when I came it was as if the whole world collapsed around me. As if the floor sucked me in, pulled me out of this reality and into some other place where darkness was the go-to hideaway.

Except, this darkness had lots of glitter.

Lots of rainbows and unicorns and leprechauns.

Of course.

Leprechauns.

It took an Irishman.

Maybe there was even a pot of gold somewhere around here.

Or could be that was between my legs.

I squeezed him so hard with my thighs that I had to admit if he survived, it was another miracle, but he didn't complain, didn't struggle.

The Five Points didn't make a man a pussy, he just rode it out with me, through me, helping me realize what it was about Aidan that I'd always appreciated. That, even though I barely knew him, I'd recognized inside him.

He was a force to be reckoned with.

An earthquake inside a hurricane.

No matter what I threw at him, he'd never break. He'd never bend. He'd always take it.

And I needed that kind of fortitude.

I'd always needed that.

He wouldn't disintegrate into a million pieces if I got sassy, if I revealed that I didn't agree with him, nor would he be disgusted if I admitted that the things he did intrigued me. He'd stay the course, butting heads with me every fucking time. Not letting me get away with shit.

It was why I'd mourned him, I realized now.

I'd known what we could have together. How perfect we'd fit one another.

Before I could come down entirely, I felt him thrust into me. It was what had me opening my eyes to look down where we were now joined. I saw that had his attention too. Him so goddamn thick and long, and me just conceding defeat to all those delicious inches.

Sex had never felt like a surrender, but right now? It felt like the best kind of forfeit. I'd acquiesce to any-damn-thing he wanted if he just wouldn't stop.

"I'm not stopping. I'm not going anywhere," he growled, making me realize I'd pleaded with him out loud. "This is my pussy," he snarled, and didn't I just melt into the massage table beneath me? "No fucker else is going to fill it but me, do you hear me?"

My eyes narrowed, tunneling into slits, and though I was probably insane, I snapped, "Takes more than one orgasm to stake a claim on me."

He made a growling noise, like some kind of beast, and I moaned at the loss of his control. As much as I loved his stalwart nature, I wanted nothing more than for him to feel as out of control as me. Why should I be the only one lost to the maelstrom? Where was the fairness in that?

Aidan grabbed my legs, hauling them high against his chest, not stopping until they were flat against his torso. The move sent him even deeper inside me, until I felt like his dick was butting my gag reflex from upside down. Then, he parted them again, making me realize he was shifting around to accommodate his bum leg, and he moved even closer, popping between them so one of my feet was on either side of his head.

Was I surprised when one hand dropped down to my pussy, and his thumb went to my clit? Nope. Did I get why he rested the other hand on my shoulder? No. Did I howl again, in pain this time, when he clamped down on my calf and bit down? Yes.

I didn't try to pull away though. Just tried not to fall off the massage table.

I squirmed against him, needing to get closer, needing all of him to be inside me, and that was when he started to drive his hips into me.

"Oh, God," I cried out as he moved hard and fast, dragging me into him with the handhold he had on my shoulder.

He invaded every inch as he impaled me on his cock over and over again. Highly sensitized flesh quivered as he raked them over the coals, not stopping now he'd started.

He growled, tension overtaking the pair of us as he started to rub my clit in earnest, hard enough to make me squeal but not so much that I felt like he was trying to detach it from my body, and when I screamed out my orgasm minutes, hours, weeks later, he wasn't long behind me.

As he pumped his cum into me, endlessly, tirelessly, I swore to God I felt the heat of him as he filled me full, and I knew, no matter what, as I soared to that glittery dark place again with leprechauns and rainbows and frickin' unicorns, that I'd fight to get back here again.

I'd lock horns with this stubborn, stubborn man, because an orgasm like this was worth fighting for.

As was, of course, the man himself.

Whether he believed it or not.

SEVENTEEN

AIDAN

AS I LOOKED at myself in the mirror over the vanity, I knew I'd made a mistake.

But regrets were a part of the life, remorse and fear and guilt too. I wore them all like badges that had been sewn into my flesh. They were points of shame, parts I disliked, but what I hated the most was that I was drawing her deeper into this filthy world of mine.

A world I wouldn't wish on my worst enemy.

In my reflection, I could see her in the shower.

Soapy.

Slick.

Fuck.

For all that I knew I'd made a mistake, I'd keep on making it.

There had to be some advantages to being a bad man, surely?

As she bent over, soaping up her calves, a place I'd bitten, then her knees and thighs, sliding her palms inward where cum had leaked onto her, I reached up and rubbed a hand over my jaw.

My dick ached already, and it had only just left that tight snatch.

Hers was the only pussy I'd ever been in without a rubber, and while she was no virgin, I swore to Christ, hers was the tightest, the best. Snug and hot and fucking perfect.

Heaven.

It was probably the closest to heaven I'd ever get as well. Da insisted that if we confessed enough, we'd get through those pearly gates but I wasn't as naive. Getting between her thighs was as much of a paradise on earth as I wanted.

A place I'd been wanting to visit ever since I'd fucking met her.

As she slipped her fingers between her legs, I watched as she cleaned her pussy. I knew I should give her privacy, but I was inherently curious about Savannah Daniels. Plus, she was pretty. What kind of penis possessor would I be if I didn't get off on watching her touch herself?

When she shivered as she cleaned up, not just a slight quiver either, but a shudder as if she were still hypersensitive, it took every ounce of control I had not to storm into that shower stall and fuck her like that.

My bastard knee was the only reason I behaved. If I fell or slipped, I was screwed, and not in the way I intended when I was with her in the shower.

Mouth tightening, I carried on watching her, taking note of the sodden bandage I'd have to change before we went out, feeling rage fill me at the prospect of that fucker hurting her, making my muscles bunch up with remembered wrath, which was when she looked up, her smile telling me she knew I'd been staring at her.

"You're a brat," I grunted.

She smirked at me, then puckered her lips, raised her wet, soapy hand before them, and blew me a kiss.

I rolled my eyes and folded my arms across my chest, trying not to think about how my filthy hands that had been covered in blood and another man's flesh just hours earlier had touched her.

Darkness was contagious.

I didn't want it to seep into her.

It would, as well.

It tainted everything. Stained it soul-deep.

She twisted around, grabbed her ass cheeks then squeezed them as she peered over her shoulder at me.

"The last thing you should try to do is draw attention to your ass," I rumbled.

"Why's that?" she taunted.

"Because it'll be the next hole I'll fuck."

Her eyes twinkled. "Who says it isn't the next hole I want you to fuck?"

Jesus.

She was going to be the death of me.

I wanted to ask if she was a virgin there, even though I had no right. I wasn't a virgin. Why should she be? It wasn't like she was eighteen, either. Both of us were definitely adults, and I liked that she knew her pleasure. I just couldn't help wanting to own a piece of her. A part that was solely mine.

Why was I this fucked up over her? With the only consolation being that she was as in over her head as I was?

It had been like that from the start, I knew. It was why I'd gotten to my feet that night when we'd dined together and I hadn't looked back.

I'd just gone.

I'd walked out of her life.

I'd known that one taste was enough to make me crave her for the rest of mine.

She was worse than heroin.

Better than Oxy.

Somehow, even before I'd had her, I'd known that.

Grunting at myself, I started stripping the second she turned off the water. Only then did I head over to the stall and enter it.

She pouted at me. "Why didn't you come in earlier? I mean, I'd even waste water for you."

Her gaze slid over me, and I felt it like a caress. Like a physical touch that I wanted on me for the rest of my fucking life. Then, of course, I saw her take in the damage to my knee.

She sucked in a sharp breath as she studied the long line that was marked with stitches down the center of it, as much as if a centipede was etched into the flesh, as well as the various other tissue that made a roadmap look neat and tidy from the bullets and the various scars they'd created.

"That's why," I said flatly. "As much as I want to fuck you in here, if I fall and fuck it up much more—"

As my words waned, she blanched. I braced myself for it, for the second that pity would slide into her gaze, but it didn't come.

I should have known she wouldn't respond like a regular person.

Instead, another smile danced on her lips, beaming into existence and filling up an empty space in my soul as she declared, "That's why benches exist."

"You're right," I rumbled, carefully stepping nearer to her.

Hauling her into my arms, I grabbed her ass, squeezed those tight cheeks and dipped my head to press a kiss to her lips. The bottom one was still pink and red from where I'd bitten her, and the sight should have filled me with shame, but it just didn't.

I wanted those bite marks all over her. Stamps of ownership so that any fucker outside these walls, hell, within them too, would know she was—

My mind stuttered to a halt.

I had no right to think shit like that, but fuck if I didn't have a say in it. If my mind already knew what she was to me even if I couldn't admit it.

"Aidan?"

I blinked at her soft whisper, the softest I'd ever really heard her get. "Yes?"

"Did you make him suffer?" She licked her lips. "I mean, *really* suffer."

"I skinned him, Savannah. While he was still breathing." Shame over the many misdeeds I committed in the family's name was long gone, something I'd stopped atoning for years ago. "I think I can guarantee that he suffered."

A shaky breath escaped her. "I liked Thomas."

Jealousy whipped at my insides, then I recalled exactly who Thomas was—the friendly doorman who always sported a smile no matter the time or the weather. Collateral damage. It never got easier to swallow, especially when an innocent was involved.

"He paid for his sins." My smile was tight. "I promise you."

Her eyes were huge in her pale face, even her rosy red cheeks from the shower had died down. "Did you find out which Sparrow sent him?"

"I did."

She huffed. "Conor lied to me."

I tensed. "What?" When the hell had she spoken with Kid? Jealousy slithered its way through me again.

She'd been wearing a bathrobe when she found me in the gym. That meant Kid had seen her like that.

"He tried to make out that he was still looking into who sent the bastard after me," she groused.

"Well, I got the name of a corporation," I rumbled, my voice deep as I tried to process exactly why I was feeling this way just because Kid had spoken with her.

"What was it?"

"You don't need to worry about that. Conor's hunting them down."

She scowled up at me. "Are you really not going to tell me?"

"What? So you can get into more trouble?" I snapped, looming over her, well aware that she was standing on tiptoes to get into my face.

"I might not know them."

"And if you don't, I'm sure you'll figure out a way *to* know them."

She ground her teeth. "I deserve to know. I have a right to know, Aidan."

"You've got a right to stay safe. To keep your ass out of the firing line. Just because you don't give a shit if it gets scarred along the way doesn't mean that I don't." I pulled back, chest heaving as I jabbed a finger into it. I'd let down my guard when I'd been detoxing, I'd had no choice, but look what fucking happened when I stopped watching out for her? She was a trouble magnet. "I'm the one who's been cleaning up after you as you stride through life like you're a bull in a fucking china shop. Well, you almost got yourself killed last night, Savannah. I think your way isn't goddamn working, don't you?"

Not waiting for a bullshit answer, I moved around her, limping as I trudged toward the shower which I slammed on. The water scorched me but it felt good as I tipped my face back and let it course over me.

I'd showered at the warehouse, but after a workout and our fuck, I needed to clean up some more.

I knew when she left the stall, and not just because she growled under her breath either. It was like the energy was less charged in here. As if, by her presence alone, she made me tune into something I'd never noticed before. Something I couldn't even begin to describe.

If I were a fanciful man, I'd say it was the universe, but there was no room for fantasy in my life. No room whatsoever.

I washed up, brisk and to the point because I needed to get her downstairs so she could grab some clothes. The thought of Kid seeing her in a fucking bathrobe—one of his, not mine—riled me up even more, but after I switched off the shower, I heard her on the phone.

I started to tense up, but then I remembered she was here of her own volition. It wasn't like I was keeping her a prisoner—well, she didn't realize that yet. She wasn't going anywhere without my ass at her side. Whether she approved or not.

As I ducked into the first aid kit to retrieve some antiseptic cream, antibiotic cream, and a fresh bandage, I heard her snipe, "I still can't believe you did that. I swear you need to go see a therapist. You're getting crazier."

"I'm so not, bitch. He was cheating on me. Did you forget?"

Two things surprised me—one, that she had the call on speaker, and two, that I recognized the voice on the line.

I didn't have men on her constantly, but I would have thought they'd have reported on this friendship.

Apparently, someone on my crew needed their ass kicked.

"I didn't forget," Savannah said with a huff. "But you're definitely crazy. It's six AM and you're calling me like it's eleven."

"What else was I supposed to do?"

"Wait until the sun had risen?" Savannah responded dryly as she toweled her hair dry, the reason, I assumed, why she had the call on speaker with Jen of all people. I knew her because I spent a lot of time at Finn's place, and Jen did as well because she was best friends with Aoife.

How the hell did she know Savannah too?

Their personalities didn't gel at all. At least, I didn't think they would.

"Like he did? My lawyer said we should discuss things, have an informal meeting. See if I can work on him to lessen the suit."

"And you listened? Shouldn't you avoid him until the day of the court case?"

"Maybe. I don't know. I can't afford what he wants, and he's rich. Don't rich people always win in court?" She huffed. "You'd know. You're rich."

Savannah rolled her eyes. "You know I'm the one who got fired, don't you?"

"For thwacking that prick's prick," Jen retorted, but she was snickering. "There's a difference. I notice the studio didn't take you to court. Just tried to wipe it under the carpet. Fuckers. If I'd have done what you did, they'd have had my ass in front of the Supreme Court."

"Not sure you're that important, Jen," Savannah consoled with a laugh.

"Oh, you bet your ass I am."

"You're not apologetic enough to meet with Damian," Savannah pointed out a second later. "How the hell can you work on him to lessen the settlement if you're not sorry for what you did?"

Crap, I remembered now. During my detox, Finn had been whining about Jen because she'd keyed her boyfriend's Ferrari.

Evidently, the court case had yet to take place...

Because I didn't need this shit show in my life, I stepped over to the dresser where Savannah had placed her phone, and murmured, "Jen, if you have him come to The 68 bar in The Sharpe, I'll sit in and adjudicate."

Silence fell at my words, and Savannah scowled at me, then shoved me in the side. "What the hell?" she mouthed.

"Aidan?" Jen queried, her voice confused. "Is that you? What are you doing at Savannah's?" She paused. "Oh, my God. You're there at six AM. Are you two fucking?"

"You know each other?" Savannah questioned, brow puckered even more.

"You stay scowling, the wind'll change, and you'll be stuck like that forever." When she harrumphed, I shot her a wink. "Trust me. It's not bullshit. Why do you think Brennan looks the way he does?"

She snickered, which fuck me, had my heart leaping in my chest.

I'd think it was a heart attack, but men like me didn't die of cardiac arrest. We endured horrendously violent passings.

The only consolation was that the most brutal of those endings would occur at my father's hands, and I highly doubted he'd ever kill me that way.

At least, I hoped I'd never be the target of that insane wrath.

A man had to have goals, didn't he?

Eyes twinkling, she mumbled, "I guess I don't have to introduce my favorite people to one another."

"Favorite people? Girl, how much have you been holding out on me? Aidan's miserable ass is no one's favorite person."

"I can hear you, Jen," I told her wryly.

"Good. I want you to hear me. It's been a while since I saw you at Finn and Aoife's but your grouchy ass made Aoife cry."

"Aoife's always crying at the minute," I discounted, but I wriggled my shoulders with discomfort. "I just said the cookies were too sugary! Jesus, you'd think I was accusing her of homicide."

Jen hummed. "You have a point about her being teary-eyed."

"Who's Aoife?"

I arched a brow. "I thought she was Jen's best friend."

Jen huffed. "Don't you be throwing shade at me, Aidan O'Donnelly. A woman's allowed to have more than one best friend, and those best friends may never meet."

Savannah snorted. "I feel like you're about to admit to cheating on me, Jen. I'm not sure my heart can take it."

"Technically, Jen would be cheating on Aoife with you. Didn't you go to school together?" I directed the question at Jen.

"We did." Jen sniffed. "Ever since Aoife married into your lot, it's not like I can take her to parties anymore. Not without Finn showing up and threatening to slice people's hands off."

"A man's got to stake a claim and protect what he avows as his own."

Savannah arched a brow at me. "Are you trying to stop being my favorite person? 'Avows as his own?' Who talks like that?"

"Me." I smiled at her. "Seeing as this has to be a new thing, I figured I wouldn't stay your favorite for long anyway."

She smirked. "Aim low and you're never disappointed, huh?"

"Something like that." I laughed. "Anyway, Savannah has a point, Jen. Why the fuck are you calling at this hour anyway?"

"I'm freaking out, Aidan, and not just because you're laughing. Did Finn tell you about that bastard I was dating?"

"Surprisingly enough, honey, Finn and I have more important things to discuss than your sex life."

"It should be the top of everyone's agenda. I'm offended it isn't."

"I'm sure." I heaved a sigh. "I do know that you keyed the guy's Ferrari. That was mean, Jen. Mean."

"He was fucking around on me. That was a way more expensive mistake than my giving his car a little love tap."

"Maybe if he owned a Ford, not a Ferrari. Changing the bumper sticker on those things costs ten grand."

"You'd know, Daddy Warbucks." Jen grumbled, "Anyway, I can't afford the settlement, so I have to go to court, unless I can convince him not to."

"And giving him a blowjob didn't work?"

"Aidan!" Savannah chided.

Jen blew a raspberry, which, without the visual, just sounded like a massive fart. "I mean, I tried, but he said no blowjob was worth that much."

I laughed. "I can't blame him."

"I need help," Jen whined. "Please? Finn won't. He says I made my own bed and I need to lie in it, but I make my bed every day and Tinkerbell hasn't popped up to save my ass."

"Why should I save it?"

"Because you like me?" she wheedled.

"Since when?"

She huffed. "Aidan! I'll ask Aoife!"

"And that's a threat, why? If Aoife can't get Finn to do her bidding, then how the hell would she get me to do the same?"

"Aoife's a pushover around Finn. He blows her brain out with orgasms or something. Lucky bitch." She pshawed. "Whereas you have no orgasmic power over her. She'll stop making you those cronuts you love. I know she will. She doesn't want me to go bankrupt as much as I don't want to go bankrupt because she'll have to feed me until kingdom come—"

"Christ, Jen," I complained. "I already told you to bring him to The 68. I said I'll adjudicate, didn't you hear me?"

"Oh. No, I didn't. I was more confused about what the hell you were doing on my best friend's phone.

"Although, adjudication might not be enough. I think he came out lucky with a scratched boy toy instead of me literally scratching that toy dangling between his legs.

"Savannah, I told you he had a micropenis, didn't I?"

"I don't think five inches constitutes a micropenis," was Savannah's amused retort.

"Well, it does in my book." She huffed. "Okay, I'll tell the prick to come to The 68. You may have to hold me back, Aidan."

"I expect nothing less from you, Jen," I commented.

"Don't worry, I'll be there too," Savannah chirped, earning herself a glower from me. She shrugged. "What? You think I want to miss out on that show? It's going to be better than Jerry Springer."

I rolled my eyes, but accepted that she was right, that it would probably be hilarious. It also meant I'd have to stack on security in the bar, but that was fine. Some fucker would probably appreciate the overtime.

"This is my life, y'all," Jen complained. "Not a daytime talk show."

"You're living your best life," Savannah retorted unapologetically. "That comes with consequences."

Jen blew another raspberry. "Okay, I'll see you guys tonight." She paused. "Thanks, Aidan." Those two words came out in a rush like she was swearing, then she hung up the phone.

I shook my head, then turned to Savannah and murmured, "You need to get on the bed—"

"Promises, promises—"

"—so I can put a fresh bandage on your thigh."

She crinkled her nose. "I'd prefer the orgasm from your not-so-micro penis."

My lips quirked. "Good to know I measure up."

"Like you have any worries in that department," she scoffed, her gaze dropping to my package which was shielded by white terry cloth.

When she licked her lips, the damn thing twitched, but I groused, "Savannah, behave. I need to change your bandage before we head down to your place for your things."

She pouted, but did as I asked, trudging over to the bed and lying down on the mattress with an artlessness that I actually appreciated.

She didn't drape herself over the covers, didn't tilt her head to the side and prop it on a tensed arm while sucking in her belly so that the space between her abdomen and ribs turned concave. She just lay there, waiting for me to do as I said.

Models and mistresses, they were all the same. Of course, Savannah was neither. That was probably why she was an alien concept to me.

A woman who wanted me for me.

Despite what I was.

In spite of what I did.

If anything, *because of* what I did.

It was almost disturbing.

But I liked it too much to really complain.

With a grunt, I ambled over and settled myself on the bed at her side.

She watched me as much as I watched her, taking in each step like a cougar sizing up a kill, and fuck me if that didn't get me harder than it should.

I tried to keep it clean, tried to be methodical with it, but she didn't make it easy on me. Every time I touched her, her skin pebbled with goosebumps and she shivered. Not an artificial one, but a genuine little quiver, as if my touch were as powerful as an electric shock.

Whenever she responded like that, it made me glance at her, and when our gazes collided, it was like the fucking world stopped.

By the time I was done cleaning the wound and bandaging it, she was trembling like a goddamn leaf and I was as hard as nails.

I blew out a breath as I rasped, "I'm not alone in feeling this way, am I?"

I could see that I wasn't, but I needed verbal confirmation that this was weird as hell.

Slowly, she licked her lips, and I swore to God I could feel the tip of that little muscle around the glans of my cock.

"No, you're not. You know that though. You know it's been like this since that first day," she whispered. "Even when I was scared of you, you drew me to you like you were a magnet. I thought it was me fangirling but that was why it hurt so much when you disappeared."

"I didn't disappear," I corrected. "I saved you from me."

She sat up, pressed her hand to my thigh. "You'd never hurt me."

"There are different kinds of hurts in this life, Savannah. You know that as well as I do."

Her brow furrowed, but then, slowly, as if it were a storm cloud marring a crystal clear day, it abated. "I've been in danger all my life, Aidan. Relatively speaking. My dad saw to that just by being who he is. You think that's the first intruder I've had to deal with? My sister was kidnapped, for God's sake. Camden routinely deals with insane stalkers." She pursed her lips. "Nothing in this life is safe. You should know that by now."

"My world is a lot more dangerous. Kidnappers don't take you because they're obsessed with your father and want whichever piece of him they can get.

"They take you because they want your spilled blood to mean something. Vengeance, a warning, a threat."

"You can't save me from myself, Aidan," she rasped. "And I told you yesterday, I'm done with you blowing hot and cold. You take me or you don't, but you make a decision fast or I'll find some other motherfucker to claim me and make me his."

A snarl was torn from me, the visceral reaction to her words firing me up much as it did earlier.

"You need to stop making that threat."

To my growl, she purred, "Why? When you react so beautifully."

Even though I knew if I didn't nip this in the bud, stop it from becoming a common occurrence between us where she thought she could have me by the balls just because she threatened me with another man taking ownership of her, I couldn't stop myself from looming over her.

The second I did, of course, pain howled through me. I'd been suffering all day and all night, but it was only now that I felt it like a blunt knife tearing through tendons and shredding muscles in its path.

I knew she saw because her expression twisted, morphing with concern as I turned around, flopping back against the mattress as the agony of my knee colliding with the bed ricocheted inside me.

As I struggled to get the pain under control, to stop that feeling of drowning, she was there, her hand on my chest, tucked against my side like she was experiencing it too. I thanked God she wasn't, but sweet fuck, it felt good to have her there. To take my mind off what I was going through.

"Is it always this bad?" she asked after a while, once my breathing had calmed down.

"You mean after I kick the bed with my fucked up knee?" My voice was so deep and so hoarse it sounded like it was being scraped over rough gravel.

"Yeah," she said softly, but there was a small bump in the middle, making it two syllables as she laughed at my phrasing.

It amazed me that I didn't mind.

The heat of her hand against my stomach was fierce, much like the woman herself.

"It's always bad," I admitted gruffly, then, I admitted what I never had to my brothers. Not even Conor when I'd showed up at his door and puked all over him. "I-It got me hooked on Oxy, Savannah."

She stiffened, then whispered, "Oh, Aidan, I'm so sorry. I thought you looked thinner. I thought it was from the pain.

"No one knows what really happened, trust me I researched as much as I could after the shooting, but everyone knows you've been limping ever since. Have you only just detoxed?"

There was no accusation in her voice, no pity either, just sympathy. It swaddled me, comforted me, let me relax and eased up the tension inside me which, miracle of miracles, diminished the pain a little.

"I'm forty-one days clean."

"Oh, dear, you're not supposed to have sex—"

I snorted. "In what world?"

"When you get clean. The NA program says you shouldn't do it. You can switch addictions."

Arching a brow at her, I asked, "Who was hooked? Your dad or brother?" There was no way she knew that unless someone in her family had been through the program, and as they were rockstar royalty, it wasn't that much of a leap. Not unless she'd researched it for an article, of course.

Her nose crinkled. "Dad. Erm, Gerry was hooked on coke for a while after his wife was murdered, and Camden had a little problem with weed before gigs. Then, Aspen got hooked on speed for dieting." She huffed out a laugh. "Drugs are a part of the lifestyle."

"So you're a pro, huh?"

"By proxy," she teased. "I don't know as much as my mom, but I know enough to know there's no sex for, like, a year. She told me she had to buy sex toys to get through it."

My brows rose. "You talk about that with your mother?"

Savannah laughed. "Just wait until you meet her." Jesus, she sounded so assured, so confident that would happen. It made me tighten my arm around her as she explained, "Mom's a sex therapist."

"She is?"

"Yep. She practices under her maiden name though or she'd never have any patients" Her giggle set my world alight. "We're very okay with sex in my family. You have to be when you're on the road.

"Before I was eight, I saw so many groupies giving the band and the roadies BJs just to get backstage that I could have given a class on how to do it the right way."

I tensed. "As much as my dick looks forward to that lesson, that's all kinds of wrong."

"It's the life. I hated it. Camden isn't the only one with a voice, but I avoided that like the plague. I couldn't cope with it as an adult as well."

"You can sing?" I cocked a brow at her. "Really?"

"Really." She shot me a smug look. "I'm a mezzo soprano."

The choir boy in me was very impressed. "You'll have to sing for me some time."

She snorted. "What? When I could be sucking you off?"

I laughed, amazed that I had it in me to do so after that blast of excruciating agony that would normally have me reaching for three Oxy, never mind one.

"You have a point."

"I'm smart, you know?" She winked at me.

My laughter died down into a grin but I admitted, "I attended some NA meetings before I decided to get clean, then I realized it wasn't feasible. I knew my brothers had their crew on me, saw them a few times, and I knew that if I carried on, it might attract attention from other people.

"I'm amazed it didn't hit any social media, to be honest." I shrugged as I tipped my head back to stare up at the ceiling. "The safest way, not just for me but the people at the NA meetings, is to do it myself."

"You went cold turkey without going to rehab?"

"Don't sound so awestruck," I said wryly. "It wasn't impressive."

"I know how hard addictions are to fight. I'm proud that you made it this far." Her hand patted my chest. "I'll do anything I can to help, and you'll need it, Aidan. Doing without NA meetings is going to be tough."

Savannah talked like she was sticking around for the long haul, but it seemed as insane as me thinking that last night's kill would be my final one.

Processing her words, I fell quiet and, to be honest, it was good to just lie there. Her at my side. It helped. I had to accept that.

"Were you really mad at me?"

"When you ghosted me?"

"I wouldn't call it that."

"I frickin' would. And bet your ass I was." She heaved a sigh. "God save me from a man who's trying to protect me from myself. As if I don't have a brain of my own to tell me that I'm making a massive mistake."

A chuckle gusted from my lips. "Thanks?"

"You're welcome. You'll be the biggest mistake of my life," she said softly. "That's what Mom always says about Dad. I never understood it until you."

I swallowed. "How long have they been together now?"

"Since she was eighteen."

"Jesus."

"Yep. You feel it too, Aidan, I know you do. That's why you're so flighty."

"I'm not flighty," I argued. Jesus, she made me sound like a pussy.

"You so are. At least I know what I want. You do too, but you're just afraid to fight for it."

I scowled at her. "Did anyone ever tell you you're a know-it-all?"

She smirked. "Yep."

"Figured as much."

EIGHTEEN

SAVANNAH

HAVING Aidan in my personal space felt right.

Not oddly so, just right.

How could it not be?

I hadn't lied to Jen when I'd said he was one of my favorite people.

The psychologists called it a parasocial relationship, and though it was a fairly new phenomenon, I'd rubbed up against it throughout my entire life because of my dad.

Much as Conor stanned on my pop, I stanned on Aidan.

Conor wanted to see my dad perform a song, I wanted to see Aidan jack off in the shower.

As long as he didn't find anything wrong with that, I didn't either.

I just had to get Aidan to agree to it.

I wasn't fussed about which exact shower, it just had to involve him being wet and soapy and I'd probably feel like I'd died and gone to heaven.

Thoughts of which stopped me from feeling like I was going nuts.

My apartment had been breached. It was no longer safe, no longer a protected area.

I wasn't sure if it'd ever feel right again, and though the Points had tried to clear it up—the living room was back to normal. No blood stains, no broken glass. The only proof of what had happened was the missing coffee table—the place was tainted with my fear.

It might as well have soaked into the walls, seeping into the air itself so that every breath I took, reminded me of last night's attack.

Of how close it had been.

Throat thick with stupid emotions that I really didn't have time to process right now, it was far easier to imagine Aidan jacking off in a shower.

So I kept that at the forefront of my mind as I tossed things into a couple of suitcases; clothes, tchotchkes, my kindle, then started sorting through the various pieces of equipment I thought were necessary for the upcoming days, potentially weeks, when I wouldn't have access to my apartment.

The prospect of being glued to Aidan's side made that less of an ordeal.

Something he picked up on.

"I'm surprised you're not arguing with me."

"I might have felt a little more constrained if we hadn't had sex," I informed him as I tucked my laptop inside the special pocket within my carry-on luggage.

"You'll have to explain that logic," he murmured, poking at one of my zen gardens that I had on a table by the window in my office.

"Now I've got you hooked on my pussy, we'll have to do it again. And again. And again. Why would I complain?"

He shook his head. "I always knew you were trouble."

"You still saved my ass though, didn't you?" I prodded, pausing my packing to shoot him a look.

"You had answers I wanted to hear." He picked up the little rake and began smoothing through the pebbles in the zen garden to form his own patterns. I didn't mind him destroying mine. Only because it was him, though.

"Didn't your dad ever ask if you'd done as he requested?"

"Da doesn't ask. He just expects. That creates many a loophole that can be exploited." He cast me a look. "Do you want to know what it was that made me come to the coffee shop that day?"

"There was something in particular? Not just a photo of my beautiful self that had you drooling?"

"Well, that too," he joked, his eyes crinkling at the corners a second before, in a flash, he turned somber as he intoned, and I knew he was quoting something, "There's a sweet kind of abyss in the unknown. In diving headfirst into whatever the universe sends one's way.

"Whether we confront that unknown or evade it, it remains there, a silent test, one that we ultimately must pass or fail. Whether it be at that moment or in thirty years' time, the test will never fade for we are that test. We are the sum of many tests that we sit through without even knowing. They forge us in fire, strengthening us like we were steel, and that is why we must embrace change.

"Today is the first change as we pass from adolescence into adulthood, and as we sit here today, or in my case, stand, we face the unknown of the future and rather than fear it, we're excited for it. Today, we're passing our first test as an adult."

"Jesus," I rasped, the words resonating with me in a way that made it click in my memory. "Is that my valedictorian speech from high school?"

He hummed, the sound oddly soothing when combined with the gentle raking of the small pebbles in the zen garden.

"How did you remember all that?"

"I like to think it's fate."

I blinked. "What do you mean?"

"I mistyped your name." He cast me a look. "Savanna Dariel," he spelled aloud. "It threw up a thread from a student forum from 2004. On it, they were discussing your speech."

"Really?" It stunned me to realize my cheeks were burning.

"Yes. Really. I read it and I don't know why but it resonated." He sucked in a breath. "Okay, that's bullshit. I know exactly why. It's just that I realized how right you were.

"At eighteen, you were more self-aware than I was in my late thirties." He shrugged. "I had to see the woman who wrote that speech. I had to know if she'd passed more tests or if she'd failed them."

"I'm not sure if I like that or not," I murmured with a scowl.

He cast me another look as he snickered. "You can't control everything. Including why I decided to hunt you down rather than have you killed. Maybe you should just be grateful, hmm?"

My nose crinkled. "When you put it like that—"

His brow quirked. "Bet your damn ass I am. That's what it boiled down to."

"My valedictorian speech saved me? Christ, it was more apt than I could have imagined. Talk about passing tests... sheesh."

He nodded his assent and carried on dragging the rake through the gravel as he said, "Then, of course, I met you. I was glad I decided not to silence you."

"Gee, thanks," I drawled. "You don't believe in compliments for the sake of compliments, do you?"

"You're probably the only person I don't have to lie to, Savannah. That's more of a compliment than you probably know."

Shit, he wasn't wrong.

I perked up. "Does that mean you'll never lie to me?"

"It means I'll tell you the truth when I can."

"I can accept that," I responded immediately.

"Good seeing as that's the only option on the table. There's shit you don't want to know."

"You say that like I'm not an aficionado."

"Reading it in books, seeing it on TV, it's not the same as knowing about it." He placed the rake down with a care that told me he didn't want to fling it even though that was his current mood. "And it's not the same as fucking a guy who—" He sighed. "Never mind. I'll tell you what I think you need to know. That's a hard limit, Savannah. I want to make that clear here and now."

I narrowed my eyes at him. "I have hard limits too."

"I'll bet you do," he sniped back, rolling his eyes at me. "Let's hear it. What are they?"

"No bullshit. Keeping things from me for my own good is one thing. Bullshitting me is another. I managed to wade into the world you tried so hard to keep me out of. I'm in it now, and I'm in danger. The truth is my vocation. Don't lie to me when the only reason I'm doing any of this is to break these bastards apart."

With his back to the window, he leaned against it and folded his arms across his chest. "You sure you didn't get involved just to rebuild your reputation?"

"At first, sure. Star got in touch with me and said she had a way to help me claw back some of my name.

"Right now, I'm *persona non grata* in most newsrooms, and I don't blame them. There are a lot of toxic workplaces out there, and someone who's willing to burn their reputation and their career isn't exactly going to gel well with a touchy-feely editor who's been there for thirty years. Who's also a key player in steering the paper through the evolution of newspapers to digital formats... He'd definitely be the priority.

"Then, Star explained to me what was going on, and I saw, first-hand, the women who'd been brutalized..." My voice waned but I sucked in a breath before I started up again, "Star's told a lot of lies over the years. She was a soldier, that much I knew to be true because she went to West Point.

"The rest, well, couched within the lies she told, most of us stopped listening to her, and when she cut herself off from us, I think we thought it was an extension of that." I swallowed, guilt choking me and making it hard to admit, "We had no way of knowing that she went quiet because she'd been kidnapped and sold into slavery."

Aidan stilled. "Star Sullivan was one of the women who was trafficked by the Sparrows?"

I found it just as hard to believe as he did. "Yeah."

"She's why you're doing this,' he rasped.

And unable to lie, unable to deny it, I nodded. "It's why, no matter how many times they try to come after me, that they try to shut me up, I'll carry on."

Aidan's nostrils flared as he stalked toward me. "Couldn't she have found a different fucking way to bring them down?"

"This is the tried and true method." I shot him a weak smile. "We let her down, Aidan. We let her down so bad. All of us. Gerry turned his back on her, she just didn't know it because she was too busy being a fucking sex slave."

Despite myself, despite how I viewed the world and respected how wicked it was, just as I knew and was cautious of the evil people were capable of perpetrating, I knew I'd never, ever forgive myself for letting Star down so badly.

I didn't even know I was crying until his arms came around me, until he propped me up and I felt the wet fabric of his shirt clinging to my cheek as I wept in his embrace.

I wasn't a cryer. I didn't do tears. There was little to no point in shedding emotion that way. But everyone had a breaking point, an Achilles' heel that proved just how vulnerable they were even though they'd reported some of the many cruelties that proved to me society was devolving.

Family was my breaking point.

And *noxxious*, for all its sins, for all that it was the most toxic thing in my life, everyone in it, the group, the band members, the roadies who'd been with them since the beginning, they were all family.

None more so than Star.

Gerry's goddamn daughter.

The man whose legacy my dad, one of the most integral cogs of the band, said was impossible to replace. Impossible to emulate. Impossible to forget.

So I cried. Because we'd let her down. The one foundation we all had, the one unchanging fact, had abandoned her, but just as I promised myself as we'd FaceTimed that day when I'd met her as well as some of the other Sinners' MC Old Ladies, Star would never be alone ever again.

NINETEEN

AIDAN

SAVANNAH WASN'T the kind of woman who cried, so when she actually did, it took me by complete surprise. I had no alternative other than to hold her. To give her what I'd never been given—a shield of safety, a haven of comfort. The need to take her pain away was acute, but the need to hold her was even more powerful.

I had no idea how long we stood there like that, but I knew, and maybe she did too, that we reached a turning point.

She cried in front of me.

That was as much of a weakness as a creature like her was capable of.

Her walls had never been lower, and truth be told, I didn't want them coming back up.

I loved her strength, loved that she was capable of going head to head with me, but this was more of a gift than she could know.

People weren't weak around me.

They couldn't afford to be.

I was Aidan O'Donnelly Sr.'s heir.

I was the future king of the Five Points.

Weakness around me was tantamount to asking for a target to be placed on your back.

Yet Savannah, in spite of knowing all this, hell maybe because of this, lowered her walls and handed me the key to the door that was her. Presenting me with something more precious than she could begin to imagine.

"I'll help you make it up to Star," I told her, rubbing my lips along the still-damp hairline at her temple. Rage fluttered through me when I brushed against the Band-Aid I'd put there last night.

She gulped. "You will?"

Once upon a time, my word had been a promise. Pain and drugs had skewed that. Made me unreliable. Had taken away the power of the words that spilled from my lips. But she made me want to change that. If, for no other reason, than to help her claw back what she thought was broken between her and Star.

"I will," I promised, gently squeezing her. Curiosity had me asking, "You said you saw it firsthand. How?"

"I wasn't talking to her and she finally got me to bite with news of the NWS. She knows I live for that shit. Anyway, I wasn't sure whether to believe her or not, and I wasn't about to risk the last of my rep on some of her BS, so she arranged for me to have a video call with some of the victims the Sparrows trafficked.

"I met them and I believed *them*." She rubbed her forehead against my chest. "We let her down so badly, Aidan." Guilt rippled throughout the admission. "Until that video call, I didn't believe her. Not until she showed me proof. What kind of a friend am I?"

"We always hurt the ones we love the most," I murmured, trying to soothe her but knowing nothing would other than her being proactive in this and bridging the chasm that had been allowed to develop between her and her childhood friend. "You have time to resolve things between you."

A shuddery breath escaped her, and I felt the heat of it against my chest as the warmth seeped into the fabric of my silk shirt.

That heat resonated on so many levels.

I'd been cold for years. Internally frozen in survival mode. Had she just started a thaw?

What was it about her that made me feel human again?

How did she do that?

How did she make it feel so right?

I'd never believed in chemistry other than the sexual kind. I saw a woman, wanted to fuck her, we fucked, that was it. Orgasms usually cleared up most cases of it, but not only had this chemistry not abated after we had sex, I'd actively avoided getting involved with her for years.

She'd triggered a level of selflessness in me that I didn't even realize I was capable of. Maybe I wasn't ordinarily, and maybe I was always bound to be different around her.

When she sniffled a few more times, then squeezed my waist in quiet thanks, in silence, we drifted apart and finished up in her apartment.

I carried most of her things, only letting her drag the cabin bag she'd used to store her IT equipment. Conor broke the security seal on the maintenance elevator so I didn't have to walk up the stairs to the helipad, which I was fucking grateful for after kneeing the bed the way I had, and we were spat out into what could be considered a mud room that had a locked door.

Conor was standing there, his gaze on us both as he held out a phone for Savannah.

She frowned at it. "Who is it?"

"Star." He waggled the phone. "Take it. It's yours. I cleaned it up so that no one can hack it. There's a secure messaging app on there, and I imported your contacts—"

"How the fuck did you do that?" she growled, her hands snapping to her hips as she stared down my brother.

I snorted. "Stick around. He's capable of worse."

And he was, but Kid definitely wasn't on his A-game.

It had been building for a while. I couldn't blame him.

He was the keeper of our secrets, our first defense against attack, and the one we most relied on to protect the Firm.

There were only so many plates a person could keep spinning before they started to fall. Conor, right now, was definitely standing amid some ceramic shrapnel. I knew how that felt, and wished there was something I could do, but the family as a whole was facing this tsunami.

The difference was, Conor and I were doing it alone. Eoghan had Inessa, Declan had Aela, Finn had Aoife, and Brennan had Camille now.

I cast a look at Savannah.

Could I have her?

She'd implied I could, but last night was just a taste of what this world was like. An amuse bouche before the appetizer. I wasn't sure, as street smart as she thought she was, she could ever be prepared for the entree.

Unapologetic to the last, Conor grinned at her. "Just consider it a convenience. At least you won't have to transfer all your data over onto the new device. I did all the hard work for you."

"Exactly what you'd get at an Apple store," I mocked, gently squeezing her shoulder. "Genius Lab 2.0. This is better, Savannah. Only fuck knows what's on your old phone."

She huffed. "No way they'd be able to hack it."

Conor's brow puckered. "I thought you were smart."

"Kid!" I barked, the warning clear.

He shrugged. "What? It's true! Everything can be hacked. Fuck, *everything*. Whether it's physically bypassed or code manipulation. Pacemakers, TVs, baby cams. It's all a playground for hackers." He rolled his eyes. "You think someone couldn't get into your phone? How trusting are you?"

Because his disapproval sounded genuine, I wasn't surprised when Savannah blushed, but he'd embarrassed her enough into snatching the phone and grimly muttering, "Thank you."

"You're welcome," Conor replied as she stalked off down the hall.

Seeing she was heading for the room I'd tucked her in last night, I accepted that she needed space.

Unfortunately for her, she wasn't about to get much of that.

"You could have done that nicer, Kid," I grumbled.

He scoffed. "I cloned her phone last night. She's got more shit on it than a fucking terrorist being hunted by the FBI. They were tracing her calls too. If she discussed anything sensitive, scheduled anything with Star on her old one, then you need to tell her to change her plans because they'll know about it, and will likely be there to gain access to her."

I thought about the meeting tonight with Jen, but merely queried, "Couldn't you have started with that?"

Conor grinned. "If she's going to be hanging around, I figure she needed to get used to the way we work."

"The way *you* work," I corrected dryly.

"Same difference."

"No, it isn't," I retorted, unable to stop myself from chuckling because he was such a fucking pain in the ass.

Conor frowned at me. "Did you just laugh? Jesus, is that all it took? An orgasm?"

I blinked. "What?"

He wafted a hand. "I heard you two fucking like two goddamn screeching cats earlier. Do you mean you haven't had sex since the drive-by shooting?"

"If you hear us fucking again, turn your goddamn music up. Don't listen in, perv," I snapped, irritation buzzing in my ears like turbocharged white noise.

"I wasn't listening in," he argued. "I heard you over *noxxious*, Aidan. Christ."

"Well, turn the volume up more," I snarled. Even her sounds of pleasure belonged to me. No fucker else. Certainly not Kid.

"Okay, I'll just rupture my goddamn ear drums because you can't keep it down." He released a scoffing sound. "Although... if she keeps you smiling, I'll let her clean your pipes out regularly and will make my ears bleed for the cause."

I growled under my breath. "I made you a promise a long time ago, Conor, that I wouldn't beat the shit out of you ever again. No matter how annoying you were. Well, you've reached that point so I'd walk away if I were you."

He squinted at me. "You really are weird about her, huh? I was only joking about the penguin shit last night."

My mouth tightened. "You're not making this any better."

Conor shrugged but took a wary step back, as if he sensed I wasn't pissing around—Kid's brain finally decided to kick in. "You should probably get that seen to."

"What seen to?" I rumbled, my hands tightening about the handles of the bags I was carrying. They started creaking—thick leather straps began creaking as they bit into my flesh because of how hard I was clenching down on them.

"The fact you're possessive enough about her to be jealous of me, to be jealous that I heard her like that. Throw in the fact she can make you smile, maybe she's what you need to get over the Oxy."

I scowled at him. "That's so unhealthy."

He hitched his shoulder again. "Whatever gets you through the day, Aidan. Our world ain't like another person's, is it?

"If it were, you'd be tucked away in some fancy rehab facility, drinking virgin piña coladas at the side of an indoor pool while you talked about your feelings and how your daddy fucked you up when you were little.

"Instead, we're dick deep in a war with a secret society and you had to detox in my living room in a blanket fort. Take the wins as they come," he intoned, arching a brow at me as I scowled at him even harder than before.

Not that he let me have the last word. Fucker never did.

He sauntered off, retreating to his office, leaving me in the hall with all of Savannah's stuff.

Technically, I had two choices.

Take her things to the room I'd given her last night, or to mine.

But I'd already made the decision when she was weeping in my arms—my room it was.

TWENTY

STAR

I DIDN'T LIKE FEELING guilty.

In fact, I really fucking hated it, but aCooooig, *Conor*, brought it out in me.

The ability to feel.

Katina, my foster daughter, had started to wear down my walls, so I couldn't solely blame Conor—although I'd deny that in a court of law—but there was an urge inside me that was growing.

I dealt with urges all the time.

Kill that bastard—*go for it. He beat his woman.*

Throat punch that barfly—*why not? He was stalking one of the servers.*

Most of the time, I acted on those impulses. It was why, instead of counting my losses once I freed myself from the Sparrows' clutches, I dove back into the fray, determined to bring them down or to die trying.

However things had swiftly grown complicated.

Along the path of learning how the Sparrows worked, I'd found women dotted around the States who'd been bought and sold like they were T-shirts from Walmart. That was how I'd found Katina.

Then, still on the hunt, I'd sniffed around the Five Points as I tried to determine whether they were the Sparrows' illegitimate front.

Because I'd breached Conor's security that first time, I'd brought them down on me. The Irish Mob had me in their crosshairs, so I'd escaped to the haven of a serving buddy/old boyfriend—the Satan's Sinners' MC compound in West Orange, New Jersey, dragging Katina along with me—CPS be damned.

Since then, more shit had gone wrong. I'd started to care about the MC. Started to *feel* like they were family which meant I'd killed, dug my way deeper into shit, and had sorted through their personal laundry as if it were my own.

Throughout it all, Conor had been there.

Once he'd forgiven me for breaching his security, we'd started a playful relationship. I hacked into his systems, he hacked into mine.

It was fun.

Fun.

Something I didn't allow myself to have, not when there was a secret society of asswipes out there to take down.

But he invited that side of me to come out to party, and we'd grown close.

Closer than close.

Which was where those urges came into play.

I wanted to meet him.

I wanted to... *touch* him.

Just hearing his voice on the other end of the line was starting to do weird things to me.

I'd never been an overly sexual person. Most of the time, I'd used sex to manipulate men into doing things for me, and because they were beautifully predictable, it worked like a charm. Having been raised on the road with my rockstar family, I knew how the world worked.

A groupie sucked off a roadie, then suddenly, they had access to the band if they gave good head. That groupie fucked the band, got passed around, and got to travel around the world for lying on her back.

Transactional.

What I was feeling for Conor wasn't transactional, and that was dangerous.

"Star? Are you listening to me?"

I blinked at the rumble in his voice.

I knew what he looked like.

One word: YUMMY.

And I never used that word.

Not even to describe Phish food or candy corn, both of which were life.

I even thought he might be hotter than Atomic Fireballs, which was pretty goddamn sacrilegious.

"I'm listening," I retorted. "I'm always listening."

He grunted. "Was that supposed to sound creepy?"

"Of course," I assured him. "What would be the point otherwise?"

Conor snickered, then asked, "Did you patch up that back door you hacked into my server?"

"I did." That was where another round of feelings came into play. Squirming on my seat which only made my broken leg and bruised hip ache all the more—long story short, I'd been blown up along with the Sinners' MC compound—I muttered, "Conor?"

"Yes?"

"Are you okay?"

He paused. "Huh?"

We'd never really done personal stuff. Not until recently. He knew I was Gerard Sullivan's daughter now, and I knew he'd been molested as a kid. That changed things.

"Are you okay?" I repeated.

"Why are you asking?"

I huffed. "No need to sound so damn suspicious. It's just a question."

"Why are you asking though?"

I squirmed some more, wondering why this was hard when, ordinarily, I'd have taken great pleasure in bruising a guy's ego. "When Savannah called me and asked me to hack into your security so she could gain access to your helipad, I noticed something."

"What?" Conor asked warily.

"Your code's weak. I think someone's been trying to get in, but they're not good enough. They're trying to circumvent it, but I don't think you've noticed."

I heard his hesitation, then he rumbled, "Thank you for telling me. I know that must have been hard for you."

It was when he said shit like that, that I wanted to melt in a puddle of Phish food. Seriously. Hackers were arrogant, cocky SOBs with massive egos and small dick syndrome.

They didn't thank you for looping them into a weakness in their system.

But Conor did.

Conor did and it made me feel weird inside. All warm and shit.

It wasn't comfortable.

He couldn't have a small dick, could he? That just wouldn't be fair.

Maybe if I prayed that he did, I'd stop feeling all these weird things about him.

Because thinking about his cock wasn't helpful, I cleared my throat. "I mean, I was toying with keeping it as a fail safe. What if I ever needed to get to you in an emergency, you know? But these attacks have been going on for too long. Your security's been strong enough so far, but I noticed a pattern. They're trying to get to you specifically."

"I'll work on shoring up the defenses."

I almost choked on the words. "I'll help you."

He almost choked on the words. "I'd appreciate that."

We both gusted out a big breath at the same time.

Silence fell, then he muttered, "I finished up with Savannah's phone. I can't believe you let her keep her old model."

He didn't sound triumphant, more disapproving, and I squirmed again. That shouldn't be hot. It really shouldn't be hot.

"I dropped the ball," I admitted to him when I'd admit that to no one else. This was the second time I'd done so, each instance had been about Savannah and her security.

She was family, and I'd sent her out into this shit show with a target on her back.

I really hoped these mistakes with her safety weren't a Freudian slip. My brain, which functioned at a high level, purposely choosing to let her down like the *noxxious* family had let me down...

I really hoped I wasn't that much of a bitch.

"We've both been dropping a lot of those, haven't we?"

"That's what happens when you've got to keep juggling so many things at the same time." I shrugged. "It's a fact of life, but these situations... they're life and death.

"We're both tired, we've both been barely sleeping, and we're working constantly. We're at the end of the marathon, but that doesn't mean someone couldn't still beat us to the finish line."

I heard his breathing on the other end, so I knew he hadn't hung up, but he was quiet for a long while before he murmured, "Do you trust me, Star?"

I paused at that. "I trust you as much as I'm capable of," I explained slowly.

Which was not only true, but concerning.

"I trust you as much as I'm capable of too," he replied. "We've teamed up against the Sparrows but we're both acting as individuals, aren't we? Instead, I think we need to act as a collective."

"I'm listening."

"I think we need to have each other's backs more. We both have other things we need to concentrate on. For me, Acuig and Five Points, for you, well, I'm not sure but I'm certain it's terrifying—" I grinned at that. *He knew me too well.* "—but with the Sparrows, we can join forces more. When you're working on it, I can sleep. When I'm working on it, you can rest."

Slumber was such a simple concept for most people. I wished it were that easy for me.

Maybe, if we slept more though, we'd both be able to react faster, hit back harder, and be more responsive in general to the constant flow of information that was streaming our way.

Even if I'd seen proof that his defenses were lowered, he was the only person I'd trust my vendetta with. He was also the only person who'd ever understand how hard it was for me to rasp, "I think that's a good idea."

"Right. We'll figure the next steps out but I need to give Savannah her new phone. She just came back."

I blinked. "I need to speak with her. Put her on the line?"

He hummed. "Two secs."

The call disconnected, then a number flashed up on my screen that was different than Savannah's usual one even though it still used Savannah's name on the Caller ID, and I answered.

Before I could say anything though, I listened in to Savannah's outrage at having her phone cloned and rolled my eyes.

Seriously.

People.

Fully on board with Conor's scorn, when she snatched the phone away, I was mostly disappointed at how Conor's voice faded as she stalked off.

Had I really reached the point that most left behind in adolescence?

Creaming over a guy's voice?

Fuck.

"What?"

Her snapped retort had me scowling at my screen. "Hey, don't take it out on me that your phone had more bugs than a termite hill."

She released a sharp breath, one that I knew was one of those healing breaths. I'd heard her mom spout that shit sooo many times over the years as she tried to get me to stop internalizing my anger.

That was back when my anger had just been over regular life stuff.

Like my mom being murdered...

Not, ya know, at being kept as a sex slave with the US government's approval.

"Sorry," she muttered. "He just really pissed me off."

See, I knew I liked him.

Grinning at the thought, I murmured, "He's definitely not everyone's cup of tea."

"I hate being talked down to. You know that."

I blinked. "He wasn't."

"He was. Men." She growled. "Always treating us like we're idiots because we have a pussy."

"Conor totally isn't like that. If anything, he thinks you're a dick for not recognizing how easily penetrable phones are." Surprise still welled inside me though at how angry she sounded. "Honestly, Conor's different. He isn't a jackass."

She harrumphed. "What's wrong, anyway? Why are you calling?"

For the second time in as many minutes, I blinked. "You being serious? Did you forget you were almost murdered less than thirty-six hours ago?"

"Shit," she muttered under her breath. "Sorry, it's been an eventful week."

"Conor said you were out cold for a while."

"I was. Eighteen frickin' hours. I fell down the goddamn stairs." She huffed out an impatient breath. "Stupid. I hit my chin."

"You must have seen stars."

"I did. Ibuprofen's a miracle worker so a lot of my discomfort's gone, but I've got a wonky wrist, a nasty slash on my thigh, and I'm a bit shaken up. Compared to what I could be, I think I'm lucky."

"Glad to hear it." I sucked in a breath. "This isn't easy for me, Savannah, but I want to say I'm sorry."

"What for?" she replied, her tone confused. Then, it darkened. "What the hell did you do now?"

I grinned at nothing before I murmured innocently, "Nothing."

"Jesus, Star. Tell me before I blow a gasket."

"You're already inches away from doing that without my help. Don't let me stop you."

She growled. "I swear, you're such a pain in my ass."

I was. And she was in mine.

Jeez, I'd missed her.

Smirking at my screen, I murmured, "I'm just pulling your leg. I actually meant that I'm sorry for not taking into account how you'd be the public face of all this. I never... I just figured outing them this way would protect you. I was myopic, and it almost got you killed." My father would be so ashamed of me for not looking out for her more.

"Star, I'm a journalist. We put ourselves in danger all the time. It's what we do. The truth is perilous, but it's our duty to uphold it."

"You sound like Captain America."

"I'd make that outfit look so much better."

"Than Steve Rogers?" I snickered. "Yeah, if you say so."

Softly, she chuckled. "Honestly, Star, it's all good. I knew I was putting myself in harm's way; that was why I holed up in my apartment. I just didn't think they'd get into my building like that."

"No, it came as quite a shock all round." Conor wasn't the only one taken aback at how they'd gotten in. "Problem was, they went old school."

"Meaning?"

"Security footage shows the intruder pretending to be a delivery man. The doorman got up, let him in, got clocked on the head for his pains and stabbed." I heaved a sigh because it was always the innocent who suffered. "The bastard stole his key cards and his passes, then headed for your floor with them. Conor's men looked at the door, and all four locks were picked."

"So it was a low tech home invasion?"

"Pretty much."

"Ironic considering I had a termite temple for a phone."

"Right?" I scoffed. "How dare they?"

"This phone... is it really secure?"

"Yep. As secure as the Pentagon."

"I know they killed the guy."

"As they should have."

She heaved a sigh. "Do you have any information on them?"

"What kind of information?" I hedged.

"You're not going to tell me anything, are you?"

"Nope." I laughed when she growled. "There's no need for you to know. Leave it to the people who don't mind getting their hands bloody, Savannah. You just focus on the exposés. That's where you'll make the most difference.

"Speaking of which, I was thinking... their attack deserves a response."

"Yeah?" she asked warily.

"Yeah." My tone was firm. "Let's drop them faster than we were going to. Let's get their faces and names splashed everywhere. And, while you're at it, let's go nuclear."

"You want me to drop DeLaCroix's name? I thought we were saving that as the grand finale?"

"We were. But this just moved the goalposts. Let's drop his on the 25th." I smiled with delight at the chaos that was about to ensue over my least favorite holiday of the year. "Let's destroy Christmas, huh?"

"Grinch," she grumbled.

"You know why."

She fell quiet, and it was, I'd admit, nice to talk to someone who knew everything. All my past history, all my lies and truths, all my secrets. There was no hiding from Savannah, not when she'd been there at the time.

"I do know why," she said eventually. *Sorrowfully*. "What are you doing for the holidays?"

"Nothing. I'll be staying with the Sinners. What about you?"

"The fam's going to Hawaii. But I'm not."

"Why?"

"Camden pissed me off."

I whistled under my breath. "Isn't that what Camden does best?"

"Well, he can go fuck himself. He's all up in arms about me trapping Wintersen."

I snickered. "Probably channeling that time you whacked him in the balls too."

Savannah cackled. "Oh, shit, how did I forget that?"

"Guaranteed his balls have muscle memory or something." My laughter deepened. "I wish you'd seen his face when you smacked him instead of the piñata. I thought he was going to be speaking at a higher octave for sure. You probably helped his singing career."

She released an amused sigh. "Good times."

"Not for his penis. You're welcome around here if you want to. I don't know what they'll be doing for the holidays, but the offer's there."

"I'm not sure what's happening for Christmas to be honest."

"She'll be coming to dinner with me."

I arched a brow. "That Aidan Jr.?" I knew he was staying with Conor even though, and this was quite sweet, Conor had tried to hide that fact from me.

"It is."

"I'm on speaker?" I groused. "Savannah, you're supposed to warn someone when they're on speaker."

"He sneaked up on me," she defended. "I thought I was alone."

I huffed. "That reminds me... talking about sneaks. If you arranged anything for the holidays, made plans for Christmas, just for a coffee or whatever with friends, reschedule. Even if it's a delivery from a store, change the times. You don't know who was listening in or what they were scoping out."

"Damn."

"I know it's tedious," I murmured apologetically. "But it's for the best in the long run."

"I guess."

"Do it," I ordered. "Don't fuck around either. I'm being serious.

They went old school last night but that doesn't mean they'll keep going with that MO."

"Yes, *Mom*. I'll change scheduled times and things."

"Good. Now, hop to it. We have Christmases to destroy, don't forget."

"As if I could," she said wryly.

I hummed with delight then disconnected the call.

Like a real anti-Santa, I had mayhem to reap, chaos to sow, and havoc to dispense.

It was all in a day's work.

TWENTY-ONE

AIDAN

"WON'T IT RAISE EYEBROWS? My going to Christmas dinner with you?" was the first thing she asked after Star cut the call.

I shrugged. "Does it matter? Either way, you're coming with me."

Her lips twitched. "Is that what a masterful Aidan looks like?"

"If you haven't seen that already, then I'm doing something wrong."

She eyed me up and down. "At the moment, you just look like a porter."

"A well-dressed one," I corrected, retreating out of the doorway to her room and starting down the path to mine.

"Where are you going?" she called out, the words hitting my back as I trudged down the hallway.

I didn't answer, because I didn't particularly want to call it 'our' room. That was adding connotations and pressure to things that I wasn't ready to deal with yet.

Just because it felt like I'd been waiting five years to fuck her against the wall didn't mean that was going to happen.

Not just because of my knee, either.

She caught up with me just as I entered the room, and tugged things off my shoulders and unlooped them from my arms as she dumped them on the floor in front of the bed.

She shot me a look then asked, "Next thing you know, you'll be giving me your class ring."

I snorted. "Do I look like the kind of guy who'd have a class ring?"

"No, you look like the kind of guy who'd have given that away at the time. I bet you had so many girlfriends back then, your dick almost dropped off from exhaustion."

My brows rose at the sudden acid in her tone, but I'd admit, I liked hearing it. Liked it too much.

Unencumbered now her things were on the floor, and I could tell she wasn't about to argue with me about staying in here, I carefully lowered myself to the bed, resting my leg out flat as I did so.

"You didn't know me back then. I could have been an angel."

She grumbled, "You've never been an angel."

I had to grin. "You'd be wrong. I was good until I hit the terrible twos. Or, at least, that's what Ma says."

"I'll be sure to ask her on Christmas morning," she chimed in, but she was still shooting me dirty looks.

"You can't seriously be jealous of high school girlfriends," I mocked, unable to believe that was the reason for her scowls.

She huffed. "You don't want to think about TV executives fucking me, well, I don't want to think about chirpy cheerleaders fucking you behind the bleachers."

I squinted at her. "There's a difference. Mostly it's about twenty years."

"Okay, so do you want to hear about how my high school boyfriend tried to screw me in the teacher's lounge?"

Irritation washed through me. "No."

She smirked. "I think I made my point."

"That we're both highly irrational where we're each concerned?"

"Yes." She unzipped her bag and started pulling clothes out of it. "I knew that five years ago though."

"So did I," I admitted, and I'd been running ever since. Or, hobbling, I guessed, was more appropriate. Rubbing my bottom lip with my thumb, I asked, "This is going to get intense, Savannah. I overheard a lot of your conversation with Star. You need to prepare yourself for the fallout."

"Will you have my back whatever happens?" she asked, her eyes meeting mine with a calm that sank into my bones.

"Of course."

"Will you stop anyone from killing me?"

"Now I know you're in danger."

"Well, then—" She paused. "You hadn't heard about my exposés?"

"No. Not until you went flying down the stairs. I've been keeping away from the business."

Her brow furrowed. "I didn't think you'd be able to do that."

"My brothers shielded me from the worst."

"You're lucky," she said dryly. "Mine wouldn't."

I *was* lucky. I guessed that I knew that, but it resonated more when she looked at me with envy.

"You ever been to a war zone?"

"The nearest I got to one was a Macy's on Black Friday," she joked.

My nose crinkled. "Okay, that example won't work then."

"No, I was teasing. Tell me what you wanted to say."

"Brothers-in-arms." I blew out a breath. "They're not just siblings to me, you know? We're in a war zone together. Nobody gets that but them."

Eyes wide, she asked, "You're not talking about with the other factions, are you?"

I shook my head. "Whether it's the Italians or the Russians or the fucking Haitians, we're always at someone's throats. In this instance, I just mean being an O'Donnelly. It's a war. A constant fucking battle." Tension clawed at me. "I can deal with it. I've always found it easy to compartmentalize my life, but things have been difficult ever since..." I broke off, gesturing at my knee.

"It makes sense," she told me softly. "The pain, the addiction... they're bound to add a lot of pressure to an already intense situation."

That she got it resonated on a soul-deep level.

"I've never really talked about this shit with anyone. Not even my brothers."

"Well, we've already established that we're weird together, haven't we?"

I laughed a little as I snagged her hand in mine. "We have."

"You ever think that sometimes shit just works out how it's supposed to work out?" She tangled our fingers together as she took a seat beside me. The bed jostled and I winced as it jarred my knee.

Voice rough with pain, I muttered, "No, it's not in me to dream like that. I live in the real world, and it's nasty and cruel. I'd like to think that way, though."

She fell silent, before, on a sigh, she asked, "Question, but don't shoot?"

"I already promised I wouldn't let anyone kill you, so I don't see why I should be the one to break that promise."

"Reassuring," she grumbled under her breath. "When was the last time you went to the doctor's about your knee? Not just for pain management?"

Chin tipping upward, I admitted, "Too long ago."

"Maybe there's an advancement... something they can do to make it better?"

Grinding my jaw, I rumbled, "I doubt it. The joint was completely replaced after they tried pins that didn't stick."

"So? They have problems with joint replacements all the time. Sometimes they're outright rejected, and sometimes they're just not aligned right. What if you're in all this pain and it's something that could be easily resolved? Or maybe you just need to have more surgery to fix what's going on with it—"

"Savannah," I rumbled, "I know you mean well, but don't."

She heaved a sigh. "Men." When she pulled her hand away, I grasped her fingers tightly in mine.

"Don't."

"Don't, what?" she retorted. "Have an opinion?"

"I didn't say that."

"No? I fell down the stairs and twisted my wrist, *slightly*, and you're all, 'We'll get you to a doctor if the injury doesn't heal.' But your knee looks like a fiber optic network of scars, and I can't say anything?"

I rolled my eyes. "There's a difference."

She shrugged. "If you say so."

"I do," I growled, and I tightened my fingers around hers even more when she tried to pull free of me.

"Let go," she snapped. "I'm pissed at you."

"You're pissed at me? I'm the one who should be pissed," I retorted. "Look, just leave it alone. It sucks. That's life."

"If you say so," she repeated.

"How can you be even more annoying when you're not arguing with me?"

"It's a gift," she sniped.

My cell buzzed in my pocket, and though my fingers stayed attached to hers, she jerked back as I reached for it, freeing herself as she began bustling around, picking up clothes and depositing them in drawers where there was space.

Partly relieved and partly surprised that she didn't storm off back to the room she'd slept in last night, I answered the call. "What?"

"Is that any way to greet a long lost friend?"

"Wait a second," I said into the phone and, wincing at my stupidity in not checking the Caller ID, I leaned up on an elbow and asked Savannah, "Could you give me a few minutes?"

When she simply arched her brow at me, I rolled my eyes.

"You're the one who wanted me in here," she told me sweetly.

I grunted, and because she was being difficult, was about to head out when I noticed her peeping under her lashes at me.

I didn't have a clue what she was gaping at, but it was making her squirm.

No way was I about to cut that short.

"Apologies, Lucifer. How are you doing?"

"I could be better. I'm pregnant and I'm way too old for it, but what the hell? You only live once, don't you?"

"Hopefully you don't die twice."

"That's true. Although I wouldn't talk about my dying around any of my men. They'll probably shoot you first then worry about killing an O'Donnelly later."

"Like any good husband," I drawled.

She snickered. "I do like dealing with you, Aidan. They palmed me off on that jackass, Brennan, but I can't get along with him at all."

"He's definitely not for everyone's palate."

"Understatement of the year." She harrumphed. "Missed you at the wedding too. Anyone else would think it was rude that you didn't show up."

"I sent Eoghan in my place. And his wife."

"Very pretty girl, that. I'd complain about the age gap and her looking like she belonged in a school uniform still but who can I judge? I fell for mine when I was her age, and Ama's no better."

"They're very happy together," was all I said, unsure why she always did this. I wasn't that great at chitchat on a good day, never mind after the last twenty-four hours. I just put it down to her being from the South.

Lucie hummed. "Glad to hear it."

"Eoghan said the nuptials went well."

"They did. If it makes them feel better, then who am I to judge? Never understood the need to formalize these things, but that's the rebel in me I think."

"You never thought about marrying one of yours?"

"Well, they didn't give me much choice," she joked. "But we never did the whole group marriage thing.

"Anyway, enough about our personal lives, I know how you New Yorkers cringe when things dare go beyond business. I have news and

I didn't feel like speaking with Jackass so I thought I'd see if you were taking calls."

"Hit me with it." I sat up straighter, curious now.

I'd been the brother tasked with handling our business with the Hell's Rebels' MC, but this was one of the chores that had been spread among my siblings. Not that Lucie was all that difficult to deal with. Not like that fucker Wolfe, the MC's Prez.

"It took long enough, and I apologize for it, but we've finally managed to get the shipment of ghost guns together."

"You don't have to apologize," I rumbled. "I already told you my father was willing to wait for the merchandise to reach his direct specifications."

"Well, it's finally happened. We're going to be bringing them up to New York mid-January. I just need to know where you'd like them delivered."

"Can I get back to you with logistics?"

"Of course." She cleared her throat. "I wanted to get them to you faster just out of gratitude for what you did for Ink. I know your brother was injured, and it seemed... well, the delay pissed me off more than it did your family. I appreciate your patience."

"No need. I'm pretty sure Declan would thank Amaryllis and Ink right now. He wouldn't have his family if it weren't for that calamity."

"Calamity's the word. Okay, get in touch with the specifics, and we'll meet in January."

My lips curved slightly. "That a threat?"

"Maybe. I like to put a face to the name."

"You looking to add to that harem you've got?"

She cackled. "They'd chew you up, boy."

"You know you're younger than me, don't you?"

"Some souls were just born to be ancient, and that's me. Comes with the name, I figure. Okay, Aidan, speak soon."

"Will do."

As we cut the call, I found myself skewered in place by Savannah's curiosity, and I prepared myself for her questions.

Only, I didn't get any.

Confused, I watched as she went about her task of unpacking her bags, and then, calm as you please, declared, "I need a room to work."

"Yes, your highness," I intoned quietly, mostly relieved that she wasn't going to make me talk about a shipment of illegal guns.

Christ.

Just because she was under my roof didn't mean she was within the umbrella of our business.

I clambered to my feet, hissing as my weight settled on my knees, then ignoring her pointed look, headed for the dining room. We never used it and the table was massive, large enough for three workspaces, never mind one.

After I showed her the space, she turned to me and asked, "It sounds as if your stay of grace is over."

"It couldn't last forever. I was fortunate to have the time I did."

"I'm sorry if I triggered—"

"You weren't the catalyst. Business stops for no one." I cast her a look. "Will you be all right in here?"

"Yes. I need to reschedule the meeting with Jen."

I nodded. "Just make it an hour or two earlier."

"You'd be okay with that?"

"Yes. We can eat there. I've had enough of Conor's housekeeper's food. She only makes pies."

"Pies?"

"Yeah. Pies. You know, pastry with a filling?" I joked, trying to make up for sniping at her earlier.

"That's all she makes?"

"Variety isn't Conor's strong point. He's getting better though. Our nephew, Shay, is making him try new stuff. It doesn't always work. Con used to be obsessed with steak, but now it's pies."

She laughed, and the sound filled me up like my insides were an empty well and she was rainfall.

The urge to go to her, to slip my hands around her waist and haul her into me was strong. I fought it though.

We might be weird together, might mean more than either of us knew how to deal with, but some things had been out of bounds for so long that this was going to be a hard habit to break.

TWENTY-TWO

SAVANNAH

MY FEELINGS WEREN'T HURT.

They weren't.

They—

Christ.

They so were.

Even after I unpacked and got myself settled in my makeshift office, and I'd proofread the four exposés I had written and planned to release over the following weeks, I was still butt hurt. Which was saying something because what these four bastards had done was a crime against humanity, so Aidan should have been tucked away at the back of my mind, not at the forefront.

I didn't deal well with being butt hurt, so I decided to act on it instead and bought him an impromptu Christmas gift that was a silent 'fuck you' and had it shipped express.

Because I didn't want to be dealing with my work over the holiday period, I also scheduled my blog posts to automatically go live over the next four days, settling on six AM, just in time for breakfast news.

Mostly that was a snub against TVGM who emailed me three

times as I worked, among other networks and papers who'd somehow gotten a hold of my personal email address.

Deciding that the next time I saw Conor I was going to ask him if there was a way to block the people who'd emailed me thus far, somehow bypassing the spam filter, I finally remembered that I had to reschedule things with Jen.

Calling her because I didn't understand the only messaging app on my phone, and I figured it was new to Jen too, I called her when I knew she was on her lunch break.

Crawford, Lewis and Jones was where we'd first met. She was my accountant's assistant, and she'd complimented me on my shoes whenever I went in for a meeting. A mutual adoration for Louboutin had her triggering a friendship with me.

As someone who was naturally cautious around people because they tended to want to befriend me to get close to my dad, there was something deliciously artless about Jen. I wasn't sure how she'd started working for the staid corporate firm, to be honest.

Knowing her, I wouldn't be surprised if she'd sucked off her boss during the interview or something. There was a reason she'd said very little about the TVGM fallout, and I had to think that was how she'd gotten her job otherwise she'd have been all over the gossip like gonorrhea.

"Girl, please don't be calling to cancel."

It was mean, but I laughed at her panic. "No, I'm not canceling."

"Thank God. I wanted to ask you something but I didn't dare call—"

I arched a brow. "That's not like you."

She huffed. "I'm scared, can't you tell?"

"You don't have to be scared. It's only money. I'll lend it to you if need be," I told her calmly.

"You told me that before but I don't think it's right to take money from friends."

I rolled my eyes at her obstinacy. "Okay, okay, we'll see what happens but know the offer is there."

"I really appreciate it, Savannah. You've no idea."

My lips curved because I knew she meant it. She was a cat, but when it boiled down to it, a kindhearted and loyal one. "What did you want to ask me?"

"The jerk says he can't meet me at eight."

"Oh, that's perfect! I need to reschedule."

"Really? Jeez, fate is working on my side." She muttered under her breath, "Let's hope it stays that way. Will six be okay?"

"Yeah, that's fine," I agreed. "I'll see you then."

In the background, I heard a barista call out her name and after she muttered her thanks at him, she told me, "I can't believe you held out on me about Aidan O'Donnelly."

"There was nothing to hold out on," I admitted. "We reconnected a short while ago."

"For a one-night-stand?" Jen squeaked. "But you never have those."

"No. I don't. It was... well, it felt right at the time."

"Not now? You regretting it?"

"No. Just wondering why things feel so right with him."

The bustle of the coffee shop disappeared and was replaced with the sounds of a New York street.

Over a horn and a gaggle of foreign voices that made me think she'd just dived into a crowd of tourists, she hollered above the noise, "I didn't hear that, honey. Did you say he fucked you wrong?"

Chuckling at how she'd mangled up my words, I retorted, "No, he fucked me *very* right."

"Okay, good, because that would have been very disappointing. I've been sniffing around him for years but he never took me up on it. That would have been depressing if all that yummy promise was for nothing."

That stupid wave of irrational jealousy took over me again, much as it had when we'd been talking about his cheerleader exes, and I gritted my teeth to contain it.

I had no right to be jealous.

It was insane.

Maybe if I repeated that a thousand times, I'd start to believe it.

"So, come on. What did he do wrong? Why are you calling, Aunty Jen? I can't fix it if you don't tell me what's going on."

"He did nothing wrong." I admitted, because he hadn't done anything. It was on him if he didn't listen to me, and I was only butt hurt because I wanted things that weren't possible.

Too fast, too soon, just too damn much.

"Savannah?" Jen called. "Are you still there?"

"Huh? What? Yeah, I'm still here. Sorry, just thinking."

"About what?"

"Have you ever loved someone?"

"Girl, you can't love a one-night-stand. That's just asking for trouble."

I snorted. "Trust me, I know, but it's different."

"We always think that. I swear, it's the patriarchy's fault. Men can fuck whoever and whatever they want with no feelings involved but we have to get in our feelings just because some dick gave us an orgasm."

Because this wasn't the first time I'd listened to a diatribe about a woman's right to attachment-free orgasms, I muttered, "I know, Jen, but this is really different."

"How?"

"We met five years ago because he decided that instead of having me killed, he wanted to pick my brain." At her prolonged silence, I choked out a laugh. "Have I done the impossible? Robbed you of words?"

"You mean, you did something, *wrote* something that made the O'Donnellys consider taking a hit out on you?"

Her squeaky whisper was indicative of the fact that you didn't say shit in this city about the O'Donnellys at top volume.

Even a mouthy bitch like my friend knew that.

"Yeah," I admitted. "It was weird."

"Sounds like it," she groused. "What happened?"

"Well, I'm still alive."

"Har-Har," she grumbled. "Come on, Savannah. Tell me! You can't keep shit like that on the downlow."

"That's exactly where I probably should keep it," I said with a sigh as I reached up and rubbed my tired eyes. "Have you ever looked at someone and felt like you've been hit with one of Cupid's arrows? Like, out of nowhere, all the songs make sense?"

"Songs?"

"Yeah. You know, music?" I mocked. "Every love song ever written somehow resonates where it didn't before. Have you never felt like that?"

"Not really. I mean, there's been plenty of guys I want to bang. I don't think you mean those kinds of songs, though, huh? Less Lizzo and more Carrie Underwood?"

Though I snorted, I said, "Yeah, more Carrie." Agitated, I fiddled with the necklace I wore, a tiny pendant of a paw my dad had bought me when Teabag, my cat, the one he'd bought me to keep me company when I left home and had gone to college, had died. "I was scared at first, but then we went out to dinner and he was different."

"Why did he take you out to dinner?"

"I don't know. I guess he was interested in me."

I heard the soft noise of her sipping coffee, and then she asked, "You love him now, that's what you're saying, right?"

"No. I don't know what it is. It can't be that. It takes time for love to grow, doesn't it?"

She hummed. "Well, I mean, you're asking the wrong person. I'm not even sure it exists. It's probably some hormonal wizardry that the doctors figured out how to put into the pill. That damn patriarchy again."

I rolled my eyes. "I'm not on the pill."

"Bullshit. *Ain't on the pill*, she says. You get the shot, don't you?"

I knew I'd pissed her off if she was saying 'ain't.' She worked hard to sound like she fit in her corporate office.

"Yeah, but I wasn't back then when I first met him." Considering he'd fucked me raw this morning, it was probably for the best I got the shot, now that I thought about it. "So your logic is flawed."

She scoffed. "Maybe they pipe something in the chemtrails."

"Jesus, Jen. What is this? Conspiracy O'Clock?"

"Sorry," she muttered, sounding unapologetic. "Okay, so these feelings, what was it then?"

"Like I wanted to fuck him, and I know he felt the same, but he didn't. We didn't. Not then."

"You didn't screw him back then? Jesus. I never met him before the shooting, but I saw pictures of him. He was hawt."

"He's hot now!" I defended.

"Yeah, but he has that look on his face. Ya know, like he's suffering?"

"Because he is?" I grunted. This was exactly the reason why he needed to go to the doctor again. "Well, we didn't fuck, even though I wanted to, and then he ghosted me.

"I had his phone number, so I called twice just... well, you know his line of work, only he never picked up, then like a week later, it was disconnected. I figured out he was ignoring me and wasn't just lying in an alleyway somewhere."

"Jackass."

"Yeah," I said softly. "It hurt."

"It usually does."

"Worse than usual." I blew out a breath. "Then, I got the job offer with TVGM, and even though Wintersen eyed me up like I was his version of jelly beans, he never, ever touched me. I know that's because Aidan got me the job. Earlier on, Conor told me that Wintersen has gone missing."

"Missing as in... he thinks Aidan had him killed?"

My tone turned hushed. "That was the inference."

"But Wintersen didn't come onto you," Jen reasoned. "You came onto him. He never did anything against you like he did the other women, your friends, right?"

"Yeah, he left me alone."

She grunted. "Okay, so you reconnected recently—"

"Last night."

"You had sex, and what? You're questioning the universe? You really need to stop that, honey. Just accept the orgasm and get on with your life."

"We're going to be stuck together throughout these exposés."

She paused. "The O'Donnellys are protecting you?"

I knew she wasn't aware of the repercussions of my exposés. Though she'd been raised in Hell's Kitchen, and like any smart kid from that neighborhood, knew to leave the O'Donnellys well alone, she was just an average citizen.

Learning that her other friend was Finn O'Grady's wife came as much of a shock to me as it did to Aidan. That Jen kept some things to herself was a given. I did the same, but that still surprised me. It also told me that Finn's wife kept her in the dark about her husband's business practices. Natural, but still, something to learn.

We all had our secrets.

Me included.

"They are."

"Why? Are you in danger?"

"Maybe. It's just a precaution."

"Jesus, should you come tonight?"

"It's in my building. I think it'll be fine." I doubted Aidan would let me go if something changed between now and then.

"Are you sure?"

No. But... "I'm not going to miss out on meeting your mystery schmuck. Plus, if you spill margaritas in his lap, I want a front row seat."

"You're so supportive."

I huffed out a laugh. "And you are? My feelings for Aidan are not induced from the contraceptive pill."

"Well, that'd make far more sense than instant love," she retorted, making me roll my eyes.

"If you say so. I'll see you later, Jen. I gotta get going."

"Yeah, my lunch break's over. Speak later, babe. And Savannah?"

"What?"

"If he makes you feel good, and not just with orgasms, then what's the harm in seeing how things unfold, huh?

"It's in your nature to overthink everything. It goes with the job, I guess. But you shouldn't. Sometimes, you just have to embrace what's happening and throw caution to the wind. Where's the fun in life if you're always second guessing everything?"

And as she put the phone down, I was reminded of my valedictorian speech. Her words and mine were similar enough that even though we were polar opposites, I was prodded into remembering why we were close friends. How something disingenuous had morphed into an all-out friendship.

Our thoughts sometimes, *sometimes*, aligned.

God help us both.

As I got back to work, my brain was whirring in many different directions, and I was actually glad when my asshole brother called. Until, of course, he spoke. Which made me remember why I wanted to smack him.

Repeatedly.

With one of his beloved Fenders—the one he'd grabbed at auction that had once been a part of some special project Bryan Adams was involved in.

"What do you want?" I sniped as I put him on FaceTime.

He glowered right back at me. "To speak to you."

"Why? I thought you made it abundantly clear that I was an idiot for sacrificing my career for something I believed in?"

"I can still love you if you're an idiot. Mostly, I just want to know why the hell you're not here."

"Because I didn't want to see you," I retorted.

He huffed. "Savvie, come on. Don't be stupid."

"Don't you dare call me stupid," I snapped. "I'm not stupid just because we don't agree on something.

"I told you, Camden, I wouldn't put up with your bullshit

anymore. You might be my big brother, and a million groupies might want to suck that skanky dick of yours, but I'm not going to let you belittle my beliefs."

He scowled. "I didn't do that!"

"You totally did."

"You worked hard to reach that position." *I really hadn't.* "I just hated to see you throw it away."

"Some sacrifices are worth making." I pursed my lips then, deciding to change the subject, I told him begrudgingly, "You look good." The last time I'd seen him, he'd been strung out on something I didn't want to know about.

He shrugged. "It did me good to get away."

"I'd roll my eyes but I'd do it so hard that they'd never go back to being normal again. Did you really have to go to a monastery in Tibet for some R&R?"

"Hey, don't knock it until you try it," he said with a smirk. "Although, you'd go crazy there. You can't talk so you can't ask any goddamn questions."

"Sounds like hell for sure," I agreed, smirking right back at him.

"Seriously though, you should come here. There's still time. I'll send the jet—you can be home tonight."

His eyes softened, and for an instant, I understood what it was that had millions of women around the world losing their sense and their panties even if I thought they were all crazy.

Camden was my dad reincarnate, only without all the good stuff Mom had bred into him over the years together. Just all the nasty rocker shit that made him questionable to touch without gloves.

"Please, sis."

If someone hadn't tried to kill me, I'd probably have said yes, but instead, I shook my head. "Camden, I know you've been in Tibet so you haven't read the news, but I've got a lot of shit going on right now that I don't want to bring down on the family."

"Like what?" He frowned. "Are you in trouble?"

I shrugged. "It's all good. But I want you guys to have a great day, okay?" I smiled at him. "Merry Christmas, bro."

"Same, little sis. It'll suck without you here."

"Maybe, or you could have the time of your life."

He pretended to ponder that, then, slowly murmured, "You know what, you could be right."

"I have your Christmas present for you before I forget." I flipped him the bird. "There you go." I flipped him the second one. "Never let it be said that I'm not generous."

TWENTY-THREE

AIDAN

I WAITED for her by the private elevator that would take us to The 68. The elevator only stopped on five floors in the entire building—Conor's apartment, a communal gym and spa, The 68, the ground floor and the private parking garage.

The second I saw her though, the last thing I wanted was to walk through those doors and step amid the patrons of a busy bar.

She looked like sin and fire and lust personified.

Dressed in a pantsuit, sharp and tight, tailored to her every curve, she had a white shirt beneath it and a black tie around her throat.

Even though it was a masculine look, I'd never seen anything more innately feminine. Her make-up shielded all the bruises, and she looked like a goddamn angel sent to torment me with those golden brown eyes that saw too much I wanted to hide from her.

Her tits looked huge, her ass round, and everything else was delicate, from her small wrist which housed a man's Rolex, to the necklace she wore that hovered above her tie, and, when she approached, I saw was a diamond pendant shaped like a paw.

Her heels were high stilettos and she moved toward me atop them like she was floating, not wearing torture devices. Considering she'd mentioned her ankles were sore from last night, I wasn't sure if she was just insane or trying to drive *me* crazy.

Still, she walked in them with ease, and a scan of her face revealed no micro-expressions of pain, so I didn't call her out on them because, to be frank, she looked banging.

She was expensive, she reeked of it, and I was more than willing to pay for everything that went beneath that goddamn suit. Christ, I even wanted those spikes to be burrowed in the small of my back as I fucked her.

She smirked at me when she was within touching distance, and I couldn't find it in me to give a damn.

"Thank fuck you never looked like that on TVGM or I'd have had to kill that co-anchor bastard," I growled as she pushed the button for the elevator and strolled inside when the doors parted for her.

"I only got away with wearing the suit because they were all afraid of me. They wanted everyone in dresses, but not me. Something to do with you, I assume," she told me calmly as I moved to stand beside her.

"I didn't think I threw that much weight around, but I must have made it known you were off limits. I'm glad I did."

"I think when you tell people to jump, they don't just obey, they drop off the side of a cliff too to make sure they don't piss you off."

"Why do I think you like that?" I drawled as I pressed the button for the bar.

"You know I like that."

"A therapist would have a field day if he knew that Isardo's death brought about the obsession with the mafia and now, somehow, you cream your panties over the craziest mobster shit." I kept my eyes fixed on her, not even bothering to glance at the floor numbers that counted down as we traveled.

"Oh, trust me, they've had a lot to say over the years." She stepped closer to me and pressed a hand to my chest. "Doesn't take away from the fact that my pussy's wet, does it?"

My nostrils flared as I thrust my good leg between hers and slowly walked her back into the wall.

"You want to play with fire?"

"You know I do," she crooned.

"Thought you were giving me the cold shoulder." She'd been quiet all day, which made me think she was still sulking over our little argument.

"What about me feels cold to you?"

"True. Did you change the bandage on your thigh?"

She rolled her eyes. "Yes."

That eye roll had me frowning at her, and I reached up and traced my finger along the line of her jaw. "Don't judge me for caring for you, Savannah."

She gulped. "No. You're right. Sorry."

I grunted, but carried on with my investigation.

Her make-up was exquisite. Perfect. Utterly beautiful.

I wanted to wreck it.

I wanted to mar it, because the second we walked through those fucking doors, there'd be men there who'd see her. Who'd want her. Who'd want something that everything inside me screamed was mine.

My thumb twitched as I reached her lips. Bright red and glossy with it, they parted at the digit's approach, and I let my gaze drift from the gleaming, pouting morsel and up to her eyes.

Nostrils flaring when I saw the challenge in hers, I growled under my breath and did as my instincts insisted.

I let my thumb slide through that gloss, dragging it aside and onto her cheek, smearing perfection. Sullying it.

"Feel better?" she rasped, no anger, more like amusement lacing her tone at my antics, as her hands came around my hips, lowering to my ass as she pressed harder, making sure that both of us were well aware I had a boner.

Much as she'd done, I threw that back at her: "Does it feel like I feel better?"

She shook her head, her eyes darkening as she rolled her hips.

"You'll get burned," I warned her.

"Maybe I want to. Maybe that's exactly what I need."

I stared at the smeared lipstick, at the mess I'd made, then I leaned forward and pushed my cheek against her clean one. "There'll come a time when you'll push me too far and too fast."

"I hope so. Where would be the fun in taking things slow?"

I had to smile, but before I pulled back, feeling the deceleration of the elevator, I darted forward, nipped her earlobe hard enough to make her squeal, then murmured, "Do not reapply the lipstick when you head to the restroom." I saw her mutinous expression and warned, "Pick your battles, little one."

A shaky sigh escaped her, and I knew why. It had nothing to do with my dictate, and everything to do with the term of endearment. It hadn't slipped out by mistake. It just felt right. Seemed she agreed because it turned her to goo in my arms.

She reached up and touched my cheek. "Aidan?"

"Yes?"

"I know it's crazy, but I want you."

"I want you too."

I wanted to tell her that, sometimes, in this life, just because we wanted something, didn't mean we could have it, but as I stared into her eyes, drowned in them, I knew I couldn't do that.

The doors opened with a soft ping. The sound was oddly gentle, as it merged with the bustling noises from the restaurant.

As I stared down at her, I heard incoming footsteps, and when someone called out, "Sir?" I rested a hand on Savannah's waist, squeezed there, then without turning my head, rasped, "Get me a damp cloth."

A confused silence followed my demand, and I whipped my head around to stare at the maître d', then saw his frown clear up when he recognized who I was. Before I had to say another fucking word, he darted away, scurrying to do as I asked.

Left alone again, I looked into her eyes and murmured, "The only appropriate time for lipstick is when you're sucking my dick." My words triggered a visceral response in her. The back of her head tipped against the elevator wall so I had the perfect view of her pupils dilating as I continued, "No more lipstick."

Though I didn't expect her to immediately comply, she gave me a shaky nod. "No more lipstick."

With my good leg, I stepped even closer, pressing my thigh harder between hers. When she facilitated the move, then ground down against me, I gritted my teeth at her heat.

"No more fighting," I rumbled with a warning as she rocked her hips. "No more sulking."

She licked her lips. "You want to look after my wellbeing? I want to look after yours."

I grunted, then I hissed when she reached between us and cupped my dick. "On the way back up, I'll reapply that lipstick," she promised, but her gaze darted over my shoulder, which told me the maître d' had returned. Of course, I knew that already. I could scent his fucking nervousness in the air.

Twisting around once more, I reached back to grab the damp cloth, then told him, "I'll be along in a moment."

Eyes flared wide, he quickly bobbed his head, then retreated, leaving us alone.

"Let me?" I asked softly, gesturing at the cloth.

She blinked but nodded, so I lifted it and pressed it to her mouth. Her skin blanched under pressure, but stayed an oily, rosy pink thanks to the lip paint.

I persevered though, being careful with each move I made, and all the while, she watched me. All the while, her pussy stayed close to my thigh and I felt her heat drenching me.

"Thank God that we're both wearing black," she rasped, proving that our minds were aligned.

I smirked at her. "You'll always have to wear black around me, little one, unless you don't mind looking...*crumpled.*" At least, that was if I did my job right.

"Always?"

I almost shook my head at her, but there was anguish in the choked out word. So, though it made no sense, I still caught her eye and nodded. "Always."

This was insanity but I'd never felt saner in my life.

She gulped, then rasped, "Always." This time, her tone was more certain.

I had no idea what I was going to do with this woman, had no idea if she'd survive my father or Christmas dinner, but there was only one way to test her: a trial by fire.

"I thought you were going to make me walk out there with my lipstick smeared," she rasped as I gave her a few final touches with the cloth.

"I'll never humiliate you in public," I rumbled. "That's not how I work."

"Just in private, hmm?" Her eyes were sparkling as she said it, though, which made me wonder if that was her kink. To each their own. I could adapt.

"If that's what you need."

"What do you need?" she crooned.

"You'll find out soon enough."

I dropped the cloth once I was satisfied with how cleaned up she was. Her mouth was oddly pale now I'd wiped off the paint as well as some of her make-up, and I was grateful I hadn't exposed any bruises as that would have turned me homicidal, but she didn't seem to care.

Savannah would, I realized, always bewilder me. Another woman would have reacted with horror at my assholish possessiveness, but she just appeared amused, especially after I tempered it with an endearment.

Because I wanted to reward her patience with me, I reached around her waist and pulled her away from the elevator wall. Then I grabbed her ass, and asked, "You ever been fucked here?"

"That your favorite place, hmm?" she asked, grinding into me again.

"Answer the question," I demanded.

Her throat bobbed. "No."

"Why not?" She was no inexperienced ingénue.

"Because the guys I've been with barely knew what my clit was. You think I was about to trust them with my ass? That place'll bleed, and not in a good way. In a 'we need to go to the ER' kind of way."

Any other woman said that, I'd have laughed.

With her, I pushed her into the wall, dropped my forehead to hers, and rumbled, "No talk of other men."

Her breath skipped as she moaned, "But you asked!"

"I don't care. I don't care if it's illogical. No fucking talk of this pussy that belongs to me being handled by another fucker. You got me?"

"Christ, that shouldn't be as hot as it is," she admitted on a whimper, before she reached up and joined our mouths.

She was like liquid silk in my arms, flowing into me, conforming around me like she was meant to be there.

And maybe she was.

Because Savannah was prickly. She wasn't born to conform. She wasn't made to be silk.

Except with me.

I let her stake her own claim, let her thrust her tongue against mine, panting as she tried to get closer, to burrow into me as her arms slid around my neck and she ground her pussy against me some more.

When she was rocking faster, faster, I added pressure to the move, shoving my leg higher and pressing her down harder.

She winced a second, released a shaky breath, then wiggled, and I figured I'd pushed down on that shallow cut to her upper thigh. Letting her find her own comfort levels, letting her find her pleasure, I watched as she got back into the groove.

The nearer her approach to orgasm, the less insistent her kiss was, so I took it over, well aware that, though the doors were closed so no one could see us, the maître d' might be able to hear us.

But I didn't stop.

She'd come to learn that I'd always take care of her.

Even if she didn't want me to.

So I took over the kiss, fucking her mouth like I couldn't fuck her pussy just yet, and then, as she started to orgasm, I kept her tongue busy to reduce the noise she made.

No one would hear her this way.

Ever.

As she came down, I held her tight as she slumped into me, then I drew kisses along her cheekbone, moving until I reached her ear.

"That ass is going to be mine. Every fucking part of you is going to be mine.

"I'm going to fill every hole you've got with my cum, until your body is stamped with my scent, stamped with me." I nipped her earlobe. "And I know you're going to be okay with that, because you want that as much as I do."

She released a shaky breath, and her mahogany hair tickled my cheek as she nodded. The scent of vanilla and chocolate filled my senses. Rich and deep, evocative and musky. Her. Just Savannah. Better than cookies or any kind of dessert. Even my ma's.

With a final nip to her earlobe, I started to straighten up, then I asked, "Are you okay to stand?"

When she peered up at me with big eyes, I knew I'd found the way to de-prick the most prickly woman in the universe—just pet her until she purred.

Satisfied with her, so fucking thrilled with her responsiveness right at that moment, I couldn't stop myself from pressing a kiss to her lips, then helping her straighten up.

On those ice picks for shoes, I knew she might be a bit wobbly, so I clamped her to my side and said, "Come on, little one, let's save Jen from herself."

TWENTY-FOUR

SAVANNAH

SWOON.

Could I just say that again? And again?

Every time he mentioned the words, 'little one,' I felt an internal shudder, like my pussy was clutching emptiness when it really needed his dick.

Never in my life would I think I'd get off from riding a man's thigh. No other direct sexual stimulation than a kiss—like a naughty teenager who only dared to hit second base—but lawd, I should have known Aidan would be different.

Maybe that's what had always made me think of him.

Maybe he was a walking promise of sin and salvation all wrapped up together in a bundle of hot hunk that I would never be able to compete with.

I was still drooling from him smearing my lipstick, and considering that took me a good twenty minutes to perfect, I should have been pissed but because it was a move born of possessiveness, I was more than okay with him being an asshole. Especially as the only place he wanted lipstick was around his dick, apparently, and I was more than happy to oblige.

shudder

Each step we made toward the maître d's station was hard won thanks to how sensitive I was, but when the guy looked at me, I felt no shame, and neither did he look at me knowingly. If anything, he peered at me as if I were insane, his gaze darting between the pair of us, which told me he knew exactly who Aidan was.

And didn't that just make me melt some more?

He was too scared of Aidan to even judge me for getting off in the elevator.

Ugh, that was too hot.

Knowing that I'd need my wits about me, I tried not to cream my panties some more when a hush fell over the restaurant as we walked in together.

The place was trying too hard with its black on black esthetic, coppery touches of color in the overhanging lights—those exposed copper bulbs that added both warmth and an odd glare to a space—all surrounding what was clearly a custom-built baby grand piano that was a dark scarlet. Tables circled the piano that was being played by someone who was clearly in love with her job because she didn't even miss a beat though the rest of the bar did.

I'd been raised with a famous daddy. I'd grown accustomed to turning heads, even if it was just to murmur about the shit some tabloid had published about my family, and of late, whispers had always stirred wherever I was because of what had happened with Wintersen, but this was different.

This was like a court responding to a king.

And his queen.

Oh, fuck.

I wanted that.

I wanted to be that. More than I could have ever recognized.

The hush stirred and shifted, whispers flying at Aidan's possessive arm around my waist, as the proprietorial clamping of his fingers to my hip was registered. I knew we'd stand out, both of us wearing suits the way we were, and I'd never felt more like a lady boss.

Fucking untouchable.

We seemed to float toward the back end of the bar where there was clearly a VIP area.

Jen was sitting there already, watching us with big eyes. She looked hot in a kind of metallic blouse that draped over her torso, revealing toned arms and a slender frame while exposing just how big her tits were.

From that alone, I knew she was going to try to seduce her ex again if Aidan's presence didn't resolve anything.

"Hubba hubba," she mouthed at me, and I smirked as I owned my moment, that delicious, sweet high that was me feeling like I was finally taking my fucking place in this world.

My confidence, already high, soared to impossible levels. While my mouth was bare, my make-up probably patchy from his clean-up job, and my gait a little unsteady thanks to the orgasm he'd just gifted me, I'd never felt higher.

That was because of him.

Which was exactly what a man should do.

Raise you up, not tear you down.

He was right about not mentioning other guys, because they'd been boys.

For the first time in my life, I was with a real man, and it fucking rocked.

"Jen," I greeted with a little smirk, oddly pleased with how awestruck she was.

Her escapades were far more daring than mine, so that she was impressed with me was unusual.

As I clambered onto the circular bench seating, Aidan shuffled in after me.

The bandage pulled against my upper thigh, but the slash there was mostly a flesh wound. More irritating than anything, prone to stinging because I'd wrapped it up too tightly. I'd be glad when I could remove it, to be honest. It was already a nuisance.

"He's not here yet?" Aidan queried, his disapproval stark as he finally took a seat.

I cast him a look, because his voice was different, and saw his face was a little pale. Guilt hit me, because while I'd been loving that moment, he'd clearly been in pain. Now that I thought about it, his gait had been smoother.

Jesus, did he control his limp in public?

How was that even doable?

Slightly in awe of him—okay, who was I kidding?—a *lot* in awe of him, I shifted my attention to my friend, who was grumbling, "He said he had issues with parking."

Aidan grumbled right back, "You know how to pick them, Jen. The fucker can't park in a place that has valet parking?"

Her nose crinkled. "I wouldn't be surprised if he doesn't show up."

"If he doesn't, then I'll do more than fucking key his Ferrari," Aidan intoned darkly, his tone not shifting as, abruptly, he murmured, "An Aperol Spritz and do you still have the forty-year-old Midleton?"

Why wasn't I shocked that he knew my drink of choice?

I shot a glance at the server who'd rolled up out of nowhere, well aware that she was eying him like he was a king too, and rather than be jealous, I pressed a hand to his lap, making it quite clear that he was mine. Stamping as much of a claim on him as he did on me, something he compounded by entangling our fingers.

"We do, Mr. O'Donnelly. Would you like me to bring the bottle?"

He grunted. "Please." As she drifted off, he muttered, "I think it's going to be one of those evenings."

Jen perked up. "I've always wanted to try expensive whiskey."

Aidan snorted. "It'll knock you on your ass."

"Wanna bet?"

"I'm in the mood to win, so why not?" he taunted, and their manner was so relaxed, so comfortable, that something squeezed inside me.

They knew each other.

Well.

But Jen had said she'd tried and failed to seduce him, which meant Aidan was unusual. Very few men Jen set her sights on refused her.

"If you don't choke on the whiskey, I'll let you have the bottle."

Jen eyed him. "Knowing you, the bottle's worth fifteen K."

"And you need every cent, don't you?"

She huffed. "How about you let me have the bottle anyway seeing as you don't need the cash?"

"Where would the fun be in that? And who the hell would buy an open bottle anyway?"

"Remind me to warn you that I'll cut your balls off if you hurt Savannah?"

I rolled my eyes. "That's some segue."

"I'm the Queen of Segues."

"You wouldn't have to cut them off. I'd do it myself."

She squinted at him. "I believe you and I approve this message." Before I could do more than grin, Jen leaned into me and asked, "Have you seen his collection yet?"

Collection?

When she saw my blankness, her tone changed. Turned apologetic. Which was when I realized I should have had faith in my friend. She recognized I was stupidly jealous of the fact she knew more about him than I did, private stuff that no amount of Google searches would reveal, and eased it by telling me, "Finn's always going on about Aidan's whiskey collection."

I cast him a look. "You're a fan?"

"Why wouldn't I be?"

"I don't know. I thought there was a rivalry between the Irish and the Scottish."

He smirked, then he made my heart flutter by raising my hand to his mouth and pressing a kiss to my knuckles. I had no idea what had happened in that elevator, but that he wasn't afraid to make PDAs was now a given.

And hot.

So very, very hot.

Then, of course, I realized why, and I couldn't be pissed.

He thought I was hot, too. He thought I was so fucking banging, he wanted every other cock in the place to know who owned me.

Was there anything better than *mutual*, irrational jealousy?

"There *is* a rivalry, but I'm talking about whiskey with an 'e.' I do appreciate a good scotch, like a Bowman, though." He winked. "I only drink it around Da."

I laughed. "Talk about dedication to annoying your parents."

"You'll meet him soon," he said wryly. "You'll understand then."

"Not sure that worked as a deterrent," Jen retorted with a grin.

He snorted. "If you could see how starstruck you look right now..."

"She's weird, isn't she?" Jen teased. "Who on earth gets a lady boner over the—" Her voice lowered. "—Irish Mob?"

I elbowed her in the side. "Fuck off."

"There'll be none of that in these heels." She arched her foot beneath the glass table and pouted. "To think, I bought new Louboutins to impress the fucker and he isn't going to show."

"Aren't they expensive?" Aidan asked with a frown that had the waitress's arm jolting and rattling the tray as she served us our drinks.

"They are," she confirmed, after he'd asked the server to bring another glass over to the table.

"So, let me see if I get your logic. You're about to be fined, what is it? Seventy? Eighty grand? And you go and spend two grand on a pair of shoes."

Jen clucked her tongue. "But the shoes do wonders for my ass, and that might have made him lower the settlement. Hence they'd have been a smart investment."

Aidan rolled his eyes. "What kind of ass-backward logic is that?"

"You've never appreciated my butt," Jen sniped. "So you wouldn't get it."

At their bickering, I chuckled. "Are you two always like this?" Christ, no wonder Aidan didn't have the hots for Jen.

"Mostly always," Jen said with a pout. "It sucks as well, because he's Finn's best friend and I'm Aoife's. We're also their kid's godparents, not that I'd wish that dire fate on any child but she trusts me for some reason." Jen folded her arms across her chest. "Aoife makes us go into the kitchen to get away from him, which is really bad for me because she bakes like she's the star of a wet dream."

"She's the star of Finn's wet dreams," Aidan pointed out dryly as he poured himself a measure of whiskey.

"Yeah, they're so in love it's sickening."

I cackled. "Well, that's nice."

She pulled a face. "It is actually." Her sigh was a lot more poignant than I thought she knew. "If you two are a thing now... and let's face it, after that entrance, I'm not sure anyone in Manhattan can think otherwise, you'll get to meet her. She's really cool. I'd have introduced you to her but Finn's mean."

"He is?" He hadn't been mean to me yesterday.

"No, he just can't let any fucking waif and stray into his apartment because Jen's got her panties in a bunch." Aidan took a deep sip of whiskey and I watched as the tension in his shoulders eased some.

I wanted to warn him that in the Twelve Steps, they told addicts not to imbibe any alcohol for fear of them getting hooked on that, but we'd already argued once today about his knee, and I didn't want to compound that, especially not in public.

Deciding instead that I'd keep an eye on him, I watched his throat work as he swallowed, then cast a look at Jen who was eying the crowd, evidently on the hunt for her man.

No, I didn't have any reason to be jealous, I recognized. They were more fraternal than anything else.

Because I really needed the bathroom, and because I wasn't concerned about leaving them alone together, I said, "I'm just going to head to the restroom." I motioned at Jen to move, and she shuffled out from the table, revealing a dress so short she might as well have covered herself up with a handkerchief.

I was pretty sure her ex, if he did show up, would fuck her because that was what she was offering, but I didn't think he'd lower the settlement. Why would he? Getting off wouldn't change the fact his Ferrari was scratched. Still, I didn't want to argue with her. She'd just call me a prude.

Again.

"I'll come with," she declared, hooking my arm through hers. As we strode off together, she whispered, "Oh, my God, you two are so hot together."

Butterflies filled my stomach. "Right?"

"I can see why he's fried your brain. At least he looks as intense as you so I don't think you have any fear on that front." She shivered. "You strolled in like you owned the fucking place.

"Mind you, he probably does," Jen tacked on wryly, "but still, you don't own Manhattan. Not yet. Not until Sr. dies." She shot me a quick glance as we ducked into the restroom where there was an attendant waiting with a smile. Jen ignored her and hauled me over to a corner where there was a vanity section. "You might want to reapply your lipstick. Did he kiss it off?"

"Sort of."

She sighed. "That's hot." Her fingers drifted to my throat where a hickey still managed to peep through the layers of make-up I'd coated over it. "Nice concealer job."

Cautiously, I asked, "You jealous?"

"Maybe." She winked at me in the mirror to tell me she was joking. "Wouldn't have warned you about the lipstick if I wanted to sabotage you though.

"I'm going to look forward to you bringing him to his knees. Aidan's got a stick shoved so far up his ass, they could dangle him on the top of the White House as a flag."

"Nice imagery." I snickered.

She wafted a hand. "There's never been anything between us," she reassured me, "but we've spent a lot of time together just because of Finn and Aoife."

I nodded. "I get it." And I did.

As I touched up my foundation and concealer, then added some balm to my lips, she asked, "You want to borrow my lipstick? It'd look awesome with the suit.

"Damn, you look hot tonight. I'm almost proud of you."

"Thanks, but no. I'm cool with the balm, especially if we're going to eat."

"Do you think Aidan will cover the tab?"

"I'm pretty sure he will." I arched a brow, then tutted. "Jen, if money's so damn tight, then why did you buy those shoes?"

"They were on credit," she defended. "Plus they might have saved me the costs of a court case.'

Rolling my eyes, I grumbled, "How are you a feminist?"

"I'm not against using men's dicks against them. That, to me, is a form of feminism."

"More like misandry."

"Whichever way you call it, if they're dumb enough to want to fuck me because I'm hot, then they're dumb enough for me to manipulate."

"Ouch." I cast her a look, wondering if she recognized what she'd said there, how much she'd revealed about her relationships with men.

Jen had never known her dad because he'd run off while her mom was pregnant, but even if I hadn't known about her past, I'd have understood everything then and there with that one declaration.

She didn't respect the men she fucked, and they, in turn, didn't respect her.

Wondering if she knew how toxic that was, I decided not to lecture her when she had a lot going on. Instead, I told her, "If Aidan doesn't, I will, and if you promise not to waste the money on fucking shoes, I'll lend you whatever you need. I keep offering, Jen, because you're my friend, and I don't want you to be concerned about bills or paying rent."

She dipped her chin, hiding her beautiful face in a cloud of dark brown hair. "Thanks, Savannah. I really appreciate that." She peeped at me from under her lashes, making me wonder how, even though she was definitely an acquired taste, a guy hadn't snapped her up yet. She was gorgeous. A twelve out of ten. "I might..." Jen sighed. "I'll give you the details for my landlord, so you can know the money goes right to him."

I frowned. "Jen, I trust you, honey."

"I don't," she said grimly, turning to face the mirror. "I'm turning into a magpie."

"You need a rich boyfriend," I teased her.

"I need an O'Donnelly." She sighed. "Conor's the only one left. He's hot. What do you think? Would we go well together?"

"He says he's taken."

Her nose crinkled. "Damn. Oh, well, I'm not as brave as you are." She leaned into me, and her perfume, sweet but not cloying, filled my nose as she whispered, "You know Aidan's going to take over the Five Points, don't you?"

"I managed to work that out," I joked.

"I know you're weird about them," she replied, "but you've never been up close and personal with them like I have. It's a scary world, Savannah. Aoife got really hurt on her wedding day. I was there."

At her shiver, I asked, "You were?"

She nodded, but clearly didn't want to talk about it.

I patted her arm. "I promise, I think I know what I'm doing."

"Is that supposed to reassure me?"

I grinned. "It's about as much reassurance as I'm capable of."

"Good to know."

After we both used the bathroom and washed up, we returned to the restaurant and found ourselves at the center of the diners' attention once more.

"I could get used to this. I'll just stick with you and I'll find me a sugar daddy in no time," Jen teased as she tucked her arm through mine.

"I'm sure Aidan would love that."

"Possessive, is he?" She snorted. "Don't answer. If he comes from the same school as Finn, then he times you when you go for a piss."

I blinked. "Huh?"

"She says it's endearing."

"Endearing?" I repeated, laughing a little. "You're going to have to give me some backstory."

She wafted a hand. "I guess I can now. It was always weird not being able to talk about them, but Finn is mega intense where Aoife's concerned.

"Anyway, when she was pregnant with Jake, she went to the bathroom and didn't come back for a while. He just thought, ya know, baby stuff. There's lots of gross crap that comes out of you when you're pregnant." She shuddered in disgust. "Anyway, Aoife puked, somehow managed to crack her head on the toilet, then passed out on the floor. Ever since, Finn monitors her."

"Is she pregnant again?"

"Nah. He's just obsessed. It's like if he takes his eyes off her, she might disappear." She pulled a face. "It's creepy, but she digs it."

My lips curved. "Well, as long as she's okay with it, that's all that matters, right?"

"I guess." She hummed. "Who's that?"

"Who's who?" I asked, following her line of sight. "I have no idea," I replied, seeing exactly who she meant. "Jesus, he's hot."

"You're taken now."

"We've been together for less than a day!" I retorted, but I was teasing and she knew it. She also did this thing with her arms that plumped up her tits. Rolling my eyes at her, I muttered, "You're incorrigible."

The stranger wasn't someone I recognized, and neither did Aidan if his scowl was anything to go by. However, the way Aidan was holding his glass told me he wasn't angry. He was also curved slightly toward the stranger who'd taken Jen's seat, his shoulder cutting off the rest of the room while he listened to whatever the guy had to say.

I wasn't lying when I said he was hot, either. His hair wasn't long, but it curled about his ears, long enough to flop onto his forehead in a carelessly artless way that probably took him five minutes in the morning to sort out, but would take a woman four hours in front of the mirror. He had pitch dark eyes, a Roman nose, a jaw that if you bounced a ball off, said ball would crack, and he looked good in what I could tell was custom tailoring.

Every instinct in my body told me he was Italian.

Every instinct I possessed told me that he was mafia. Just not high up enough in the ranks to be newsworthy.

The bulge in his jacket that told me he was packing helped confirm that belief, but it was in the way he glanced around the room. My guards made similar moves—

Speaking of which, where the hell were my guards?

A quick scan of the room revealed three of them.

Seated in various places around the room, they were all watching me, and each had bruises on their faces.

Bad ones.

Jesus, Aidan had been at it again.

Before I could do much more than grimace with apology, Jen whispered in my ear, "Oh, my God, I think I just came."

I almost chuckled, but I realized why—he was looking directly at her.

And when I said directly, I meant it. It was like the twenty feet between us and the table were mere inches. Like the columns that had to diminish his view of her were non-existent. Whenever a waiter switched into her path, he didn't appear to notice.

Shooting a look at Jen, I saw, unusually enough, that she'd blushed. There was no coquettish pouting, no smizing, no teasing smiles or hot glances. Nope, she was bright pink.

"Do you recognize him?" I muttered, trying to figure out what was going on with her.

Jen's initial reaction to plump up her tits when in the vicinity of a hot, rich guy was her standard MO. Blushing and falling silent? Not so much.

"No," she whispered, her hand tightening on my arm.

"Are you okay?" I whispered back, concerned now.

"I'm fine," she replied, her voice thick.

About to bully her into telling me what the hell was going on, I saw that Aidan had realized the stranger's attention was elsewhere, and that led to him seeing that I was there.

His nostrils flared at the sight of me walking toward him, and I wasn't about to lie—I strutted the hell out of that short walk. With every passing second, his tension increased, his jaw hardened, and I just knew his boner grew more and more painful.

I almost sighed with delight.

This sweet agony of need was mutual.

Thank God for small mercies.

With their attention on us, we were a silent group as, finally, we made it back to the table. The Italian got to his feet while Aidan made an effort to stand but I pressed my hand to his shoulder and murmured, "Just scoot over."

His nostrils flared as he reached up and tangled our fingers together.

I blinked at him, almost forgetting that we weren't alone, that the table had other people sitting at it, and that we were in a very busy bar. At that moment, I wanted nothing more than to be back in the elevator, me on my knees, his cock in my mouth.

Almost drooling at the thought, I slipped into the booth when he finally shifted along, and as I did, I saw that the stranger's intense stare hadn't died a death at all. Proximity be damned.

Jen, on the other hand, was staring down at the table.

This was weird.

Why wasn't she flirting with him? Charming him?

"Savannah, Jennifer, please, meet Luciu Valentini."

I tensed, shot Aidan a look, received a brisk nod of his chin that involved him dipping his head forward a scant half-inch, and had my confirmation that this Valentini and the one Brennan had mentioned yesterday was, indeed, sitting at our table.

What on earth was going on?

"It is a pleasure to meet you, ladies," Valentini replied, his tone courtly but there was a lilt of an accent that made his voice sinful. It wasn't just Italian. It was far more complex than that. I'd never heard a Sicilian accent before, but I guessed today was a day for firsts.

Aidan tipped his glass down and said, "Jen, your guest sent a note. He isn't coming."

Jen didn't even scowl, just reached for the drink in front of her. Aidan, in our absence, had poured some whiskey into the glass the waitress had brought us, and that was the one she grabbed and, subsequently, lost her bet with Aidan over as she started coughing the second the liquor hit her tongue.

Aidan chuckled, but Valentini pressed a hand to her arm and asked, "Do you need some water?"

Jen tensed and, mid-cough, peered down at his arm. Her cheeks, already bright pink, flushed some more. "I'm fine, thanks."

"I think you just lost your bet, Jen," I teased her gently.

"Bet?" Valentini crooned.

It was hard to think this was the guy who routinely made a habit of slicing up people's faces, leaving them permanently scarred. What he did to them wasn't pretty, but then, hadn't Aidan said he'd flayed someone? I mean... there was very little that was more gory than that.

"Jen keyed her ex's Ferrari," Aidan murmured, his tone droll as he took a small sip of whiskey. "We had a bet going on so she could earn some money to pay him off."

As far as I knew, that was his one and only measure too.

"He was cheating on me!" Jen sputtered, some of her usual fire returning and replacing the weird coyness I wasn't used to. "What was I supposed to do?"

Valentini propped his elbows on the table. "The fool cheated on you?"

Ignoring his question, I grinned at her. "Dump his lying ass?"

She heaved a sigh. "Well, I did that afterward. Keying his car was more satisfying."

Valentini smirked. "A woman with a taste for vengeance, interesting."

Aidan rolled his eyes, then sank back his whiskey. "If the prick isn't going to show up, our reason for being here is obsolete." To the stranger, he murmured, "I'll speak with my father. You have my word."

For the first time, Valentini looked away from Jen. It was pretty amusing to be honest. Like something from an adult Disney movie. He might as well have love hearts on stalks popping out of his eyes, and she was totally doing that coy Minnie Mouse thing too. Turning all bashful and shy when Jen was about as shy as a whore in a convent.

"I appreciate it," he intoned calmly, his eyes darkening as he looked at Aidan. "Men of their word are hard to find."

"I don't disagree," was Aidan's reply. "But I make no promises. You know as well as I do that my father dances to his own beat."

Valentini's lips quirked up in a smile that, I had to admit, was breathtaking. Sultry and smoky, his eyes gleamed like they were prickled with gold dust as his mouth, those full lips, curved invitingly.

He was Jen's form of catnip. I just wondered why she wasn't taking a bite. She didn't cower in front of Aidan, and by her own admission, she knew Finn well. The O'Donnellys were beautiful men—she was used to being around them so why she was being bashful now, I had no idea.

"I can handle rejection. I just would like an opportunity to present myself to him. Court him, as it were."

Aidan smiled, and shot me a look, and I knew we were both thinking the same thing—that was how we'd met. Because I'd been trying to court Aidan Sr.

"If you're honest with your intentions, then I don't see why he'll disapprove of the move. I'll be seeing him for the holidays. I'll speak with him."

"I appreciate you marring *Natale* with business."

"It's in all our interests." To Jen, he said, "I'm taking Savannah home. I'll pick up your tab if you want to eat—"

Valentini rested his hand on Jen's arm once more, but his fingers trickled up her forearm, the tip tracing a shape that had goosebumps flickering to life there. I wasn't surprised when she gasped in response.

Either he didn't hear her, or that was the reaction he wanted because, calm as you like, as he told Aidan, "There's no need for that. The tab is on me."

Aidan arched a brow, then he smirked as he picked up the bottle of whiskey. "An Irishman never hits up the chance for a freebie."

Valentini's brows rose in surprise, more at Aidan's teasing than his cheek. "And a Sicilian doesn't mind investing in his future allies."

"Touché." Aidan nodded at him, but his smirk didn't die as he gently prodded my leg to encourage me to move.

Before I did, I glanced at Jen and, needing to give her an out—though I highly doubted she'd take it, not after our conversation in the restroom—asked, "Hon, do you want to stay or come up with me?"

I noticed Valentini's fingertips gently pressed into her wrist. Not to the point of pain, more of a caress, but either way, it was a silent indication that he wanted her to say no.

Because Jen was Jen, I was damn sure she would come with me just to spite him, even though reeling him in was exactly what she'd declared she wanted as we left the restroom, but she didn't. She shot me a wide-eyed smile, swallowed, then breathily murmured, "I'll text you later."

I leaned over the table and demanded, "You'd better."

With that, I slid out of the booth then got to my feet. Aidan made it to my side, and said, "Valentini."

"O'Donnelly."

"A pleasure to meet you, Luciu," I said softly, deciding to relieve some of the formality.

He smiled at me. "The pleasure was all mine, Savannah."

Aidan gripped my elbow and started to steer me away from the table. I got the feeling he didn't like Valentini smiling at me... I wasn't going to complain about that.

As we moved away, I tilted my head to the side and asked, "What did he want?"

Grunting, Aidan murmured, "Later."

I scowled, pretty sure he wouldn't tell me at all, and that his version of later was when I was a hundred, but before I could chide him, someone called out, "Savannah!"

I knew that voice.

I'd had to listen to it every goddamn morning for four and a half years.

Stewart Allsheim had been my co-anchor through blizzards, hurricanes, presidential campaigns and TikTok.

For all that he'd played one of the biggest parts in my life of late, we'd never liked each other. While he never did or said anything to indicate he was a creep, that was because he was too smart. Smarmy, to boot.

Grimacing as he approached from a table that was near the door —something I recognized as being low on the real estate at the restaurant—I plastered on a fake smile because people were watching.

His hands were outstretched, his arms wide as he moved in to give me a hug, but before he could, before he could even try to air kiss me, Aidan stepped right in front of me, and asked, "Who the hell are you?"

Stewart frowned like he didn't understand the question.

I had to smile because we'd played a large role in a massive chunk of New York's breakfasts together, and Aidan also owned a part of TVGM so there was no way in hell he didn't know exactly who Stewart was. It was a power play. God, that sent shivers down my spine.

I didn't mind him being a possessive asshole, not when it meant I didn't have to endure a hug from my creep ex-co-worker.

Resting a hand on the center of his back, I peered around him to ask, "Stewart, long time no see."

"You know how it goes, Savannah. The news never stops. Seeing as you're front and center of it right now, I guess you'd know that more than me." He beamed at me like he was on some kind of deranged happy pills. "I know the station's been trying to get in touch with you."

"I'm well aware, Stewart. I have no desire to talk to the people who fired me for raising awareness about the toxic workplace that TVGM has been for the last few years." I made sure I didn't lower my voice, and because people were listening in, the hush that fell at that moment was classic. As was how Stewart's face fell. "I won't be selling my story to TVGM any time soon, and if you think you can try and hoodwink me, well..." I leaned around Aidan and pressed a hand to Stewart's chest before I gently patted him there. "...you and I both know we never had that type of friendship. Now, I hope you enjoy your meal, but you can tell TVGM from me that they can go straight to hell."

I strode off, aware that Aidan was at my back, and the doors opened wide like they were being pulled open by magic as I stalked through them.

The maître d' looked like he was going to bow, but if he did, I didn't notice, I was too busy storming into the private elevator. I turned around when I felt it dip slightly, and seeing Aidan pull out a pass and swipe it, I watched as the doors closed, and relaxed at once.

"I didn't expect to see him tonight," I grumbled.

"No love lost between you, was there?"

There was a faint growl to his voice, and it was second nature to reach for his hand and to slide my fingers through his. "He never said or did anything to agitate me."

"A miracle in itself," Aidan half-mocked, making me grin up at him.

"He was just a creep. That's all."

"That's enough."

I shrugged. "It wasn't that bad that you need to repeat whatever you did to my guards... You did beat them up, right?"

"Their incompetence almost cost you your life." He arched a brow at me. "What do you think?"

"And Wintersen..." I eyed him beneath my lashes. "What did you do to him?"

"Culpable deniability. I know you've heard of—" Before he could finish that sentence, the elevator jerked to a halt.

"Oh, great," I growled, sure that it was a power shortage or something.

Then, the lights cut out, before they flickered on again and the elevator car rattled once more, jolting us both. Aidan let out a gasp of pain which told me he'd rocked back on his bad leg.

Before I could even screech that this was weird, and I'd been in a broken-down elevator many times—this was New York, after all—it dropped.

Literally dropped.

Heart in my ears, I fell back against the corner, hands coming up to cup the wall, flattening them there. The glass was slick beneath my palms thanks to the perspiration beading my skin. My reaction was as instantaneous as the breakdown of this fucking machine.

"Aidan," I screamed when the damn thing jerked to a stop.

"It's okay, little one," he thundered, sounding anything but okay as he fell back against the corner before sliding across to me.

His arm tunneled around my waist and he hauled me into him as the elevator car rocked once more. With his other hand, he dragged his cellphone out of his jacket pocket, pushed the button on the side, then hollered at Siri, "Call Conor!"

His arm tightened around me as the mechanics beneath us made a groaning sound that was like nothing I'd ever heard in my life, a sound that I never wanted to hear again, a noise that would haunt me for the rest of my life if I even lived that long.

My mind flashed back to Emilio Estévez at the beginning of *Mission Impossible*, all the while I tried to tell myself it was like that fucking ride at Disney World. The one where your stomach felt as if it were falling through your body as you were plummeted tens of floors at a time before being dragged up the tower again.

This time, when it dropped, I screamed. It was squeezed out of me by gravity, like I was an overripe orange in need of juicing.

The lights flashed on, then off, and Aidan's arm tightened around me before he let go, and twisted around so he was facing the door. I could feel his heat, so intense, such a forceful amount of energy as if—

God.

I felt the protection coming from him.

I felt the way he pushed me into the corner, shielding me with his body.

Oh, God.

He thought we were going to die, but not by this elevator crashing.

He thought it was going to be stormed.

Tears prickled my eyes as the car came to a juddering halt, and then Conor hollered, "I'm on it!"

"Are we going to be boarded?" Aidan snarled, his ass shoving me deeper into the corner as if by squeezing me, he could make me a smaller target.

As grateful as I was, my terror soared.

What if he was hit?

What if he was shot again?

I sobbed, unashamed to be dealing with my terror at that moment, needing simply to let it flood out of me as I shoved my forehead between his shoulders.

I'd have called myself a pussy, but two murder attempts in less than forty-eight hours was just too much for me.

I pressed my arms around his waist, holding him close, needing his solid strength, his staunch resolve.

Aidan wasn't scared.

He was in fight mode.

He was *angry*.

Hell, that was an understatement.

He was fucking FURIOUS.

He throbbed with it as Conor snapped, "I don't have time to talk."

Over the thunderous beat of my heart in my ears, I could hear the pounding of his fingers against the keyboard.

When there was another groan, a creaking snarl from the mechanics beneath us, I tensed, preparing myself for that horrendous feeling of the floor being stolen out from under us, and then, out of nowhere, there was a whining, screeching noise and the entire mechanism shuddered like we were in the middle of an earthquake.

Except, we were fifty stories up.

Maybe less, considering I had no idea how far we'd fallen.

The jarring halt had Aidan releasing another snarl and I grabbed a hold of him, trying to steady him so his bad knee didn't take as much of a hit, but it was no use.

The lights flickered, before they flashed off permanently. The elevator made a whining sound, the floor beneath us released another creak, and then there was silence. Aside from my harsh exhalations and his.

"Conor? Talk to me!" he demanded, calmer this time, which told me he thought the danger was under control for the moment.

In turn, that surety settled inside me and I released a snotty sob as I hugged him harder.

We'd almost died, hadn't we?

Again.

Those fucking bastard Sparrows.

Those motherfucking pussy assholes.

I was going to fuck those fuckers up. Tear them to shreds. Rip them to pieces—

"I had to pull the kill switch."

Aidan rasped, "What does that mean in regards to our security?"

"The system was being overridden. The only way to kick out the intruder was to enter the kill switch sequence. The elevator's a brick now so you're safe because you're locked in there."

"A brick?" I whispered brokenly.

"It means it's useless. We'll need firefighters to fish us out," Aidan explained calmly, and though I had no idea how he was so fucking calm at that moment, it dramatically cut down on my panic.

I didn't let go of him, my hold on him absolute as I clung to him, feeling weak and like a pussy but SOMEONE HAD HACKED AN ELEVATOR TO TRY TO KILL ME. I thought I was well within my rights to feel goddamn shaken.

"We're going to have to change the internal computer. It's fried," Conor rumbled.

"How did they get in, Conor?" Aidan asked quietly.

I didn't know Conor, not at all in the grand scheme of things. But he released a snarl that was so like his brother's, it came as a surprise. Throughout that crisis, he'd been calm aside from the pounding of his fingers as he tried to save us.

"I'm working on it," was all Conor said.

"Da'll find out if we need firefighters."

"I know."

Aidan released a breath. "Prepare yourself for his bullshit."

"I'm already prepared," Conor snapped. "I'm going to work on shoring up the building's defenses, but though we can use the other elevators, it's not ideal—"

"Did they want us to freefall or did they want to board it?"

"They were taking you to the eighteenth floor."

"You've sent some of our men there?"

"Yes. I'll keep you updated on who was waiting."

"Trap them inside the building then take them to the Hole," Aidan commanded.

"Will do. I'll call Brennan's crew to get their help with hauling them over."

"Good. The Fire Department is on their way?"

"Yes. They were notified when I realized someone was hacking the elevators."

"This needs to stop happening, Conor."

His younger brother released a growl. "I fucking know, Aidan."

"Maybe we need to tell Da you have to have a break."

"A break?" Conor's laugh was the angriest sound I'd ever heard, and I'd been around a detoxing hair band that used coke like it was oxygen. "How's that going to go down, Aidan? We're neck-deep with the Sparrows.

"Look, I recognized someone had infiltrated the building's security. I was on it. I was just concerned. You were about to hit the eighteenth floor. I needed to not let that happen.

"Code was written to be broken. The expectation that mine is unbreachable is beyond unrealistic. I'm not a magician, and my work isn't sanctified. If it was, maybe then it'd never be breached. Unfortunately for us, I'm just a guy."

"You're not just anything to Da."

Conor growled. "Did you hear what I said?"

"I did, and I get it," Aidan soothed, using a tone I'd heard him use with me which was interesting. "I'll tell Da."

"This isn't about the fine," Conor growled. "This is about expectations, and his being impossible."

"Like they aren't for all of us," Aidan retorted.

Conor released a sharp breath. "You're not wrong there. Look, you're in between floors now. It's going to be awkward to get you out of there," he warned.

"Oh, my God, we dropped sixty floors?" I squeaked, my hands clutching Aidan's jacket as my brain finally allowed me to do math.

He reached down and patted my hand, his calm in this storm so clear that I recognized how he wasn't flustered by any of this.

I thought I knew what to expect from the mobster world. I'd spent more than half my life reading up on it, for God's sake. But this was so much more than I'd anticipated. Myopic, sure, but being in the spotlight was a hell of a lot different than researching light bulbs.

"You'll be stuck for a while," Conor finished, almost as if I hadn't spoken.

"We can't get any lights on in here?" Aidan rasped.

"No," came the brusque reply.

A soft whimper broke free from my lips, and it shamed me. The noise fucking shamed me as much as if I'd just pissed myself. They didn't need me to be weak, they needed me to be brave. Yet here I was, whimpering.

Neither of them wanted this.

Neither of them would even be involved in this if it weren't for me.

Aidan could have been killed and Conor was going to have to replace an expensive machine because of me.

I reached up and pressed a closed fist to my lips, but like he knew, like he felt what I was doing, Aidan shifted around, moving so that I knew he was facing me because I felt the flaps of his sport coat drift apart.

"Conor, get them to work as fast as you can, okay?"

"Of course. I'll pay them extra to get a move on."

"Keep me in the loop?"

"Will do. For the moment, I'm monitoring all elevator traffic. Only faces that pass the security metric and are identified as residents of The Sharpe *or* as recent visitors to The 68 will be allowed to use them. Even then, the elevators will only travel down, not up. Speak later."

I rocked my head back against the mirrored wall the second Conor's voice disappeared, and the only word that came into my mind was, "Sorry." I licked my lips. "I'm so sorry, Aidan."

He moved with a precision that I wasn't sure why I was surprised by. Aidan seemed like a magician to me, capable of pulling moves out of thin air like they were rabbits out of a top hat. His hand came up to rub his thumb along my cheek as he asked, "What are you sorry for?"

A bark of harsh laughter escaped me. "For putting your life in danger. For the inconvenience? For the expense?"

Aidan grunted. "I told you you weren't ready for this world. They're all costs of doing business, Savannah. It's a first that anyone's gotten into one of our buildings and done this, but people fuck with us all the time. Today's no different other than the elevator was carrying precious cargo."

I swallowed. "Your father would have been so mad at me—"

He released another grunt as he dipped forward and pressed a kiss to my temple. "Wasn't talking about me, little one."

A shaken sigh escaped me as I pressed into him, sliding my arms around his waist again and huddling into him. He immediately facilitated the move, holding me close, and as I pressed my ear to his chest, I heard the steady beat of his heart and knew that he really wasn't scared, knew that he really meant what he said.

To him, I was precious cargo.

Which settled me, somehow.

Deep inside, where all the shit was riled up, all the fear from yesterday and now this, all the adrenaline from the initial release of the exposés, the rush of writing the articles, it seemed to settle down.

Which was ironic because nobody rattled me more than he did.

Figuratively and literally.

I wasn't even sure how long we stayed standing there like that, but eventually, we heard knocking on the doors, some kind of creaking that had my heart pounding again, and someone called out, "We're working on getting you out of there."

Aidan's cell buzzed at the same time, and as he let go of me with one arm, I saw that his screen was lit up and could read Conor's message:

They're predicting it'll take over an hour.

Gulping, I whispered, "Aidan?"

As he put away his phone, he hummed. "Yeah?"

"Does nothing scare you?"

He grew quiet. "You really want to hear the answer to that?"

"Of course. I wouldn't have asked otherwise."

Slowly, he said, "Very little scares me."

"I want to be like that."

"You're fearless in your own way," he disregarded. "But you're used to being protected, and you're used to that protection being silent and hidden. There's a difference."

"Maybe."

"No 'maybe' about it."

"Pain suffocates me, but it doesn't trigger fear in me, just..." He sighed. "Desperation. That's a new Achilles' heel of mine.

"You weren't made for this life, Savannah. I'm not sure any woman is. I see my ma, she's been in this world since she was born, and it's broken her. The shit that's happened to her, the crap that's befallen us all things considered..." He hesitated. "You know that evening we ate together?"

"How could I forget?" I wasn't even teasing.

"You went to the restroom, and I was just sitting there, minding my own business, when two things happened." At his sigh, I braced myself for the worst. "This guy got on one knee and proposed to his girlfriend. She said yes," he muttered absentmindedly as his hand came up to toy with my hair.

I had no idea how he even saw the strand well enough to play with it, but I wasn't about to complain. I wouldn't have been shocked if he'd have pushed me away when he uttered those initial words, but instead, he was hauling me closer by connecting with me.

"That was a good thing, wasn't it?" I queried, nestling into him, not wanting any space between us. For all that this terrified me, the only thing that felt right was his presence.

His touch.

I didn't want to be anywhere other than with him—whether that was in an elevator or in Conor's apartment, it didn't matter.

"It was, I guess. I'm not exactly a romantic," he mocked. "We're not bred that way."

"You are, actually," I corrected quietly. "Everyone knows how much your parents love one another."

He grunted. "For Ma, it's more like goddamn Stockholm

Syndrome. Da, well, she's his. He loves her, but his love isn't the clean kind of Hallmark love everyone thinks about."

"No love is the Hallmark kind of love," I chided. "He went to war for her."

"After his business got her kidnapped and gang-raped," was Aidan's harsh retort. "She was a goddamn shell for months afterward. He had to hospitalize her at one point."

"Jesus, I didn't know." Everyone knew about the Aryans and how Aidan Sr. had annihilated them, just not the personal aftermath under the O'Donnellys' roof.

"Why would you? We paid a lot to make sure it never came out. God forbid, we look like humans to the rest of the world."

"Humans can be hurt. Gods can't."

He grunted. "True that."

I reached up and pressed my hand to his lapel. "I'm sorry about your mother."

"She's never been the same. Hopped up on meds most of the time. You'd never know it to look at her. Well, you'll see tomorrow. She plays a good game."

"Tomorrow?"

"Yeah. Conor has to replace the elevator, but we'd have been moving out regardless. We spend the 23rd at the family estate."

Jeez.

"You know, two days ago, I'd have been so excited about that."

He snorted. "I'll bet. Weirdo."

I wasn't offended. I'd been called worse over the years. Instead, I tugged on his lapel. "Carry on. Tell me what happened at the restaurant."

Aidan sighed. "It doesn't really matter."

"It does to me," I countered with a growl. "Aidan, that was the best first date ever. I-I never felt like that before or since. It was... jarring when you disappeared. I fully expected you to realize you'd made a mistake, but you never did," I ended softly. Sadly.

"Men in my family don't really propose to their women," he said with a grunt, his fingers still playing with my hair. "We don't get the chance. This generation is a little different but I've been reared knowing that my woman will be picked for me.

"I'd never get to do that whole bending down on one knee thing—ironic, of course, because now I couldn't fucking do that if I wanted to—but still, as I saw how much freedom that bastard had, I was envious. Envious because things were so right with you.

"I went into our initial meeting with zero expectations. I knew you were beautiful. Hell, a Google search told me that. But in the flesh, you were different. More different than anything I'd come across.

"I could see us dating. I could actually fucking see me reaching a point where I wanted to do that whole restaurant/engagement meal thing, and it freaked me the fuck out because I didn't know you. You just felt...right. It made no sense to me, and it still doesn't.

"What I knew back then was that Da already wanted you dead because of Paddy. If I wanted you in that way too, he'd have had double the reason to get rid of you—"

"He wouldn't have hurt me if he knew you had feelings for me, surely?" I argued, heart racing at his admission that I hadn't been alone in being crazy where he was concerned.

What I'd felt, this insta-lust/insta-need combo, he'd experienced too.

The validation soared inside me, taking away that weird sense that I'd been a creep or something, incapable of judging a good date from a bad one, reducing how big of a fool his ghosting me had made me feel. I mattered. His words mattered. More than he could know.

"Of course, he would have," Aidan rumbled tiredly. "You asked me if I ever get scared, Savannah. I don't because of my father. You can't be raised by him without learning what the real fear of God is like. There is no bigger monster in this city than him—" He gritted his teeth, I literally felt him grinding down as he rasped out, "then there's me."

"You're not a monster," I snapped, pissed on his behalf.

"I am," he countered. "I'm what he made me. We're all what he made us. The laws don't count for us, Savannah. What we do on the daily would make a normal man have nightmares and send him running to his therapist. I told you what I've done, that's not even a whisper of the other shit I've pulled over the years.

"Had he learned that I was dating you, I just knew how it would end."

"If you loved me, he wouldn't—"

"He doesn't care," Aidan ground out. "The Firm is all he cares about."

Tension hit me, freezing me up inside before I managed to get out, "Is that different now?"

"Maybe I'm different now. Maybe I needed to feel pain, to know what it was like to be addicted, to have to go through withdrawals, to really embrace what I needed to do."

"What's that?"

"I'm a monster's heir. I've been in his shadow all my life, but there reaches a point where you have to step out into the sunlight. I think now is that moment."

My breath rushed from my lungs. "Because of me?"

"Because of a lot of things," he corrected, "of which you are a large fraction. This isn't on you, Savannah. I don't want you thinking that you're the reason for a falling out between me and him. That's not your responsibility. It's been a long time coming, and you're my catalyst but there are a hell of a lot of reasons why this showdown is about to happen. You understand?"

I did, and I thought that was the exact moment when I knew that all these stupid feelings I'd had for him was love.

Insane, but true.

The feelings choked me, swamping me, drowning me, and I clung to him like a life raft, well aware that adrenaline might be the reason they were overwhelming me as my heart flushed my body with chemical-laden blood, but I didn't care. I didn't give a damn if it was insane or stupid. My feelings were my feelings, and he'd just validated them.

"I do," I whispered, and I slipped my hands up and around his neck. "What was the second thing that happened that night?"

"During the proposal, one of our enemies walked into the restaurant."

'Who?" I remarked, shocked.

"Benito Fieri. Striding in as cool as you fucking like into a restaurant on our territory. Tensions between us had been building for a while."

When he broke off, I frowned, and managed to piece together what he wasn't saying. "That call you received? It was something the Italians had done? Him walking in was a 'fuck you?'"

"Spoken like a true mafia aficionado," Aidan commented dryly, finally tucking that piece of hair behind my ear with an unerringness that had me wondering how brilliant his night vision was.

"That means I'm right," I whispered.

"It does. It was more than a fuck you, though. It was a reminder."

And yet, here he was, standing close to me. Not pushing me away.

"What's changed, Aidan?"

"Me. You. You're a little less bright and shiny than you once were. Time and the job has had an effect on you.

"On this occasion, you weren't poking your nose in the corners of our business, trying to figure shit out and coming face to face with a mousing cat. No, you stepped into my world, and I'm the only person who can keep you safe."

My throat bobbed. "Are you going to hold that over me?"

He laughed. "From what you know of me, what do you think the answer to that is?"

"Yes. But I'll like how you do it."

His laughter deepened, and then he reached down and stole my breath by pressing a kiss to my nose. "I'll hold it over you for an eternity, Savannah, because I'm not letting you go this time. I tried, and it failed, and it..." He growled. "I don't want to do that again. Whether you like it or not, you've waded into something that's bigger than you—"

"I know. But when I'm with you, I'm not afraid." Not for my life. *For his.*

My lips curved, and even though I was shaken inside, and even though my words frightened me a little, there was a wholehearted truth to them.

This man would die for me. He'd proven that tonight when he'd stepped in front of me, shielding me with his body. What other man would do that? It was a testament to who he was.

What he was.

So for all that I believed my next words as I uttered them, to me, he'd only ever be Aidan. *My Aidan.* "Why do I have to be afraid when Manhattan's second biggest monster is at my side?"

TWENTY-FIVE

AIDAN

THE SECOND WE WERE FREED, we took the general maintenance elevator to the penthouse.

Savannah, unsurprisingly, was exhausted, and to be frank, I was too because I hadn't slept the night before. Still, the exhaustion went deeper than that. The hits were coming at us from all angles, and though my brothers were on the case as well, the rest of the Five Points too as we dealt with the Sparrows, it was different now.

Savannah was involved.

The woman I'd tried to protect all these years.

The woman I'd kept my eye on all this time.

The woman who, despite all the shit I'd tried to do to protect her, to keep her out of this life, was here anyway.

If that wasn't fucking fate, I didn't know what was.

So, when we made it upstairs, I came to the decision that we could spend the night here.

Tomorrow, we'd have been heading to the family estate in upstate New York anyway. With one of two access points to this apartment out of commission, and Conor having done something to make sure that the general maintenance elevator we'd used was shut down, I knew we were safe for one night.

Especially as, knowing him, that meant he was sleeping in the damn contraption, and I couldn't complain. I figured he knew what Savannah meant to me, or at least, he did after we made it upstairs, with her shaken and quiet, huddling under the arm I had hooked around her shoulders.

Either way, I knew no one else would be getting in here tonight, not without going through Conor, so that enabled me to let my guard down a little. Just enough to get a few hours rest as she did too.

None of this was expected.

None of it.

Didn't take away from how fucking right it felt.

Especially with her curved into me. Somehow apart but connected.

I'd shared my bed with very few women, but each time, they'd been clingers. As if clinging to me there was a way to cling to me through the day.

Spoiler alert: it hadn't worked.

Savannah was huddled on her side into a tight ball, but she was distinctly on her half of the mattress, while one hand drifted toward me. Not invasive, giving me space, so whenever I woke up, which was every hour or so because I rarely slept the full night through, I knew she was nearby.

Close enough to touch.

Exactly what I'd needed these past five fucking years without her.

After I woke up for the eighth time in two hours, I decided that my body was warning me about something.

Not one to let my instincts be ignored, I got out of bed with as much stealth as I was capable of. Which was to say, not much.

I grunted as pain slammed into me, but I gritted my teeth and blew out a breath, trying to let out the discomfort, manage it the best way I could now—through breathing and shit that Conor told me was beneficial—fucking meditation. A goddamn mobster meditating. Talk about a joke.

Either way, it spoke of how tired she was that she didn't stir regardless of the fucking shit show that was me in stealth mode.

The urge to protect her was strong. Stronger than it had ever been before.

I'd never thought I could feel so much for someone after such a short length of time, but that was the difference. I'd watched her for so long that I knew more about her than she would ever imagine.

Just as, I realized, she was with me, because I highly doubted that inquisitive mind of hers would have stopped researching the family—she'd just have been quieter than before.

We had a five-year courtship under our belts. Without either of us realizing it.

Huffing at the thought, I hobbled into the hall and trudged down toward Conor's office. When I found it empty, I checked the sofa first before I headed to the room off the kitchen where the other elevator was situated behind a locked door, figuring he was in there like I'd thought earlier.

As I ambled into it, I heard a faint noise coming from the walk-in freezer and, rolling my eyes at the sound, knocked on the door to the elevator, calling out, "It's me."

A minute later, Conor opened the doors. His hair was all over the place like he'd been tugging on it, and his eyes were red-rimmed from fatigue.

I was used to him looking wired but this was getting beyond a joke. When a guy looked worse than the addict in the family, that was fucked up.

I didn't say anything though, because he was guarding Savannah while I'd rested, and instead asked, "Who's in the walk-in?"

He blinked. "The two guys who were waiting for you on the eighteenth floor."

He said that like it was obvious.

"Why did you bring them up here? I told you to have them taken to the Hole."

"I wanted to try something."

"Try what?"

He smirked. "You sure you want to know?"

"Wouldn't have asked if I didn't," I grumbled. "Spit it out."

"I've been fucking with a Taser."

"Suping it up?"

"Yep," he replied cheerfully.

"You tested it on them yet?"

"Nah. Wanted to freeze them a bit."

I snorted. "Sick fuck."

He winked. "Takes one to know one. Plus, I don't know, I thought it would alter the impact on their system."

"Wouldn't it dampen it?"

"Maybe. It's a test. I have the freezer up here, so why wouldn't I try it? Brennan can always experiment on one of the other poor fuckers who end up at the Hole. This is a good opportunity."

Interested, I asked, "Wanna try it now?"

"Shouldn't you be asleep?"

"Yeah, but I can't settle."

"Your penguin okay?"

I scowled at him a second, thinking he was joking, then I remembered what he'd called her when he'd first learned her identity, so I heaved a sigh. "No nightmares or anything. She was freaked in the elevator."

"You really do like her, huh?" He eyed me curiously. "Not seen you so protective of someone before. You're normally a bit of a selfish asshole."

I smirked and threw his own words back at him, "Takes one to know one."

He shrugged. "I make no bones about it. Either way, don't hide from the question."

"I'm not. You know she means more to me than usual otherwise I wouldn't give a fuck about her situation and would have dumped her on Brennan or Declan."

"True. Funny how you're skirting the conversation."

"Mostly because there isn't a conversation to have yet."

"You're taking her to Christmas Dinner?"

"Yes."

A knowing gleam appeared in his eyes. "Aidan and Savannah, sitting in a tree, K-I-S-S-I-N-G."

I scowled at his mockery. "What are you? Eight?"

"In spirit if not in body," he retorted, moving into a sweeping bow. "Either way, if you're willing to take her there, that says more than you not dumping her on Dec or Bren. Da will have questions. You know we don't take people over there unless they're about to become a part of the family."

I pursed my lips. "You finished?"

"No. I mean, let's face it, I'd prefer him to focus on you and Savannah. It means he'll give me less shit about the hack. I'm just trying to warn you. That's all."

"I know. I appreciate it, Kid." I clapped him on the back. "Let me worry about Da."

"Well, I will, but you know he's gonna have ideas about you and I marrying someone."

"I know."

"Probably an Italian someone," he prodded.

"That's not going to happen. Anyway, in the chaos, I forgot. Luciu Valentini was waiting for me at The 68."

"The Valentini Bren was talking about the other night?"

"Yesterday," I corrected dryly. "It just feels like a fucking week ago." I grunted. "Anyway, yeah. He has a proposition for us."

"I'll bet." Conor's tone was dry. "Either way, I'm more interested in this declaration you're about to throw down with Da. As long as you know what it means..."

"He's going to think she's my girlfriend. He's going to think this is a run up to me proposing," I retorted, annoyed with the conversation.

"I know, Conor. Trust me, I know. I'm still going to do it. I should have fucking done it years ago."

"Really?" Conor arched a brow. "Hmm. You known her long?"

"Five years." I tipped my chin up. "Like you didn't know that already, which means this fishing session is over."

"You gonna marry her?"

"Maybe."

"Unlike you to not be decisive. Although, the Oxy's changed you, of course. Don't think it's made you less of an arrogant schmuck."

Despite myself, I snickered. "Thanks, bro."

"Welcome."

"And yes, maybe. It's way too soon."

"You see it heading that way?"

I'd seen it heading that way five fucking years ago. It was as insane then as it was now, but that didn't take away from the truth of the matter, did it?

"You ever meet Star?" I asked softly.

"No. We only recently talked on the phone."

Well, that was a new development. "You like her, don't you?"

"Yes."

"Wanna fuck her?"

"Yep."

"Know what she looks like?"

"I get where you're coming from," he said dryly. "I wanted to fuck her before I knew she was Star Sullivan and knew what she looked like."

"Attraction, chemistry, need, lust, love, it doesn't have to make sense."

"Agreed."

"Sometimes, you just have to go with what feels right, and something has felt right about Savannah for a long ass time."

"I'm glad, Aidan. You were lost for a long time and I wasn't sure what would bring you back to us. I'm glad that you cleaned up before she came along. I'd like to think that was for a reason. I'd like to think that you were preparing yourself for her."

"Didn't know you were a romantic, Kid."

He hummed. "Only for the people who matter most to me." His hand came up to my arm and he squeezed my bicep. "You know I'd go through hell for you, Aidan."

My throat closed. "I know, Con. I know."

Our eyes clashed, and the years skipped away. My stomach churned as I remembered Kid's face back then, so way back in the past when he'd been young and innocent, before that had been defiled. Christ, that was when I'd been young, not so innocent, not so pure, but I hadn't killed yet.

Father McKenna was the start of a slippery slope, but for all my sins, his was probably the worst in the eyes of God, and yet, I'd never atone for it. If it sent me straight into the Devil's clutches, I'd go. A thousand times over, I'd go.

For Kid.

For what had been done to him.

To my baby bro.

He'd always be that. No matter his age or mine, he'd always be Kid, and would always be someone I'd die for.

"You wanna taze some assholes?" I rasped.

"I'm down for that," he said softly.

So we did, after grabbing the semi-frozen bastards who thought they could hurt my woman, we headed to the one room in his apartment that was soundproofed—his bedroom—to do the deed.

There really was nothing like brotherly bonding over torture.

TWENTY-SIX

SAVANNAH

"YOU NERVOUS?"

"No," I muttered with a huff, peeking into the mirror to check my make-up.

It had taken a while to conceal the rainbow of bruises on my jawline, never mind the hickeys Aidan had given me. I wasn't complaining, but they made me a little nervous.

Who wanted to meet the parents for the first time with their throat looking like something Dracula had been gnawing on?

It was all fun behind the bedroom door, but for Christmas dinner? Nope.

"Why do you keep messing with the hem of your jacket then?"

I heard the amusement in his voice, and rolled my eyes. "I'm about to meet a hero."

Aidan shook his head. "Fucking Isardo."

My lips curved. "Hey, if it wasn't for him and years' worth of therapy, we'd never have met."

He smirked at the road, and I had to drool a little at how the veins and muscles in his forearms were in stark relief as he commanded the wheel of his Range Rover. I already knew this was a secured version, because it drove heavy as if it were a tank.

"What did you really do with Wintersen?" I asked, curious because he'd raised the subject of Isardo.

As we pulled up at a stop light, he shot me a look. "What do you think?"

There was such disdain in his voice I had to laugh.

"Guess that was a bit of a 'duh.'"

He shrugged. "Least I could do."

"Funny how you've swept through my life like you pick up trash for a living, but you always stuck to the sidelines, never coming forward, so I didn't have a chance of seeing you in the full light of day, did I?"

"For your own safety."

"I'd have preferred you."

"You say that now," he intoned quietly as he set off again.

"No, I know that now. I knew it back then. The last few nights gave me a taste of mob life, sure, but Aidan, I've always been in danger. There's no difference. One of my father's psycho fans is just as likely to torture and rape me as much as one of your enemies—"

"Jesus, Savannah!" He slammed on the brakes, making me grateful no one was behind us in traffic. "Don't even fucking talk like that!"

Touched, I turned to him with a soft smile. "I didn't mean to freak you out."

"No? Well, you did."

"Thought nothing scared you," I mocked, deciding that if the bear wouldn't poke me, then I could poke him.

His hands tightened on the wheel. "I don't want you even thinking shit like that."

"Thought it for long enough. I think we all accepted it after one of the twins got kidnapped. You know how fans are about my father and the rest of *noxxious*."

"I do," he grumbled, and his tension flooded the car, intoxicating me with how much he cared. "Conor's not exactly stable where they're concerned."

My smile widened. "Didn't realize any of him was stable."

Aidan laughed a little. "Don't make me laugh."

"I'm only teasing. He reminds me of Einstein."

"If Einstein had any idea what a computer was."

"Well, he would have. The Antikythera mechanism was discovered in the nineteen hundreds."

He blinked at me. "The anti-what?"

"The first analogue computer." I wafted a hand. "Never mind."

His grin made an appearance and, like always, on the few occasions I'd seen him smile, it felt like I'd won an award. That was, I saw, the moment you knew how much someone meant to you... when their smile felt like a Pulitzer.

"We almost there?" I asked.

"Yeah."

"I feel like a kid going to Disney," I admitted.

"It's really not that impressive."

"I'm about to go to the Five Points' mothership, Aidan," I groused. "This is about as impressive as it gets."

"You keep it up, I'll start to think you're only in this for my father."

I snickered. "You keep on thinking that." I fidgeted with my suit jacket. "I really should have worn black like you warned me."

"I was only teasing. It's not a funeral," he scoffed. "You look hot."

The low rumble in his voice had me squirming in my suit. "That was my intention." I cast him a look. "I didn't forget about what was supposed to happen in that elevator last night."

"You mean before we were hijacked?" was his droll retort.

"Yes, I mean before then. I have a very fertile imagination," I told him with a pout. "I was looking forward to applying lipstick to your dick. It was going to be the prettiest in the city."

He snorted out another laugh, then did something that made my pussy clench. There was nothing complicated about the move, nothing intense either—Aidan just rested his hand on my thigh, then squeezed. *Gently.*

But it stayed there.

His hand stayed there.

Oh, my God, it didn't move.

His fingers were tipped in, tilted up toward the apex of my thighs, and it was hot. So hot. So much like a brand that I knew I needed to have sex soon again because apparently, I'd been sex deprived before.

"I can deal with having the prettiest cock in the city," he told me.

"Won't be a score against your masculinity?"

He grinned at me, and that grin told me that he was entirely unaware about how his simple claiming affected me. "Maybe if I applied it myself. But I think it can handle it if you were the one who put it on for me."

His eyes were twinkling and my heart just plopped in my chest.

Love, I could confirm, made you stupid.

Seriously.

I had a Masters in Journalism and Mass Communication. I was a seasoned reporter, had broken countless stories, had been a news anchor on the most watched morning show in the nation, and was now going to be the face of the New World Sparrows' end of days.

Things were about to go Revelations on their asses, and I was going to be the face of that, so, no, Aidan had no right to tangle my ovaries in a bunch. Seriously.

"Well, it's a shame we're staying in your parents' place."

He arched a brow at me. "Why is it a shame?"

I gasped. "Well, we can't have sex under their roof."

His brow arched higher. "We sure as fuck can. I'm not sixteen. As far as I know, you're not either."

"Time hasn't turned back on me," I confirmed. "You can't expect me to make sex noises in your parents' home. I'm loud. We both know this." I mean, I wasn't usually, but yesterday, it'd been like the office in NASA when one of their rockets launched successfully.

"I'll kiss you to keep you quiet. Last thing I want is anyone hearing you."

My eyes flared wide, and I squirmed some more. "I mean, I thought they were really traditional?"

"They are. But I'm not a kid, and it's time they realized that. I'll handle them. There's no way the night is ending without you in my bed."

My lips curved. "Such a rebel."

"Oh, yeah, rebelling at forty-fucking-two." He rolled his eyes. "Tells you how under the thumb we all goddamn are." His hand tightened on the steering wheel. "Well, not anymore."

I gulped. "I thought the goal here was to make your father like me."

"It is. But if he doesn't, it's tough shit. I've decided."

He said that like it was a blanket statement. So, curiously, I queried, "What have you decided?"

"That I'm not accepting anymore of his bullshit." He grunted as he took a turn that would maneuver us off-road and onto a private street.

Nerves hit me, and I asked, "Are we almost there?"

"No. We're ten minutes away. I want to head to my place first. My—*Our,*" he corrected quickly, "gifts for the family are there."

I blinked, trying not to melt at his inclusion. "Why don't we just stay here, then?"

He turned to look at me as we pulled up outside a massive set of gates. "Because it's Christmas." Those words were uttered with the utmost severity. Like he was a kid awaiting Santa Claus.

"Okay, then," I said sheepishly.

Everything about this was crazy to me. We were heading upstate to the family estate for dinner today, and we'd spend Christmas Eve there, but we'd return to Manhattan for Midnight Mass, then drive back, and spend the weekend there.

Why we weren't just staying in the city until Midnight Mass was beyond me. Not that my ecological-loving ass was complaining—even though I really was trying hard not to imagine how much gas this tank was guzzling—because I was too excited about meeting the O'Donnelly patriarch, but still, it was clear to me they took the holiday seriously.

The house itself was like a dream. Once the gates opened up, it revealed a garden that was pretty much landscaped to high heaven.

There were large patterns in the lawn that reminded me of regal crop circles, because they were all surrounded by privets, and they all stood in a deep cascade, high to low where the house was, to shield the property in a kind of manicured neatness that belonged in the Queen of Hearts' yard in Alice in Wonderland.

Then there was the mansion.

I was rich. My family was rich. My dad had a sixty-two room property in Santa Clara, for God's sake, but this place looked as if it had been dragged, brick by brick, from the UK to here.

The only way I could measure it was that it had fourteen windows across and was three stories high.

It was antique stone, had cast iron decorations, and more stone molding than Notre-Dame Cathedral. There were even gargoyles, for Christ's sake.

At the front, there was a fountain, and it was a roundabout that he drove around to park.

"Holy shit," I breathed.

He rolled his eyes. "Ostentatious, right?"

Surprised, I laughed. "A little. I wouldn't have expected—"

"No, me either. Da had it built after the accident. He wanted me close so that if there was a problem, I was nearby."

"It looks like he dismantled a house from the UK."

"Probably did, knowing him. The masonry is definitely from another property, but the design inside is more modern. We even have running hot water and everything."

Chuckling, I unfastened the seatbelt and asked, "Is the place empty?"

He nodded. "I sent the staff away while I was with Conor."

"There are rehab centers with crazy strict NDA rules," I mused, "strong enough that most of the times my dad and his band mates attended, no one even knew, so why did you do that? Why go to your brother?"

His jaw tensed, and I knew, point blank, that he was going to lie to me. "He's one of the few people I trust."

I frowned at him. "Don't lie."

"I'm not lying," he grumbled as he climbed out of the car.

When I hopped out and met him at the front steps, I groused back, "You totally are lying. I just don't know why."

"It's insane," he groused as he pulled out his keys from a pocket.

"I can deal with insane."

"You say that now," was his droll retort.

"Aidan," I growled, exasperated because I sensed something was going on. My spidey senses were tingling. "Tell me!"

He shot me a mutinous look. "You were on the floor below."

I blinked. "Yeah. What about it?"

"I've known you lived there for fucking months, Savannah. I've avoided Conor's building as a result, even though I know there was little chance of us ever meeting because the penthouse has different entrances, but when I cleaned up, I just... it sounds insane to me too, but I wanted to be close to you."

For a second, I just stood there, processing his words, and then I pulled my arm back and socked him in the chest.

"You jackass," I yelled, doubly pissed when my socking him in the chest didn't even rock him back on his heels, which then made me gasp as I grabbed a hold of him as I remembered his injury. Oh, my God, I was such a bitch! "I'm so sorry! Did that hurt your knee?"

His hands came up to cover my wrists, as both sets of fingers were clutching and creasing his very expensive jacket. "Savannah, it's okay."

"I could have hurt you."

"No offense, sweetheart, but Brennan is starting to train my brothers' women in self-defense... You really need to take that class."

I squinted up at him. "Are you trying to tell me I have a weak right hook?"

He smirked. "I'm not trying to tell you anything. I'm telling you."

"Don't make me forget about what you just said, you asshole. Not only did I not move from my old building for years, I was in The Sharpe for months! I picked that building to be close to a goddamn O'Donnelly. I was hoping it was you but didn't know for sure.

"You felt that much for me that, at your lowest, you wanted to be close, yet you still didn't reach out?" I wanted to rail him, and then, when I saw the gentle amusement in his eyes, I processed why. "I need you to stop looking out for me, Aidan."

"Not going to happen."

"No, seriously." I grabbed his shirt. "If it means you don't get to be a part of my life, then you need to stop it. Now."

His lips twisted into a smile, but then, something snagged his attention. His head whipped to the side, and he peered at the grand glass and cast iron-curlicue door. Whatever he saw had him dragging me behind him.

Scowling, I cupped my weak wrist, the one he'd grabbed, and peering into the house so I could see what had scared him, muttered, "What's going on? I can't see anything."

"I thought I saw movement—"

He started scanning the property line, the exact opposite of inside the house where I thought he'd been looking, but I stood my ground and bit off. "Is this you not looking out for me?"

His head whipped back to face me, and there was fire in his eyes as he snarled, "The day I stop looking out for you is the day we die. Even then, it's not going to stop. I'll haunt your ass to keep you safe if you outlive me."

"If anyone could do it, it'd be you," I whispered quietly, eyes big in my face as I looked up at him, knowing he meant it.

"Exactly," he rasped. "I think I've done enough of the Devil's work for him to owe me some favors."

"Maybe I can help, though?"

"You can. By doing as you're fucking told."

His cell buzzed.

"Conor?" he barked, after scanning the Caller ID.

"Someone just walked through your gates. I have men on their way. Two minutes' ETA."

Aidan unlocked the car with the fob. "Savannah, get your ass in the car." To Conor, he said, "Divert Savannah's guards. They don't need to see the bloodshed."

"Done," Conor replied as he cut the call.

Having heard his brother's side of the conversation, I bit my lip, then just as I started to step away, I heard something too. I twisted to look over Aidan's shoulder and finally saw the guy from last night walking across the manicured lawn toward the driveway as if he owned the place.

"Is that the Italian from The 68?"

His nostrils flared as he turned to look where I pointed, then when he caught Valentini's eye, he twisted back around and unlocked the front door. "Get inside."

I was about to do as he demanded, his words different now, not just a command, but one that was uttered from his soul—the heir had spoken and everything in me responded.

However, as I stepped away from him, I soon saw four men circling the Range Rover and I grabbed his hand. "Aidan! Look!"

"I see them. Get in the house!" He shoved me away, but I wouldn't let him.

"No, I can't leave you—"

A growl escaped him and one hand grabbed mine again, his fingers curving about it to the point of pain as he rumbled, "Stay close to me."

Call me crazy, but in the middle of a gunfight, I'd prefer to be stuck at his side anyway, so there wasn't any place I wanted to be more than right here.

The prospect of seeing him being cut down by these men—

God. No. I couldn't do it. I couldn't stand to see that. Even if it meant my death too.

"If this is your idea of trying to get me on board with you taking over the *Famiglia*, Valentini, then you're fucked in the head," he snarled, somehow projecting confidence when all I felt was horror at his belligerence.

Valentini just arched a brow and stepped closer. "You have a beautiful property, O'Donnelly. It's not what I expected, antique on the outside and," he paused as he peered through the glass door, "ultra modern on the inside, but I think that makes sense. It's very fitting for the Irish Mob. Old and new." He hummed. "I approve."

"Well, I can rest easy tonight knowing you approve of my home," Aidan snapped. "But you might not be resting so easily—"

Valentini lifted his arms in surrender. "I mean no harm."

"Coming onto my property like this is an act of aggression. Fuck that, it's a declaration of war. The only thing saving your ass is that you didn't break in."

"By no means is it an act of war, Aidan. I think we should call each other by our first names, no? We're going to be working closely together after this...

"Your house is too secured for even my greatest code cracker to begin the attempt, but slipping inside the gates once you pulled through them is another matter entirely. We have done no harm. I intend no harm, either. Actually, I have a Christmas gift for you," he finished when Aidan scoffed.

For all that my heart was in my lungs because I knew this was us being in a situation that went beyond deep shinola, a part of me, the part that was fascinated by all things mafia, was breathless with anticipation.

I'd come to realize, through a thousand hours of therapy, that sometimes, the thing that made you the most scared, that terrified you to death, was also something that made you feel alive.

Messed up, but so true.

"What kind of Christmas gift?" Aidan rumbled, and this close, I could practically feel how pissed he was.

Close to vibrating, Aidan O'Donnelly Jr. was the antithesis of a happy camper. Which was very sad, because he'd been happy before.

While I knew I should be running screaming for the hills, this, if anything, confirmed that I was in the right place.

Of course, I might have changed my mind if Valentini wanted to skewer me on a spike, but lucky for Aidan, that wasn't happening.

Phew.

Valentini lowered his hands and with a placating motion, swept them aside. "He's in my van, waiting to be transported to wherever you'd like him."

"He?" Aidan intoned, his surprise clear.

Valentini smiled, but it was nothing like last night's—the one that had made Jen undergo a personality transplant.

It was cold, cruel. Calculating. Twisted and bent.

This man I could envisage slicing up another's face.

Shivering, I wondered how Jen had fared after we'd left. I was such a shitty friend for not having checked in sooner. Although, come to think of it, she hadn't texted me either.

"I listen to the chatter from the Vatican." He tapped his temple. "I distrust the church, but we Italians, what can I say? Catholicism is in our blood. But my men have kids, and I'm not about to let them be preached to by some pedophile *cazzo*."

Aidan tensed up, making the way he was vibrating before look like a purring cat in comparison to the outraged tiger in front of me now.

"What are you talking about?" he thundered, his hand tightening around mine again. It hurt, but when I squeezed back, I knew it soothed him.

Not outwardly, but he shifted toward me the faintest inch. Like magnets, we stuck close together.

"The Archbishop of St. Patrick's Cathedral has helped shield seven priests from being thrown in jail. When my *consigliere* discovered this, they went hunting, and uncovered a neat little connection that I'm sure your family wouldn't like to be out in public."

Aidan grated out, "Watch your mouth."

I cast him a look, and realized that someone in the family had been abused by a priest. One of his brothers? From his fury, I'd guess so.

"I'm watching it," Valentini almost crooned, but he was being placatory, not incendiary. Although, I wasn't sure it mattered. Aidan was acting like a hand grenade with the pin pulled. "But that's why I brought him as a gift for you.

"Seven priests went without justice, but how many children?" Valentini shook his head. "I would ordinarily deal with this kind of thing myself, however I know how you O'Donnellys work."

"A favor for a favor," Aidan ground out.

"Exactly." Valentini smiled, warmer this time. Satisfaction lacing it. "If it makes it any better, he's also a Sparrow."

Aidan straightened up. For that matter, so did I.

"He is?" I demanded.

Valentini cast me a curious glance. Not dismissive like I might have expected, just inquisitive. "He is." He tipped his head to the side. "You were doing the Lord's work from an early age, Aidan. Culling the perverted from the flock. Apparently, the Archbishop was well aware of what you did with Father McKenna. They were words spilled during confession."

As his words waned, Aidan rasped, "Who?"

Valentini pulled a face. "This is compounding the favor."

Aidan's mouth firmed. "I've already told you that I'll do what I can with Da. He's a loose cannon. There's no controlling him."

"But this is one way I can earn his gratitude. I understand that the Irish and the Italians haven't been friends for a long time, since before he was even in the Mob, however our grandparents were not like this. The Valentinis ruled with honor. The Fieris—" He spat on the ground. "—were devious fuckers. We are not like this."

"Da won't listen to reason." Aidan growled. "But if he isn't open to the suggestion of us backing you, then you can rest assured that I'll at least arrange a meeting between you where you can argue your position."

"That is all I need to make him see sense." Valentini's eyes lit up. "A man of honor would not make such a statement lightly."

Aidan scowled at him as he snarled, "I'm aware of this. Now, tell me—*who?*"

"Your Uncle Padraig."

TWENTY-SEVEN

AIDAN

THERE WAS one consolation to this situation—the property's security hadn't been breached.

Valentini's van and his men's vehicles were all outside the gates, lined down the road, something I saw when, after calling Conor and getting him to stand the guards down, I accessed the cameras on the border walls through the app Kid had built for us.

I even watched the footage of Valentini sneaking through the gates. He'd flashed a light onto the sensor which made the gates retract. Normally, I had a guard standing there so that was a loophole that wouldn't reoccur but still... I was pissed.

Not just at Valentini's break-in, but at his news, and at Savannah's disobedience.

Relieved that she was inside the Range Rover now that I'd shoved her difficult ass in there—a vehicle that could double up as an armored tank—I cast Valentini a glance and said, "If you tell anyone, anyone about what you know, Da is the last person you'll have to fear."

Luciu turned to me. "I know what it is to protect family, Aidan. Conor should never have gone through that. If anything, you have my sympathies." His glance turned curious. "Is it true you are allied with the Satan's Sinners' MC? The one operating in Jersey?"

"Why?"

"I heard about that pedophile hunter." He rubbed his chin. "I might have some work for him."

"I don't deal with them. My brother, Declan, does. If Father accepts you as an ally, I'll get you an in."

Valentini straightened his shoulders. "What's the likelihood of that happening? We can cut the bullshit now it's just us talking."

My jaw clicked as I worked it. "Before this, I'd have said you didn't have a snowball's chance in hell."

"So I was right to make this move." He laughed softly. "Interesting. This is good to know. Now the Italians and the Russians are dealing with turmoil, the Irish are the strongest influence in Manhattan.

"We all know the Triads aren't that interested in our petty squabbles. They're more concerned about the Yakuza. It would be in my best interest to remain friendly with your father. If he likes gifts, I can give him plenty of those."

"Little interests him."

"I'm not an ass kisser, but my family has been waiting sixty years to reascend to its rightful place. I will do whatever I must to make that happen. I've already got the *Famiglia* under my thumb, but acceptance as its leader comes in different ways."

"I'm surprised. I thought one of the Genovicos would have taken the top spot."

Valentini smirked. "There are very few made men remaining in the top hierarchy. Our churches are busy with many funerals right now."

"Leading by fear." I grunted.

"A sad but true fact of life. Of course, in twenty years, I'll have to deal with pissed off sons. Much as they're dealing with me now, but I'm unafraid of borrowing trouble."

"Lead by example, then. Don't trigger resentment."

"Once I'm in power, once my place is consolidated with a brokerage of peace from the Irish and the Russians, this I can do. As it stands, I still have to play the politician, and I'll carry on doing that until my position is secured." His jaw tightened. "They'll never be able to disband the Valentinis ever again."

Disinterested in his power grab, I cast Savannah a look and found her peering down at her cellphone in the Range Rover.

A nerve ticced at my temple when I thought about her disobedience from before, a disobedience that could have gotten her hurt, and I knew I'd be late getting to the family estate.

If neither of us were okay with my family hearing her moan, then being okay with hearing us fuck nasty was another matter entirely.

"Can I borrow the van?" I asked when it pulled up. Innocuous, like any of the million other white vans that roamed New York City, it would blend in easily with traffic.

"Of course. I'll be trashing it after anyway. Can you deal with this?"

I arched a brow at him. "You trust me to do that?"

Valentini smirked. "We're going to be allies, my friend. We're going to own the city again.

"Your father won't live forever, so it will be you who sits at the Summit the next time we convene. The old generation fucked up NYC, but now there's young blood waiting to take over it, we can start anew."

Smirking at him, I said, "If you want Da to like you, don't say shit like that."

Valentini smirked back. "I know my audience."

"Which prompts me to ask why the fuck should I trust you?"

"Because I don't want war with you. You hate the Fieris as much as me, which means you're the enemy of my enemy, Aidan. Plus I have no beef against the Irish. The Valentinis and the O'Donnellys always played nicely together...

"I just want to take back what's rightfully mine." He turned to me with his hand outstretched. "I truly hope you make the asswipe pay for covering up what he did. Knowing your reputation, I'm sure you'll do all those children proud."

My hand snapped out to grab his and we shook on it, gaze held firm as we both took each other's measure. I knew it was a little like a pissing contest, but after a few minutes, we both reached a semblance of peace, and we pulled free at the same time.

"He's drugged for the moment. It should last three more hours max." He cast a look at Savannah as if he knew how I'd be using that time, before he shifted his gaze.

Smart man.

I wasn't exactly rational where she was concerned.

Jumping down the steps to the driveway with an ease I envied, I watched as he gathered his men together. Savannah's interest was stirred and she peered around, watching the Italians disperse, getting into their vehicles so they could head back to the city, leaving only the white van behind.

I'd met the Archbishop several times over the course of my life, and though I didn't know him well, it was hard for me to imagine he sheltered pedophiles.

He'd always seemed so upstanding, but then, what those priests did to protect the church was sickening. One of the many reasons that I wasn't as devout as Da.

When the Italians disappeared down the driveway, I closed the gates manually through my phone, shot off some messages, and then, I stood on the top step, watching Savannah.

My one, true priority.

It didn't take long for our eyes to clash and when they did, she ducked her head and opened the car door after unlocking it.

Biting her lip, she climbed out then, without me having to say a word, muttered, "I couldn't just leave you. I needed to know what was going on."

"That car is bulletproof, Savannah," I told her calmly, even though I felt anything but calm. "It's also wired up with more security than you can imagine. You get in there, it's like a fucking tank. There's no getting you out of it unless you open the door.

"They could even drop it in the river, and water wouldn't get in. You might die of oxygen deprivation, but that's how airtight it is. So, when I tell you to get your ass in there, you fucking do it, do you hear me?" I snarled at her.

She ground her teeth together. "And what? I was just supposed to watch you get shot or stabbed?"

"What if you were pregnant, Savannah? What if you were carrying our baby?" My dick needed to not get hard at the thought right now. We had bigger fish to fucking fry. "You think my life is worth more than our kid's?"

She gulped. "I get the shot. I couldn't be pregnant."

"I'm sure you do, but that doesn't take away from the question."

Her mouth worked. "I don't want to answer it."

"No? Well, tough shit. That's the mafia life, little one," I growled. "You have to answer the impossible questions because that's what it boils down to. You have to accept that I'm going to look after you no matter fucking what.

"I did it when there was nothing in it for me other than knowing you were goddamn safe. I did it when you weren't mine, so now that you are, how the hell do you expect me to stop?"

Her eyes flared wide. "I'm yours?"

My mouth tightened. "What do you think? And trust you to focus on that rather than anything fucking else."

Was I surprised when she pretty much flung herself at me?

Not really.

She collided with me like we were two stars merging, and the energy that triggered nearly cleansed my soul of its sins, that was how goddamn powerful it was.

"You were mine five years ago, Savannah," I rasped in her hair as I hugged her closer, so tight neither of us could begin to calculate exactly where she started and I ended. "You think I'm going to let go now?"

"I feel like you're ready to run off."

"That's because I did it once, but don't punish me for trying to protect you—"

"You could run off to protect me."

"I told you in the car—you walked into danger. It's not going away. Even if you release all those exposés, Savannah, there's no guarantee you'll get every Sparrow.

"Let's face it, it's actually unlikely that you will. Did you know the Archbishop of New York was a Sparrow?" When she stiffened in my arms, I had my answer. "Exactly. You're going to have a target on your back for the rest of your life, and I can't have that. As my woman, as my wife, you'll be safe" I growled under my breath. "From everyone but me."

She didn't tense up, if anything, she snuggled into me. "I was scared for you."

"I don't care," I told her coldly, even as I tightened my arms around her, because Christ, I did care.

I cared so fucking much.

I mattered to my family, but to no one else.

To know I counted to her filled me with some messed up emotion I couldn't begin to describe.

"Your safety is my priority. Do you understand me?"

She pressed her forehead into my chest. "I'm sorry."

"You should be." I muttered, "Come on, let's get you inside."

"Inside? We're not going to your family estate?"

"You're worried about screaming too loud there. Here, I can make sure you're as loud as you want to be."

She sagged into me. "Oh, God, don't say stuff like that."

Rolling my eyes, I directed her through the front door and into the foyer. It was a massive vestibule with a central staircase that led to upper mezzanine floors, but I rarely used those steps, and instead hobbled down toward the elevator.

As I did, I rested some weight on her, and I had to admit, it helped ease the pain in my leg, making the walk smoother and less harried.

As we walked down the hall, I felt her gaze touching everything, drifting along the art and the ornaments that lined it, then dipping into the rooms that had opened doors.

When we reached my whiskey room, she paused, and asked, "Is this the room Jen was telling me about?"

"It's where I house my collection, sure."

When she pulled away, I let her, because this was my favorite room in the house and, now that I thought about it, it was pretty fucking fitting that we christened this room first.

This, the first of all of them, because there was no way we weren't about to scatter DNA throughout the entirety of this place. Maybe then it'd feel like a goddamn home instead of something I rattled around in by myself.

When we strode into the black on brown exterior, the woods dark, the metals cast iron, a hint of copper here and there, I started to tug on my tie. As I did, she oohed and aahed at the space.

The side wall housed two massive windows that let in a lot of light. Rich black velvet drapes diminished some of the glare on the back wall which housed backlit cubby holes in varying sizes. Small nooks that housed precious bottles, some that Napoleon himself had handled.

I turned on the lights so that the backlights popped on and she oohed at the warm amber gleam which filled the space, even in the daytime.

Opposite the shelves, there was a massive TV, but in between, there was a black corduroy sectional. That was going to be our destination. Leather would have been more fitting, but I hated the cold chill against my skin, and this was always more comfortable in winter.

As I ambled over to her, I murmured, "Savannah?"

She turned to peer at me. "Yes, Aidan?"

Her tone was meeker than I expected, and it sank to my dick, settling there, and making it pound in fury.

Holy shit, her eyes were lowered like she was a naughty girl.

That should not have been as hot as it was, but goddamn, it was like fire flushing through my veins.

"You know you shouldn't have done that, don't you? You know you're going to have to listen to me in the future if we're going to make this work."

She bit her lip. "I do. I'm sorry. I'm not used to—"

"Listening to people? Obeying someone when they're more cognizant of the danger in a particular situation than you are?" I growled under my breath as I pulled my tie free from my collar. "I'm not people. I'm me. I'm not just anyone. My primary directive in this fucking life is to make sure you keep that pretty head of yours attached to that sinful body, so with that in mind, I want you to get naked."

Her eyes flared, but not with fear, more in excitement. She pretty much started stripping the second I made the damn request, and I wasn't about to complain.

Her neatness didn't come as a surprise, either, not after seeing her apartment, and especially as I knew she wanted to make a good impression on Da.

She placed her clothes carefully on the back of the sofa, laying them flat so they wouldn't crease, and every time she twisted and bent, swaying and dipping to make sure the fabric wasn't ruffled, well, it shouldn't have been as much of a turn on as it was.

Catching glimpses of her tits swaying, the line of her hip tautening, the way her belly scooted in then popped out, everything about her, every goddamn inch that was revealed to me was like finally catching a glimpse of paradise.

I wanted to watch this woman undress every fucking day. I wanted to watch her apply her make-up in the morning and take it off at night. I wanted to see her screaming with pleasure, and I wanted to watch her face puckered with distaste when she tried a new food she didn't like.

I wanted it all, I realized. Wanted everything she had to give, and even that wouldn't be enough.

How I kept my hands away from her, I didn't know, but I wanted her naked, out of that sexy as sin pink suit that had a weird blend to it so it took away from the severe cut and made her look more feminine than last night's ladykiller outfit.

She was soft and approachable, everything I didn't want her to be when I had an enemy in the vicinity.

I knew men would already have begun to arrive from Da's compound after I shot off some messages to Finn once Valentini was on his way.

I'd have preferred to ask Conor, but I didn't want him knowing who was in the van.

Finn was sending guards to sweep the land to make sure there were no other intruders as well, with one also tasked with driving the van to the estate, but leaving it at the back of the garages where I knew, sometimes, Da did some wet work if a situation was particularly personal to him.

Knowing we were safe, knowing I could let my guard down, I watched my woman, *my* goddamn woman, strip. It was time to remind her of exactly who she was now, what she was to me, and what that fucking meant.

I just had to hope that, by the end of it, she didn't give up on me entirely.

TWENTY-EIGHT

SAVANNAH

MY BOOBS WOULDN'T STOP jiggling. Every heavily-panted breath, every time I moved to undress, when I laid my clothes out as flat as I could, everything I did made me hyper aware of their jiggle.

I was even more hyper aware of Aidan who was watching me, his necktie in his hands. Didn't take Einstein to figure out what he was going to do with that, and I was so beyond down for it, for everything and anything he wanted to do to me.

I'd had good sex in my time, but kind of bland. Vanilla. I had a feeling that the devious flames that fanned to life behind Aidan's eyes were just the start of what was to come.

When I was totally naked apart from the bandage around my leg and the one on my wrist, I turned to him and deciding to be smart, I held out my arms for him to bind. He arched a brow at me though, and stepped closer, the necktie still in his hand but he moved so that all of my backside was exposed to his clothes.

His heat.

His strength.

God, he was like a furnace and it felt so good because it was cold in here. While my nipples were already budding into tight peaks, it had nothing to do with the temperature and everything to do with the man, and he hadn't even touched me yet.

Shivering, I waited for him to make his next move, but I could never have anticipated what he did.

Looping the necktie around my waist, at the smallest part, he made a knot that proved he'd gone sailing at some point in his life and that I hadn't, because it held fast, adjusting as he slipped the flap down between my legs.

I yelped when the silk brushed my pussy and then it tunneled between my asscheeks as he hauled the fabric straight up and had it acting as a thong, before he looped the remaining length into another knot.

"I could have just kept my G-string on," I complained breathily, but as I moved, I felt the difference.

When I shifted, the knots adjusted, tightening, always tightening, never loosening. I could even feel a slight compression around my waist that made me feel slightly breathless.

The necktie was pulled so taut that there was no give either, and I squirmed against the compression, even though that felt both better and worse.

"You can squirm all you want. I'll even let you get off that way if you can." There was a shrug in his voice. "You need to apologize to me, Savannah. I need a good apology so that I'll forget that you pissed me off by disobeying." His hand reached up and curved around my loose-swinging hair. He gathered it around his wrist then tugged my head back. As he did, he brushed his lips against the curve of my jaw, and breathed, "Do you think you can do that?"

I gasped as he tugged on my hair hard enough to hurt and when I squirmed some more, I felt it like a jolt to the pussy. "Y-Yes, I know I can do that."

"Good." He let his fingers tangle with my necklace. "What's this?"

"My dad bought it for me after Teabag died."

He sighed and pressed a kiss to my temple. "I wanted so bad to come to you when she died." I felt his remorse, but I didn't necessarily forgive him for not helping me through that time.

"I wish you had," I rasped, tilting my head back so that I could peer at him.

I didn't want to get upset, so I reached up and nipped his chin, which, because he knew me so well, had a knowing, but understanding look drifting into his eyes, and it prompted him to drop his hand so he could squeeze one of my tits.

"Fuck, these are so juicy. If I were okay with some son of a bitch seeing these, I'd ask you to get them pierced." I squirmed some more. "You like the idea of that, huh?"

"Maybe," I whispered shakily.

His tongue trailed along the length of my jaw. "You're an O'Donnelly's woman now, Savannah. I don't think you know what that means."

Shakily, I let my head fall back against his shoulder. "Tell me."

The fingers that had been toying with my nipple dropped down to between my thighs. When he patted me there, I moaned.

"This belongs to me. No fucker else. Everything that is you is mine." He nipped my jaw. "If you have a gynecologist that's a guy, you need to change that. I don't want a woman touching you, never mind a fucking man."

I gulped. "That's irrational."

"That comes as a surprise?"

"N-No, I guess not."

He nipped me again. "Eoghan told me once that he'd only be okay with Inessa, his wife—although, knowing you, I guess you're well aware of who she is—going to the doctor's office with him there. I get it now. I thought he was insane, but this is mine," he thundered in my ear, his hands delving between my silk-covered folds. "And I think you like the idea of that as much as I do," he whispered, his fingers finding slick pussy juices that really were unseemly.

I mean, he'd barely done anything other than say shit that'd piss any modern woman off, and yet, here I was, creaming like I was an eclair being squished in the middle.

My mouth trembled as I rasped, "Do I get to visit the doctor's office with you?"

A chuckle escaped him. "Why do you never say what I think you will? Want to see me bent over as the fucker checks my prostate?"

Why did that make butterflies dance in my stomach?

"I wouldn't say no." I moaned when he patted my pussy with the flat of his hand.

"Or do you want to be the one with your fingers in my ass, hmm?" he crooned. "That'll take a lot of good behavior. Like ten years' worth."

Dancing around his grip, trying to get him in a spot that directly affected my clit, I pouted. "That's impossible. No one can behave for ten years."

"You'll learn to, because otherwise I'll die of a heart attack first."

I stilled. "Well, I don't want that."

"No? Then, behave. Simple answer." Slowly, he leaned forward, which pushed me forward too. I let him, and groaned when the tie pulled on different areas, some pinching and some compressing the right spot. "If it were a longer tie, I'd have knots that bumped your clit." He hummed. "You're going to look good tied up on my bed, Savannah. Maybe that's one way to make sure you behave."

"D-Don't you have anything here we can use?" I asked around a gasp, surprising myself by how he lowered my inhibitions.

He hesitated. "I've not been a saint, Savannah. Those things have touched other women, and nothing, and I mean, fucking nothing, that's been used on anyone else is ever going to touch you."

I groaned. "You say stuff like that and it makes me melt."

"Good. I was born to make you melt." The nails of his spare hand scraped down my side, making goosebumps surge into being. "Just like you were born to make me burn."

I liked the idea of that. Still, I couldn't let him get away with murder. "Sounds like a UTI."

He chuckled, but then he bit my throat, hard enough to mark.

"D-Don't!" I complained. "Your parents will see."

"Good. The more marks on you, the more likelihood they'll figure out what the fuck you mean to me without me having to spell shit out."

Tension eased in me, tension that came with relief and need that he made me feel with his wholehearted acceptance of something he'd been fighting for five years. The way I relaxed eased the pressure on the tie, and had it brushing up flat against my clit. I groaned, shuffling my legs together to take full advantage of the delicious sensations that the new position triggered in me, then he bit down on my shoulder and I arched up on tiptoe at the sweetly blissful pain his branding me triggered.

"Didn't realize you were a werewolf."

"Gotta mark what's mine," he grumbled in my ear.

"So long as it's mutual," I muttered, then gasped when he rocked his dick into my ass.

"Yeah, it's mutual. I expect it," he retorted, squeezing my tits together in his palms. "Never gave a fuck before, but now I want every pussy in Manhattan to know I'm taken."

Heat swirled inside me. "Y-You do?"

"O'Donnellys go big or go home."

"We're at your home now," I pointed out on a rasp.

"Don't be literal." I smirked as he bunched my breasts together again then moaned when he whispered, "Spread your legs wider."

I did as he asked, then recoiled at how that made the fabric dig into me. The way the silk went up my ass reminded me of the first time I'd worn a G-string, but the pressure on my clit was acute, borderline painful.

"How's this?" He gently touched the bandage, which he'd been carefully doctoring.

"Fine." That was no word of a lie. My current discomfort was definitely clit-centric.

I blinked, bowing forward onto my forearms, resting my weight there to ease the strain between my thighs, then I felt him move back, and his fingers dipped between my ass cheeks.

Rubbing the now-covered rosette, he murmured, "I'm glad this is untouched."

"Not for long, though, I think."

He reached down and I yelped when he bit my ass cheek. "Yes, not for long."

"G-Good. I want you to own every part of me, Aidan," I whispered, meaning it, but also needing him to stop teasing me and I wasn't averse from using my words against him.

He rewarded me by raking his short, blunt nails against my flesh again, which made the blood flush to the surface and had me dipping up and down on tiptoes as I tried to both avoid his touch and lean into it.

He bit down on a fleshy part of my ass again, then he growled and straightened up. "Fucking leg."

Aidan stepped back, then limped around the sofa. About to ask what the hell he was doing when he was getting to the good stuff, I watched him strip out of his shirt, which he flung to the ground without a care unlike me, then unfastened his zipper.

When his cock bobbed out, free from boxer briefs getting in the way, I licked my lips as he maneuvered around so that he could lie flat on the sectional.

"Come and put that pussy where it belongs."

Eyes wide, I whispered, "On your dick?"

He arched a brow. "My face, baby girl, my face."

Melting, I quickly dashed around the sofa and clambered over the armrest. He chuckled when my knees pinned him on either side of his head, and then his hands were on my ass—in a hold that was coming to be a signature move of his—and he was urging me down against him.

His tongue flickered against the silk, which was delicate enough that I could feel it, but it was dampened by the fact that something was between his tongue and my clit.

Like he knew, he sucked harder, but as much as it pleasured me, it was a tease. I thought he was aware about that too, and I knew why: I wasn't sitting on his face. His hands urged me to rest on him, to settle *right there*, but I kept some tension in my thighs. However, the way the tie dampened the sensation had desperation overtaking me.

Flinging caution to the wind, I ground my pussy into his face, uncaring if he couldn't fucking breathe, just needing more of him, needing him to give me what I was dying to have, forgetting that he was supposed to be punishing me for not behaving, not even realizing that this had been his intention all along.

As I rocked against his face, my arms clung to the back of the sofa for support, and then, his finger made an appearance.

Goddamn that finger.

It swiped deep between my thighs, just by my perineum which I knew had soaked the silk through with my juices, and then tunneled higher to my ass. His thumb prodded the rosette through the silk, forever ruining what had probably cost a couple hundred dollars, and then his wily pointer finger slipped beneath it and flexed until it was inside me. Just the tip at first, but it had me clenching down around it.

I screamed when, for whatever godforsaken reason, that triggered my orgasm. The wail that escaped me was compounded by heavy grunts as I carried on grinding my pussy into his face, uncaring and oblivious, unashamed to chase my pleasure at that moment, more than I'd ever been in my life.

As I soared, he carried on, teasing me and taunting me, not stopping until I was a panting mess and was pulling away from him.

I arched up, evading that goddamn motor mouth, and I sobbed out, "No more, Aidan, no more!!!" When I saw his evil smirk, I wagged a finger at him. "No more orgasms." Then, realizing what I'd said, I quickly muttered, "For five minutes."

His smirk turned into a grin. "I don't know, I'd hate for you to think that I didn't listen to your needs." He grabbed the tie and pulled it tight, making me arch higher. "Get that pussy back on my face."

I moaned. "N-No."

He growled and I sobbed, but I almost flopped down, and this time, I realized he'd done something that meant his tongue was straight on my clit because the tie was digging into my labia in a way that hurt, but it made blood gather throughout my sex, making me hyper aware of the area as I squirmed on him.

There was no pretty way to describe the sounds that flooded around the room. If anyone could hear, they'd think a cat in heat was being bred or something, but sweet Jesus, the man's mouth was a crime against nature in the best possible way.

As he dragged on my clit with his teeth, I yelped and that set me off so hard and so fast I sobbed as I rocked against him, using his fucking nose to help prolong the delicious agony.

When he thrust a finger inside me, managing to work one into my slit, I growled when he pushed down hard on the front wall of my pussy. All the while, he rubbed down against it, until I felt the weirdest sensation.

A squeal escaped me, and this time, I didn't just try to haul ass, I nearly flung myself off him as the weirdest urge hit me.

It was like...

Jesus.

No.

I didn't need to pee.

But he wasn't letting me go, so when I moved, it just increased the pressure of his finger against the front wall of my pussy.

I felt it.

The second it slid free from me, I felt it and I blushed bright red then blanched with mortification. It poured out of me in a high pressured spurt, and that was when it hit me and I almost sagged with relief, never mind painful pleasure.

It wasn't pee.

I'd squirted.

Onto his face.

His face.

And from the sounds Aidan was making, he was into it.

Big time.

I'd never felt like a meal before, but that was exactly what was happening here. I was being eaten out. What other guys had done to me was the dieting equivalent of having your pussy licked. This was a full on banquet. I was appetizer, entree, and goddamn dessert. Maybe even after-dinner coffee too.

As he munched on me, I felt electric sparks start at the base of my spine, and then it came again. That weird feeling, and like he knew, the fucker, he pressed another two fingers inside me. The added pressure had me screeching, but there was nowhere to run and nowhere to hide. He ground them against that pleasure spot, the one in my ass pushing down hard too, not stopping until I felt the release and I felt it trickle onto his face.

I'd never been more mortified and more turned on in my life, and those were two such discordant reactions that I didn't know what to do with myself.

Aidan did.

Before the embarrassment could hit, he got busy, sending me to the stars again, engaging my mind and not just my body.

I was suddenly soaring around a solar system that he'd built for me alone, and all the while, I knew just how fucked up this man was because his tongue had to be part-Cyborg.

When minutes, hours, decades, centuries later, he let me back down again, I realized I was sobbing. That was why he'd stopped. Big sniffly gulps had escaped me as my sensitized body shuddered through another orgasm.

After pulling out of me which triggered another mini-climax, his hands came to my ass cheeks and he helped me move.

My thighs were like spaghetti, limp and overcooked, and every muscle in my body ached like I'd endured a four-hour HIIT class.

When I flopped on top of him where he wanted me, making my sore wrist ache slightly with the force of the move, his cock prodded my slit and took my mind away from such plebeian thoughts. I felt it, felt the thickness of it, knew what that felt like inside me, and I realized something weird.

I wanted him to fill me up.

I wanted his come inside me, dripping down.

I wanted it...

Jesus.

I wanted to put my pant suit on and have that cum dripping down my thighs as I met his parents.

What the fuck was wrong with me?

He wanted to brand me, and I just wanted to be full of him.

As his cock nestled into my slit, his cautiousness now spoke of how sensitive he knew I was.

Even though he was to blame for my current state, I couldn't stop myself from crying out, "Aidan?"

"Yes, baby," he hummed, sighing with relief as his cock made its way inside me.

"I-I-I l-l-l-ove y-y-you," I stuttered out as the stark heat of him made me burn up again. I didn't need him to reply, just needed him to know the truth as I shivered then, a little helplessly, before I pushed myself into a sitting position, using his hard chest and abs to hold me up.

I couldn't ride him, but I could rock, and I could squirm, and I could feel from the thick pulse inside me how ready he was to burst.

His hands came to my hips, and he helped me grind into him, which was exactly what I needed.

I couldn't handle my clit being touched, couldn't handle him rubbing my nipples or doing much with any other part of me, but the way my pussy clung to his shaft was just enough to torment us both.

Panting and sore and tired, I carried on, grabbing onto that thick shaft that was made just for me, not stopping until he hollered his pleasure too.

When his cum filled me, I knew it was impossible, but I'd watched way too much hentai not to think of all that seed dripping down inside me, and I groaned as a tiny orgasm hit me hard, dragging at his cock, milking him of every drop.

Then, when I flopped onto him, and his arms came up to hold me, he gave me the greatest gift of all.

He kissed my temple, and whispered, "I love you too, Savannah."

And that was when I closed my eyes and napped.

TWENTY-NINE

AIDAN

I LET her into the shower and cleaned her up, but I used the nozzle to direct where I needed her clean.

That pussy was staying full of my cum, and she seemed to be into that as well because she didn't redirect the shower stream.

When I grabbed another necktie, one that wasn't wet, she let me tie it in the same way even though it wasn't long enough for full coverage and would pull on her waist.

"The second it gets uncomfortable, tell me."

She blinked sleepy eyes at me. "I'll tell you."

She wouldn't. She liked it.

I didn't tie this one as tight so it was more manageable for at least an hour, but knew I'd have to check on her and make sure that she was doing okay.

The prospect of dragging her into a bathroom at my parents' home and 'checking' on her made my dick twitch, but there was no way she could handle more.

She already looked spaced out, her eyes slowly blinking like she could just crawl into bed, and I almost felt guilty because she was about to meet one of her weird anti-idols, but she'd needed to learn a lesson.

Positive reinforcement worked the best in my opinion.

Sure, I could have denied her any pleasure at all, that would have worked, but instead, she'd remember the intensity of what I'd made her feel, and it would sink in.

Delighted with her, delighted that she'd squirted, I petted her as I cleaned her up, taking care to smooth soap over her arms and legs, just keeping that filthy pussy stuffed full with me, taking special note of all the bites on her body, most of which were between her legs so for my eyes only.

I dressed her, then readied her to leave, and when I found the white van gone, satisfaction of a different kind hit me. For all that she looked exhausted and ready to nap, I was prepared for the fuckfest that was about to go down.

Da was not going to be happy, but I wasn't averse to twisting the situation to my own advantage.

If it meant diverting him from the fact Savannah wasn't dead when she was supposed to be, and if it meant that Conor finally got some vengeance, then so be it—I'd ruin his Christmas.

Before we left, I handed her a can of Monster from the fridge, telling her, "You should drink all that. You'll need the energy for what's about to go down. Christmas in my family is crazy."

She blinked at me, smiled sleepily, and popped the tab.

Fuck me, I wanted to kiss her. I wanted nothing more than to haul her ass upstairs to the master bedroom and just go to sleep with her, but that was for later. For another time.

I took a deep breath.

We had many other times coming our way.

I knew it. I had, for the first time in a long while, faith.

She'd survive today, she'd survive the family, and she'd live to see another day.

Who wouldn't?

New York's Archbishop.

Both buried in our thoughts, neither of us spoke all that much until we made it to the family estate. As the gates loomed up ahead, she whispered, "Does he think I'm dead?"

I cleared my throat. "I try not to bog him down with information that isn't necessary for him."

"Meaning that he does," was her dry retort. "Didn't he see my reports?"

"Probably not. He might have skimmed them, might not. While he has the memory of an elephant, because you write under S. Daniels, and because he's a sexist asshole, he thought you were a guy.

"Anyway, in the grand scheme of things, you were a blip on his radar and we have massive whales on that goddamn radar on the regular." At least, I really fucking hoped that was the case.

"I shouldn't be offended by that, should I?"

I snorted. "No. It's a good thing not to be on our shit list."

"Let's hope you're right and that he doesn't remember my name." She took a deeper sip of Monster. "I can see why you gave me this now. Better that than a bottle of vodka."

I leaned over and pressed my hand to her lap. Squeezing gently, I murmured, "All will be fine."

"You don't know that."

"I do." I shrugged when she shot me a disbelieving scowl. "Look, you were a problem before, but now you're helping us get rid of the Sparrows. Wasn't he lucky I was disobedient?"

She chuckled. "That's one way of looking at it."

"Mostly, he's not going to like that I've brought you to the house. I doubt he'll remember your name."

"He won't like it because of what he thinks it means for you to be bringing someone home to meet the folks?"

I hummed as security finally walked out of the gatehouse, eyed the car up and down, then checked us out with one of Conor's gadgets. After it was done, I opened the window, and asked, "Jonesy, where's Da?"

"Don't know, Aidan, but I know that a van rolled up an hour ago. Maybe he's with that?"

Smiling, I said, "Good." I rolled up the window, then drove through the gates once Jonesy had opened them.

"You think the Archbishop is going to detract from my presence?"

"He is." There were no two ways about it.

I felt her gaze on me, felt her curiosity and braced myself for what was coming. "It was Conor, wasn't it?"

I tensed. "What about him?"

She sniffed. "Don't play games. We both know what I'm asking."

We did. My mouth tightened. "Yes."

Blowing out a breath, she whispered, "Oh."

"Oh."

"What happened?"

"You don't want to know. Safe to say the priest who hurt him didn't get the chance to hurt any other kids ever again."

"See, it's when stuff like this happens that I like this world." She grunted. "I talked about so many shitty situations on TV, had to read out so many atrocious stories where people just didn't get any justice at all, that I understand the satisfaction of jungle justice.

"Then, I recognize that we can't have everyone going around killing people in the name of an eye for an eye."

"No, you can't," I agreed. "But that's the mobster way. Mafia 101, little one."

"I know," she said with a huff. "I'm just talking out loud, trying to reason why I'm so glad you killed that sick fuck when I really shouldn't be happy to know you murdered a priest." Despite myself, I had to snicker, and when she slapped her hand against my thigh, she muttered, "Hey, don't laugh!"

I snatched her fingers and raised them to my mouth as I steered one-handed.

"I've done a lot worse besides that, and it won't stop, but they're not good people. Anyone in this world isn't good by proxy."

"Your sisters-in-law are innocent."

"Are they? They wear fancy clothes and live in fancy buildings on the backs of a lot of spilled blood. We all make a choice. That's why I gave you the option to take a step back." I cast her a look. "Do you regret not taking it?" I worded that carefully, making sure she knew the time for leaving was long in the past.

"No, but I don't think wanting to be with you means I'm like the next Don Corleone. I don't want to kill anyone."

"You almost killed that guy the other night," I pointed out. "If you'd had a knife close at hand, wouldn't you have stabbed him?"

Slowly, like she was processing the situation, she whispered, "I guess."

"There's no shame in that. I don't get off on killing people for the sake of it, Savannah. I'm not like Da—" I froze the second the words spilled from my lips and I pressed my foot to the brakes like we were driving a hundred miles an hour instead of a sedate twenty.

I'm not like Da.

Jesus.

Those words.

Four of them.

Four fucking words.

They hit me deep inside. Resonating, echoing, spinning around and around—

"Aidan? What is it?" Savannah demanded, her concern clear.

"I'm not like Da," I repeated, turning to her, unaware that I looked like death warmed over, which was ironic because for the first time in a long while, I felt alive again. "I'm not like Da."

She blinked at me then said, "Okay, well, I knew that already, but why do you keep saying it?"

"Because I thought I was," I said softly.

"Oh." She bit her lip, then her hand found mine and she twisted our fingers together. "I mean, I knew that but you're definitely not like him," she confirmed, then she bit her lip some more. "I didn't stop my research, Aidan, just because you ghosted me.

"In fact, I determined that I'd carry on but with more stealth." She cleared her throat. "I bribed a couple of coroners in Hell's Kitchen to slide any deaths they thought were mob-related my way."

"Jesus," I hissed, my hand tightening on hers. "What the fuck did you think you were doing?"

"I just, I don't know, I was curious. I always am. It's a failing." Her nose crinkled. "But either way, I quickly discerned a pattern."

"There's no way you could do that."

"If you're mathematically inclined, sure there is."

I thought about how she'd had all those autopsy reports on Paddy, and then wondered why I'd been so slow to fucking realize that she had an in with, not just the one coroner's office I'd threatened if they kept on feeding her files, but several.

I growled under my breath. "I don't believe you, Savannah!"

She scowled at me. "Why would I lie?"

I released a sigh as I reached up and pinched the bridge of my nose. "I don't mean that I think you're fucking lying. I mean I can't believe you did that shit. What the hell? I was trying to keep you from that—"

"I'm a grown ass woman, Aidan. I don't need someone to tell me what I can and can't see or do or read." She grumbled, "It's that kind of thinking that made us lose five years, buddy, so change the record. Anyway, I enjoyed it. I know it's weird, but I did."

"I've heard of weirder shit that people do in their off time. Although, granted, reading autopsy reports and itemizing them between mobsters definitely takes the cake. Never thought about pottery classes? How about learning how to macramé?

"Jesus, Savannah, we need to work on getting you some new hobbies." I scowled at her when she scowled at me. "No way in fuck you can maintain those links now. It'll bring shit back to us."

She huffed. "I only did it to keep an eye on you. There's no need to do that if I'm sitting on your face, is there?"

Even though I was beyond pissed at her, I had to laugh. "You're such a fucking pain in my ass, do you know that?"

"Well, takes one to know one," she sniped, huffing again and folding her arms across her chest with a petulant pout that made me want to bite her bottom lip. "I was only trying to tell you that I quickly discerned the deaths your father was involved in."

I reached up and rubbed my forehead where a headache was starting to gather. "You did?"

Did I even want to know how?

Just the idea of having to read reports was enough to make me want to puke. I spent most of my life avoiding the written word, and whenever I could, I listened to text.

The last words I'd read, in bulk, were from Uncle Paddy's fake autopsy report.

"I did. He has a flair that speaks of enjoyment. Your father would, in all likelihood, always have been a killer. Whether he was a part of the Irish Mob or not. So, when you say, 'You're not like your da,' I know you're not."

"You can't know that. Not really. Because I only just figured it out myself."

"I'm not saying you're not cruel, Aidan. The shit you did is terrifying, but there was no enjoyment to it. You didn't prolong people's deaths."

I thought she was old enough to know better, but she'd just proven to me that she was capable of some dumb fuck moments so I decided to test the waters, push her buttons, and tell her, "The guy who came into your apartment—I prolonged *his* death. He paid for what he did to you. He paid for not only hurting you but for scaring you. When I was torturing him for information, I made it slow and I made it hurt, but I did that for one reason."

"Me," she said softly, her smile pure when the topic of conversation was anything but pure.

"Yes," I said gruffly.

"Your father's a psychopath, Aidan—"

"You're the one who's excited about meeting him," I drawled, watching her shrug.

"He fascinates me. I can't help it." She chuckled, but it was sheepish. Embarrassed. "I know it's odd."

I could no more stop the soft laughter falling from my lips than I could stop night from turning into day. "I'm the one with the psychopath for a father, little one. If anyone should be embarrassed, it's me." When her warm gaze collided with mine, I teased, "Anyway, you're no stranger than those guys who like true crime novels."

Her nose crinkled. "Thank you for trying to normalize it, but I'm pretty sure they don't go to the extents that I have."

"I guess it was all just homework for the real thing, huh?" I jibed, feeling a little lighter, enough that I could joke about something that definitely wasn't funny, but then, she did that to me. For me.

Somehow, amid the darkness of my world, she shone a flashlight over it. Not to illuminate the nasty stains but stumbling over it like Nancy Drew. Except, this particular Nancy Drew had the hots for the bad guy. Not the good.

"You're not your father, Aidan," she assured me. "Not saying you're a good person, but you're not him."

I had to laugh. "Gee, thanks."

Sending me a wink, she murmured, "Just telling it how it is."

"Brutally so." I snorted, but I eased off the brakes and started trundling down toward the house.

"Aidan?"

"Yeah?"

"I don't—" She paused. "I can't—" When she hesitated again, I shot her a look. "What is it?"

"I'm just trying to find a way to phrase it."

"Phrase what?"

"I don't care what you do. I know I should. I know it's bad, but there's so much bad in this world. So much of it." Her head tipped back against the rest as her eyes fluttered close. "I've read so much of what the Sparrows did to women, and I've learned some things that I didn't want to know a human could do to another living being—some of which were in the files I got from the coroners—but I just ask one thing of you."

"What, little one?" I asked quietly.

She gulped, tilted her head toward me, then whispered, "That you don't get caught."

I released a breath, then reached for her hand and raised her knuckles to my mouth so I could brush my lips over them. "Your wish is my command."

THIRTY

SAVANNAH

THE DAY HAD NOT GONE how I'd imagined, but I was starting to see that that was the way my life was going to be from now on.

It wasn't even Aidan's fault.

It was mine.

He was right—I was the one who had dived into this with the Sparrows. I was the one who'd brought just enough danger to myself that Aidan had pushed aside his guilt, and had let his fear for my safety trigger him into acting because, in his mind, it was far better for him to be the monster in my life than the ones waiting out there in the shadows.

I didn't regret it, was truly fascinated by the turnabout, and when I walked through the front door to the family home and was confronted with seemingly hundreds, maybe even thousands of photographs, it was like ET had phoned home and had gotten a direct ride to his planet.

Eyes big, I stared at them all, scanned them for the faces I knew, ones I didn't, eager to absorb as much information as I could. When Aidan started laughing at my side, I didn't even notice, but someone else did.

Someone I didn't see until she stated, some confusion to her tone, "Junior?"

Tearing my attention from the photos, aware I was salivating and that it was weird, I came face to face with Magdalena O'Donnelly.

The matriarch to Aidan Sr.'s patriarch.

The woman he'd gone to war for.

The woman in whose name he'd committed unspeakable acts.

She was his wife, the mother of his children, but everyone knew she was more than that to Aidan Sr.

She was his queen.

"All right, Ma?" Aidan left my side and dipped down to kiss the cheek of the woman who'd appeared in the doorway. "Merry Christmas."

I gaped at him, at his ease with her, then shook myself because this was his mom. What was he supposed to do? Bow? Just because she was unofficial royalty didn't mean her kids treated her that way.

She narrowed her eyes at him. "And what about Thanksgiving, hmm? Not a call or a message."

He winced. "I'm sorry."

She scoffed, but begrudgingly muttered, "I'm sure you'll have a damn good reason for it. I'll leave you to explain that to your father. Merry Christmas, son." She reached up and grabbed his cheeks, her thumbs digging in. Not to hurt, but so she could tilt his face this way and that. "You look brighter." Her lips pursed as she assessed him.

"Feel it."

I didn't see what silent communication they had going on with their eyes, but Magdalena hummed and let him go. Then, she turned to me and with a false smile, asked, "Now, who's this?"

"She's trouble," Aidan teased, limping over to me and tucking me into his side.

I shot him a sheepish look, then untangled myself from his grasp and walked over to her.

A part of me really wanted to curtesy. And the way she was looking at me didn't help matters. I half expected her to call out,

"Aidan, come lop off her head," but she didn't. Just carried on looking me up and down as if I were a gnat.

"My name's Savannah. It's a pleasure to meet you," I greeted, then when she said nothing, I tacked on, "Merry Christmas."

"Ma," Aidan warned, strolling over to me and tucking his arm around my waist again.

"You boys are going to be the death of me," Magdalena muttered, her gaze on the way he held me close. "He's already up in arms about Brennan. Now you bring another girl over?"

I cleared my throat. "With respect, I'm not a girl."

"You are to me." She pinned me with a glance. "You're from that TVGM show, aren't you? The one who punched the executive in the nuts?"

I had no idea why, but I really wanted to laugh at her question. Instead, I politely murmured, "That's me."

"You have a good right hook."

"She doesn't actually," Aidan countered.

"You'd know, would you? What did you do to piss her off?" Magdalena asked, shooting him a gimlet stare.

Because I could tell the woman liked bullshit as much as I did, I was honest with her. "He told me that instead of being with me for the last five years, he was watching over me."

Magdalena's brows fluttered. "Watching over you?" she repeated. I felt Aidan grow tense at my side then yelped when she reached up, grabbed him by the ear and hauled him down to her height. "Aidan, did I raise a stalker?"

"No! He wasn't stalking me!" I cried out, shocked at how she started dragging him down the hall. But it was too late. "His knee!" I warbled, stumbling along after them as Aidan let her, *fucking let her*, clip him around the ear.

The necktie around my waist made it hard to walk fast as it squished me, so I was breathing heavily by the time we made it into a kitchen.

There were six women sitting at a table who immediately jumped to their feet at the spectacle.

Magdalena stormed toward them, son literally in hand, then she ground out, "Sit down!"

I figured she was talking to Aidan, but the women all obeyed, dropping into their chairs with an immediacy that would have been hilarious if I wasn't stunned by the turnabout.

Still with her fingers nipping his ear, she forced him to sit down, and I darted over, hands dithering as I tried to figure out how to fix this.

"He didn't hurt me!" I cried out.

"I didn't raise no pervert," Magdalena barked.

"Aidan's not a pervert," a red-headed woman chided.

I cast her a grateful glance, and as my brain tripped into gear, I realized it was Aoife O'Grady.

"He's not!" I confirmed.

Aidan smirked up at me. "I appreciate your defending my honor, little one. You too, Aoife." It was clear this was not the first time he'd been in a similar position, but Jesus, what if Aidan Sr. came in? Would he do something worse?

Imagining a very bloody Christmas—well, bloodier than whatever was going to happen to the Archbishop of New York—I snapped, "This isn't a joking matter, Aidan."

He snorted out a laugh. "It's pretty funny from where I'm sitting."

I growled at him, then to Magdalena rasped, "I promise, he was just watching over me."

"Why did you punch him then?"

"Because I didn't want him to watch over me. I wanted him to..." I gulped. "...*be* with me."

She squinted at me, but didn't let go of Aidan's ear, and behind me, I heard someone ask, "Aidan's smiling. It's weird."

I twisted around to glare at the table, and realized Jen was there. I scowled at her. "Shut up, you. What are you even doing here? And why didn't you text me about last night?"

Jen grinned, but a shadow invaded her expression at that last question. At any other time, I'd have been all over that, but the situation was dire, and my breathing was still out of whack.

"Aoife invited me. Said I couldn't spend the holidays alone worrying about my impending bankruptcy."

"I think we should get back to the matter at hand," another woman retorted, and when I shot her a look, I blinked when I recognized Camille Vasov, purportedly the latest O'Donnelly bride. She slipped out of her seat, moved over to Magdalena and gently cuffed the woman's wrist. "Let go, Magdalena. You know Aidan isn't a pervert."

Magdalena's mouth tightened. "Five years she said he was watching over her. Aidan O'Donnelly Jr. who set you up as a guardian angel?" She finally let go of his ear, and I winced with relief when he straightened his head, and wiggled his neck a little.

"I could say God, but you're not Da so I don't think you'd accept that as a legitimate excuse."

Magdalena huffed. "No, I wouldn't."

"How about that I was in love with her? That I couldn't be with her, not without bringing the poison from this fucking world to her front door, so I had to look over her from afar?"

"You'd still be talking to the wrong person," was his mother's waspish retort even if it made my heart flop around in my chest in a way that told me I needed to go visit a cardiologist—stat. "Since when was I a romantic?"

"At least you identify that it was romantic," Camille said softly, reaching over to pat her mother-in-law's shoulder. I wasn't sure why Magdalena looked at her, when she was the newest member of the family, but Aidan's mother did. Their glances collided and Camille sent her a gentle smile as she said, "And we all do crazy things when we're in love, don't we?"

Aidan rolled his eyes, but he reached up to rub his ear as he asked, "You stopped taking your meds or something, Ma? You're more snippety than usual."

"Shut up. You'll make this worse," I grumbled at him.

"There's no making it worse with Ma," he countered, his gaze fixed firmly on hers. "She knows we're not cattle at the market. She knows what an arranged marriage feels like. And she knows what it means when someone dark comes into your light and stains everything in sight."

His mother glowered at him, but she merely asked, "If you're such a stain, Aidan, then why did you darken her door at all?"

"Because she's helping us. She almost died yesterday—"

"Oh, my God, bitch! What the hell? Why didn't you tell me?"

I cast a glance at Jen. "Sorry," I mouthed, well aware that I deserved her glare. But there wasn't really an optimal moment to tell someone that you'd almost been killed.

Or, if there was, I'd never received the memo on that particular social nicety.

"What happened?" Magdalena demanded. "And don't you dare say it's business because if you do, Aidan, so help me God I'll let your father do worse things to that ear than I just did." She folded her arms against her chest. "Let's face it, you need me to smooth things over because if you're bringing girly over here for Christmas dinner it's more serious than you're letting on."

Aidan's lips curved up. "Ain't seen you this riled up for about ten years, Ma."

She squinted at him. "Don't smile at me and think you can worm your way out of things." His smile shot up a few megawatts, and Magdalena groused, "Why do you have to look like your father?"

"Well, he had to have something that'd make you weak at the knees, Ma. Sure as hell wasn't his sparkling personality, was it?"

Her lips curved. "He can be amusing in his own way."

"His own psychopathic way," someone muttered behind me.

Deciding to grab my balls back, I stopped pleating my fingers together and murmured, "Can we start again?" I held out my hand. "I'm Savannah."

"I'm Magdalena—"

"Lena," Camille chided, and her mother-in-law huffed.

"You can call me Lena though."

Unsure why Lena was listening to Camille, I shot the younger woman a smile first, then, the matriarch of the family. "Thank you so much."

Receiving a grunt for my pains, I watched as she wandered over to the stove.

"Do you want cake?"

Cake was the last thing I wanted, but Aidan nudged me with his elbow and nodded.

Quickly, I replied, "Please!"

Lena grumbled as she cut out a slice of cake, and that was how I found myself sitting at the kitchen table in a three-thousand dollar Valentino suit eating cranberry crumb cake while everyone—even though I already knew their names and most of their life stories—introduced themselves to me.

Because I was me, I was so tempted to turn my voice recorder on so I could listen to this again, but deciding that would be weird, instead I hyperfocused on everything that was said, and came to see another side of Aidan.

For all that he was at a table full of women, he was well at ease with each of them, and they with him. Aoife and Jen more than the others, but that fit seeing as they'd known each other a long time.

It was also clear to see that he was a momma's boy, but rather than being creepy as all hell, it was sweet. Caring. It showed another side to the man. Never did I think I'd meet his mother, and within seconds, he'd be hauled down the hallway by his ear! Talk about a baptism by fire.

"I was supposed to send you to your father when you arrived," Lena said after a short while.

"Is he in the office?" Aidan asked lazily, no rush in his voice.

"No. He's sniffing around that present you sent him."

Any laziness disappeared and he straightened up. "Sniffing around it?"

Lena shrugged. "They all are."

"Shit." Tension throbbed through him, and I reached over and patted his good knee.

"You go and sort that out, yeah?"

He shot me a glance, and as our eyes collided, the heat in his was at war with the ice. The heat was for me, the ice for what was about to happen. "Are you sure?"

"I won't clip her around the ear," Lena crooned, but that wasn't much of a consolation, was it?

A laugh escaped me though, because the tension that had Aidan sitting straight up seconds before was nothing to now. He shot his mother a glower that would have disintegrated a lesser person into dust, before he snapped, "No, Ma. Watch it. Don't even tease."

"How else am I supposed to get my fun?" she retorted with a huff.

"How about you don't terrify the mother of your grandchild?"

I froze, then elbowed Aidan in the side. "What the hell?"

He ignored me. "Give her some respect!"

Mouth dry, I rumbled, "I think we've gotten our wires—"

"She's pregnant?"

"She has a name!" Aidan countered.

I heaved a sigh. "I'm not pregnant."

"We don't know that."

Uh, yeah. We did.

I frowned at him, wondering what the hell his game was, then, of course, I recognized that if a woman could get pregnant by a look alone, it'd just happened.

I had no idea what he was doing, none whatsoever, but he'd apparently decided the way to get his mom on side was to lie to her.

Christ.

The last thing we needed today was a birth by immaculate conception. I was quite happy leaving that to the Virgin Mary.

As he leaned into me and pressed a kiss to my cheek, I muttered, "Thought you were Catholic. *Thou shalt not lie.*"

He snorted, and didn't reply, but turned to his mom and said, "You need to look out for her."

Lena was glaring at him, not me again. "Did you get married the way Brennan did?"

"No."

"Why not? If she's pregnant, your father will go mad."

"Yes, at me."

Lena sat up straighter. "What's going on here, Aidan? Is this a joke?"

He shrugged. "If you think my becoming a dad is a joke."

She sniffed. "Don't guilt trip me, boy. Go and play with your father but tell him the second it hits ten PM, that work stops. No excuses. Remember?"

"How could I forget?" he questioned wryly.

"What happens at ten?" I asked the woman beside me—Aoife.

"It's when the guys turn their phones off. No business until after brunch on the 26th."

My brows rose, but I said, "Thanks."

She smiled at me. "Don't worry about it. Lena will calm down. She's probably still in shock."

"I'm not pregnant," I muttered, aware mother and son were sniping at each other.

"Aidan clearly wants her to think you are," was Aoife's dry retort. "God knows why but these men are wily." She chuckled. "Method to every madness."

That had me frowning as I turned back to Aidan when his arm slid around my shoulder. He turned me into him and kissed me sedately on the lips.

A glint was back in his eye, cold and hard, which made his soft kiss all the more powerful. "Be good."

I blinked. "What can I do here?"

He smirked at me. "That's exactly what I'm asking myself." Sniggering, I watched as he clambered to his feet. "Okay, ladies, I'll see you back at dinner."

"There's a golf cart waiting outside for you to take to the summer house," Lena told him. "Your da sent it over to save your knee. Why you won't just use a goddamn cane I'll never know."

"Not this again," Aidan sniped as he limped off, letting me realize that when I'd spoken with him about his leg, I wasn't the first to get in his face about it.

Lena pinned me with her stare the second the French doors that led to a very lovely patio area slammed to a close. "Don't you care that he's hobbling around like that?"

"I do. We've already argued about it," I confirmed, well aware that I had to find my footing here.

Fast.

Lena wasn't any scarier than the guy who'd infiltrated my apartment and I'd managed to hold him off with a mop and a coffee table book. How much worse could this be?

"Argue a lot, do you?"

"Lena," Aoife chided. "You've got to give her a chance."

"I don't have to do anything." Lena sniffed. "He brings a girl to my doorstep and—"

I didn't want to start on a lie. "Lena, I'm not a girl, and I'm not pregnant. I don't know why Aidan said that. I don't want to lie to you though, because I'm going to be a part of your son's life for a long time, and eventually, you're going to realize that I'm not pregnant," I said wryly.

Lena pursed her lips. "Remind me to clip his ear again?"

I winced. "He was just trying to protect me."

"No, he was trying to manipulate me into twisting his da's arm to the idea of another non-arranged marriage." She grunted. "Only my Eoghan was a good boy."

Inessa, the youngest wife here, murmured, "I can promise you he isn't a good boy, Lena." Her mother-in-law cackled, surprising me. Inessa shot me a smile. "Let's not lie to ourselves, hmm?"

"It was good to see Aidan smile though, wasn't it?" Aoife prompted.

Lena huffed, but she did concede, "Thought my ears were deceiving me when I first heard him laugh." I received a gimlet stare. "So there's some use to you, at least."

"Better than Prozac, that's me," I confirmed, something settling inside me as the other women started taking some of the spotlight off me.

"The boy's been on worse than Prozac," Aela retorted.

"His eyes were clear, weren't they?" Inessa asked.

So, they'd known he was taking drugs. "He's clean. Has been for about six weeks," I informed them.

Lena pursed her lips. "You the reason for that?"

I shook my head. "No."

"Well, unlike my son, at least you're honest. Used to be a time when they were terrified to lie because their da used to tell them he'd cut off their fingers if they did."

"Christ," Aela muttered.

"You know that's not a good thing, don't you, Grandma?" I turned to see Seamus, Declan's son, pausing in his attempts to lick a spoon clean of what looked like cake batter.

The female population in five years' time was going to swoon whenever he walked into a room.

These O'Donnellys and their goddamn genes. Talk about blessed.

"There are worse things in this world, my boy."

Victoria said something that had Shay smirking, and they turned to each other, chuckling in a way that had both their cheeks burning with heat.

Teen crushes were so cute.

"I won't be telling Jacob that I'll cut his fingers off if he lies," Aoife muttered.

Lena shrugged. "Different times."

"Not sure there was ever an era where that *wasn't* politically incorrect, Lena." Camille pursed her lips. "You were upset when you found out about Eoghan's beating—"

"When was he beaten?" Inessa burst out, bristling.

"Before your wedding," Aoife murmured as she bit into a sugar cookie.

"How did you know that?" Jen asked.

"Finn was mad at Aidan Sr."

Lena's mouth tightened. "Keeping them on the straight and narrow is one thing, but beating them into—" She sighed. "I know you were beaten too, child, for not wanting to go through with the marriage."

Eyes wide, cake forgotten, and fascination at fever pitch with this conversation, I tried not to feel like I was living in a reality TV show.

Talk about bliss.

"It's never right to beat your child," Aela grumbled. "Even if he's a pain in the butt and won't ever do as he's told," she called out so Shay could hear.

He grinned at her. "Mom, you know you love my BS."

She rolled her eyes. "If you say so, kiddo."

"I didn't like it," Lena admitted. "But I wasn't as brave as you all back then."

"Hard to imagine you not being able to chew nails," Aoife commented with a soft laugh.

"Well, Junior wasn't wrong about the darkness staining everything, was he? We talked about that."

Damn, I wished I'd been a fly on the wall for that conversation.

Lena drummed her fingers against the scrubbed oak kitchen table, which made her nails clack against it and, clearly wanting to change the subject, asked, "You were dating all those years ago?"

"No. It didn't work out." I shifted in my seat. "But I'm glad we're together now."

She tipped her chin. "Did you really argue with him over a cane?"

"Yes—" Sheepishly, I admitted, "I bought him one for Christmas, but it will be delivered to my apartment in The Sharpe."

"You bought him a cane?" Lena repeated, and I wasn't sure why that surprised her, but it did because her brows were doing a salsa dance on her forehead.

"I did. My mother taught me that if you can't make a man listen, you just make him do instead."

Lena processed that but slowly grinned. "She's a smart woman."

"She is actually," I agreed dryly. "She had to be smarter with a man like my father."

"Why? What's wrong with him?"

"He's a famous musician," I explained quietly, aware I had everyone's attention.

"Famous is an understatement," Jen tossed out after she finished dissecting a cookie on a paper napkin with her fingers and popped a piece into her mouth. "Her dad is Dagger Daniels."

At the center of everyone's attention again, I glared at Jen. "Thanks for that."

She winked. "Welcome, bitch."

I groaned, because she wasn't going to forgive me any time soon for not telling her about my almost dying. That's what good friends were for, I guessed.

"Why do I know that name?" Lena questioned, brow furrowing.

Aoife chuckled. "You know his music, Lena. He's Conor's favorite, isn't he?"

"Not with those *noxxious* men?" Lena grunted. "Good God, I had to listen to their music on repeat when he was a boy. It's no wonder I don't remember. I purposely gave myself amnesia."

Amused, I toyed with my necklace. "Well, their music isn't for everyone."

"Still, Conor must be happy," Aoife said with a laugh. "Bet he's jealous he didn't get to you first."

"I think he'll cope. Anyway, he's taken, isn't he?"

Silence fell again, and yes, it was awkward, enough that I shuffled in my seat. Something about Lena made me feel like I was thirteen and had been caught trying to record the principal and the high school secretary having sex so I could print it in the paper.

Something I'd deny in court.

Lena loomed over the table. "My baby's taken?"

I blinked. "Well. That's what he said."

Aoife cleared her throat. "Oh, dear."

THIRTY-ONE

AIDAN

I DIDN'T WANT to leave Savannah with my ma. Mostly because she was in a finicky mood—it had been years since I'd been clipped around the ear—but also because nobody should be dumped on family as fast as Savannah had been, when their partner had to head on out.

I had a feeling if anyone could survive a trial by fire with Magdalena O'Donnelly as the judge then it was her, but still, I knew it was cruel abandoning her, and only did so because if Da opened up the fucking van and found the Archbishop of New York in there, then my ear wouldn't have been the only thing being clipped today—my balls would be next.

The golf cart had wind whipping around me as I traveled over the large acreage toward the summer house. It had a nice name, but a not-so-nice purpose.

Ma used it tongue-in-cheek, but there was nothing tongue-in-cheek about what Da was capable of doing there.

By the time I reached the property, my nuts had almost frozen off despite my thick winter coat, and the van was still outside, so relief hit me as I clambered off the cart and headed inside the building.

About the size of a small house, Da had an office in here as well as a man cave for when he was in Ma's bad books. I'd never looked, but I was sure he had a bedroom for that purpose as well.

"Merry Christmas," I greeted Liam, one of Da's usual guards, who was a bit beaten up after that shit show at Coney Island two months ago.

"Same to you, Aidan. They're in the office. He's chomping at the bit," Liam warned, making me pull a face.

"Thanks for the heads-up."

Liam just grinned as I hobbled into the house.

Sound alone would have told me where my family was, because, Jesus, they were loud.

As I made it to the end of the hall, I cast a look in the office first, and had to hide a smile because amid the whole chaos, Jacob was fast asleep on Finn's chest, not even flinching whenever Da boomed with laughter or Declan and Brennan began bickering over fuck knew what.

That kid, I swore.

Finn and I were on a wavelength that didn't exist for anyone else in my family. I wasn't sure if that was because of what we'd done together, of the demons we'd fought side by side, or if it was because we were the eldest, but he cast me a look the second I popped my head around the door, like he knew I was there.

Then, of course, Jake being a traitor stirred, hauled himself around his dad's knee and garbled, "Un-cail, Un-cail!" Da had taught him that I was *uncail* in Gaelic, so the poor little fecker had to get his tongue around that now. He'd proved himself to be stubborn when I'd tried to unteach it, and he still used the butchered Gaelic.

Conversation came to a screeching halt at Jake's call, and Da, who was sitting on his office chair, surrounded by maroon leather and mahogany wood like he was Colonel Mustard in Clue, kicked his legs off the antique desk and straightened up. "Junior!" he boomed. "What's this gift you've sent me? Is it to make up for missing Thanksgiving?"

"Where's Kid?" I questioned, rather than answering.

"At the house. He's working," Finn explained.

"So he should be as well. Fine mess he's gotten us into," Da complained, twirling a cigar between his fingers before he took a deep puff.

"Thought Ma forbade you from having those," I groused, folding my arms across my chest.

"It's Christmas," was his retort.

"Exactly. Don't think it's fair Kid's working, do you? When it's Christmas?"

"His system was breached—"

"And he acted the exact way he was supposed to. There's no code-version of Fort Knox, Da. Everything can be deciphered." I huffed as I limped into the room and perched my ass on the side of his desk. "You can't keep fining him."

"Of course, I can. He's my boy. Little prick would get too big a head if I didn't." Da frowned at me. "What's with you, anyway? Bringing me a gift then telling me off all in one go?"

I grunted. "Sometimes you need to be told. No fucker else will outside of this room."

Da grinned at me, which was always a surprise. His changeability was worse than the fucking weather. "Need my boys to keep me grounded, do I?"

"You need us to do something, that's for fucking sure," Eoghan retorted, getting to his feet and mirroring my position on the edge of the desk. When he crossed his arms too, he tipped his head to the side and asked, "What's with the white van? You going Dexter on us?"

Ordinarily, even when I was high, I'd have flipped him the bird. Today? Well, it was too opportune with Kid not being here. As much as I knew he deserved the retribution, I wasn't sure if I could...

Jesus.

This was one of the few promises I'd made in my life that I'd kept.

He'd begged Finn and I never to tell Da, he'd made us swear.

After that day, when Paddy had helped clear up the mess I'd made of that piece of shit, we'd never talked of it again. I'd tried to be there for him, but Kid was Kid. He went his own way, seeming to do that even more so in the aftermath.

Reaching up and rubbing along my bottom lip with my thumb, I rasped, "Da, I need to speak with you alone." I shot Finn a look. "You too."

"Fuck off," Eoghan scoffed. "Ain't we old enough to hear whatever shit you've been up to?"

I cast him a look. "No. You're not."

Eoghan frowned at me, but the prospect of sharing this with my brothers was... impossible. *Heinous*. A betrayal to Kid.

Brennan and Declan got to their feet, clambering around me, evidently thinking that would intimidate me into speaking—because, yeah, that'd work on me.

Instead of rolling my eyes, I shot Finn a look. His head tipped to the side with confusion, but he knew I was sending him a message—he just didn't know what I was saying.

Letting my gaze drift down to Jake, I murmured, "Eoghan, can you take Jake back to Aoife?"

Finn frowned. "She's baking. I was supposed to entertain him."

"He looks real entertained," I said dryly when I saw him tearing bits of paper apart. Fuck even knew where he'd gotten it from. "Plus, he doesn't need to hear any of this." My jaw clenched, any amusement fading, and I said to my other brothers, "You need to back off."

"If this is about business," Eoghan growled, "then we have as much right to be here as anyone else."

"It isn't." I knew then they weren't going to fuck off. So I lied. "I want to tell Da about what's been going on with me."

Declan's brows rose. "Yeah?"

I hummed.

"Why does Finn get to stay?"

I shot him a mocking smile. "Back up?"

Brennan squinted at me. "This sounds like bullshit."

"Well, you spout enough of it," I retorted, "to recognize the smell. Now, fuck off all of you. I just need a half-hour is all. When playtime comes around, you can have fun with us if you want. Or like any goddamn regular person, you can enjoy a pre-Christmas Eve lunch with your women."

Eoghan cleared his throat. "He has a point."

Brennan grunted. "He does." To me, he muttered, "Fucker."

I just smirked at him, then to Declan and Eoghan said, "When you get back there, I brought a guest. Be nice." I was careful not to use pronouns.

"What the hell's going on, Junior?" Da rumbled as I micromanaged his boys.

Looking at him, I murmured, "I need privacy."

We weren't the closest, even though I was the eldest and had been around the old bastard the longest. I'd also been at his side for the most time, reared by his own hand as it were. Da was... I almost sighed. He was just Da. Insane, deranged, violent, but I knew he loved me. I knew he loved his boys, it just wasn't the type of love that another father would understand. Not even one in the life.

His concern was clear though. My words had any festive jollity fading as he said, "Boys, do as your brother asks."

Eoghan, Brennan, and Declan headed out, scowling all the while, with Eoghan grabbing Jake and tossing him around a little which had the kid squealing with joy.

"Your boy likes me better," Eoghan boasted as he grabbed the many tons of layers the kid needed to step foot outside. By the time Eoghan was done dressing him, he looked like a padded starfish.

"For now he does," Finn jibed, then tacked on, "fuckface."

I grinned a little as Eoghan flipped him the bird, which Jake snagged in his hand, then gnawed on it like it was a pacifier.

When they drifted out, I asked Finn, "Check they've left?"

Frowning at me again, he got to his feet and wandered over to the door. Beyond, there was the hall I'd just walked down and it had windows, so I knew he could see them make their way back to the main house.

He turned around and said, "They're leaving."

"What's going on, Junior?" Da rasped.

I rubbed my chin. "This is hard to talk about, Da."

"I know about the Oxy. You don't have to tell me—"

I wasn't altogether surprised that Da figured it out. He was watchful around me anyway. But it still had me wincing. "The boys will be pissed. They thought they did a good job of covering for me."

He shrugged. "Know you too well. Like looking in the mirror."

Deep inside, I winced, but I clung to the conversation Savannah and I had had together in the car.

I wasn't like him.

We *weren't* a reflection of one another.

"I'm clean."

"Figured as much when Conor kept making excuses for you every time I called." Da took a deep drag of his cigar before he ground the glowing tip into an ashtray. "It's the only reason I let you get away with missing Thanksgiving.

"I'm not sure I like how you'll all lie to me to protect each other, but what can I say? I did the same for my brothers, and I wouldn't want your relationships to be weaker for it." He grunted. "Let's not make a habit of it though, hmm?"

"What? The lies or the drugs?"

"Both, preferably."

His calm surprised me, but to be honest, I was past caring if he knew or not. I was clean now, nothing to hide. If anything, the truth being out would be easier on us all. Pussyfooting around Da was never a simple task.

It was only then that I realized how much of a weight had been lifted off my shoulders. Doing without the Oxy was hard, but there were some advantages to living without it.

And with Savannah around, well, it wasn't difficult to stay distracted. Not just because her pussy was like the fucking mothership calling me home, but because thus far, it had been the opposite of all quiet on the Western Front thanks to her exposés.

"Surprised you let me get away with it for as long as you did."

"Knew you'd get yourself right when you were ready." He scratched his jaw. "Had a problem with Angel Dust back in the day. Managed to clean myself up before it got to be too big an issue."

Finn snorted, but it was soft and I heard him mutter, "Explains a lot," as he drifted past me.

I hid another smile.

Da eyed me. "Been thinking about visiting that orthopedic surgeon of yours."

Surprised, I jerked back. "Why?"

"I'm sure he fucked up your surgery. My boy don't get hooked for nothing. I figure he messed up the procedure and the hospital is covering his ass." His gaze turned mean. "Figured I'd break his knees, let him see how much pain you were in—"

Scoffing, I told him, "Da, that's insane."

"He fucked up. You shouldn't be like this all these years later. Hobbling around like a goddamn cripple. It's not right."

"Maybe it is, maybe it isn't." I cleared my throat. "I should go in for a check up."

"Thought you had to go in regularly," Da pointed out as Finn mirrored my position on his desk, much as Eoghan had earlier.

"I do, and I haven't been."

Da growled. "Dipshit."

"I know." I ducked my head. "It was easier just to pop some pills, but I'm gonna have to do something. The pain's bad. But... either way, don't be breaking any surgeon's knees, okay? It's not necessary."

Da grumbled under his breath but, otherwise, stayed silent.

"The reason I wanted to talk with you... it's not about the drugs." Reaching up to rub the back of my neck, I rasped, "Do you remember when Father Doyle went to the Vatican? Finn and I were about fifteen?"

I felt Finn's tension—didn't even have to look at him to sense it.

"Jesus, that's ancient history, boy. What the hell do you want me to be thinking about that for? Wasn't that when Paddy was—" He swallowed. "When those bastards slaughtered him like he was a fucking pig?"

"Aidan, what are you doing?" Finn asked softly.

"I gotta tell him, Finn. I ain't got no choice. So much is wrapped up in this story. It's such a fucking mess."

"What are you two talking about?" Da growled. "Don't keep me in the dark. Fucking hate that."

"It's entangled, Da. It's not that easy to explain."

"Start at the beginning," he said, calmer now, which told me he saw how genuine I was being. None of this was going to be easy to talk about.

"That year, when Doyle was in Rome, there was a priest. McKenna."

"I remember him. Odd." He scowled. "Shifty eyes. What about him?"

For a second, I couldn't even get the words out, and then I didn't have to because Finn, in a whisper, said, "He molested Conor."

The office was so silent that I felt like I could hear mine and Finn's racing heartbeats as if they were a starting pistol. Da's chair creaked as he rocked back.

"This isn't some joke that you're both going to regret when I break your fucking noses for daring to even say that out loud, is it?"

I shook my head. "I wish it were, Da. I wish it were."

THIRTY-TWO

AIDAN SR

MY HANDS TIGHTENED around the edge of the desk as I processed the unthinkable.

He.

Molested.

Conor.

I felt each word like a punch to the head. In fact, I'd have preferred that. I'd prefer the pain, I'd take that a thousand times over—

My boy.

My goddamn boy.

Ruined.

Defiled.

Broken.

The roar escaped me without my even knowing it, and the desk, loaded down with papers and picture frames, went flying as a piece of furniture that weighed two hundred pounds was suddenly no longer in front of me.

It was tipped up on its side, both my boys having staggered back at the suddenness of my move as I turned it over with my bare hands.

With a scream, I twisted around, picked up the desk chair then hurled it against the wall behind me.

As it caught on the window, the glass shattered, but it wasn't enough. I picked it up again and slammed it there, over and over, over and fucking over, each slam not enough. Never enough.

My poor, goddamn boy.

Abused.

Violated.

With the broken wreckage of the chair in my hands, I dropped it to the ground and with a keening wail that penetrated the haze in my head, I slammed everything on the dresser in front of me to the ground, the beloved photographs, the crucifix my grandmother had given me at my confirmation and which I'd framed, I threw it all to the floor like it was trash.

At that moment, it was.

Tearing out the drawers that were loaded down with documents, I slammed them there too—each one of them strewn on the floor like garbage. Then when they were bare, I hurled them across the room with a strength that was born of rage.

For the first time in my life, I understood why wrath was one of the seven deadly sins.

As I stood there, panting, my lungs burning, my heart pounding, my fists tightened into balls that made my nails prick my skin, my feet buried within papers that had made the Irish Mob into the powerhouse it was today, feeling wilder than a rabid wolf, I snarled, "Find him. He has to die."

"He's dead, Aid—" Finn paused. Corrected, "*Da*. He has been a long time."

Jesus.

None of this was a lie if Finn couldn't call me by my name. If he had to use a title that he'd never used before and in front of Junior. But I didn't even care that my oldest had heard it.

If anything, Finn's use of that had my knees wobbling, cascading out from under me as I pressed my back to the wall and stared blindly ahead.

If the fucker was dead, then there was no retribution.

How was I supposed to avenge Conor?

How was I supposed to fix this?

How was I supposed to make it right for him?

I'd spent their entire lives trying to make my boys bulletproof. I'd done shit no ordinary parent would ever condone, I'd forged them in hell to make them ready for heaven, making an enemy out of each of them to protect them from the fuckers out there.

They thought I was a monster?

That was nothing to the Fieris of this world.

I had standards. I didn't touch kids. I didn't sell sex slaves.

My boys were my heirs. The city was my bequest to them. They'd rule over it together. Just like I should have done with my brothers until they'd been torn from me.

Ripped away.

I never wanted that for my boys, so I made them strong. I made them tight-knit. I made them a unit. Sacrificing what I should have had with each of them. I'd done that to protect them, but on my watch, under my fucking eye, a man of God had touched Conor.

My boy.

My fucking boy.

My head slammed back into the wall.

Once.

Twice.

Four times.

Six.

"Da! Stop it!"

Junior was there, in my face, his hands on my shoulders as he grabbed me. Finn was there next, both of them hauling me away from the wall, but I fought them both. My two boys, for all that one was injured, were normally both stronger than me—not at that moment. I tossed them both aside and twisted around, my forehead slamming into the drywall.

Two times.

Five.

I didn't even feel the pain.

Grief robbed me of it.

How did I fix this?

How could I fix the unfixable?

"Conor," I shouted, tears in my eyes, burning like acid, sinking through soft flesh like they were made from cotton candy. "My fucking boy." Judders of emotion rolled through me as I pulled back from the wall, then slammed one fist into it before letting the other rip.

"Da! Stop this. I ain't finished explaining," Junior hollered, grabbing me by the shoulders again and trying to stop me, trying to keep me still.

But there was no keeping the monster still.

He was out.

He needed blood.

I twisted around so I could snarl, "Fuck your explanations." I snatched Junior by the collar, hauled him close, and snapped, "Did the fucker touch you?"

He shook his head, his hands coming to my arms, his fingers pinching the flesh of my biceps. "We think it was just Kid."

Mouth wobbling before I firmed it, I demanded, "Finn?" My boy had already been through that once, had the priest taken advantage of him too?

"No. He didn't touch me." Our eyes clashed and held with the secret we shared. With knowledge I'd never divulge.

"What about Brennan and Declan?" I grated out.

"No. We made sure to ask."

"I trusted him with my soul, my eternal spirit," I ground out. "But he defiled one of my boys..." My voice turned hoarse. "Who killed him?"

"I did," Junior rasped. His mouth worked a little. "I saw red."

"What happened?" I tipped my head back so I could look at them, catching the glance they shared, but before they could think to hide anything else from me, I rumbled, "Tell me. Everything."

There was no peace to be had, but retribution had to be measured.

McKenna might be gone, but there'd be someone in his family who could pay for his sins.

And if all his kin were dead, then their graves could be defiled. Anything to unsettle their souls and rip them from the comfort of death.

When Finn whispered, "We caught him in the confessional," time seemed to fracture. Splintering. Shattering. "We dragged him out, Aidan grabbed a candlestick." He swallowed, like he was nervous. Like he hadn't done a thousand worse things than this in his time. Like he knew my sanity rested on his next few words. "He beat him to death."

Pride wasn't something I often felt, because it was the lesser of the seven deadly sins in my opinion and seeing as I had a hold of most of the worst ones, I figured pride was something I could do without.

At that moment, pride began to swell inside me.

Like father, like son.

Nostrils flared, jaw clenched, I sought out my son's eyes, and I rasped, "Did you do me proud?"

"It was nothing to be proud of."

Some semblance of peace settled inside me. Junior wasn't as bad as me, and I hoped he never would be either, but when he saw red, it was the same shade that always plagued me.

That meant the bastard had suffered.

As much as a teenaged Junior was able to make a man like that suffer. Which, now I thought about it, wasn't much. Wasn't enough.

My eyes grew wet, and unashamed of the emotion flooding me, I let the tears gather.

"How did you make him pay?" I needed to know, more than I needed Lena to take her next breath.

"He was a bloody pulp by the time Uncle Paddy got there and helped us clean it up."

I tensed. "Padraig knew?"

"He did."

Had this been his first kill?

I remembered sending him to the optometrist because the boy couldn't shoot in a straight fucking line, then there'd been that phase where he and Paddy had gone to the boxing club every couple of days —both him and Finn now that I thought about it.

This must be the reason why. Paddy had taken them away to help them.

My poor boys.

This had made them men.

And they'd gone to Paddy, not me.

Fuck.

I knew I was a monster. The Five Points needed that. They didn't need some pansy-assed wimp sitting on the throne, but a man who knew how to lead through fear. Who had the whole city at his feet, who made them scared of what the O'Donnellys would and could do next.

I'd done that.

I'd been all that.

I'd even treated my sons like they were toy soldiers and I was their general.

I'd forged them in fire, strengthening them until they were ready to take over in my stead, but they'd gone to my brother when they should have come to me.

That had the stuffing in my joints disappearing as I dropped to my knees, sagging over, panting as I rested my hands on the floor.

It was only then I saw the blood on my fists, the wrecked skin, the busted knuckles—but I felt no pain. I rarely did. Blood spattered against the wooden slats beneath me, the garnet red drops dark as night against the mahogany floor.

Junior muttered, "Conor made him swear that he wouldn't tell you. You know Uncle Paddy took being a godfather seriously."

"Why didn't you tell me? I could have made him pay. Made him suffer. Made him fucking hurt."

"Because Conor made us promise not to. He didn't want you to know," Junior whispered rawly.

The shame that triggered in me almost made me twist around so I could slam my head into the wall a few more dozen times.

"Why not?" I cried, unaware that tears mingled with blood as they coursed in rivets down my cheeks. "He had to know I'd burn the church down for him."

How the fuck was I supposed to confess there now?

How the fuck was I supposed to get to my knees, admit to my sins and atone for them, in the place where my boy had to get to *his* knees? Had to—

Dear God.

How many times had Conor confessed in that booth?

How many times had I made him go to the place where he'd been abused? Made him confess for his sins, *atone*? Seek penitence in a church that must have been his personal hell?

"I don't know why. I wanted to—" He heaved a sigh and pinched the bridge of his nose. "You know what Kid's like. He moves in his own way."

"I'd have made him pay," I raged. "He had to know I'd kill for him. For all of you."

Anything for them.

My boys.

My fucking boys.

Didn't they know the only warmth this broken soul of mine ever felt was when I was with them and Lena? Didn't they know that my family was the only light in the darkness? The only thing that kept that fucking pit of blackness that threatened to swallow me whole every day at bay?

"I'd have made that bastard pay. He has to know that. How couldn't he know that?" I sobbed out.

"The only way to find out is to ask him yourself," Junior whispered.

Finn cleared his throat. "Why'd you break that promise now, Aidan? Neither of us have even spoken about it together, never mind telling someone else."

Junior skewered Finn with a look. "I found out today that the Archbishop of New York is a Sparrow."

"Monsignor Masters is a Sparrow?" I repeated dazedly, needing to know for sure.

I clung to the statement like the saving grace it was.

McKenna was dead. I couldn't kill him again.

The Archbishop still breathed and he was one of those secret society sons of bitches. That put a nice, big fat target on his forehead. At least, it did as far as I was concerned.

Junior nodded slowly. "He is."

"How do you know?"

"It's been a busy couple of days," my eldest said with a grunt.

"Start at the beginning," I snapped. "Just tell me what you know."

"You heard of Valentini?"

"That Sicilian who slices up one side of a fucker's face?"

"That's him. He's making a power grab for the head of the *Famiglia*. Says that peace with the Irish will help him cement his position if we grant it."

"Why would I grant any Italian bastard peace?" I rasped, confused. My mind already felt fractured, but the out-of-the-blue topic jarred it even more.

"Because it's good business?" Finn questioned softly. "It's doing no one any favors for us all to be at war, and with the Russians having new leadership as well, it'd be a good time to broker a deal between the top factions. A mini-Summit, as it were, but with anything other than the Sparrows as the subject on the table like last time."

"That," Junior agreed, "as well as the fact that Valentini's the one who told me Monsignor Masters is a Sparrow?"

"He did?" I whispered, my brow furrowed, blood dripping through the wrinkles.

"He did," Junior confirmed. "He wants to speak with you, see if you can come to some sort of arrangement together." He hesitated. "The Archbishop is in the white van... Valentini said it's his Christmas gift to you." Tension riddled me like cancer through a bone but before I could say a word, Junior carried on, "He said that the Archbishop has sheltered several pedophiles within the church."

Wrath howled inside me again.

Conor didn't want me to know about this. If he did, he'd have come to me and shared the truth years ago, and that was my failing. My flaw as a father. Junior had done my job for me, getting rid of the predator who dared prey on my son, so that option wasn't open to me either.

The Archbishop was the only remaining pawn on the chessboard. He was the only piece I had left to play and play him I would. So fucking brutally the Devil wouldn't be able to tell the difference between him and one of his demons when I was done with him.

Nostrils flaring wide, I growled, "Sheltered seven sick fucks, did he?"

"Apparently," Junior muttered, eying me warily.

That was when purpose flooded me. A sense of direction that helped me clamber to my knees. I ignored the blood, ignored the mess of my office, instead, I demanded, "It's time to open my Christmas gift, boys."

And time to make one sick bastard pay.

Ho, ho, fucking ho.

THIRTY-THREE

SAVANNAH

WITH JEN IN THE BATHROOM, and all the other women assigned tasks that were more appropriate for people not wearing Valentino suits—seriously, why hadn't Aidan told me this was an informal get together? He'd been wearing a suit, so I'd dressed up as well. Men, FML—I was out of it while also in my element.

Observing was what I did best, and as I sat there, watching Lena direct the troops that were her daughters-in-law, a grandson who was more interested in looking down Victoria's blouse, Inessa and Camille's sister, while blushing whenever Inessa talked to him, and Aoife who took it all in stride while doing most of the work, I absorbed the moment.

Yes, I had stars in my eyes.

These were the people I'd been investigating my whole life.

I was under their roof.

I was inside their kitchen.

I was going to break bread with them.

This was turning biblical, and all without me schtupping one of their sons.

When a cup of coffee was placed in front of me, I shot a smile at

Camille who, rubbing a hand over her forehead, took a seat at my side.

She was sweaty and flour-covered, and when she took a sip of her drink, she sighed like she'd been working down a coal mine.

Not that I could judge—I was tired just watching all the women work.

The orgasms Aidan had given me had definitely stunned the shit out of me, but so was being breathless, which was why his necktie now graced the trash can in the bathroom.

Squirming while around his family wasn't something I'd try again. Especially not when Lena kept glowering at me.

"She's a hard taskmaster," Camille commented quietly, her smile warm. Welcoming. *Kind.*

Was it horrible that I'd never imagined a Bratva Pakhan's daughter being kind?

Now I knew how David Attenborough felt in the wilds of Africa, monitoring lions and lionesses in their natural habitat. Although, I didn't imagine those lions ate a lot of Beef Wellington with special, home-made cranberry sauce.

"She looks like it," I agreed. "I'm not sure whether I want to smack Aidan for failing to tell me that I'm overdressed, or relieved that I am."

Camille grinned. "He probably did it to save you from having to cook. Brennan wasn't so kind to me." Her nose crinkled. "I quite enjoy it though."

"You do?" I asked dubiously. "You're all sweaty."

"I'm not very good in the kitchen, but I like learning."

"What are you cooking?"

"All kinds of things. You know Brennan and I are married, yeah?"

"Well, news hasn't hit Page 6 yet, but that rock on your finger gave it away." Plus, of course, Lena had said that Brennan's marriage had caused a ruckus with his father. I wasn't a journalist for nothing.

She hummed, but she played with the massive gemstone. "Lena

was hard on me too at first, just so you know. I'm sure she'll warm up to you soon. It helps that you didn't lie to her."

"Men, right?" I clucked my tongue. "Why on earth Aidan would think starting my relationship with his parents with that lie between us would work is beyond me."

Camille chuckled. "I think it was more the desperate act of a man who was trying to shield you from his mother. She can be brutal when she wants to be."

"You know her well?" I asked, curious because if she did know Lena well, it meant the Bratva and Irish Mob had been friends longer than they'd let on to the public.

As far as I knew, a truce had been drawn when Inessa had married Eoghan. They said the Irish had colluded with the Russians to take down the Colombians who'd been behind the drive-by shooting that had wrecked Aidan's knee, but I wasn't sure how accurate a depiction that was yet.

Most of what I knew was from secondhand reports.

That I was sitting with someone who was a source made me salivate.

"Not particularly, but recently, I think all of her daughters-in-law have grown closer."

I tipped my head to the side. "Do you mind me asking why? Because, to be frank, I need me some of that."

"You're truly with Aidan?"

"Well, yeah, that's why I'm here."

"No, I mean, you're with him. Seriously?" Her look was measured, and I got the sense that she wasn't going to tell me shit unless I flashed an engagement ring in her face.

"Well, I'd like to be. I mean, I love him if that counts."

Camille's mouth quirked up at the corners. "It counts. I do not know him well, not like Inessa, and she said that she hasn't seen him laugh in many moons."

"He's in pain," I excused. "I knew him before. He was... different back then. I like this new Aidan to be honest."

"Why? In what way is he different?"

"I mean, don't get me wrong. He's arrogant now, and he's got a bit of an ego. I'm not blind—but that's part of the problem. If I were a guy and I looked like him, I'd be egotistical too."

Camille snorted. "And you're not beautiful?"

"Well, he's Aidan O'Donnelly." I drooled. "I mean, he's Aidan frickin' O'Donnelly."

She blinked. "I don't understand?"

I wafted a hand. "Some kids have rock stars, some have authors, I fangirl for mobsters."

A snicker escaped her. "Seriously?"

I grimaced. "I promise, it's loaded in psychoses."

"Is that supposed to be reassuring? That it comes therapist-approved?"

"I might not see a therapist," I pointed out, even though I had *two* therapists.

"You're Dagger Daniels' daughter," she countered with a laugh. "Of course you have a therapist."

"I feel pigeonholed," I complained. "I don't think you should only drink vodka because you're Russian."

She grinned. "I do drink vodka. A lot. Just not in front of my mother-in-law."

"That's very smart thinking." We both shared a laugh. "Anyway, Aidan is Aidan. But before, he was, well, a fuck boy."

"I don't mean to be rude, but he still is, isn't he?"

While I couldn't get mad when Aidan and I had basically claimed each other within a period of time that could still be counted in hours, I sniped, "They all are. They can be reformed, can't they?"

"True." She smiled at me. "Okay, you passed the test."

"I did?"

"Yep, you'd have blown smoke up my ass if you were just gossiping. Instead, you were really pissed at me just then." She laughed. "I deserved it, but still, you're authentic."

"A lot of people would say I'm more brass balls than authentic."

"I saw what happened on TVGM. I think it's disgusting what they did to you. I was so glad when you smacked him in the balls." Her smile turned sheepish. "I wasn't sure I'd have the courage to ever do anything like that."

I cracked my knuckles. "It was fun, let me tell you."

Her smile warmed, a strange glint appearing in her eye. "I'll bet."

"The old bastard deserved worse," Jen inserted as she slipped into the chair opposite me. "If anything, I think you should have done a one-two punch to the gonads." She made a pow-pow sound as she jabbed her fists in front of her.

"He crossed his legs too soon."

Camille and Jen started snickering, but Camille eventually murmured, "Lena will soften up. She just takes time."

"You're the newest O'Donnelly. She seemed to respond well to you."

"I was involved in an altercation recently. It's made her be nicer to me."

"Sheesh, really?"

Camille nodded. "Just let her calm down, you know? Aidan's the eldest but after what he's been through, she's very protective of him. They all are."

"I'll bet."

"Brennan's taken on a lot of his workload too, so they're all feeling the pinch of Aidan not being at the top of his game."

"It isn't like he did it on purpose," Jen pointed out, which made me want to blow her a kiss.

"No, but it was years ago and he's not..." Camille grimaced. "Look, I've not been around here a lot, but you can tell he doesn't exactly help himself."

I grunted, because I couldn't deny that. "I'm not sure if Aidan will let me go to my apartment building to grab the gift I overnighted for him. I really need to get that. Maybe I can guilt trip him into using a cane."

"It's more than that," Aoife stated as she took a seat at the table with us, her hands cupping a mug of what smelled like peppermint tea. "I think he's scared of doctors or something."

"No way," Jen retorted. "Aidan's not scared of anything."

"Contain the admiration or I'll have to sock you in the vagina," I groused, laughing when she pouted. "I'm good at socking."

Aoife snickered, but she shrugged. "I think so. He won't go in for check ups, and I know Finn has gone so far as to make appointments for him when his knee's bad."

"It was probably easier to take a pill." I winced. "Sad but true."

"A cane will help," Aoife replied. "If you can get him to use it."

"I'll work my magic somehow." I didn't like the idea of him not going to the doctor's either. Crap, was I supposed to be this involved this fast?

"You already worked magic today so best not to exhaust the daily quota," Jen said wryly as she leaned into the table. "Is Conor really seeing someone?"

I shrugged. "I think so. He said he was."

"Conor doesn't say anything he doesn't mean," Aoife pointed out, her tone thoughtful.

"I'm surprised Lena didn't haul him downstairs and ask him," Camille said.

"Savannah's good at deflecting," Jen remarked with a laugh. "That whole '*oh, I must have misunderstood because I hit my head*,' BS worked like a charm."

"Clearly not if you didn't believe me," I sniped.

"She wanted to believe it," Aoife retorted with a laugh. "They're all protective of him. I never understood why. It's as if him being crazy smart makes him dumb or something." Her brow puckered. "Weird."

She wasn't wrong. A sigh escaped me as I took in the kitchen, its occupants, as I thought about Aidan, and Conor upstairs, then the brothers I'd met the other night. It was like a dream, but a really good one, not the usual shitty ones I was plagued with.

"I didn't think it'd be like this," I admitted. Not just what I felt for

Aidan, but was starting to feel for his family too. All of this was too fast, like I was about to hit the gas while going over a speed bump, but there was no stopping it mostly because I didn't want it to stop.

"What?" Aoife's gaze softened. "Love? You do love him, right? I could see it when you were sitting next to him, but like, you might just be putting on a show for Lena."

That had Jen elbowing her again. "Hey bitch, are you calling my other BFF a liar?"

Aoife snorted. "No. But she worked on TV, and I'm going to assume that someone as woke as her knows what a creep Stewart Allsheim is but she still smiled at him like she didn't want to skewer him with, what are those fluffy-headed mikes called?"

"You mean a wind muff. We don't use those so much in the studio," I explained.

Aoife nodded. "Thanks. But yeah. One of those."

I grinned. "You're not wrong. I've got a good poker face."

"Just never let her play poker with you," Jen muttered.

"Lose big?" Aoife queried.

"Lost my shirt and any rights to bitching about how bad her coffee is too."

"Ouch."

Camille shot me an interested glance. "You play poker?"

"Texas Hold 'Em. My brother and I were on the road a lot as kids with the band, you know? Gerard Sullivan, Sully, he was a card shark." I whistled. "One of the basics of poker is the ability to count cards—he taught me how." And that was nothing to what Star could do.

"Okay, I'm going to encourage the guys to start a poker game," Camille said with a cackle. "Just so you can whoop their asses."

"You guys need to not get jealous because I mean no harm, but it might take more than a couple of meals to get me over the fact I'm surrounded by O'Donnellys."

Aoife frowned. "What do you mean?"

"Like, you probably had a crush on Justin Timberlake as a teen. The O'Donnellys were my thang."

She snorted. "Really? I grew up being terrified of them."

"Smart girl," Camille drawled.

"Well, I wasn't so smart, and they were bigger than my boogeyman so I fell for them."

"Who's your boogeyman?" Jen questioned with a frown.

I waved a hand. "It doesn't matter." It totally did, but now was not the time to overshare. I had to impress these women. If I had my way, they'd be my sisters-in-law soon enough.

"I think you'll find it does."

"So, you think because you fangirl over them you wouldn't be able to win?" Aoife queried, ignoring Jen.

"Maybe." I shrugged then, leaning into the table, whispered, "The other night, I woke up surrounded by them. It was scary until I realized who they were and then I'd never wanted to be in a bukkake flick more in my life than at that moment."

Jen snickered, so did Camille, but Aoife frowned. "What's a bukkake flick?"

"Jesus, Aoife, how are you still so fucking innocent with me as a friend?" Jen groused, but she was chuckling as she grumbled. "Bukkake is this Japanese porn where, like, this girl gives a group of guys a blowjob. They're all standing around her in a circle. Basically they come on her face, jack off on her, shit like that."

Aoife's cheeks turned pink. "Oh."

"We need to hook you up with better porn," Jen said with a sigh. "Finn is obviously not educating you right."

"He's educating me well enough," Aoife countered.

Camille arched a brow at me. "I guess I should be jealous seeing as we're talking about my man too."

I hitched a shoulder. "I was and probably still am concussed so you can't hit an injured woman."

Her laughter boomed from her, which told me I'd really tickled her and, like moths to a flame, her amusement drew Inessa, then finally Aela over. Aela was dipping her fingers in a jar of—

I blinked. "You're eating Nutella."

"Yeah. Pregnancy craving."

"From the jar," I finished.

"That's not a craving," Aoife scoffed. "How is that a craving? It's just regular food."

Aela flipped her a distinctly chocolate brown-covered bird. "Fuck off. If my kid wants chocolate and hazelnuts, I'm not going to waste time by not giving her Nutella."

"I really hope it's a girl," Lena murmured, bringing herself over to the table too with a coffee cup in hand. "I'm not sure Declan would survive, but him and Brennan would make good daddies to baby girls."

"Hey!" Aoife complained. "Finn would so rock that too."

"And Eoghan," Inessa groused.

"Why are you bitching?" Camille retorted. "You don't want kids yet."

"I'm not even twenty. Why the hell would I want a kid now?" Inessa blew out a breath that had a piece of golden hair flopping on her forehead. I almost heard Seamus sob into whatever it was he was making for his Grandmother General.

"You girls are lucky you had a choice," Lena intoned, then she cast a gimlet glance my way. "How old are you, Savannah?"

"I still have functioning eggs," I argued, immediately knowing where she was taking this and not about to deal with that particular bullshit. "Mom had my youngest siblings in her late thirties, and she was a late baby as well for her parents."

Lena harrumphed. "Better to have them when you're younger."

"Respectfully, that option isn't open to me unless you know of a portal that cuts through time and space?" I shrugged. "My career was important to me."

"Still is," Jen insisted. "And why shouldn't it be? You're rocking the shit out of it too." She heaved a sigh. "I wish I were. I swear I do half the work for my boss and he gets all the credit and the directors just look down my blouse while I tell them that."

"Maybe you should start wearing blouses with a high neckline?" Aoife drawled, earning an elbow in the side from Jen.

I grinned at my friend when she winked at me, thankful she'd changed the subject because I wasn't about to throw down with Aidan's mom on this matter.

Seriously though, what did she want me to do? Apologize for being in my thirties? Aidan wasn't exactly young, either. Damn nerve.

"If I wore a high neckline, then my boss would realize that I've got a high IQ." She blew a raspberry. "This way, I'm learning as much as I can so when I strike out on my own, I have alllll the information at my fingertips. I can count on you as my first client, right, Savannah?"

I grinned at her. "I wouldn't dare stick with Crawford, Lewis and Jones over you."

"That's a wise choice." She wagged her finger. "I'd have to put Ex-Lax in your coffee until you agreed."

"With friends like that, who needs enemies?"

That deep voice had me wishing that were Aidan, but when we all turned around and saw guys coming in through the kitchen door, I didn't see him, but was instantly reminded of why fangirling was a problem.

Oy vey.

The interesting thing was, of course, I didn't want them. I was even disappointed when Aidan wasn't one of the men walking into the kitchen, but that didn't mean I didn't salivate over all of them.

The O'Donnellys were rarely photographed out of suits, so to see them, en masse, dressed in sweaters and jeans just had my teenaged self fanning her face.

Plus, Eoghan was carrying a baby that looked like he was dressed for Antarctica. How fucking cute was that?

Although, I had to admit, their comfortably casual clothes did make me question why Aidan had dressed so formally. Not that I should complain. He looked like sin itself in a suit.

"So, you're the guest Aidan mentioned."

I peered up at the guy who was purposely looming over me.

Okay, so that was one way to cut down on my fangirling.

I scowled at Brennan. "Yeah. You got a problem with that?"

Brennan smirked as he encouraged Camille to get off her seat then to slip onto his lap. "I ain't got no problem so long as you're not dicking my brother around."

My scowl deepened, but Camille elbowed him in the stomach. "Hey, leave her alone, Brennan. She's cool."

"She is, huh? You ladies bonded over crumb cake and Beef Wellington?"

Camille nodded. "We did. So be nice."

Brennan stopped trying to stare me down and shot his wife a look.

As he did, I'd admit to melting a little, and when I looked at all the women who were accompanied by their men, most of them now sitting on their laps, well, hell, my fangirling eased some more.

My crushes of old were married now. Happily. Even though they were all murdering monster mobsters, I was happy for them.

Yes, weird.

I knew that already.

I was weird by nature. But, I realized, I was supposed to be that way. I was supposed to think these guys, who were the villains in anyone's story, were actually heroes because Aidan was mine.

And I was his.

A belief that sank into my bones, resonating on a deeper level than I'd ever experienced before.

So, sure, our time together *could* be quantified in hours and minutes, but that didn't matter when the universe had decided thousands of millennia ago that we were destined to be a pair.

Which, to me, was pretty fucking awesome.

Of course, the second I came to that decision was when we all heard it. Like a punctuation mark in my thoughts, it shot everything into high relief. Slashing through the room with all the power of a chainsaw.

The roar of pain. The roar of agony. The smashing of glass and what felt like the trembling of the earth as one man's fury seemed capable of making the tectonic plates beneath us vibrate alongside him. That was the power of this family. That was the magnitude of a man like Aidan O'Donnelly Sr.'s wrath.

As one, we all looked at each other, silence falling where, moments before, there'd been festive joy, and the craziest thing happened.

Once the roars died and the smashing stopped, everything went back to normal.

Everything.

But while they appeared to be able to switch off that side of their brains, not digging into business they didn't consider their own, reverting to peeling carrots and whipping mashed potatoes, turning back to the gravy they were sweating over and the cakes they were praying didn't sink as they baked in the oven, I didn't work that way.

Aidan Sr., I knew, had just learned about his son's child abuse, and I had a feeling in my bones about what that meant for the holiday period.

No one was safe in New York City tonight.

THIRTY-FOUR

AIDAN SR

I FLUNG open the van door with a force that had the vehicle quivering.

Raising a leg, I heaved myself into the vehicle, not even taking in what I was seeing—a man, the lower half of his face covered in duct tape apart from two holes at his nostrils that breath whistled in and out of, lying huddled on his side.

A scream of fright had escaped the guy as I dragged open the door, which was music to my fucking ears, but I grabbed his foot by his bare toes, twisted the big one until it crunched and he howled, then jerked his ankle until that was broken too.

With that same foot, I hauled him off the back of the van, his cries of pain serenading the demons inside me as I jumped down to the gravel driveway once again, taking a moment to steady myself, before I dragged him out into the light of day.

His body collided with the ground in such a way that a dull cough escaped him, the shock of the move, of momentum and gravity making him land flat on his back had him choking for air seconds later, but I ignored that, and carried on dragging him by that broken foot.

It took me longer than if I'd asked my men to carry him inside, but where would the fun be in that?

His coughing came in handy—it shielded his screams of pain from the main house.

I didn't even make it to the summer house before he passed out, which was more convenient for me in the long run too, so when he was in the room I called a garage—it only housed the golf carts we used to get around the estate faster—I had Aidan grab me a chair while Finn helped me put him on it, holding him up while I duct-taped him into place.

Chest heaving, heart pounding, lungs burning, I stared at this motherfucker who'd helped protect a predator shielded by a cassock.

My brain whirred with ideas, with plans and expectations, but all I knew was that this was the appetizer. The main event needed to be cataclysmic. Just like how this cocksucker had helped burn my boy's childhood into ashes, I needed to make him feel that pain too.

I heard footsteps and from gait alone, knew it was my kids settling into place, readying themselves to watch their da at his most insane.

In the heat of the moment, I wasn't sure if Junior had registered what Finn had called me, but I felt the label like it was a crown he placed on my head. A crown I didn't deserve.

I was his da.

Not his dad or his father, his fucking da.

That was two of my kids I'd failed to protect now. Two boys that were molested by people I trusted. By people in whose care I'd placed them.

My thoughts turned red with rage. Aimed at myself. Aimed at the world. At the shit choices I'd made and the decisions that had failed them.

I let that fuel me because if I didn't, then I'd just want to slam my head into the wall again, and that'd get us nowhere. I didn't deserve the peace of a coma, of death by brain damage at my own fucking hand.

I deserved to burn too.

I deserved to suffer.

Just like this fucker did.

Picking up some pliers from the back wall where tools were stored to upkeep the golf carts, I walked over to him and held the jaws to his nose, then I pressed down, knowing that he'd either sink into unconsciousness or switch online fast as he struggled for air.

Within seconds, I had my answer. His eyes popped open. I smiled. The stench of shit soon made itself known to me, and my smile deepened.

As the struggle in his eyes, the desperation for air twisted into being, I leaned down and whispered, "You know who I am?"

He bopped his head forward, panic making it flip back and forth like a beach ball being hurled at a wall by kids.

"Then you should know that picking the Church over a man like me was a very stupid thing to do. God won't protect you from me, and your death won't be fast. He won't shield you in his loving embrace. He'll just watch over us as I make you pay for your sins."

Panicked squeaks escaped him, until they grew sluggish with oxygen deprivation, and finally, I released his nose, then I grabbed the duct tape at the side of his face, and tore it off, which split his cheek even more as I saw that Valentini had gotten to him first.

Ordinarily, I'd be pissed, but instead, I was grateful.

Grateful because if I didn't have someone to release this rage on, then I was fucked, and I couldn't be fucked yet.

Junior wasn't ready to take the seat at the head of the Irish Mob. Not yet. He had to get over his addiction first, had to get married and have kids before he had the pressures of my position.

Before he had to become the most feared man in all of New York, he needed a woman who'd love him. A woman who'd understand him. Who'd accept him.

That clicked in my head like a light switch.

An arranged marriage wouldn't suit my eldest.

He needed someone who'd take him as he was, and accept him as he morphed into the King of the Five Points.

As blood gushed when I tore off the duct tape, I stared at the wound, then I stuck my finger in it. He howled, but I ignored him until I felt his teeth then I pulled back before he could bite me.

Peering at the wound, I saw that Valentini cut all the way through and found myself more impressed than I should be.

Italians were all SOBs, but this one had mettle.

It took a strong man to face his opponent in the eye and to make such a personal cut. Having someone held down and beaten was one thing, but when you got your hands bloodied, that was the act of an honorable man.

I'd raised my boys that way.

They were willing to get dirty, willing to sully their hands and it meant that we had an army of men who'd been loyal to us. Until the Sparrows had come into being, that is, and as far as I knew, they'd been around since my own da's reign.

"I want to know how the Sparrows work," I rasped as the Archbishop panted.

"I-I don't know what you're talking about," he slurred.

Hand snapping out, I dug my fingers into his nostrils and pushed his head back. As he yelped, I loomed over him, staring him straight in the eye and I said, "Don't fuck me around. You ain't seeing the light of day, so you can either make sure that your brothers rot in hell at your side or they can stay in the shadows until Lucifer brings them home."

The Archbishop whimpered as I pulled my fingers back then snapped his nose clean to the side. He graced me with another howl, then as I pressed the pliers to the broken cartilage, he yelped, "W-We're just a group of men who help each other!"

I narrowed my eyes at him. "You are? Just a bunch of guys who help cover up sex trafficking and use law enforcement as a way of turning people to their side? Sounds like a real honorable cause, boys, doesn't it?" I asked Junior and Finn, not expecting an answer and not getting one either.

"I don't know anything about that!" he squeaked.

"I'm sure. There's been rumors about you for years. I thought it was bullshit. How could the Archbishop be fucking gay? Is that how they got you? Caught you with your pants down?" I sneered at him. "How does the hierarchy work?"

"I-I don't know," he squealed, then he screamed himself hoarse when I twisted his nose the other way.

"Don't fucking lie to me."

"I'm not," he screamed. "Nobody knows! We don't get together. We don't meet. We never see each other, just know that if we're called on our phones, it's a conversation regarding business for the NWS."

I squinted at him, at the hint of truth I heard in his voice, but I turned to my boys and asked, "What do you think? Is he lying?"

"I'm not!" he shrieked. "I'm not, I swear it! P-P-Please don't kill me. P-P-Please! I swear, I won't tell the cops—"

Laughter barked from me as I loomed over him again. "You bet your ass you won't tell them." I smirked. "Of course, you don't mind having your ass played with, do you? Maybe you want to go to jail? Maybe we'll find a nice big motherfucker who'll make you his bitch. Get you hooked on Big Daddy cock until your asshole's bigger than the craters on the fucking moon—"

"I swear, I didn't do anything," he yelled, "I just facilitated meetings when they requested them, put people in contact—"

"What kinds of meetings? Who did you put in contact?"

"I don't know. I just arranged for hotel rooms and made sure restaurants were booked for private events."

"You mean to tell me they treated you like a fucking concierge?"

He swallowed, something shifting in his eyes that told me he'd just given me a semi truth. Semis didn't work for me.

Wandering over to the wall of tools, I found a blow torch, then as I returned to his side, I knocked him so he was on his back, feet raised. I clicked the blow torch on and pressed the flame to his heel.

As his skin wept and blistered while I broiled his soles, he screamed, "I shared what I learned in confession!"

Pulling the flame back, I shot a look at my boys. "What do you think? The whole truth and nothing but the truth?"

"I think so," Finn rasped as he moved toward the Archbishop. When he kicked him in the head, I watched on in surprise.

My second eldest didn't like wet work. It wasn't his style, even if he'd come through the ranks like every good Five Pointer, but when he pressed his shoe to the Archbishop's throat and added his weight to the guy's windpipe, I knew he was about to displace his own rage, was going to project his own abuser onto the fucker lying here.

"And what about the pedophiles you helped shelter?" Junior intoned, hobbling over so we were all peering down at the bastard. "What about the kids who were abused on your watch?"

My hand tightened around the canister as Finn loosened his step on his windpipe so the fucker could talk.

"That was the Church. Not the Sparrows," he gasped, like that made it much better.

I pressed the flame to the flesh between his big toe and second toe, and listened to his screams as if it were a choral symphony from the angels above.

His pain soothed my own.

His blood stemmed mine as if I were pressing the flame to my wounds and cauterizing them.

His screams made peace flood my ears.

That was when I pressed the flame to his cassock and I let it catch fire. As he screamed, I grabbed the fire extinguisher and when his roars of pain reached fever pitch, I extinguished the flames.

I did that two more times over the next three hours, and I didn't stop until he was one big boiled blister. Until his skin morphed from red like a lobster who'd been thrown in with a crawfish boil into a nice charred black.

That was when Junior found the salt we threw on the driveway when it was snowing.

If my boy had a signature move, it was rubbing salt in the

wound. I figured that said a lot about him. Figured it told me the manner of the man—a sin couldn't just be repented, it had to be felt.

As I watched him drag his hand along the raw exposed flesh of the Archbishop's torso, that was when the Archbishop slurred a name, "Justin DeLaCroix."

Finn stopped helping Junior by dredging the bastard's body in salt, and stilled. "The Chief Justice of the Supreme Court?"

The Archbishop rocked his head forward. "Please, just kill me now. Please."

"What does DeLaCroix have to do with anything?" I rasped.

"I didn't lie," he whispered, tears puddling on either side of his face where it rested on the floor. "We don't meet, we just wait on calls. We're directed where to go, what to do, and when. But we all know who DeLaCroix is."

"And what's that?" I snapped when he took a few seconds to reply, pressing the flame to his feet again until he howled:

"Our Commander-in-chief."

A knock sounded at the garage doors, a soft knock, one I'd heard many times in the years of our marriage, and though my brain reeled at what the fucker on the ground had just revealed, I snapped, "Keep him quiet."

Finn's foot covered the Archbishop's mouth, and he twisted his face to the side with the pressure as I rushed over to the garage entrance.

When the motorized doors rolled up, I saw her, and when she caught sight of me, she didn't even flinch. Lena had seen me look worse than this in her time, and she loved me despite the shit I did.

Of course, I loved her too.

I was a monster. Monsters didn't love, or so they'd told me at my Catholic school when I was whipped for the various shit I did, but Lena held my heart.

She held it in her fucking grasp, and even though I'd broken her, even though my actions and my job had led to her experiencing some things that no woman should have to endure, she still looked at me with love in her eyes.

She was why I had to go to heaven.

She was why I needed the boys to get there too.

Because for all she'd let me make them into the men they were today, and for all that would make her a sinner in another mother's eyes, there was nothing more important than the eternity in paradise that was awaiting us once this miserable life was over.

What mother, who loved her kids as much as Lena did, what father, who loved his boys as much as I did, wouldn't want those same children to be in heaven with them? To be at peace after a lifetime's war?

"The children can hear, Aidan," Lena told me softly, and I heard the chiding note to the words, a reprimand that she'd never have given me at one point.

It'd taken a rolling pin to the head to make me see her for what she was—my soul mate. Only when I'd pushed her past her limits had she opened herself up to me, revealing that we were two peas in a pod. Two beings capable of the worst thing humanity had to offer. Two monsters who could only find peace in each other's arms. "Jacob won't stop crying, and Shay's nervous. He knows what you're doing."

"I have no choice."

She frowned. "It's Christmas. Of course you have a choice." She tutted as she raised a hand and pressed it to my forehead. "What have you been doing with yourself?" Uncaring of the gore on me, uncaring of the mess, the blood on me, she stepped nearer and repeated, "I thought I told you you weren't allowed to do that anymore?" She was talking about banging my head into walls. "You promised me you'd stop that, Aidan."

I swallowed at her reprimand. "I know I did. I didn't even know I was doing it."

Her scowl deepened. "What's going on?"

Once upon a time, I'd never have told her.

Then the Aryans had taken her. Then they'd broken her. Then

I'd broken them. Then I'd taken them. There was a symmetry in everything, but only the truth had helped my Lena. Only knowing what I'd done to them had helped her sleep at night, better than any chemicals the doctor could prescribe.

I pushed forward until my bloody forehead was pressing against her clean, unmarred, unsullied brow.

Raising my hands, I cupped her cheeks while she slipped her arms around my waist and held me close, bracing herself for what was to come.

She knew me well enough to know that something was coming.

Something bad.

Something heinous enough to make me ruin Christmas.

"Conor was..."

"Conor was, what? What's he done now? That boy, I swear," she heaved a sigh. "If he's broken into that NSA place again, then—"

"No, nothing like that, sweetheart." I pulled back and pressed a kiss to her lips. "He's a good boy."

"The best," she said immediately, her smile turning misty. "They all are. We did a good job, didn't we, Aidan?"

A choked breath escaped me. "We did. We did the best we could. We saved them from what we went through."

I reached up and tucked a strand of her hair behind her ear. It was no longer the scarlet of our past, but a faded amber, and I loved it as much now as I had when I'd unveiled her on our wedding day. She'd been a possession back then, though. Now she owned me.

Funny how the good Lord worked.

"What's he done, Aidan? You're scaring me."

"I didn't mean to, sweetheart." I hushed her and tightened my arms around her. "I just learned something that we have to keep between ourselves. Only Junior and Finn know the truth."

She tensed. "What is it?"

"Our boy—" I gritted my teeth as tears burned my eyes. "Our beautiful boy..." A sob escaped me. "H-He was molested."

She tensed in my arms. "Why are you saying that? Don't say

things like that! Why would you say that?" she screamed as the salt in my tears made my eyes sting harder.

"It's true, baby, it's true." I held her tighter, keeping her so close that I could rock her in my arms. Soothe a pain that couldn't be soothed. Heal a wound that would always be open. Necrotic. Turning our living flesh into a blackened mass. "One of the priests—"

"No!" she wailed, struggling in my grip. "No!"

I felt that pain in my soul. I felt it in my heart. I felt it in my fucking head. In my eyes. In my mouth. In my hands and in my feet.

Her pain let me feel it too, let me experience it through her as I held her close, fighting her when she slapped at me, trying to get free, trying to loosen my grip on her, but I was stronger and I wasn't about to let go of the one person who'd never let go of me.

"Not again, not again," she sobbed, and I knew she meant Finn. I knew it and I felt that too.

Our guilt. Our shame.

We'd done our best but it wasn't enough.

I was the most feared man in New York City and still, some fucking bastard had come into my parish and had forced my son.

My fucking son.

When I started sobbing, I'd never know. I didn't understand that I was breaking down in my woman's arms, that we held each other through a storm that would never cease, and I didn't know when her grief turned to hate. Didn't see it happen or feel it. I just heard her silence.

I knew what that meant.

Another mother might think Lena unworthy of pity or sympathy. She might think she was cruel for forging our boys in fire, but Lena was a realist. A pragmatist. Our boys making it to their eightieth birthdays was more important to her than anything else. But she was also dangerous. More than her sons knew, because I'd made sure they didn't know. What she'd gone through had scarred her, made her impulsive, decisive and dangerous.

She'd acted on it once.

One single time.

And Aoife's mother had paid the price of an irrational jealousy that I understood.

We were evil, Lena and I, twisted and corrupt, but we were made for each other.

How couldn't that be right?

When I pressed a kiss to her sweaty temple, I pulled back to see that look in her eye. A look that promised death. That promised an end and a new beginning.

"Who?" she rasped. "Who the fuck dared? Is he in there? Is that who—"

She pulled free from my grasp and I let her. I let her storm into the garage, and let her see the Archbishop even though, by this point, he was unrecognizable. Christ, his own mother wouldn't know him from Adam.

"Ma?" Junior queried, his voice panicked. He tried to stop her, but I didn't have to turn around to know that my Lena wouldn't let our eldest get in her way.

"Lena? What are you doing?" Finn demanded, his confusion clear, his surprise evident.

She didn't reply, just fell silent, which was when I turned around and saw her staring down at the Archbishop.

"Who is he?" she asked. "Is he the one who touched my boy?"

Finn cleared his throat. "He's the one who helped hide the priests in the church. He's Archbishop Masters."

"How did he hide them?" she rasped, but when Finn started to answer, she raised a hand and then, very carefully, lifted her foot and pressed the heel of her shoe to the man's eye socket.

My Lena had funny feet. Put her in a pair of slippers, her bones ached. Let her wear some heels, she could walk around as if she were barefoot.

At that moment, the short kitten heel dug into Masters' eye and as he squirmed around like a dying fish, she screamed, "How did you hide them?"

"I moved them around!" he screamed back. "The second I heard of any rumors, I shuffled them from parish to parish."

"To maximize their abuse?" Lena whispered.

"N-No, just to hide them. If they moved on, they could never stop anywhere long enough to condition a child."

I frowned at that logic, logic he hadn't uttered to us.

"How many other priests have you done this with?" Lena demanded, her heel burrowing deeper into the bastard's eye.

"S-S-Seven," he stuttered.

Her nostrils flared. "How many came to our parish? Served in our church?"

"T-Two."

Her eyes clashed with mine and I saw the hellfire begin to burn in them.

The Archbishop was about to pay for his sins.

He'd wish that I was the one doling out the punishment. He'd fucking wish he'd come to me rather than being the Church's whipping boy.

By the time my Lena was done with him, the Archbishop was going to be praying for Satan's embrace.

And maybe, just maybe, I would too.

THIRTY-FIVE

AIDAN

THE CLOSER WE got to Manhattan, the more I felt the miles between Savannah and me.

She was safe.

That was my only consolation.

She was in no danger on the family compound, surrounded by my brothers and their wives.

If anything, she'd be in her element, and I wouldn't have been surprised if she was asking my siblings for details on shit she shouldn't fucking know about.

I had to take comfort in that. *Needed to.*

My da was off the rails, and as much as I expected that, it was Ma who concerned me.

Ma who I kept looking back at to see if she was okay.

Her face looked as if it were carved from stone as she remained tucked under my father's raised arm, and it hit me then, after watching her dig her heel into the Archbishop's eye, her own face dotted with what I assumed was Da's blood, after watching her set a blowtorch to his dick, that my ma was as much of a psychopath as Da was.

Psychopaths didn't know how to love, and in all honesty, that explained a lot about how we'd been raised. We'd been toy soldiers with a general, reporting back for duty, aware that if we misbehaved, well, we'd be punished.

Brennan's wrist was one such act of terrorizing, Conor's scars another. I'd been whipped a few times myself, and I knew Declan had as well—plus, he'd been bullied for his love of the arts.

Eoghan was the one who'd been spared the most, I thought, but as I looked at them, the pair huddling together, reacting to the news I'd shared, it was a strange moment to feel loved.

To see, for myself, how these two monsters were shaken, broken by what I'd shared.

It hurt to admit that I'd expected Da's ego to be pricked. His rage to be based on the fact that someone had dared defile an O'Donnelly.

But it wasn't.

I'd seen that when I'd watched him slam his head into the wall.

I'd seen that when I'd watched him tear his office apart, just as his soul was splintering into a million pieces with his grief.

Everyone knew Aidan O'Donnelly had a short fuse, but what I'd witnessed was like nothing else. Was indescribable.

The brutality with which he'd tortured the Archbishop was beyond anything I'd ever witnessed from him, and I'd seen a lot. I'd watched him cut off toes with a blunt knife, and I'd seen him piss on people when they were on fire to blot out the flames.

Tonight, he'd been pure rage.

And that was for us.

His boys.

It made it easier to accept that I'd broken Conor's promise. Especially as we were heading to St. Patrick's Cathedral in Manhattan without him.

A part of me hoped Kid would never have to find out that I'd told Da, but I wasn't so lucky. I knew that. He'd find out eventually. Secrets had a way of doing that, didn't they? Coming to the surface?

As Finn drove us in a town car, the white van following us with one of our men behind the wheel, I kept glancing back, watching Ma.

Seeing how broken she was, it made me question shit. Why they'd raised us the way they had. Why, when they clearly loved us, they'd had to be so fucking mean.

I didn't ask them, didn't say shit. Didn't even mention the fact that, for some reason, Finn had called Da, *Da*. Whatever reason for that was something I couldn't deal with yet. Tonight was for this problem, and I had no idea how it was going to end.

As I tugged on my bottom lip, we drove through Midtown and made our way toward Fifth Avenue where the cathedral, the Catholic Church's most visible symbol within the city, was found.

At six-thirty, it was already way past dark, and while the area was bustling as people did their Christmas gift shopping, I knew the cathedral would be silent by now, the dress rehearsal for tomorrow's Midnight Mass having been completed hours earlier.

Finn took us around the back of the cathedral, and while this wasn't our main place of worship, we'd been here for enough weddings and funerals to know the lay of the land.

Da, I knew, even had a key, and I didn't want to wonder why the hell he had that in his possession.

The car and the van merged down a dark alleyway, the tires rustling as we drove over some glass and whatever else was in the shitheap behind the cathedral.

As it started to rain, a storm cloud appearing from out of nowhere, thunder rattling along in the sky in a season where thunder was as rare as a boiling hot day, Da whispered, "There, you see, baby? God's crying with us."

I had no idea why that made me feel like I was choking, but it did. I sat there, stoic in silence, wondering what his and Ma's game plan was, because they were clearly in sync, while the windshield wipers tried to fight off the sudden deluge.

This would take care of the crowds at least.

When we made it down a certain street, like Da actually knew where the fuck we were, he rumbled, "We'll park here. In the trunk, there's a jammer."

I frowned. "There is?"

"Conor gave it to me as an early Christmas present." Da's laugh sounded as choked as I felt. "Thought it would make me fine him less."

"God love that boy," Ma rasped, before she broke my heart by weeping.

The soft sounds were a torment I didn't want to ever hear again, because every time she cried, it was when the worst shit in our lives went down.

When my uncles died, when she'd been kidnapped, the drive-by that had butchered my knee and Aoife's guts, when, when, when...

"You're going to get wet, sweetheart," Da soothed. "Are you sure you don't want to stay in here?"

Ma didn't answer, just scurried over to the other side of the car and got out of that door when Finn unlocked it for her.

As she stood there, in the pouring rain, I asked Da, "What's the game plan?"

"You'll see soon enough."

I climbed out of the car, and hesitated when I reached Ma. She stood there, so isolated, staring up at the cathedral, and it made me whisper, "I hurt the priest who did this to Conor, Ma." Shit, why was it parents had the ability to make you feel like a little kid again?

"Your father told me." She cast me a look. "You make me proud of you every day, Aidan. Every day you get up, and you fight, you make me proud." She reached forward, her hair soaked and swirling around her face, her clothes drenched, everything about her slick with rain, as she cupped my chin. "But I've never felt that more than now.

"Your da's funny about pride," she whispered, but somehow, even over the rainstorm, I heard her voice. "He might not tell you, but you've earned the right to be his heir today."

Jesus.

Was that supposed to be a compliment?

Rather than disrespect her, I dipped down and brushed my cheek against hers. She held me close, squeezing me, until Da called out, "Get the jammer, Junior."

I hobbled away, feeling oddly bereft, feeling as if something were about to happen, something I could only dread.

I'd started building a snowball tonight, that somehow had turned into a boulder that could flatten the city.

Where this was going couldn't end well, but it was too late for that. It had been too late since I was fifteen.

Grabbing the jammer from the trunk, I saw the six men in the van behind us clambering out too.

From the town car's trunk, they retrieved a wheelchair and they shoved our captive into it.

The Archbishop was dressed in a robe and slippers, his head tipped forward and covered by a hat. He was unconscious, had been ever since Ma had set that torch to his dick, so I knew we were good for the time being—he was no threat to exposing us, especially because he just looked like an old man in a wheelchair.

While one guy, Anthony, pushed him, the other five carried only fuck knew what in duffle bags. Four apiece in their hands, they were loaded down with them, and they were clearly heavy as hell as they lumbered with us along the grim walkway that had slick floors which had Da gripping a firmer hold on Ma while we walked toward the cathedral.

The looming spires, the neo-Gothic architecture that took up an entire block on Fifth Avenue, was wasted on me.

Even its beauty meant little.

For all that Da had tried to make us be Catholics, none of us felt the faith like he did. His belief system made no fucking sense to anyone but him though, so considering we weren't born headcases, just taught, I took it as a good sign that his logic and ours didn't compute.

It was ridiculously easy to disrupt the local electronics. I even saw the snap as a camera close by burned out with whatever the hell it was that Conor had made.

It was the size of a tablet, and had a manual red button that Da directed me to push every few minutes. Because I had no desire to go to jail, I did as requested and we lumbered into the cathedral like a rag tag bunch of thieves once Da used his key to let us in.

The second we were within its cavernous interior, we were graced with the silent halls that, on any given day, held up to three thousand souls. Beneath our feet, cream marble gleamed even in the shadows, because hundreds of stained glass windows let in the meager light from outside.

Overhead, the arched dome was supported by dozens of archways that were grounded by decorated columns. A carved stone pulpit loomed over the rows of shining wooden pews, which led down to the high altar.

I knew there were several altars in here, but I doubted Da wanted any other than the largest. With its famous bronze *baldachino*, an intricate Sanctuary that shrouded the altar, it was on a higher level than anywhere else in here, surrounded by marble so pure in color that cream looked filthy against it.

Beside the high altar, there was a *Pietà*, a sculpture of Mary mourning Jesus' passing as she wept over his body, and, considering my mother's tears, I couldn't help but find that fitting.

"Spread out," I told the men who were with us, my voice gritty with repressed emotion. "Make sure the place is empty. Any guards on the premises must be freaking out about their security system being down, so go and sweep the place, yeah?"

The guys obeyed, leaving the duffle bags behind while Anthony pushed Masters along the aisle, as we trudged after my parents, each of us in the dark as we made it to the high altar.

The silence in here was more overpowering than the bitter cold. Insane, really, because the wheelchair squeaked and our feet clicked against the stone tiles on the ground, but it was like a vacuum. Everything was swallowed up by the shadows.

Only the main stained glass windows really let in any light from the streets, but the columns were so thick that it didn't allow for easy maneuvering, and was enough for our cell's flashlights to barely penetrate the gloom.

"All clear," one guy called out softly.

"All clear."

"All clear."

By the time we made it to the fifth 'all clear,' there wasn't as much need for silence, so I demanded, "What are we doing here, Da? Did you want to check out his sacristy?"

Da didn't answer me—no surprises there.

Instead, to Anthony he directed, "Wheel him onto the high altar's dais then go and help the others."

Behind me, I could hear zips unfastening, and then I heard sloshing.

Shit.

"Da, is this wise?" I rasped, peering up at the ancient edifice, wondering if my da was insane enough to think even we could get away with torching New York's main cathedral.

Who was I kidding?

Of course, he fucking was.

"You know the rectory and the Cardinal's residence are connected to this place," I pointed out.

"They'll get out as soon as the alarms go off," was all Da would say.

"Well, we need to hurry the fuck up, then." I just hoped Conor's jammer didn't stop the alarms from working.

God, this was a nightmare without an end.

Anthony grunted as he hauled the wheelchair up the few steps to the altarpiece, and when he was done, he slipped into the background like the good grunt he was—Da preferred his crew to be doers rather than thinkers—and I assumed Anthony began helping the others spread what scented like gasoline.

"He's really fucking lost it this time," Finn whispered at my side, his shoulders hunched against the cold as we both watched the scene unfold.

I couldn't disagree with him. This had the makings of a disaster, the likes of which we'd never seen in the Five Points, written all over it.

Scrubbing a hand over my chin, I murmured, "Let's see what they do. They're more—" I heaved a sigh, because this sounded insane to me, never mind Finn. "—fragile, than I thought."

He grunted. "I know what you mean. I didn't think they'd react like this."

We shared a look and, even though it was pitch black and impossible to see his features without flashing the light right in his face, I knew we were both on the same page.

I had no idea how much time had passed, but the sound of matches being struck had me turning to see what was happening, and I winced when I realized they'd started lighting candles on the altar.

I pushed the jammer for prosperity a few times, hoping to God they fucked with the cameras, which was when Anthony walked up and hovered behind me.

"Tell Sr. that the guards are handled." He worked his jaw. "Might be a shit storm there. They were armed like they were a fucking militia." He shrugged. "I went around the cathedral and I think we got them all."

I blinked. Great. Communicating with Da was down to me. How lucky was I?

"You took them out?" Finn demanded.

He smirked. "Conor gave me a gift too. Said it was better than getting sent down for another aggravated assault charge." His lips curved up like he was proud. "Said your da needed me too much for that to happen."

Conor said that?

Suspiciously, I asked, "What was it?"

He raised a hand and wiggled another of Conor's goddamn

contraptions. This one was a lot smaller than the jammer. "I press this button, and it fucks with people's ears."

"How didn't it fuck with yours?"

"He gave me some special ear plugs." He tapped his ear. "Go equipped."

When he thumbed the button, I snatched out and grabbed his wrist. "I don't need a test run." Then, I frowned. "Did you knock out any of our men?"

"Nah. They're wearing the ear plugs too."

"How didn't we hear it?"

Anthony shrugged. "Too far away. I went into the rectory and the offices."

My mouth tightened. "Are the guards dead or passed out?"

"Like they were fucking dead." He grinned, then he looked around and that grin died.

Yeah, it was one of those nights.

"Where are they?"

"Dumped them outside."

"Are they visible from the street?" I demanded, worrying about that whole 'grunt' shit seeing as Anthony wasn't the smartest cookie in the jar.

Figured that Conor would give the bastard a tool to help him out, but wouldn't think Anthony'd try to give us some 'show and tell' so we could see it in action.

"No. I shoved them in a couple dumpsters around the back."

"All of them?"

"They were out like lights."

Jesus. He wasn't a grunt for nothing.

"They can breathe?" I clarified, not wanting the extra hassle of their deaths.

Anthony shrugged. "I taped up their mouths, but not their noses."

"You wheeled them far away enough so that if this place explodes, they won't get caught in the blast?"

"This ain't my first arson attack," Anthony growled like I'd offended him.

"What about the rectory? The common areas? Were they clear?"

He nodded. "Didn't see anyone other than guards."

"You checked every room?" Where was everyone?

"You trying to tell me how to do my job?"

Raising my hands in defeat, I stepped closer to the altar, murmuring, "Da? Security is dealt with."

He just grunted as he tugged off the hat on the Archbishop's head, then slapped him until he was conscious.

Unlike before, he now had a matching Cheshire Cat grin thanks to Ma. I'd seen her use a knife in the kitchen, and she'd certainly learned some skills while cooking was all I'd say.

The dull thwacking sounds sent blood spattering everywhere, but Da didn't care about blood evidence. Why would he when he was going to torch the ancient edifice anyway?

Masters came awake with a slurred, "Where am I?"

Da rumbled, "You're at the gateway to hell." His head tipped back as he peered at the Sanctuary's ceiling.

A sacrifice was going to be made tonight, but it was anything other than Catholic in origin. Far more pagan than I thought Da was capable of.

Like those words brought him to full wakefulness, though, the Archbishop sobbed, "No, please, no. Last rites, I need—"

Da punched him in the face, not that the bastard had to be feeling all that much by now. Brain damage was already underway especially with how fractured his orbital bones were.

A bag appeared from his pocket and it was placed around Masters' head, then Finn and I both sucked in a sharp, surprised breath, as Ma, wielding the duct tape, began to tape it in place.

As the Archbishop made agonized sounds as he gasped for air, the bag grew fuller and fuller, turning into a balloon as he started struggling in the wheelchair.

Da raised his arm and tucked Ma under it. "See him squirm, baby?"

"I do," Ma confirmed. "Wish Conor could see it. Wish Conor could know." Her cheeks gleamed with tears that flowed non-stop. Tears that had nothing to do with the rain that had wet us all through.

Nervously, I licked my lips. "You're not going to tell him?"

"Your father told me you promised Conor to keep it a secret from us."

A harsh sob escaped her, one so loud and so surprising after the calmness of her earlier tone that I flinched at the sound of her agony. It made me close my eyes as I felt her pain with her.

I'd never processed what it had done to me to see Conor being abused like that.

I'd never processed how it had felt to kill that son of a bitch.

Uncle Paddy had taken Finn and me boxing for a while, but then he'd died.

Well, *pretended* to die.

Christ, I still had to tell Da that.

Scrubbing a hand over my face as Ma sobbed out her fucking heart, falling forward with the agony of her sorrow, needing Da to prop her up and stop her from sinking to her knees in a puddle of grief, I felt Finn huddle nearer to me.

At that moment, I knew we both felt the same way. Like small boys who were seeing our parents break down. We didn't know what to do, where to turn, not when our constant was suffering, so we found solace in each other. As we'd often done over the years.

"You're my brother, aren't you?" I whispered to the soundtrack of my ma's grief.

"Yeah," he replied just as quietly.

"I always thought you were anyway."

"Me too."

"Fitting, I guess. To find out tonight." I turned to him and reached up and drew him in for a hug. "No matter what, blood aside, you've always been my brother." I pushed my forehead against his and muttered, "Always, Finn."

He nodded, our foreheads dragging against each other, before he rasped, "Why don't I think tonight's going to end well?"

I pulled back and said, "Because you've got a brain between those big ears?"

He smirked, his teeth glinting in the meager light surrounding us. "Mine match yours."

Grunting, I turned back to my parents, and watched as the Archbishop began to take his last few breaths of air. I knew because they were slower, lethargic, *strained.*

My jaw clamped down as I watched, but then I couldn't just watch. I couldn't just let him die. Not when kids had suffered because of this bastard. Not just my brother, but only God knew how many.

And he'd allowed it.

He'd let it happen.

He'd even facilitated it.

Again and again.

Over and over.

It fueled me, much as the gasoline would fuel the fire that'd make the seat of this bastard's archdiocese burn like the gateway to hell Da had declared it as being.

Like a phoenix who was reborn in flames, I needed that. I needed the Archbishop to die in agony just so he could experience a smidgen of Conor's pain.

So I hobbled along to the Sanctuary, and I drew out my knife. It gleamed in the candlelight, and I prodded the bag with the tip, watching as air whistled in through that hole and Masters gulped it down like it was a torrent rather than a trickle.

Turning to my parents, I declared, "Let him feel the fire. Let it eat him alive." My jaw clenched again. "Just like it's eaten Conor alive, and just like what we had to do has eaten us alive."

Finn rasped, "Hear, hear."

Da rumbled, "You dealt with McKenna, so it's your decision, boys." He gritted his teeth. "I'll even let you light the fire."

I shook my head, knowing they needed that release. "You can have that honor."

Stepping away from the altar, I retreated to Finn's side, unaware that tears crawled down my cheeks, merely watching as the men stopped sloshing gasoline around the place, bringing it right to the altar. One of them went the extra mile and poured it on Masters too.

I was surprised when none of them argued because this was a sacred place, but like good children, they behaved themselves before Da told them, "Go and wait in the van."

They retreated like robots, silent and deadly ones, then Da pulled out a box of matches, and asked, "Lena?"

She took the box without a word.

Expecting them both to head down the steps to the aisle, to my horror, I watched as Ma didn't move an inch away from Masters. Stayed right where she was as she lit the match and threw it onto the Archbishop.

A howl escaped him as he went up in flames, and the roar of the fire was so sudden it scorched my eyes as I staggered back, blasted by it. Finn too. My folks stood their ground as much as they could, watching him burn, until I yelled, "Get the fuck away from him!"

"What the hell are you doing?" Finn shouted, a scant second later.

Ma didn't listen, just reached for another match.

"This is suicide," I screamed, hobbling forward, wanting to get to them before they did something fucking stupid. Something that couldn't be taken back.

Some days, I hated them. Others, I loved them.

Either way, I didn't want this to be my last day with them.

For this to be our final memory.

She tossed the flame to the left of the altar. It shot up as Da called out, "Go, boys. Go. We'll be fine."

We'll be fine?

The light of the fire, the fucking heat of it, gleamed on Finn's face as we stared at each other in horror while we both rushed forward. The flames licked at us when we made it up there, and we tackled them both.

Ma shrieked as Finn grabbed her around the waist, hauling her up onto his shoulder. Her howl of agony as she was denied something she wanted, made the sounds coming from Masters seem pleasant. I wanted to close my ears against the noise, but I couldn't, instead, I focused on the fire that was beginning to rage, that was starting to make my skin tighten with the heat, that was going to hit my father soon if I didn't hurry.

About to tackle him, I saw something in Da's eyes that I never thought I'd see.

Regret.

Resolve.

Remorse.

"No," I snarled at him. "No."

His hand came to my shoulder. "Leave, Aidan. Leave. I deserve to burn with him."

"It's suicide!" I barked, coughing and choking on the smoke that was already filtering through the air. "You'll go to hell."

"Exactly where I belong," he rasped, and he moved closer to Masters, closer, closer.

Which meant he left me with no choice.

As fucking usual, the man couldn't even atone for his sins without fucking me over.

Well, not this time. Not again. Never fucking again.

THIRTY-SIX

SAVANNAH

THE SOUND of alarm started while we were playing poker.

Because this felt like the calm before the storm, and I always hated that part the most, I was glad for it in all honesty. Aidan had been gone for hours, and while I enjoyed observing the family, something was going down. Something nobody was talking about and which we were all pretending wasn't happening.

Lena had gone off hours ago to grab Sr., Aidan, and Finn, but she'd been away for so long that we'd eaten without her.

Conversation had been stilted, not as free-flowing as earlier, and I almost resented Valentini for not having the decency to wait until after Christmas because everyone was on edge now.

Aoife was worried about Finn, and I was concerned about Aidan. The other women stuck close to their men, which had given me ample time to pump Jen for any info on Valentini but, for once, she was being close-mouthed and had been avoiding me as much as she could.

Everyone seemed on edge about the noises coming from the other side of the property—quite understandably—and we weren't even telling Conor to come down to play or eat because, in Eoghan's words, "He'll be happier with his code than with us."

I didn't think I'd heard anything sadder, but I got it. We all had our coping mechanisms, didn't we? Conor clearly needed his, just as I needed mine.

So when the poker suggestion was thrown on the table by a smiling Camille, I was relieved for a change of pace, for a reason to switch off the part of me that was filming a mental documentary intended for my eyes only.

But before I could even begin lulling them into a false sense of security, a flurry of pings sounded from the brothers' cells as they received a text message.

"We need to get the women and kids to the safe room. That was the front gate," Eoghan muttered, having reached for his phone first.

My eyes rounded in surprise, but that was nothing to everyone else's reaction. Only Shay was slow, which confirmed what I already knew—he was new to the life. Aela dragged him along, while the rest of the women hurried after them. Only I lagged behind.

"What's going on?" I demanded, slowly getting to my feet as I tipped my chin back to stare up at Eoghan.

Why were they all so goddamn tall?

Declan shuffled the women and kids away, and I bit my lip as I heard one of them start crying. Fear didn't fill me, but at that moment, I felt alive again. Like I did when I was in my apartment. When that bastard had come for me.

My breathing wasn't fast this time, my heart wasn't pounding. If anything, I felt a bizarre kind of clarity. I was safe. With the O'Donnellys, I was safe. Just like they'd protected me before, they'd do it again.

"You need to get to the safe room," Brennan said grimly, his eyes on his phone now as well. "Thank fuck we didn't switch them off," he muttered to Eoghan.

"Did you hear the alarm?" Conor called out from the doorway to the TV room where we'd set up after dinner, another room that was covered in wall-to-wall photographs which I'd explored after we'd eaten.

Eoghan barked, "What's going on?"

"Some motherfuckers are trying to storm the gates."

To punctuate his statement, gunfire sounded.

My eyes rounded as my heart began pounding in reaction—how was this upstate New York? It sounded more like downtown Benghazi.

I dropped to my knees and crawled over to the window, not stopping until I could peer outside.

"The fuck do you think you're doing?" Brennan thundered as the lights went down in the room.

"Who did that?" Eoghan snapped.

"Me." Conor's tone was grim. "The electric fences just did their job."

"What's that supposed to mean?" Brennan demanded.

"That the lights would go off if the fences were tripped," Declan explained gruffly, telling me he'd deposited the women in the safe room and had returned.

I felt someone move over beside me, the heat of him brushing against me as he stood next to the window and peered out. When he spoke, I recognized it was Declan too. "The estate's completely blacked out."

Conor hummed. "First line of defense tripped. If they have a second wave, then they'll reach the next part."

Why did he sound like he was enjoying this?

Someone dropped beside me, making me jump because I thought they were hurt. Then, a laptop screen lit up, and I saw Conor's face glowing in the blue light.

He cast me a glance before his fingers started flying across the keyboard. "Having fun, Savannah?"

"Had better times," I countered.

"Aidan'll kill you for being out here and not in the safe room. You're his penguin."

"His, what now?" Then, deciding I didn't have time to learn exactly what he meant by that, I muttered, "He can't kill me if they kill me first."

Conor scoffed. "As if I'd let that happen." His brow furrowed. "Don't let the elevator thing make you think I'm not damn good at what I do."

I blinked. "I didn't think that." I was now, though. Shit. The unmistakable sound of guns cocking ricocheted around the room, and I muttered, "Can I have one?"

"What so you can shoot us in the foot?"

Brennan.

I narrowed my eyes at nothing, because I didn't know where the hell he was, but I sniped, "Sexist, much? My dad's a hunter. He made me learn when I bitched at him for the senseless killing of animals."

"What a weird way to get you to shut the hell up," Declan mumbled. "He made you learn to shoot as, what? Retaliation?"

Conor, as he tapped away, said, "You should tell them what he shoots instead now."

"Shut up," I hissed at him.

"It makes a difference," he retorted.

"What does he shoot?" Eoghan asked, and I felt him approach the window too.

"Paintball pellets."

The guys cackled and I elbowed Conor in the side. "Shut the fuck up. I bet I'm a better shot than you."

"Probably," he confirmed. "I don't like guns. Never have."

Of course, he didn't. "What kind of mobster doesn't like guns?" I complained.

"This kind of mobster?" He grinned at me. "Give her a gun. She might let me concentrate then."

I rolled my eyes at him. "Too kind." But a weapon was shoved at me, and I took it with a muttered, "Thank you."

"You're welcome," Declan retorted.

"Where did you even get the guns from? Aren't you supposed to store them in a safe?"

Before I recognized the ridiculousness of my question—but they had kids wandering around, surely they locked them up?—Conor murmured, "Hidden in plain sight."

"Where?"

He groused, "You're supposed to be letting me concentrate."

"Sorry."

"Grandfather clock," Declan explained. "I don't see anything, do you guys?"

"No. Nothing. You sure it wasn't some bird or something?" Brennan demanded. "Or is that wishful thinking?"

"Definitely wishful thinking unless it was a pack of fucking emus," Conor grumbled. "My fences are hardcore."

"Actually, it's a mob of emus, not a pack," I corrected softly.

He snickered. "Fitting. But still, no emus were harmed in the blowing up of my fences."

Eoghan grunted. "How many men did the sensors pick up?"

Conor called out, "Six."

"Shit. We're outnumbered if they got to the guards."

Just as Brennan finished his sentence, Conor's fingers sped up even more, then there was a massive explosion that had me jerking backward, flopping onto the floor. It didn't shatter the windows, which told me they were made of reinforced glass, but beneath me, the ground trembled a little with the force.

Winded thanks to how I collided with the ground, a bit like I'd belly-flopped, I rasped, "What the fuck was that?"

"Good, old-fashioned illegal substances that are punishable by forty years in a state penitentiary," Conor chirped.

"Da's gonna be pissed if you wrecked Ma's daffodil flowerbeds," Declan muttered.

"We're in the middle of a siege!" Conor growled. "What am I supposed to do? Let the daffodils survive while we get shot up?"

My heart flipped a little, but I hurled myself onto my stomach, flat to the ground as I scurried forward like I'd been taught during my own training—all those goddamn classes Dad had made me take to defend myself from kidnappers and such were coming in handy as I returned to the window. Aidan was so wrong about my right hook. Ex-SAS soldiers had taught me and my siblings how to fight. When I peered over the sill, just a scant inch, I wasn't sure if it was fate or not, but I saw something.

He was dressed all in black and the smoke from the explosives made him stand out in stark relief.

I knew Eoghan was the family's sharpshooter. "Do you see him, Eoghan? Over by that ornamental duck pond?" I asked softly, and received a hum of assent.

Now, my heart pounded. The figure in black was quite clearly disoriented, enough that he was staggering from side to side rather than striding forward, but I felt the cold brush of air as one of the windows was opened, and then a loud ricocheting bang sounded, one that made me jolt almost as much as the bomb that had gone off in the yard had done.

"I can only see one more sign of life," Conor said, confirming Eoghan's kill.

I blew out a breath at the thought, but found myself still not scared. Mostly just relieved I was on the O'Donnellys' side. Although, I wasn't sure what kind of a death wish the Sparrows had by doing this. It was clear they were after me again, but dear Lord, breaking into the O'Donnellys' compound was like asking to be killed.

As I gnawed on my bottom lip, a move that belied the lack of fear I purportedly didn't feel, I turned to Conor and saw he was monitoring a screen.

I frowned as I saw it was like a sensor, with dots of heat here and there. I quickly surmised that where we were, there was the biggest cluster. I also saw that around the perimeter of the building, there were guards, but toward the front, there was only one sign of life.

"Does that mean some of your guards are dead?"

We shared a look. "Sadly. Yes."

"Oh," I whispered, guilt spearing me in two.

The day before Christmas Eve, my presence here had led to some of their men's deaths.

Conor patted my knee, and while the gesture was awkward, he said, "You're exposing criminals within the justice system, within the government and only God knows what other parts of American society, Savannah. Sometimes, blood has to be shed to liberate the truth."

Gratitude filled me as I rasped, "Thank you, Conor."

He shrugged. "Only being honest."

A loud gunshot sounded, one that had me ducking my head, my shoulders coming up to hunch around my ears.

"Who the fuck was that?" Brennan called out.

"I don't know. The remaining intruder's not doing too well. His heart beat's too slow—" He grunted. "It's petering out. There's another shooter out there."

"Shit!" Brennan snapped. "We're sitting fucking ducks in here."

"There are ten behind the gates," Conor called out, and his calm stunned the hell out of me.

"Where the hell did they come from?" Brennan snapped.

"Must have been waiting in the wings—reinforcements. It makes sense. I have sensors as far down the roads as I can go, but shit starts to get dicey when we hit the highway. Because it's an Interstate route, if I put them there and they're discovered, which they will be, it gets federal."

Maybe I should have realized there was more to him than that diamanté-studded cat he carried around. Knowing he was a genius was one thing, but seeing it under fire was another.

More gunshots sounded, but it was weird—they didn't seem to be getting closer.

"Someone's picking them off," Eoghan muttered, his calm just as intense as his older brother's.

In fact, they were all relaxed. The only one who wasn't was me.

Or, at least, my heart was starting to throb a little more, but not like it should have been.

This kind of adrenaline buzz was better than anything Red Bull could do.

"Someone on our side? Is there a sharpshooter in Da's protective detail today?"

Conor replied, "Let me check—" He grunted. "Robertson, but he's at the back of the property. I can see him. He's approaching, just not from the front."

Another gunshot pounded through the sound waves, followed by another one, and three more in sharp succession.

"Who the fuck is that?" Brennan rasped.

"They're on our side, so does it matter?" I snapped.

"Yeah, it fucking matters."

"Two intruders still alive. The shooter's just outside my network."

"The other guards have finally made it to the front yard," I commented, relief hitting me as I pointed to the dots on the screen.

Conor hummed. "It took them long enough."

"Think the golf carts were sabotaged?" Eoghan queried.

"Maybe. Can't see it, though. They're stored on the property, so someone would have to have sneaked in earlier."

Declan grunted. "We already know we've got a rat problem."

"Shit," Brennan spat, hissing the curse under his breath.

"You have Sparrows in the ranks?" I gasped.

"Somebody remind me why the fuck she isn't in the safe room?"

"Are you always a jerk?" I spat.

"Pretty much," Conor confirmed with a cackle. "He can't help it. In his defense, it's in his job description."

Brennan shocked me by snorting. "Jackass," he grumbled.

"You know it," Conor retorted, but he sported a smug smile, like... well, as if being teased by and teasing his brothers was his raison d'être.

"I thought Sparrows were only in law enforcement and politics, spheres of influence."

"No," Conor disagreed. "They're everywhere. Law enforcement uses patsies within the various factions inside the city. I'd imagine, within the country as a whole.

"They fit them up for crimes they didn't commit, then if they don't comply with the Sparrows' wishes, they get shafted and sent to jail."

"So, they either ask for the death sentence by betraying their people, or go to jail for a crime they didn't commit?" My eyes widened. "I hated them before, but that's just mean."

"Yeah, they don't play Polly Pocket," Brennan sniped.

"Leave her alone, Brennan," Declan grumbled. "What is it with you, anyway? Aidan likes her."

"Aidan loves her," Conor corrected, which made my cheeks turn pink.

"Love?" Brennan spat, scoffing. "He barely knows her."

Conor cackled again, and I had to admit, I was growing addicted to that sound. It was everything cheeky and naughty combined into a laugh and, as if it were contagious, made my lips twitch in response. "Yeah, says the man who's been married for two minutes and is all over his wife like he's herpes."

"Shut up, Conor. This ain't about me."

"No, it's about Aidan. It's about him finally finding a woman he doesn't just want to fuck but that he actually wants to be with. I mean, Da gave you shit about Camille, and it pissed you off, so why the hell are you bitching at Savannah?" He scoffed. "Hypocrite."

"Well said," I cheered, grinning at him. "See, I knew we liked each other."

"BFFs for life," he concurred with a snicker, his fingers still flying, until out of the blue, he whistled under his breath. "Someone's approaching."

I felt Eoghan's tension soar, then when someone's cell buzzed, I was curious enough to watch and see if he flinched—he didn't. Christ, that was cool.

"It's me," Conor muttered. "Star, now's not the time—" He paused. "Shit. Stand down, Eoghan. She's on our side."

"Who the hell is it?"

"Dead To Me." Star's voice filtered through the room now Conor had put her on speaker. "She's a sniper—"

"We know who she is," Declan answered. "That psycho who gives her kills gifts before they die."

Oh, my God! I knew about her. She was wanted in all fifty states! Before I could fangirl again, Star retorted, "I wouldn't call it psycho, more artistic. Hey, we all have our own creative flair. You never work a day in your life if you love your job, am I right?"

I chuckled. "Not sure that's the same with snipers, sweets."

"Savannah? The fuck are you doing there?" She growled under her breath. "Conor! You were supposed to look after her. She's, like, the one person in the world I don't hate all the time."

Snorting, and feeling surprisingly light-hearted given the situation, I told her, "Feeling's mutual, babe."

Conor's shrug was in his voice, "We told her to go to the safe room."

Star heaved a sigh. "I told you you had to get forceful with her. She's got the self-preservation of a fly eying a pool of honey like it's a treat."

"Hey!" I countered with a huff. "I *am* here, ya know?"

"Yeah, where you shouldn't be. Are you trying to get your ass killed?"

"No, I just..." I frowned. "I don't know. I didn't want to miss out."

Star groused, "Savannah, at some point, you're going to have to switch off the whole journalist thing."

"I can't, it's who I am—"

"This is a real touching conversation," Brennan growled, "but is now the time?"

"Why not?" Star countered, definitely not afraid to go toe to toe with him. "You're safe now. Dead To Me confirmed the kills. That patch we added to your code, Conor, held."

"I noticed. Thanks, Star."

"My pleasure. They didn't get through, but I'm surprised they even tried."

"You must have some information on the wrong people," Brennan intoned, sounding calmer now Star had shared that piece of news. "Who's left on your shit list, Savannah?"

"Andrew Litten, Laurence Ozarc, James Lindenstein—" I listed the next ten Sparrows who were scheduled and ready to be published. I'd already written those exposés.

Conor wheezed, "You mean to tell me the Speaker of the fucking House, two of the Joint Chiefs of Staff, and the Head of Homeland Security are Sparrows?"

I shrugged. "Well, yeah."

"Why the fuck didn't you start with them?" Conor snapped, for the first time losing his composure. "Jesus, talk about burying the lede!"

"I wrote what I was fed," I shouted back, unafraid to get in his face. "In the order Star gave them to me. It's not my fault if she gave them to me ass backwards."

"Why would you even do that?" Conor demanded of Star.

"Because I picked them in order of how much I hate them."

Despite myself, I had to snicker.

That was such a Star thing to say.

"Your arch-nemeses, huh?"

"Exactly," the woman who was almost a sister retorted, a shrug to her voice.

"When are you due to publish those names?" Brennan asked, and I was surprised by how pleasant he sounded now we were supposedly out of danger.

"Within the week. I was supposed to space them out over the next month, but we decided to flood the news over Christmas."

Declan remarked, "Maybe now's the time to start hitting 'publish?'"

A knock sounded at the door and I heard Eoghan slip away.

When there was no gunfire, I assumed it was Dead To Me, because though she came in with the muzzle of Eoghan's sniper rifle buried in her neck, she swayed in like she was striding down a catwalk.

I eyed her with envy because she totally owned the room at that moment, somehow giving her outfit of all black a panache that'd have made me look like a trash bag.

With an oversized sweater over some slimline sweatpants, she wore Doc Martens' shitkickers and an asymmetric kind of woolen poncho that made her look stylish.

"Star? Can you ask this fucker to take his gun out of my neck?"

"Eoghan O'Donnelly! How could you be so rude? She saved your asses!"

Conor cleared his throat. "She has a point, baby bro."

"How the fuck do we know she is who she says she is?"

"Duh, because I said so," Star groused.

Eoghan sniped, "Do you have a picture? I'm not about to let her loose with my family unless I see some ID."

Star heaved an impatient sigh, but Conor's cell pinged. He scrolled it open, then shone the flashlight in Eoghan's direction, letting it scan the woman's features.

"That's her," I confirmed before he could. Instantly, Eoghan retreated, moving away and back to the window so he could peer out of it once more. "See, Brennan, Eoghan trusts me."

"You'd have to be a dumbass or a Gestapo double agent to lie when Conor was looking at the screen too," was Eoghan's cool retort.

My lips curved despite the seriousness of the situation. "Not just a double agent, but in the Gestapo too?"

"Eoghan's always had a thing about WW2. He cries whenever there's a documentary on TV," Conor informed me.

"Fuck off, Conor," Eoghan growled, pretty much confirming his brother's gossiping with that one curse. "Or I'll take that goddamn cat of yours and shove it up your ass."

"So aggressive." Conor smirked at me, his grin unholy in the blue light, and I grinned back, appreciating that we had a kind of rapport.

"What's going on?" Star complained. "I can't see anything, remember?"

"Stop whining," I retorted, then I cleared my throat. "Dead To Me's just arrived, duh. The guys are trying to deal with the ego-slam that two girls saved their butts."

"Well, I figured that out already. Surprised you don't have a lady boner."

"Maybe I do, maybe I don't," I said with a sniff, but I totally did.

Dead To Me was reported to have over eighty kills to her name, and each one had been foreshadowed by her victims receiving a gift with balloons attached to it. The theatrics were astonishing, the gall? Admirable. Well, if you were a weirdo like me.

"Dead To Me," Star called out. "Did you get them all?"

"Yeah."

"You sure?"

"Sure."

Woman of few words apparently... damn, there went my exclusive scoop.

"Our guards are approaching," Conor warned.

"How did you even know to send someone to help us out?" Eoghan demanded, his gun back in his arms, the butt nuzzling his shoulder.

"I'm helping patch up Conor's system. Happened to see one of the security feeds he's got running about twenty miles away. As luck would have it, Dead To Me was in the vicinity."

"Star?" I grumbled. "Don't bullshit. We've known each other way too long for you to even think of pulling the wool over my eyes. What's really going on?"

She huffed. "Nothing! It was like M*A*S*H or something. Military truck loaded down with fucking mouthbreathers, hustling down a goddamn residential road? It stuck out like a sore thumb."

"What's a mouthbreather?" I asked.

"Nasty way of saying someone's a grunt," Dead To Me intoned as she stepped over to the window where Brennan was standing.

"And grunt's a nice way of saying soldier?" I asked wryly.

Conor snorted. "Nice and the army don't go hand in hand."

"True fuckin' dat," Eoghan rumbled.

"You planted Dead To Me here for me, didn't you, Star?" I prodded nervously, Eoghan's severe tone shaking me where nothing else had so far.

I didn't even know why, but that, as well as the fact soldiers had been sent after me...

I already knew the Sparrows meant business, but sending the Army after me? Holy hell.

"Well, I wasn't going to get caught out twice. Fool me once, shame on me," she said, her words waning, before she barked, "Conor? You seeing what I'm seeing?"

"Yeah. The guards are checking out the gates and the soldiers."

"I have a visual," Eoghan confirmed.

"Is that a bad thing?" I whispered, asking no one in particular.

Conor said, "They went straight to the scene of action, not to the house. If they were coming to the house, it's more indicative that we're not their targets. I.e. they're not working for the Sparrows, but for us."

I sucked in a sharp breath at his explanation, which didn't make me feel better at all.

"Unless, they're not morons and can figure out that the way not to look guilty is to go to the dead people first then the alive ones?"

Dead To Me's droll tone had me biting my lip. I twisted around, not liking being in the dark, and peered over the sill once more.

"You okay, Savvie?"

"God, it's years since you called me that."

"I know."

"I could be better."

"Next time, go to the safe room."

I hummed. "Maybe."

Conor snorted. "You really are bad with self-preservation, aren't you?"

"Told you," Star sang.

I harrumphed, but with another flourish, Conor did something that had the lights coming back on.

As he did, floodlights drowned the area, revealing a scene of carnage that looked like it belonged in a third world country. Blood was everywhere, but that was nothing to the number of men who were strewn around like rag dolls.

The guards were clearly tossing them over, checking pulses, seeking out threats from the soldiers which meant, I had to assume, they were on our side... At least, I hoped that was what it meant.

"Lodestar?" Brennan called out.

"Yeah?"

"Could you ask Cruz to come and visit us? We'd owe the Sinners big time."

"I can ask. Probs best to go through Rex, though. For a bunch of rebels, they can be pretty fucking sticklers for this kind of shit."

Brennan grunted, but Declan said, "I'm on it. Padraig should be able to hook us up."

Padraig?

Who the hell was he?

The only Padraig I knew was Aidan Sr.'s brother. The one who was supposed to be six feet under but was living it up in Canada.

A few seconds later, he moved toward the other end of the room, murmuring, "Sorry to disturb you, Padraig, but we need help. We need someone to get rid of a bunch of bodies fast, clean, and efficiently."

"You shouldn't listen to things you can't print," Conor murmured softly, his gaze anywhere but on me as he apparently sensed my eager curiosity.

"That's a good piece of advice," Star agreed.

"Look, the only people with death wishes in this vicinity are already dead. If you think I'm insane enough to publish any kind of shit about the O'Donnellys, then you truly believe I'm fucking stupid."

Conor cackled. "Da's reputation does precede him."

"Yeah, just a little," was my dry retort. Plus, it was clear they didn't get it yet.

I was going nowhere.

You didn't rat on family, but that didn't mean I wasn't fascinated still.

Everyone with a Daniels' surname knew Dad had had Aspen's kidnappers killed—I hadn't printed that in a goddamn paper, had I? Sheesh.

"Holy shit, have you seen the news, Conor?"

"Been in the middle of a gunfight at the O'Donnelly Corral, Star. Most of the news has been happening in our front yard."

"New York cathedral is on fire. Your da's going to go apeshit if it was arson."

"Jesus. Apeshit ain't the word. He loves that place. It's like his Holy Grail."

Did I think it was a coincidence that the Archbishop of New York had been brought to the O'Donnelly house in a white van, and then the leader and his heir disappeared with said Archbishop and then there was a fire at the cathedral?

Did I look like I was born yesterday?

What the hell had Aidan done?

THIRTY-SEVEN

AIDAN

MA'S SCREAMS would haunt me until the day I died. Her rage at being dragged out of the cathedral, like she wanted to burn alongside it, would never leave me.

And Da's resolve that he should burn too was something else that was going to stick around for a long time to come.

You thought you knew someone, and then when you learned you knew fuck all about them, it turned everything on its head.

My entire world was forged on the fact that I was an O'Donnelly.

This city would be mine once Da died.

I was more heir than son. More a leader in the making than his kid. But here, now, I came face to face with the harsh truth.

Da was an unconscious sack of shit as I dragged him down the aisle, the shiny marble tiles helping me slide him along its impressive length. I figured it was fitting considering he'd tried to haul my ass up it enough times with goddamn arranged weddings, but as the temperatures surged in here, my panic increased because not only was it getting harder to breathe, I knew we had to get out of here soon before the cops and fire department showed up.

My leg ached like a fucker as I hauled him along the tiles, and when Finn came back, relief hit me as he grabbed Da's other leg and took over, letting me hobble along faster now I wasn't encumbered with Da's deadweight. He didn't ask questions, didn't waste time, just took over.

As always, we were in tune. The Oxy had broken that. Maybe Aoife had too. Finn's priorities had changed. Only having Savannah made me see that a change of priorities wasn't always a bad thing. Sometimes, it was what kept you getting up in the morning when you had no other reason to do anything but stay in bed. Both Conor and Finn had told me that—I'd just never listened.

I was choking by the time we clambered out of the cathedral, and Finn doubled over with a coughing fit as we were blasted with the cold night air. I felt it on my lungs as well, but I felt more panic than anything else. In the distance, I could hear them—sirens. Our fucking death knell.

Da's crew grabbed him and I saw Anthony was carrying Ma. I figured Finn had slapped her or something because she was dangling in his arms.

Any other time, I'd have beaten the living fuck out of him, but from her screams, I knew she was hysterical. A mirror image of Da.

"Come on," I rasped, beginning to choke on the cold air too as oxygen flooded smoke-filled lungs. "We have to get out of here."

I grabbed his arm and, together, we started staggering down the alley, much the way we came.

At our back, one of Da's crew was messing with the jammer, jamming the frequencies or whatever miracle Conor had wrought within that control panel, and I hobbled with Finn toward the town car so we could get the fuck out of here.

Consequences weren't something we often dealt with, but this was a New York goddamn landmark. It'd be treated as an act of terrorism. Plus, everyone knew Da took his Catholicism to the extreme. They'd expect him to be up in arms over its destruction.

By the time we fell into the town car, Ma and Da were slumped over in the back seat. Finn shoved them aside so he could fit too, while I jumped into the passenger side, coughing all the while.

Anthony, who was behind the wheel, drove off with squealing tires, and even though he'd been complicit in the cathedral's destruction, muttered, "What the fuck was he thinking?"

I didn't imagine Da's crew often questioned him, but in this instance, I didn't have it in me to argue.

Anthony wasn't wrong.

This was a fucking disaster in the making.

Finn coughed, and the hacking sound had me twisting around to make sure he was okay. The veins protruded on his forehead as he choked, seemingly unable to catch his breath. I opened the windows, letting fresh air in so he could flush out his lungs and mine too.

As the chill hit me, though, and I began coughing, a sense of clarity came with it.

An arson attack against the cathedral would look like a slight against the city.

An attack against the cathedral *and* St. Patrick's, our local church, would look like it was against Catholicism, and because of the churches in question, more that it was against the O'Donnellys and the Irish Mob.

Allaying suspicion wasn't something we usually had to do, but fuck, we had people in our pocket, enough to make the Sparrows look innocent of corruption, however this was too big to shield.

We needed a fall guy, and before I could figure out who exactly, we needed a solution in the meantime.

As we drove through Hell's Kitchen, I directed Anthony, "You got anymore gasoline left?"

His head twisted to the side as he shot me a bewildered look. "Two canisters."

I rubbed my chin. "Take us to St. Patrick's. Our parish, not back to the cathedral," I clarified because he was a moron.

"You can't be serious," Anthony rasped.

"Are you fucking questioning me?" I barked, satisfied when his shoulders hunched.

"No, Boss."

"Good," I snapped, coughing a little before I rumbled, "Now take us to the fucking church." I reached for my cell, called Donall, and told him to make a shell out of the white van.

Driving through our territory, our neighborhoods, I felt safer than I did being in Midtown, but that wasn't saying much. Even here, we could be picked up. If Conor's gadget had let us down for just a few seconds, we might be fucked if we were caught on camera.

In the distance, I could see the church spires, and started pressing the jammer as I recognized just how much of a mainstay it was in my life.

Everything was celebrated here, the end of the week, births, deaths, marriages.

Seven days didn't pass without me having to come to the godforsaken place twice, and I had to sit in that goddamn booth where Conor had been raped.

I had to sit there and atone for shit when I was already fucked. When I was already going to hell because I'd never confessed to McKenna's murder. Not because I was scared of the consequences if Da ever bribed Doyle into sharing secrets he learned in the confessional—and I wouldn't put it past him—but because I felt no regret.

I'd willingly burn for an eternity because McKenna had gotten everything he deserved.

Now, maybe, it was our chance. Maybe Finn and I could have some of that. Some peace. Some goddamn freedom from our pasts.

As we pulled up outside the church, Finn rasped, his voice hoarse from coughing, "What's the game plan, Aidan?"

I didn't answer, just said to Anthony, "Keep the jammer working. I'm not concerned about the church, but about any residential cameras."

He blinked but reached for the gadget and pressed that red button while I was there.

I nodded in thanks, then struggled out of the car, the agony in my knee fading as I stared up at a place that was a personal source of misery. Which was when, at the worst possible time, I realized the Oxy hadn't just helped me blot out the physical pain, but the psychological too.

Throat thick, from emotions as well as the smoke, I whispered, "Can I ask you a question, Finn?"

"Of course," was his immediate reply.

"You never told me why you ran away from home. Did you?"

He stilled. "You know that fucker was beating me."

"Did he know you were Da's?"

"Apparently."

I grunted. "That's why you ran away?"

Finn reached up and tugged on his shirt collar, pulling away the already loose necktie. As he did, I knew the desire to lie was strong in him. I could fucking feel it.

Just like when Da had been looking at Finn and me, there'd been a different kind of hell in his face when his gaze had glanced off me and pinned itself to Finn.

A hell that made me wonder shit.

"You got married here," I said softly.

"I did."

"Why?"

"Because it was expected of me. Just like Jake's baptism." He hissed. "What would you have had me do, Aidan? I couldn't tell your da."

"*Our* da," I corrected.

He heaved a sigh. "Today was the first time I ever said that out loud. When I learned what he was to me, he wanted me to call him Da but I've never wanted to say it, didn't want any of you guys to know."

"Why not?"

"I don't know. I didn't want anything to change, I guess, and Da just doesn't sit well on my tongue. Maybe because he's Aidan Sr. to me? Either way, it, well, I-I just couldn't not call him that today. It wouldn't have been right, not when he was going through...*that*."

"Fucker lost the plot in the cathedral."

"Your ma wasn't that much better," Finn groused, his head tipping back as he looked up at the church which was picture perfect thanks to the cold midwinter night. "I have no idea how she managed it, but she hurled herself off my shoulder. She didn't land right."

"She hit her head on the way down and passed out?"

He sighed. "Yeah. I checked her over before I went in after you. She's got a nasty crack on her forehead, think that's probably why she passed out."

I scrubbed the back of my neck. "Thanks for coming and helping me with Da."

"You know I've got your back. Always."

And I did.

"We should talk about what happened," I rasped, everything inside me needing to *never* talk about that fucking day so long ago at this very site but maybe we should. We'd covered it up for so many years... The destruction we'd left behind in Midtown spoke loudly about how bad it was to repress shit like this.

"Since when did we grow pussies? I don't need to talk about that day."

I winced because I was grateful. Then, a thought occurred to me. "Do you resent me?"

Finn blinked. "Huh? Resent you? Why the hell would I? You saved me. We didn't have to be this close, Aidan. We're brothers by fucking choice. It's just sealed by blood now. That's all."

It settled something inside me that he was right. We were exactly that. I was, in all honesty, closer to him than I was the rest of my siblings. I didn't know if it was an age thing, or if it was that Finn and I had been together since nursery, whereas Brennan had been a pain in my ass since he was a toddler. Being an only child would have suited me down to a tee and that little fucker had been a crybaby on steroids.

Finn and I had gelled. I'd kill for my brothers. They were the only reason I'd gotten out of bed these past couple of years, but family and friends came with different expectations. You chose your friends, after all.

I didn't have a say in being irritated by Conor, or having to listen to Declan waxing lyrical about Swan fucking Lake.

Me and Eoghan could argue over football where he was always wrong, and Brennan and I would forever butt heads. I had no say in that. Didn't want one, to be fair, but that was the reality of family.

Whereas Finn and I had chosen to be close over years spent loyal to one another while supporting each other during crises.

"I've got your back too, Finn," I promised him. "Always."

He smiled and clapped me on the shoulder. "Tell me something I don't already know." He peered up at the church though. "You want to burn it down?"

"Don't you?"

"Wanted to burn it down long ago, but got used to it." He shrugged. "I can deal with putting up with stuff I don't like better than you can."

"Is that the privilege of being an heir?" I winked at him when he just snorted.

"It's either privilege or you're a spoiled ass." He folded his arms across his chest then winced and barked out a cough. "Fuck, I got a mouthful of smoke that last time. Feels like I've been sucking on cigarettes for the last fifty years."

I shot him a concerned look. "Do you need a doctor?"

He grunted. "I don't think so. I don't think I'm bad enough to call the whole guard in." By whole guard, he meant the ghost hospitals we constructed when one of us was mortally injured. Much as Declan had been treated in a ghost hospital when he'd been shot.

"Well, the option's there if need be."

He clapped me on the back. "I know, Aidan. I know. Now, what's the game plan?"

"Arson attack against the cathedral, the night before their biggest mass of the year, gives it a terrorist vibe. Wouldn't you agree?"

"Shit, yeah, it does. Last thing we need to stir is that hornets' nest."

"Agreed." I scratched my stubble, grateful as always for the relationship we had because talking shit out with him let me think with a clear head. "Target that and this church, people won't suspect us, if anything they'll think it's an attack against the Irish Mob. That's better for a whole host of reasons," I explained, giving him my logic. "Namely that the city won't lock down again like it did after 9/11."

When he didn't argue, just said, "We need to get on with this. It's more residential here so we run more of a risk of getting caught," I knew my thinking was sound.

"No one would squeal in this neighborhood," I pointed out.

"There's always a first so let's not rock the boat."

"True." I sighed, and began limping over to the trunk where the gasoline was stored. As I pulled out one of the tanks, Finn grabbed the other, and I asked, "You good?"

"Been better but this makes sense."

"You know it's probably a thirty-year prison sentence if we get caught at two arson attacks," I pointed out softly, needing him to know because Aoife and Jake were at home, waiting on him.

"We ain't gonna get caught," he denied, "but it's fucking freezing and I think we need to do something about that."

I smirked at him as we hauled the gas canisters over to a place that was our personal hellhole, and forty minutes later, when it was burning up real good, I wasn't ashamed for tears to prick my eyes, tears that had nothing to do with the heat from the fire, smoke, or the glare.

It was simply relief.

Like I could take a deep breath at long last because I'd never have to come to this place ever again.

It was gone.

The past wasn't, it would always be there, would always shadow us, but this church didn't have to plague our future.

"A fresh start," Finn rasped, coughing a little.

I turned to him, saw the gleam in his eyes and nodded.

It felt good to be free.

THIRTY-EIGHT

SAVANNAH

"YOU'RE FUCKING WEIRD, do you know that?"

I ignored Brennan as I watched the biker who'd pulled up twenty minutes ago with a few other brothers from his MC—all of them making up a cavalry of hogs with a pick-up truck trundling along behind them—being shown the battle scene by Declan.

I wasn't sure why he needed a guided tour, but Declan kicked over a few bodies, exposing lifeless faces and gesturing at them all the while.

"You morbid or something?"

Folding my arms across my chest, I asked, "Why? Is it an issue if I am?"

Brennan grunted. "Not if you make Aidan happy. Conor's right about that."

Tilting my head to look up at him, I admitted, "We haven't been together long enough to know that. Not really. But I want to make him happy if that gives you any peace."

"Women aren't peacebringers," he disregarded, his focus on the scene ahead. "You're warmongers."

I snorted. "White male privilege talking there. AKA, bullshit."

He smirked. "You stick around this family and you'll realize it's the women who are the troublemakers. We men are just humble servants, doing business and keeping a roof over your heads."

"If you say so," I mocked, but my lips twitched a little because I realized Brennan was joking.

Actually joking.

What the hell?

"Surprised you're not out there, asking questions."

"Declan told me to stay here." I pouted.

"He got a read on you fast, huh?" Brennan scoffed. "What's with the morbid curiosity, anyway? You know I'll have to slice your head off if you dare publish anything about the family?"

"Do you know how many times I've been threatened with that?"

"Decapitation?"

"No," I complained, "with retribution if I publish anything about the O'Donnellys. It's already happened three times today, and I'm getting pretty sick of it."

"Once a journalist, always a journalist."

I nodded. "You're right, and I'm not ashamed of that."

"Why not?"

I stared at him, dumbfounded by his lack of awareness. "Don't you know how important the free press is?"

"I vote Republican, Savannah," was his dry retort, "what do you think?"

I made a puking sound. "Did you seriously vote for Hewett in the last election? His head was so far up his own ass you could see it when he was talking."

"You do know who my father is, don't you?"

Despite myself, I had to grin. "I haven't met him, but I can imagine."

Brennan murmured, "I vote red for the tax breaks."

"Of course you do."

When I rolled my eyes, he snorted. "Yeah, I really feel bad Ms.

Trust Fund Baby. I'm sure your job at TVGM paid for that twenty-million dollar apartment you live in."

I really wanted to flip him the bird but instead, I said, "Dad wanted to know I was safe."

"You can do that without spending twenty million dollars."

"True, but I'm his favorite," I mocked, prompting him to grunt.

"Of course you are."

Outside, they started gathering the bodies together, dragging them over to a little cavalcade of golf carts which they were using to transport the corpses only God knew where on the property.

"How will they dispose of them?"

"Sure you want to know?"

"Wouldn't have asked otherwise. Do you have pigs nearby?"

He laughed. "We do, actually. Two towns over. But for a job like this, we need a deep clean."

My stomach churned. "I don't need to see that."

"You sure?" he asked dryly. "I mean, you like to watch, don't you?"

This time, I really did flip him the bird.

"Aidan's going to kill you when he finds out you didn't go to the safe room." He smirked. "I hope observing was worth it."

"Seeing as Dead To Me did most of the work, I'm not sure if I was ever in danger," I sniped, then I hummed, *Sisters Are Doing It For Themselves*.

He dipped down and whispered, "You're showing your age."

Then he swept away, leaving me to glower at his back.

"My age? How old am I? An antique?" Huffing under my breath, I stayed where I was, watching, learning.

I had no intention of doing anything with the information, but breaking the habit of a lifetime was next to impossible. I had an infinite amount of curiosity, and in my world, asking questions was the way forward. In this, I'd already seen how the women didn't even bother formulating the thoughts required to make a question, never mind actually verbalizing it.

That wasn't to say they didn't have opinions, didn't have feelings about a certain situation, but they just knew that the answers weren't something they wanted to hear.

Was ignorance really bliss? I didn't think so. I'd have preferred to have been shot today while knowing what was going on, than being tucked inside a safe room, unsure about what was happening.

Maybe that was just me.

After the bodies disappeared from the driveway, leaving behind blood stains that reminded me of Grand Theft Auto when I played it with my brother and sisters, one of the MC brothers sloshed something on the ground which began to eat into the substance.

As far as I knew, getting rid of bloodstains was very difficult, and more often than not, there were always trace amounts left behind. From the heavy duty gas mask the guy wore, I got the feeling these chemicals made bleach look like drinking water.

When that guy disappeared too, the bustling around the house died down. I knew the brothers had left to do God knew what, with only Conor staying behind.

"When will you let them out of the safe room?" I questioned.

"The guys will make that decision when they know they've got the all clear."

I traipsed over to the sofa. "Will you get fined for this?"

He scowled up at me. "No." His answer was belligerent. "My fences stopped them. My explosives stunned them. And if Dead To Me hadn't shown up, I had three more rounds of physical defense. Da can go fuck himself if he's gonna try to fine me—"

I raised my hands. "Hey! I didn't mean to piss you off. I was just curious."

His cheeks were burning with color and he grunted at me. "Sorry. I didn't mean to blow your head off."

"Thank God you didn't," I told him with a smile. "I like it attached."

An alert sounded on his computer, and he murmured, "They're coming back."

"Who are?" I jerked upright. "The Sparrows?"

"No," he said wryly. "It's Da's town car. It just came through the gates. I'm guessing Finn and Aidan are with him."

I said nothing, just walked over to the window and saw a car that was too short to be a limo, but too large to be an average sedan driving along land that had recently seen bloodshed.

As it pulled up, I waited, peering out to see who exactly it was that was climbing out... then I saw him, and I felt like a whoopee cushion someone had just sat on.

All the air was squished out of me, all the oxygen taken away as I looked at him, which, of course, was when I fell apart. I started sobbing because if I had gotten my ass shot, I'd never have seen him again, and five years of being away from him was already too much.

I hauled ass, running out of the living room and out into the hall, then dragged open the front door so I could throw myself at him.

And like every Prince Charming, even if this one smelled of smoke and gasoline, his arms immediately came up and curved around me. He tucked me so deep into his chest, I almost coughed from the smell of soot and the compression of my lungs, but damn, what a way to go.

In his arms, though it was totally irrational, I felt safe. *Safe*. Safety was more of a commodity than ordinary folk even knew.

"What the fuck's happened, Kid? Has Brennan upset her?" He squeezed me tighter, like just the thought was enough to infuriate him—I even heard the rumble in his chest when he snarled out the words.

Conor, who must have come out for the show, probably hoping to watch Aidan rail me a new one for disobeying, snorted. "You really think Brennan would make her cry?"

"He can be a bastard when he wants to be," was all Aidan said. "What the fuck's happened if Brennan isn't to blame?"

Ignoring him, Conor demanded, out of the blue, "Is Finn okay? What the hell? Ma and Da are unconscious!"

"It's a long story. Why is Savannah crying?" he barked, making his priorities very clear.

Me.

I was at the top of them.

Naturally, that made me cry harder.

"The compound was attacked."

"What?!" Aidan bellowed, and because of the way the yard was constructed, that made noise echo around the place.

"I can match your long story," Conor murmured, "and play hard ball."

"Sparrows came for me," I sobbed out, uncaring that I was snotty and sticky from tears. "L-L-Lots of people died."

Aidan tensed. "On our side?"

"Guards, mostly. None of the women. Why was Ma with you? Why are they all unconscious?"

"Finn's just asleep," Aidan muttered. "It took him a long time to stop coughing, then when he did, he passed out. As for the folks, it's... the Archbishop of New York was a Sparrow."

Conor whistled under his breath. "No fucking way."

"Yes way. Da was naturally upset."

"I'm assuming that's why the cathedral's in ruins? Heard about it —it's all over the news."

"Da wanted to send a message," he confirmed rawly.

"Why the fuck was Ma with him?"

"Why does Da ever do anything? He thought she should come along for the ride." He squeezed me tight then pressed a kiss to my temple. "You're safe, sweetheart."

"She always was." He scoffed. "Damn nerve."

"Wasn't slighting your security, Conor. I was just trying to be reassuring."

"Well, get more creative."

Aidan grunted, "Stop being a jerk." Another kiss was bestowed to my temple. "Everything's going to be okay."

"I know it is," I whispered, my voice clogged with emotion.

"Then, why are you scared?" He paused. "In fact, why the hell are you out here and not in the safe room?"

Conor laughed. "You can take that out on her ass later. We have work to do."

"Jesus, I've already done a day's work."

"It sucks to be the heir, doesn't it?" Conor retorted, mock-sympathy lacing the words.

Because I'd been involved in the process, I knew he wasn't wrong, knew there was still a lot to do before the night was out, especially if their parents were unconscious—what the hell was that about?

Instead of causing more of a scene than I already had, and now that I knew he was here, I whispered, "It's okay. I'll go to the safe room now."

Aidan squeezed me once more. "I'll come and get you out as soon as I can, all right?"

I peeped up at him. "I missed you."

"The feeling's mutual," he rasped, his gaze locked on mine. "Thank you for not running for the hills."

"She didn't have a choice. Those hills were more dangerous than the estate," Conor muttered, and I let out a snot-laden laugh.

"He has a point."

Aidan growled under his breath and shot his brother a death-ray glance, then he heaved a sigh. "He usually does."

THIRTY-NINE

AIDAN

TODAY HAD PROBABLY BEEN the longest day of my life.

One of the worst and the best too.

What a day to realize I had daddy issues.

After a very busy night, one that made the day feel like it had run slow, I headed to my parents' room before I went to the safe room to get Savannah out.

Putting an ear to it, I heard moving around, the sounds of drawers being opened and closed, even the shower, so I knocked and braced myself for what was about to come.

I'd received the lowdown on tonight's events, and had given a cleaned-up version of what had happened at the cathedral to my brothers, all while Cruz, one of our allies, made sure our place was spic-and-span with no forensic DNA evidence.

Star had even telecommuted in on the meeting, and had hacked into Savannah's website, releasing all the exposés in one swoop.

I wasn't sure Savannah would appreciate that, but once I informed Star that the Chief Justice of the Supreme Court was the fucking head of the Sparrows, had explained how they worked using the information the Archbishop had spilled under torture, there was no stopping her.

The exposé on DeLaCroix, the Chief Justice, we'd learned, had already been scheduled to drop on the 25th, but this recent intel changed the timeline and sped up the urgency.

We needed that bastard behind bars.

With no head, how could a body work?

Savannah and Star's source was an ex-trafficking victim of the Sparrows. A Sinners' Old Lady with a quirk that, with her past, must be torturous. Definitely more of a curse than a gift. The ability to remember every face I'd ever seen wasn't something I'd wish on an enemy, never mind an ally. Star had promised that she'd be pumping this woman, Amara, for more faces so we could truly start to annihilate the NWS from the inside out.

With the compound cleaned up of forensics, Conor's chatter confirming that the NYPD believed the attacks against our church and the cathedral were considered gang warfare—retaliation against the Irish Mob—that there'd been no casualties so far aside from the intended one, of course, and my brothers believing that Da had gone off the rails because the man we'd learned was a Sparrow was Catholic, things were wrapped up as well as they could be. Especially once I'd seen Finn rattling around, stooped a little as he hacked up his guts some more.

I wasn't as badly affected, and half-wondered if my detoxed body had assumed the smoke was a type of drug. I sure as hell wasn't coughing as much as he was.

In fact, a few coughs sounded within the bedroom, but the door opened, revealing Da's haggard face to my cautious gaze. "Son?"

Nerves hit me, and I wasn't even sure why. I just felt on edge, pretty much like he did.

I'd never seen my father fragile, and after a lifetime of him being an inferno that blazed out of control whenever he walked into any room, far worse than the fire he'd started at the cathedral, this was strange.

He looked... *old.*

I didn't like it.

Not one bit.

"Is Ma okay?" I asked softly.

He nodded. "She's trying to get clean."

"Oh." Shit.

I reached up and scrubbed a hand over my face. I remembered this phase. After the Aryans, she'd take thirty-minute showers where she came out with her skin rubbed raw. Da had been the only one who could ever get her out from under the water.

"Yeah." He heaved a sigh. "She had to know, son."

"Did she? Are you sure about that?"

"I know that I needed revenge. Why shouldn't she? He's her boy too."

"You're not exactly an over-sharer, Da."

"You'd be surprised what she knows." He shot me a look that was surprisingly measured. More than I was used to. More than I thought any of us were used to. This was getting fucking weird. "Son?"

"Yeah."

He reached out and cupped my shoulder. "Thank you for saving my soul."

Swallowing, I rasped, "You're welcome."

"Finn came to see me a while ago. He told me what happened with St. Patrick's." I tensed, but he shook his head. "You did good." He did the craziest thing then, his hand curved into a fist, and he tapped it gently against my chin. I was used to a punch, but not a gentle bump. "Look at you, taking over for me before I'm dead and gone."

My Adam's apple bobbed.

Was this... acceptance?

Approval?

Fuck.

My mouth worked as I tried to figure out what the hell was happening here, and then I drawled, "You're not leaving us yet. Long Live Aidan O'Donnelly, eh?"

His lips quirked up, but the smile didn't hit his eyes. "We'll see."

"Does Ma know about Finn?" I asked, my voice gruff.

"She does." His voice turned strained. "She loves him like he's hers anyway. I wish he were."

There was something in his eyes, a deep source of regret that had me shifting on my feet. This was just too much for anyone to have to deal with in this short a time.

"I'm about to get the women out of the safe room... I wanted to check in before I did though."

"Your ma says she likes this Savannah broad. She told me all about her when we woke up."

"Thought she'd be the last thing you had to talk about."

"After the tears and recriminations about the past, sometimes, you gotta think about the future. It's cleansing." He tipped up his chin. "If you're serious enough to bring her home for Christmas, then you have my approval. Not that you need it."

"Don't I? I thought I did."

"After what you did—" His voice broke. "You earned the right to pick your own bride."

"What about Conor?"

"Think he'll ever get married?" Da shook his head. "I don't. But we'll see. He has the right to make his own decision about that too."

My eyes flared wide.

Talk about a fucking Christmas miracle.

I cleared my throat. "We'll need to show a strong front about the church attacks."

"I know. But not tonight, and not tomorrow either." It was well into the early hours of Christmas Eve by now. "Let's just enjoy the holidays."

"We need to present an image, Da. You wouldn't ordinarily let things lie like that."

"No? Well, there's a first for everything."

I was well aware that I needed to tell him about his brother, but as I looked at him, right then, right there, I knew that would just be the nail in the coffin. So, instead, I rasped, "Tell Ma I love her."

Da dipped his chin. "I will. I'll haul her out of the shower in a minute. If you're all going to bed, then we'll probably get started on the food."

"You? You're going to cook?"

He shrugged. "Used to help before I got too big for my boots. Ever there's a moment where she needs her husband, it's now."

Nodding, I made to turn away, but before I did, I twisted back and asked, "Da?"

"Yes, son."

"Did you both really want to die in that church?"

His mouth tightened. "I made a lot of sacrifices over the years to make you all untouchable, Aidan." Not Junior. *Aidan.* "I ruined relationships with you all, broke bones instead of building fences, and I did that to keep you safe. So you'd never have to feel what I did when Paddy and Frank died." I tensed, but he didn't see, his gaze was turned back to the past. "You might not realize it, but ever since Jake was born, I've felt this..." He sighed and pressed his fist to his chest. "This ache inside. It's strange. I'd kill for any of you, you know that. Especially after tonight. But for Jake? Now Shay?" He shook his head. "I'd burn this fucking city to the ground.

"Not just a pissant cathedral or a fucking church. Everything that made this city great would be in ashes if anyone hurt them." His jaw tensed. "I pray you never have to know what this feels like. What this fucking scream is like in my head. I know you have it, he's your brother, but not like this. Not like what's in your mother's head.

"McKenna is dead, and the Archbishop who put him in my parish is dead too, but it doesn't take away from what happened." He cleared his throat. "Revenge doesn't take away what happened to Conor, doesn't change the fact you saw that, that Finn did too.

"No," he rasped, his head shaking on repeat. "I pray you never have to hear this scream."

Well aware that he hadn't answered my question, I whispered, "God takes you on his clock, Da, not the other way around."

"I know, son. I know. Don't worry. We'll get through this. We always fucking do, don't we?"

His smile was tight, and as I nodded, I stepped back and away, turning my head over my shoulder as I watched him, my broken father retreat to help my broken mother... He was right on two matters. I heard that scream, but I'd never hear that as a parent because he wasn't the only one who'd make NYC burn for his family.

My mind was racing as I started for downstairs, but before I could hobble my way back down, Da called out, "Aidan?"

Not Junior.

Was this going to be a thing now?

I straightened my shoulders. "Yeah?"

"Arrange for a meeting with Valentini in the morning. You deal with him. We'll back him as Don."

My eyes flared wide. "You're okay with me handling that?"

His top lip quirked up. "I think you're more than ready for it, don't you?"

I'd been ready for years, but he'd never trusted me before.

Stunned, I nodded. "Okay. I'll get in touch with him now."

"Good."

As he closed the door, I started to make my way to the basement where my brothers were waiting to open the safe room together.

Frowning, and panting in pain from my fucking knee—goddamn, I had to go all the way back up those shitty stairs in a minute—I asked, "What are you waiting for?"

Brennan's eyes were calm as he settled them on mine. "You're the leader. You should be the one to open the door."

And fuck me, I had no idea why that meant so goddamn much, but it did.

It really did.

Finn clapped me on the back, and as I shot him a look, I realized that he'd told Brennan what had happened tonight. Eoghan and

Declan were chomping at the bit, so I knew they hadn't been informed, and I was glad about that. The fewer brothers who were aware of the night's events, the better.

I knew why Finn had told Brennan, though.

Finn would always be my right hand man. Not just because he was the Points' money man, either. But Bren? He'd be my second. If the difficult fucker agreed to it.

Nodding my thanks, I limped forward and pushed in the code to the safe room. We'd had a few models over the years since the drive-by on Aoife and Finn's wedding day, but this was the most advanced. It ran under the full length of the house, and was large enough to have small bedrooms for privacy. There was also enough gear stored down here to survive a nuclear war.

When the door opened outward, I stepped inside and found the place in silence. It was dark, as if everyone were resting, only Savannah was there, pacing, and when she saw me, even though it had only been a few hours ago since I'd deposited her here, she hurled herself into my arms.

My brothers waded into the room, their women their destination, and I guessed it was a point of trust that they all knew their men would be coming for them. That they'd always be coming for them.

That was a lesson Savannah would have to learn, too.

I just had to give her time.

FORTY

SAVANNAH

AFTER I LET GO of him, Aidan plunked his ass down on a sofa, letting his bad leg come out in front of him. He was clearly in pain, but that didn't stop him from dragging me beside him, and I went willingly.

The safe room was pretty damn luxurious for what it was: a bunker that would probably see the family through a nuclear war. It had comfortable touches, like down-filled sectionals surrounding a big screen TV which, I guessed, had all the channels you'd ever need to see out an apocalypse. If Netflix survived a zombie war, that is.

There was a kitchen that looked like it belonged in an issue of Vogue, as well as a dining room with a table that seated fifteen, minimum, and which was forged from a single piece of wood and had a delicious light blue/cerulean resin surface that looked like sea foam was drenching it. The colors were rich, the walls painted in jewel-tones, accent cushions and even a tapestry that appeared to be some kind of tribal pattern.

Behind this room was a hallway that had several doors shooting off it, and after having explored, I knew they were bedrooms. Each one as comfortable as the next with a TV that looked as if you were viewing the outside world.

All in all, I'd been cooped up in worse places, TVGM's green room, for example, but it wasn't my idea of a dream destination.

When I thought that I might have been in Hawaii if I hadn't argued with my brother, this definitely fell short off the mark, but then Aidan wouldn't be here either.

My hand tightened around his as his brothers all headed to rooms that I thought they were allotted, and retreated with their wives and families. It took a good long while for them all to leave, wishing us a good night as they trudged out, yawning as they went to their own beds, leaving us alone in the silent space.

I figured I knew why, even though it could have been because of his knee...

"Is this place soundproofed?" I queried interestedly.

"It is," he confirmed, his tone calm if tired.

I peered at him, saw his head was tilted back against the rest and that he was staring at me.

Smiling at him, and I'd admit it, a tad mistily, I murmured, "You gonna whup my ass?"

"How will you learn if I don't, little one? Apparently you need some pain with your pleasure to make you learn a lesson."

Well, didn't that just send shivers down my spine?

Humming, I asked, "I didn't want to miss out."

"Miss out on being shot? Isn't that a good thing?" he drawled.

"I didn't get shot. I had faith in your family's security," I lied. His brothers, sure. I'd had faith in them.

He snorted but his eyes were twinkling. "Make that two whuppings."

"Two? Are you sure you're not too tired for that?"

"Never too tired to make sure you're safe."

"I'm in a safe room. Can't get much safer. In fact, the only person who's threatening my butt is you."

"Yeah, but I'll make you like it," he said, and he wasn't teasing. He was deadly serious.

Mouth watering a little, I murmured, "I'm glad you're okay."

He blew out a breath. "Not sure I'll be okay for a while, but physically, sure, I'm well."

I tipped my head to the side. "Want to talk about it?"

His jaw worked, and I got the feeling he was going to say no, but then, he surprised us both by murmuring, "I learned Finn was my blood brother tonight."

"Your dad cheated?"

Aidan hummed. "A long time ago. I'm ancient, don't you know, and he's only a few months younger than me."

"Is it true about the rolling pin?"

A laugh escaped him. "How did you find that out?"

"Do you really want to know?"

He cocked a brow. "What do you think?"

"There's this coffee shop in Hell's Kitchen where these women get together and talk about shit. They're there every day." I shrugged. "They're loud."

"Jesus, are they all old?"

"I guess. Most of them, at any rate. Some are in their fifties?"

"That's the Old Wives' Club. They're the wives of the guys who died on the job. So long as they don't marry again, Da provides for them." He rolled his eyes. "Guess who never gets married again?"

"All of them," I said with a laugh. "Canny ladies."

He grunted. "You overheard the rolling pin story?"

"I did. Guess that means it's true? That she hit him over the head and it knocked some sense into him?"

"Apparently. I wonder if she knew at the time he was cheating. We never got that version of events, truth be told."

"You really didn't know that Finn was your brother?" I asked softly.

"No. I really didn't."

"I mean, you look alike." I bit my lip. "I just thought it was something you guys didn't talk about. You know, a dirty secret?"

"Did the Old Wives' Club say that?"

"Nah, I've got eyes, don't I?" I tapped my nose. "Plus, I've made it my business to look into everything O'Donnelly."

"True." He grunted. "So, for all that I'm surprised, you're not at all... Typical."

"Sorry," I said with a grimace.

"Don't be." He heaved a sigh. "Jesus, Savannah, tonight has been a real fucking night."

"I'm sorry, Aidan," I whispered, edging nearer to him, and pressing myself against his side.

"I've watched Da brain himself on the wall, torture a goddamn Archbishop, and then almost self-immolate—"

"What?" I burst out. "He tried to kill himself?"

"He did. Ma almost did as well," he rasped, scrubbing a hand over his face. "I had to knock him over then drag him down the fucking aisle."

I reached for the hand that was trying to wipe away his fatigue and pressed it to my cheek. "You saved him from himself."

"I did. He called me Aidan as well."

"That's your name?"

"He calls me Junior." His brow furrowed even further and he let out a nasty-sounding cough. "What a weird motherfucking day."

Even though I knew he was processing something, something he wasn't comfortable sharing, my lips curved. "Funny how it's the fact that your dad stopped calling you by your nickname, and not that you burned down a cathedral that was weird about your day."

He scoffed, "You're not wrong. Jesus. You should run away, kicking and screaming, Savannah."

"You going to let me?"

My heart felt like it stopped beating as he peered at me. Making me wonder if he was trying to find my soul, as if my eyes really were the window to it, then he smirked, slipped his hand away from the gentle clasp I held it in against my cheek, pressed it to the back of my neck and hauled me into him.

"What do you think?" he rumbled, which was when my heart started pumping once again.

He didn't let me answer what I figured was a rhetorical question, but I was relieved anyway.

The second our mouths collided, I groaned with wonder, content to breathe his air and for him to breathe mine. Neither of us were at our freshest, he stank of smoke still and my Valentino suit looked like I'd been rolling around in a washing machine for a few hours, but I didn't care, and I was happy he didn't either.

It meant this was real.

It meant that he wanted me when I looked like a million dollars and when I was doing a pretty good impression of a bag lady. Well, a rich bag lady. This suit definitely hadn't been cheap.

His tongue thrust between my lips, making me sigh as he tasted me, savoring me, sampling me.

I let him, content to feel him against me, holding me, needing me just as much as I did him.

Sighing into his kiss, I reveled in the moment as he stoked the flames of need all while staying true to it.

One hand remained at my nape, while the other roamed down my arm, along my side. The heat from his palm sank into me, warming me up as if I'd been frozen with cold the entire night, and I huddled closer, needing more, needing everything.

As he pulled away, I groaned, sinking deeper into him, but he nipped my bottom lip and rumbled, "Why did you put yourself in danger tonight?"

Dazed, I blinked at him. "Huh?"

He tutted, reached up and dragged my bottom lip down. "Why didn't you come to the safe room with all the other women?"

"Because I'd have been scared otherwise. I don't like being scared."

Aidan tipped his head to the side. "Does anyone?"

"No. But if I can see it, I can understand it. If I can't see it, then I fear it."

"Fucking Isardo. I knew it was down to him. If he hadn't been a lying, cheating piece of shit, you'd never have seen him that day." He growled then dipped forward to press a tiny peck to the corner of my mouth. "But then you wouldn't be here, sitting on this sofa. I'd terrify the living fuck out of you." He released a breath. "I'm not a good man, little one.

“A good man would say that he wished you hadn't seen that, he'd say that he'd spare you that pain if he could, but I want you here. With me. Nowhere else."

"That's exactly where I want to be," I moaned as I clambered onto his lap, trying to be careful so I didn’t accidentally kick his knee.

As I ground into him, he grabbed my ass, molding the cheeks to his grip, making my pussy clench down hungrily, reminding me of how empty I was

"Good," he ground out, reaching up to nip my bottom lip. "You’re gonna be mine, Savannah. In all the ways under the sun." He bit down hard on the soft morsel. "But you’d better start watching out for yourself. My patience only runs so far, little one. I’ll only cut you so much slack because of Isardo," he warned.

A groan escaped me, one that was loaded with want and desire and delight, as I let our mouths collide again. His words filling me with need and lust because I *felt* his care, his love at that moment.

His hands came up to cup my waist, squeezing there before he dragged up my shirt, and his fingers slid along my waistline, drawing my shirt out from it so he could spread that delicious heat along the small of my back.

Sensation had me shivering, especially when he moved around my waist, finding the buttons that made up the fly, and began to unfasten them. The second he struck gold, we both groaned, and he slipped his fingers between my thighs, making short work of what had to be a difficult task considering how tight the gusset of my pants pressed against his hand. I didn't question how, just cried out as he found my clit.

"Down here," he rumbled against my lips, "they won't be able to hear you cry out."

A husky laugh escaped me. "That's your plan, huh?"

"I didn't think about this earlier," he whispered. "I'm surprised my brothers aren't down here too."

"Maybe they're just not as possessive as you are."

"Doubt it." He arched a brow as he tapped my clit with a finger. "You going to complain about my being possessive? Not wanting anyone else to hear those moans that belong to me?"

I swallowed. "N-No," I groaned, arching my hips so he could get more access to my slit. He took immediate advantage, and I squealed as he drew circles on the nub. "Oh, that feels so good!"

"If you don't look after yourself for me," he ground out, "then how am I supposed to let you feel good?" His fingers had me wiggling on his lap. "Why should I let you feel good, Savannah? If you make me feel bad by knowing I can't trust you to keep this beautiful ass safe?"

I groaned again. "You weren't here. What else was I supposed to do?"

"You really gonna take that as an excuse?" He leaned up and nipped the pad of my chin. "When I'm not here, you listen to my brothers. They're invested in keeping you safe because I'll beat the living shit out of them if they don't."

"I don't like being kept in the dark," I grumbled, but it quickly morphed into a yelp when he thrust a finger into my slit. It was thick and I was wet, but it still came as a surprise.

"Well, we already agreed that some things have to be kept from you."

I squinted at him. "You think I'm going to go to the cops."

"No. I don't actually," he said wryly. "I think the more you know, the more trouble you'll get into."

"What's that supposed to mean?"

"It means you'll pull that Nancy fuckin' Drew act and get your ass killed as you hunt for a story. I'm going to have to fill this belly as soon as possible just to keep you busy."

My eyes flared wide as I reared back. "Fill it with what?"

A laugh burst from his lips. "My God, if you could see your face. A baby, little one." He smirked. "Some cum might go down there too. When you earn the right to suck my dick, of course."

Holy shit.

And didn't that just send the need to give him a blowjob right to the top of the agenda?

There were so many things wrong with that statement, but Jesus, tell that to my body. Unable to bear it anymore, I started scrambling off his lap, still with enough wherewithal to take care with his knee.

"Where do you think you're going?" he growled, reminding me that we were connected as he hooked his finger against that one spot he'd found and made his bitch yesterday afternoon. I groaned as he held me in place with a single goddamn finger.

"I need to get naked," I panted, shuddering.

"I can get behind that." Aidan rubbed the area. "Looks like I found your happy spot, little one."

"Y-Yes," I rasped, feeling the electric shocks sparking up and down my spine again.

A knife appeared from out of nowhere, making me jolt as he pressed it to the seam of the fly to my pants. When he pushed down, with a care I appreciated seeing as it was near the family jewels, I watched as he sliced down the seam. It parted like butter on a hot day.

"Where did that come from?" I whispered faintly, eying the metal against the baby pink suit and trying not to melt because that'd be a disaster waiting to happen.

"I'm always armed."

"You are?" I asked, my voice high pitched.

He blinked as he stared up at me. "I'm in the mob, Savannah. Did you think I wouldn't carry at least a knife?"

I shuddered. "I guess I thought you were carrying a gun."

His lips quirked, then he hummed as he sliced deeper down the seam, straight toward where his hand bulged the fabric. "Shame, I liked you in this suit but I want to see that pussy more."

"Y-Yes," I moaned, trying not to be turned on by that knife. That sharp blade which could very much hurt me if he so much as sneezed.

In the otherwise silent room, the sound of the fabric parting was like an ASMR video or something. It made my ears tingle. And other bits of me as well.

I felt a slight whisper of air next. "Jesus," I squeaked, freezing in place. The metal didn't touch me, not until he pressed the flat of the blade to the heat of one of my labia. "Aidan!" I squeaked again.

"Da tried to look after Ma," he rasped, "but there's no trying with me. You'll never shed a drop of blood on my watch, Savannah."

"What about a paper cut?" I whispered.

"Smart ass." He tapped the blade to the other side, making me hiss with the chill, before he carefully retreated, dropped the knife on the sofa cushion beside us and rumbled, "That's better."

It was, actually.

Especially when he thrust his other fingers into the slit he'd made, and those fingers went to work on destroying me.

He ground the butt of his hand into my clit, then drew juices from my cunt onto the tips before slipping up to my ass. "I think," he stated, "that every time you misbehave, you should take my dick in your ass."

I gulped.

"Then I'll only forgive you if you come so hard you squirt again."

A wail escaped me as I rocked higher onto my knees. "Aidan!" I bit off, jittering as he ground harder onto my clit.

"Yes, little one?" he crooned, making me shudder again.

"I-I don't know."

He chuckled, then the fabric of my pants tightened before loosening as he made the hole bigger. When he prodded my ass, I squirmed, grinding my hips into him before he said, "Lean forward and press your hands onto the back of the sofa."

I blinked at him, fumbling to do as he asked because, to be frank, why the hell wouldn't I?

Aidan wouldn't hurt me—not unless it was to make me feel good in the process.

Positioning myself how he wanted, I leaned forward which had him slipping the tip of his finger into my ass. I didn't squeeze down, because I'd messed around with a butt plug a time or two, just had never gone through with anal because a man had to work for that shit.

A groan escaped him when his finger hit home, and I whispered, "I want you to fill me up, Aidan."

Our eyes clashed.

"I want your dick inside of me. Always. We wasted so much time—"

He reached up and pressed his mouth to mine, tormenting me above and below. His tongue plied mine while he filled my pussy with a taunting finger, grinding his palm against my clit, while carefully thrusting another in my ass. It wasn't hardcore, but after the long day I'd had, it had me shuddering in response.

"Only good girls get dick," he rumbled, pulling back after a few, torturous moments where he stole my breath.

"I'm a good girl," I cried when he pulled away from my pussy.

"Are you going to listen when something bad happens?"

Even in my state, I heard that word.

When.

It resonated, hitting harder, deeper than it might ordinarily, but even though I knew I was embracing the danger that came as part of the package deal of being with him, I whispered, "I'll try."

He clucked his tongue as he pressed his fingers to my mouth. As I sucked them in deep, cleaning them up and lapping at them, he whispered, "You'll do more than try. You want to break me, little one? You want me to get shot or stabbed or killed outright because I'm so busy worrying about you that I can't protect myself?"

I tensed. "N-No," I mumbled around his finger.

"Well, then. You need to remember that when you're scared because you're in the dark about something. You think all those fucking years keeping you out of trouble was for nothing? Just for me to fuck it up when I finally get a piece of you?"

Shaking my head, I whispered, "No."

"So what are you going to do when one of my brothers tells you to get into the safe room?"

"I go."

"Good." He grumbled, "If I'd been them, I'd have hauled you over my shoulder and taken you there myself."

"I slipped through the cracks," was all I said.

"Well, something's about to slip through your crack," he retorted, and despite myself, I had to giggle, and I pressed my face into his shoulder as I did so.

"Don't make me laugh."

"I wasn't joking," he said wryly.

I turned my face into his throat and pressed a kiss there. As his head rocked back, I followed, and as I anointed the area with kisses, lathing it here and there, fluttering the tip along the sinews, I whispered, "Aidan, you're not allowed to die."

"I know, little one. I know."

That was when he thrust the finger deeper into my ass, and took things to a whole other level.

FORTY-ONE

AIDAN

BY THE TIME she was crying out, literally in the palm of my hands, I knew Savannah was way past thinking about what had happened tonight.

Which was exactly what I wanted.

I needed her brain focused elsewhere because it let me forget too.

As she squealed and cried out, groaned and mewled on my lap, each squirming attempt to simultaneously avoid and to get closer to me was a sign of how far gone she was.

I took advantage of that, turned all my focus on her, then when she was a weeping, filthy mess, I pulled away from her completely, leaving her pussy and ass empty, leaving her wriggling mindlessly, needing what I wasn't giving her.

Taking away her orgasm before she could have it.

Pleasuring her but never letting her tip over the side. A sharp and undoubtedly cruel contrast to the inundation of climaxes I'd bestowed upon her yesterday. Every action had an equal and opposite reaction, after all.

"Aidan!" she cried out, grinding her sopping wet pussy against my dick, able to do so now my hands weren't down her pants.

"Get yourself off, little one," I directed, watching her eyes flare wide open at that.

But as she sensed my resolve, her hands went to my shoulders, and she did as I ordered. Riding my erection through the fly as fast and with as much pressure as she could add to it.

As she rocked against me, her breathing grew frenzied, and I reached for her tits, tearing open her blouse so I could see them jiggle. When her hoarse cries filled the room, I slipped three fingers into her mouth, loving how she sucked on them while she got herself off.

Hips bucking with her wild moves, I watched the show, delighted in her as she came, letting her follow through with the aftershocks too, savoring every moment.

When she slumped against me, momentarily spent, I held her to me for a second, squeezing her before I let her go, maneuvering her so that she was ass up, face down in the cushions.

Amused that she didn't argue, I got to my feet, grimacing after the day's strenuous activities made themselves known in my knee.

Damning the joint to hell because it made sex so fucking awkward, I twisted her some more so that I had better access, grinning when she just let me.

God, if she was this pliable in real life, it would be much easier. I already knew I had a nightmare ahead of me when it came down to keeping her safe in the future, but when it boiled down to getting her to behave how a good, proper mob wife should, I'd embrace her crazy and make it work for us.

She was worth the shit I'd get in the long run.

Tearing her pants open wider, I revealed that sweet ass of hers. Peeking between the baby pink folds of fabric, it made her pussy lips all the darker, especially now they were flushed with color, the succulent and juicy flesh an array of reds from her orgasm.

The urge to taste her was immense, but I wanted her ass. Fuck, I wanted it bad. Even if I couldn't have it all as I had no lube, I wanted some of it. Some piece of it to take as my own.

Knowing I wanted to see those cheeks turn pinker still, I didn't stop until the hole I made in her seat was big enough for her butt to peep through in its entirety, that was when the slickness of her cunt called to me, so I unfastened my cock, finally releasing it from its prison, and slipped it through her folds.

A shaky breath squeaked from her, followed by a high-pitched keening sound as I tortured us both. When my dick was slick, I pushed it home, while with my other hand, the clean one, I gathered her juices and used them to fuck her in the ass.

As I pounded her from behind, making sure to stretch out that hole good and well, I curved them down, digging them into my dick while I used my other hand to spank her.

With each thrust, I tapped that booty, making sure to get it pink and blotchy, and that mewling sound just fired on and on, the note hitting something inside me, resonating in a way that made me speed up.

Fucking her how I needed, loving that she took everything I had to give, I screwed her until the disastrous evening was nothing more than a memory.

Until all I saw, felt, heard, smelled, and tasted was her.

Always her.

And hadn't it been that way since the first time we'd met?

Always her?

I moved faster, harder, slicing into her softness, feeling it welcoming me, beckoning me where I belonged—home.

This was home.

Her.

Her cunt.

Her warmth.

Her fucking heart.

And it was mine. All mine. No fucker else's.

Unable to stop myself, I ceased spanking her and instead, grabbed her hair in a tight grip and forced her to sit up on her knees. She squealed as she straightened, and I grabbed her by the throat, being careful not to break her necklace, pinning her to me, my front to her back as, deep in her ear, I rasped, "Who do you belong to, little one?"

"You!" she screamed, detonating around me, coming so hard that I saw fucking stars as she drew me into the darkness with her.

Together, we exploded.

Together, we burned.

Which was, all told, pretty fitting for the life we were going to lead.

That was why, as I panted through my release, feeling the aftershocks settle deep in my bones, adding to my tiredness while also revitalizing me, as we both fell into the sofa, me wincing as it hurt my knee, her flopping into the cushions, I whispered in her ear, "Marry me?"

Drunkenly, she replied, "Only if you'll wear a ring."

I smirked as she hummed Beyoncé's *All The Single Ladies*.

"You liked it so you want to put a ring on it?" I asked dopily.

"Exactly," she slurred.

A thought occurred to me. "Where's my necktie?"

She turned into me, twisting so that we were still joined, barely, hooking her leg over my hip, as she muttered, "I cut it off," before promptly falling fast asleep in my arms.

I might never see the heaven that Da was so obsessed with, but here, now, I knew this was as close to heaven on earth as I could be. I was more than okay with this being the only one I ever got to visit so long as I had it for the rest of my life.

Didn't mean I wouldn't tan her ass for ruining another necktie though.

Smiling, I closed my eyes and finally found some peace of my own.

FORTY-TWO

AIDAN

"I DIDN'T EXPECT to hear from you so soon. Your father must really have liked that gift of mine, hmm?"

Not bothering to turn around, I kept my face averted, gaze fixed on the outside world as I peered out of a window that had more grime on it than the floor beneath my feet. I meant it too—this was regularly cleansed for DNA. The window evidently wasn't.

"Sometimes, a gift just keeps on giving, doesn't it?" I replied.

"Heard on the news that the cathedral got torched. Your church as well." Valentini strode toward me, moving to stand opposite me before he leaned against the wall. "They're saying that a charred skeleton was found there."

"I wonder whose bones they could belong to?" I questioned, finally catching his eye.

He grinned at me, and after sharing that smile, I took the opportunity to take a glance around the warehouse he'd agreed to come to, and to check out his men.

They were edgy, one kept flicking a knife in his hand, and though the blade was tucked inside a sheath, he was clearly nervous about being on Irish territory, in a place where bodies routinely had a habit of entering but never exiting—at least, rarely in one piece. Lean and tall, his agitation made him the focus of my men too.

Brennan was warily watching him like he was about to throw that knife, while my brother's hand had tunneled into his pocket where I knew he was probably palming his own switchblade.

The other Italian was stocky, his features blunt, his eyes dark, but his expression was blank. Enough that it drew my attention.

As I stared at him, Valentini murmured, "My *capos*."

I blinked at his explanation, appreciating it. "My second," I replied, motioning at Brennan with my chin. "The rest are guards in case you do something stupid like try to pull a fast one."

Valentini grinned. "I'm Sicilian, Aidan," he chided. "We Sicilians don't break our word."

"You identify as Sicilian and not Italian?" I queried.

"Are you Irish or American?"

Though I got what he meant, I replied, "I've never even been to fucking Ireland."

He smirked. "Still Irish though, aren't you?"

I smirked back. "Still am, for sure."

"Much as I appreciate the meeting, especially so soon, I was hoping to meet with your father, Aidan—"

"I know you were. Some business is for me to deal with now. That's not to say that you're less important to my father, if anything I think it's indicative of what you were saying yesterday—we'll be the ones who'll reign over this city together."

I'd had power in the Five Points since I was sixteen years old, but this highlighted how little I'd really had.

This was power.

Forging new alliances and breaking up others.

Valentini's eyes gleamed. "A new guard."

I nodded. "Exactly. Now, why would he broker this agreement and not me?"

He shot me a steady look. "That means a deal's going to be had? You'll back me as Don?"

"The *Famiglia's* been a fucking mess for decades. What makes you think you can reign over it and keep those animals in line?"

"Do you know how it works?"

"Vaguely. What's on Wikipedia mostly," I mocked.

Valentini laughed. "I think we'll get along for sure, Aidan." He rubbed his hands together. "There used to be five families in charge of the whole *Famiglia*. Five collectives who worked to keep the central line, the Valentinis, in check. It never failed us. Five is a check and balance, after all.

"Fieri annihilated my family, and eradicated one other, leaving behind the Genovicos and the Rossis. They were his lapdogs. His bitches."

"As far as we've come to know, the Sparrows started blackmailing the *Famiglia* back in the sixties/seventies."

Valentini nodded. "Yes, after my grandfather was killed they started to slither their way in. That would never have happened on our watch, but it is what it is. There's no changing the past, but there's letting it breathe new life into the future." He folded his arms across his chest. "My intention is to bring back the original way. It worked."

"Five families?"

"Five."

"Including the Rossis and Genovicos?"

His top lip quirked up in a snarl. "What do you think?"

"I think that, in my family, they'd be slaughtered like the pigs they are."

"And you'd be right. Now, I was raised in Sicily, but I've been back in the States for ten years." He rubbed his jaw. "Slowly, I've been building shit up to the point where I was going to trigger a war.

"Benito Fieri's seat is my rightful place, after all.

"But before I could, this entire shit show went down with the Irish and the Russians, these Sparrow fuckers came to light, and, here we stand. The Fieris taken down by you, and your allies, the *Famiglia* in tatters, and hundreds of *soldatos,* never mind *capos,* running around like headless chickens."

I nodded. "They're going to be a problem soon enough."

"You take away the elders, the rulers, and all of a sudden, you have young fucks roaming the streets, unchecked." He met my gaze. "I've gained a majority rule in the *Famiglia*, but when I consolidate power once this peace deal is brokered between us, you won't have to worry about that. We'll back off Irish territory, stick to our own—"

"What about Russian territory?" I questioned. "Your war is mostly with them."

"I know. Once I take over fully, I'll see to it that I speak with the new Pakhan, broker peace with him as well."

"You're being very conciliatory," I pointed out. "I'm not sure, in your shoes, if I'd be so diplomatic."

Valentini merely said, "I don't appreciate having to speak with the Irish Mob's golden boy to get what's rightfully mine, but I've done worse over the years to reach this point.

"One conversation with you will save a lot of men's lives, and seeing as how the *Famiglia* is already on its ass, I think that makes me a smart leader, one who'll go to bat for his people rather than leading them into a war they can't win."

I believed him, and he spoke sense.

Shooting a look at Brennan whose poker face was, as usual, in play, I saw him make the tiniest of nods, and knew he and I were on the same page.

I reached up and rubbed my chin. "What do you want from us?"

And that was when we both got down to business, hashing out an agreement that, unbeknownst to the city, would have a detrimental effect on its streets for decades to come.

Valentini and I made history together in that moment, a history that wouldn't be in the textbooks, that would never be discussed outside of this room and with these people, but it was groundbreaking nonetheless.

It also took hours. Hours of my Christmas Eve morning where

I should have been waking up with my dick inside Savannah—a new festive tradition I intended to uphold for the rest of my fucking life—and stuffing my face full of Ma's freshly baked monkey bread.

When Valentini and his men were driving off the compound of the cement factory we owned, one of many fronts in Manhattan, I turned to Brennan and asked, "Any news from home?"

He arched a brow at me. "No. Should there be?"

I scrubbed my chin. "I don't know. The folks are a lot more fragile than I like."

"They'll come around. They're not the sort to let shit gather under their feet."

True, but... "This is different, and you know it."

He grunted, then called out, "Forrest, Tink, Baggy, you can all fuck off home now."

"About time," Baggy groused. "Some of us have wives to fuck."

"Some of us have wives who'll nag about us going missing for hours on end on Christmas Eve morning," Forrest confirmed.

"Jesus. Talk about a bunch of moaners," Brennan rumbled. "Stop bitching at me and get your asses home." As his crew grunted and started rolling their eyes, he called out, "Merry Christmas, fuckers."

They returned the call, and I was left with my crew. Men I barely knew anymore. Men who I'd outgrown a long time ago, but who, I knew, would have my back.

I shot a look at Mickey, Jamie, and Connolly, and told them all, "Have a great day tomorrow. See you the day after Boxing Day."

Like I was their fucking general, they saluted me. Their formality so unlike Brennan's crew that, for a moment, I was envious.

For all that the sniping between Brennan and his men could have looked like a weakness, it was, if anything, a strength. They wouldn't ass-lick, wouldn't blow smoke up his ass and be anything other than candid with him.

Yeah, Brennan's relationship with his crew was something to envy for sure.

When they retreated, slipping out of the warehouse, leaving me alone with him, I limped toward him so we could go home as well.

"Why don't you ever use a fucking cane?" Brennan asked as he watched me. "I'm pretty sure it makes shit ten times harder on you."

"Gimps use canes."

Brennan frowned at me. "What fucked up bullshit is that?"

I scratched my jaw. "Not my words, heard them at church."

He squinted. "Someone said that and you overheard it?"

"Yeah." I shrugged.

"Which dumbfuck said that?"

"Tony said that to Paul," I murmured, referring to the men Da considered his advisors even though they were denser than rocks.

"You shitting me?" Brennan growled. "Why didn't you tell Da?"

"What am I? Fucking five?"

"They think you look more hardcore hobbling around like that?" He scowled. "God spare me from idiots. Although I'm not sure who's the bigger dipshit. Them for saying it or you for listening."

"Fuck you," I told him, but my tone was mild. "*You* go from being the Irish Mob's golden boy, expected to be perfect, expected to lead in our father's image, and then having to learn that you'll never be what you were before."

Brennan scowled. "I hate to break it to you, Aidan, but it sounds like you were listening to your fan club. Trust me, your brothers never thought you were fucking perfect."

I had to grin, and it morphed into a chuckle as I socked him in the shoulder. "Bastard."

He smirked. "True, though. You're an idiot for listening, and have probably damaged your knee more because of it. Anyway, everyone knows Tony and Paul are schmucks."

"Everyone but Da."

"Oh." Brennan whistled under his breath. "Oh, I get it."

"You do? Slow off the mark, Bren."

"You thought he'd listen to them?"

My mouth tightened. "I did. I wasn't going to do anything that would make Da take my position from me. Of course, I fucked up by getting hooked on Oxy." I blew out a breath. "But that was later on."

"You want to lead the Firm that much?" Brennan questioned.

"It's my right," I told him. "I took a lot of shit over the years for it. Wasn't about to have it snatched away through no fault of my own."

"You know we wouldn't have let that happen, don't you?" Brennan questioned, the scowl back in his eyes.

"I know you don't want to lead. I know you've resented me for putting so much work on you." I grimaced. "I'm sorry for dropping the ball, bro. Thank you for picking up the load."

Brennan's shoulders wriggled which, I knew, meant he was uncomfortable with the conversation. "You dropped the ball, but hopefully if you're back, then at least I can have a fucking life again. I got a wife now, Aidan. I want to see her. Be with her."

"I got a woman as well, Brennan. Only Kid doesn't now." I scratched my jaw. "We're going to have to work something out so that we have more of a life than Da does.

"I don't want to be like him. Don't want to rule with an iron fist at home." I thought of yesterday, and rasped, "He loves us, Brennan. I didn't think he did, not until yesterday."

"Da doesn't know how to love," he disagreed. "Ma does, but she's got some kind of fucking Stockholm Syndrome or something going on. He messed with her head. Gaslit her or some shit."

Slowly, I shook my head. "If you'd have seen him yesterday, you'd get it."

Brennan grimaced. "Maybe I never will. Maybe I'll always remember what he did, and what he said, rather than what he didn't do or say."

"I get it. We've all got a lot of crosses to bear where he's concerned," I agreed. "Now, come on. Let's go home."

He nodded. "Gotta stop off at Conor's place first. There's some shit he wants us to bring back."

"Sure," I agreed, twisting around to look at the grim warehouse that had just seen a peace like no other brokered between two of the city's biggest factions. "Think Valentini will do it? Think he'll make it as Don?"

"His birthright was snatched from him. You don't use a cane because you were worried Da would listen to some dumbfucks. I think we can guarantee that Valentini's willing to do dumb shit to get to where he wants to be."

"Wonder how long it'll take." I winced as the biting cold in here made my knee ache like a motherfucker.

Brennan sent me a measured look. "A week."

I smirked. "Want to bet on that?"

Brennan grinned. "Yeah, I'm willing to put my money where my mouth is so long as you are." We bumped fists, but it was more than just a bet we agreed on.

In this warehouse where blood was shed and truths were earned through torture, brotherly loyalty was cemented in place, and Brennan, though Finn knocked him out of the line of succession, was born to be my second, and he officially took the role I offered and, more importantly, accepted it.

For me, that meant more than what had just gone down with the Italians.

As he slapped me on the back, I muttered, "You got Cammie a gift yet?"

"Of course. Did our ma raise a fool? Wait, don't answer that. You were raised by her too."

My scowl ended with a laugh. "Fuck off."

"You need to get Savannah something?"

I nodded.

"I'll take you to the place I went. They'll hook you up."

Good. No way was I about to celebrate our first Christmas together without my giving her a gift.

FORTY-THREE

SAVANNAH

I BIT my lip as I watched Aidan from the corner of my eye.

He wasn't playing poker with us, but he was off to the side, his bad leg stretched out, his good one propped up on the coffee table in front of him.

He didn't look indecent.

I mean, he looked hot like always. But indecent, nope. Not to anyone else in the room. Not to anyone who didn't see what he was doing with the hole in his jeans and two fingers.

It had started with him tracing that hole with the tips, going around and around like it was absentminded as he read something on his phone.

Then, I'd taken twenty grand from Eoghan with a royal flush that he'd been bitching about even when Inessa had hauled him up to bed. I was left playing with Brennan and Declan who, interestingly enough, the drunker they got, grew more alert and more nostalgic.

"Remember that time O'Leary nearly got decapitated?"

Magic words that ordinarily would have pricked my curiosity, until Aidan tilted his wrist, and thrust those two fingers into the hole as if it were my pussy.

My sex clenched at the sight, and I glowered at him, then did so harder when I saw he wasn't even looking at me. Was just tormenting me for the fun of it.

"When he got that piano wire tangled around his neck?" Brennan cackled. "I remember that. How did he die again?"

"Not by decapitation," Aidan inserted wryly.

Declan started to twist around, looping his arm over the chair's backrest before Brennan muttered, "I fold." That drew his attention away from Aidan, and the finger fucking he was giving a slit in his jeans.

"It's just you and me," I told Declan calmly, feeling my cheeks starting to turn pink as I kept darting glances at Aidan.

I knew he had an ace of spades and a five of diamonds, whereas I had two tens, a club and a diamond. Technically, I was always going to win, but he didn't have to know that, did he?

"You sure you ain't stacking the deck?" Brennan rumbled, the ice in his glass tinkling as he waggled it at me.

Grinning at him, I murmured, "Always the sign of a sore loser. What is it, Brennan? Pissed that a girl beat you?"

He narrowed his eyes at me, before he replied, "Being beaten by a girl is pretty hot, actually."

Aidan's head whipped up. "Brennan!" he snarled. "Watch your fucking mouth."

My grin widened.

Brennan just rolled his eyes. "I meant figuratively, Aidan. I'm not jonesing for your woman. I got my own." He smacked his lips. "She'll bite your dick off if you so much as look at her wrong," he declared proudly.

My eyes bugged at him, because for all they were being expressive tonight, that was a whole other kind of admission. "Camille bit someone's dick off?" No wonder she'd smiled when I'd told her how good it felt to punch Wintersen in the junk.

Wow.

Brennan smirked. "Sure did. Clean off." Then he scowled at me. "If you go to the cops, I'll slice your—"

"Brennan," Declan rumbled, "you got a death wish, my man? Aidan's probably fingering his knife right as we speak."

Well, if we were going to get technical, Aidan was fingering his jeans. Not his knife.

The second eldest, well, the official second eldest—yikes, that wasn't going to get confusing, was it?—just scoffed as he scraped back his chair and clambered to his feet. "I got better places to be."

"Horizontal and with the missus?" Declan hummed. "Not a bad idea." He squinted at his cards, squinted at me, then grumbled, "I fold too."

I knew my grin beamed at him, because he blinked like I'd shone a light in his eyes. As Brennan called out, "Night, fuckers," Declan leaned forward and wagged his finger in my face.

"He's right, ya know. You sure you didn't stack the deck?"

"If I did, don't you think I'd have won every hand tonight?"

His owlish blink would have been cute if dark and moody wasn't my thing. "Seeing conspiracies everywhere," he grumbled under his breath. "Right, night you two." He squinted at his watch and groaned. "See you in a few hours."

As he strolled out, I gathered my winnings together, purring at the sight of all the lovely money I'd earned tonight. Then, when I cast a look at Aidan, I saw his gaze was on me and those fucking fingers were deep in that slit.

I gulped.

This shouldn't have been so hot.

Why was it so hot?

"You're bad for my IQ levels," I groused.

"Had worse complaints in my time," he said dryly before he scissored his fingers.

I bit my lip, but surged to my feet, only to sink between his legs in front of him.

As I peered up at him, I wondered what it was about him that made him so impressive. It wasn't just his position. Men were born to power all the time, but they didn't always command a room. They didn't always suck the air out of a space whenever they walked into it.

He was there, legs splayed, finger fucking his jeans, a glass of whiskey held loosely in his hand now he'd put down his cellphone, sitting in a paisley-patterned armchair as if he were a king in a throne.

Biting the inside of my cheek, I rocked forward and placed my hands on his thighs. One covered his, to cease the teasing, and the other just rested on the denim.

"You stacked the deck, didn't you?"

I tipped my head to the side. "In a poker game, who do you owe loyalty to?"

His smile appeared, widening as he considered me. "My grandfather would have called you canny."

I blinked. "Should I consider that a compliment?"

He nodded. "You really should." He took a sip of his whiskey, then placed the glass down on the table beside him.

In the ultra feminine space that was this second family room, dominated by floral patterns in the curtains, sofa, and even the paintings on the wall, he looked more aggressive. Hyper-masculine in a way that made me melt.

"I like your brothers," I told him softly.

"Not enough not to cheat them," he said with a laugh, his fingers coming to my nose to tweak it. Why that made me squirm, I had no idea.

"I didn't stack the deck. Poker is a game of statistics, and I'm damn good with statistics. Better than them apparently." I pouted. "You're going to tell them, aren't you?"

"No," he teased. "I'm just never going to play poker with you."

"Not even if it's strip poker?"

"That I could get behind if it wasn't me doing the stripping," he said wryly.

"I could figure out a way to even the score." I shot him a measured look. "How about that?"

He smiled. "I could be down for that. Not tonight though. You'd win without me doing much. It's been another long day."

It really had, and that he admitted that to me was everything.

I bit my lip and whispered, "It'll be okay, Aidan."

"Will it? I'm not so sure." He shook his head as he traced his fingers along the line of my jaw. "I was hoping Ma would bounce back. She's manic so she can do that."

Lena had spent all day in bed after cooking for the rest of the night while we slept. Aidan Sr. had come out for food, then he'd watch over whichever room we were in, looking misty-eyed as he saw his family having fun together, before he'd retreat to Lena's side.

My heart ached for them both, and seeing Aidan Sr.'s pain was what had taken away the gleam of the fangirling moments I had. We'd not even been formally introduced, not really, but he was human to me now. As was the rest of the family.

It had just taken a siege, an arson attack on two Catholic monuments, and a Christmas Eve spent bickering with his brothers and their families.

It was horrible to admit this, especially when his parents were so sad and Aidan was too, but I'd had a ball.

Unlike with my siblings, there'd been no real arguments. No getting in each other's faces, roaring at each other and screeching from one side of the house to the other.

There'd just been love.

It was everywhere in this house.

It tied everything together in a way that my therapist Mom would love to study.

From the breakfast Aoife had made where we'd all gorged on monkey bread and cocoa with whipped cream, to the pizzas we'd ordered in for dinner. Everyone had been together all day. Games had been played, sport reruns had been watched, poker had been ladybossed. It was like something from a movie.

"Aidan?"

He hummed.

"Do you think your family appreciates the highs because the lows sink so deep?"

He blinked at me, then smiled. "You enjoyed today, didn't you?"

I bit my lip and nodded. "I'm sorry," I blurted out.

"Why? I'm glad you like my family and don't just want to observe them," he teased. "I saw the journalist in you pop up a few times, but you kept it banked for the most part."

A gasp escaped me. "That's why you started doing that thing with your fingers." I squeezed his hand. "Cheat!"

"Talk of decapitations get your brain whirring, little one," he joked. "I had to bring you back down to earth." He surged forward, not stopping until there was a scant inch of space between our noses. "The journalist is hot. She makes you accept my fucked up world, but it's the woman who sets me on fire, Savannah. It's you who makes me hard all the time."

A shaky breath whispered from my lips as he pressed our mouths together. I groaned into the kiss, a whine escaping me as he slipped his tongue against mine.

I shifted into a taller position so that I could lean into him. His hands moved around my waist and to my ass so he could squeeze it, before they slid down my thighs and back up again. That caress zinged all the way to my toes.

I knew he wanted to feel all of me, have his imprint on me, but he didn't have to worry. He'd done that years ago with barely a touch between us.

Three meetings, one where he'd let me live, the other where he'd respected my intelligence enough to believe in my investigation and its findings, followed by a simple meal and that was it. A life changing day.

The thought urged me into moving, and I pressed my hands to his shoulders and pushed him away, gently, as I slid my fingers down his chest. He knew I wasn't pulling away, so he rocked back into the armchair, and I let my hand continue its voyage down, with his gaze on mine, as I reached for the zipper on his jeans.

Our eyes still glued together, I delved between the folds of his fly and reached inside to grab his cock.

You knew a man was beautiful when you wanted to drop to your knees the second you saw him in a suit.

But when he was in jeans and you still got wet? That was hawtness to the nth power.

With my hand around his shaft, that power in my hand, I murmured, "I know I'm not wearing any lipstick, but let me please you."

He was always so focused on me, and while I wasn't going to complain, giving back was a pleasure. An honor. I knew it was only a blowjob, but to me, it represented more. It was taking control of him and owning it. I knew he'd probably had thousands of blowjobs in his life, but none by me.

A bark of laughter escaped him, and he reached out, rimmed my mouth with his finger, then rasped, "You can wear lipstick next time."

Grinning, I dipped down and pressed my lips to the tip of his length. As I explored him, circling the glans, enjoying the thick spongy skin against my tongue, slipping down and experiencing the contrast of veins and smooth flesh, iron and silk combined, I tasted him much as he did me. Savoring him like he was a treat.

He scented of soap from the shower he'd had before dinner, but deeper than that, there was just his essence. Inherently him. It was delicious. *He* was delicious.

When he groaned as I slipped my lips along his shaft, finding the same rope-like veins and the thick flesh that I'd explored with my tongue, I lost myself in the moment. Lost myself in his pleasure.

His hands came to my hair, and he tugged and pulled, his hips bucking as I tuned into him, wanting to ease his concerns, to give him an escape from the intensity of the past few days.

He wasn't gentle, but neither was I. I nipped and sucked, using the thick saliva that coated his cock to take him as far down my throat as I could. When I nuzzled my nose in his groin, I sucked in air that was scented of him and was pretty sure I'd just gotten high.

With a gasp, I pulled back, releasing all of him, and though his hands encouraged me to return, I didn't. I pressed his length against his belly, and let my tongue trace that thick padded flesh which ran down the underside of his erection. I shuddered when he did, then moaned when he grabbed both my hands and twisted them to the side so I couldn't move them.

I squirmed, shifting slightly so that I could dig my heel into my pussy, letting me grind against it as I started to lick his balls. When he grabbed them and lifted them with his free hand, I nuzzled into them, weakly struggling against the hold he had on my wrists, not to escape, just to test him.

Knowing he'd shackle me to him until the end of time, I wanted that.

Needed that.

Craved that.

He growled as I pulled one ball into my mouth, sucking down hard on it before I gifted the other with the same treatment. His hips bucked, and I groaned, loving his taste, needing more, needing all of it. Lips traversing the length of his shaft once more, I slipped them around the tip, and sank back down. This time, I bobbed my head fast, wanting his cum, demanding it.

Just because I let him order me around didn't mean that I couldn't do the same.

This particular Irish Mob boss needed a lady boss, and I was more than willing to take that job.

When he came, his seed slaloming into my mouth, I swallowed as quickly as I could. Jizz was never going to taste like Cherry Twizzlers, but fuck, if it could taste good, his did. Which was how I knew I was a goner. For real.

He growled as I took everything, sinking it back like fine wine, and he grabbed my hair again, tightened his grip on my wrists, and bucked into me as he thrust my mouth deeper around him. I gagged, but I groaned too, loving that his control broke as he rode those final few waves, and loving that I did this to him.

When he let go of me, I knew I probably looked a mess, but his hands released me, and they cupped my cheeks before drifting down so he could press his thumbs against the various hickeys that concealer wasn't doing that great a job of hiding, touching me as if I were the most precious thing in his world.

Maybe I was.

Maybe I wanted to be that.

He stunned me by kissing me again, thrusting his tongue against mine the second I parted my lips. Apparently Aidan hadn't received the memo that guys didn't kiss once a girl had given them head, but then, why would he do anything the normal way?

Hallelujah.

FORTY-FOUR

AIDAN

"WAKE UP!"

Immediately, I jolted awake, sitting upright and doing a pretty damn good impression of Dracula coming out of his coffin as I demanded, "What is it? The Sparrows? Russians? Italians?"

"No, it's Christmas, Aidan."

I jerked back like I'd been shot, then I blustered, "Conor, what the fuck are you doing in here?"

"Waking you up," he groused back.

Casting Savannah a glance, seeing she'd somehow slept through the alarm that was my younger brother, I grabbed the sheets and hauled them over us when I saw a sliver of her nipple peeping out. Her legs were also bared, the bandage covering up some of her modesty, and I growled, "Turn away, Conor. Right this fucking second."

"I got my own woman. I ain't interested in yours," he scoffed. "Anyway, hurry the fuck up. You know we can't open presents unless everyone's downstairs."

I blinked. "Since when do you have a woman?"

Naturally, the one thing I wanted to know, he didn't answer. Just scurried away like the pain in my ass he was.

Flopping back into the mattress, I yawned as I peered at the clock, cursing when I saw it was four AM.

"Fucker," I grumbled, before I turned on my side and hauled Savannah into me.

She came, cuddling into me the second she resettled against my side. Skin to skin. Christ, did she know how good she felt?

How many bitches had I fucked just wishing they were her?

How much goddamn time had I wasted when I should have said, 'fuck it,' and claimed her regardless?

This was what happened when you tried to pretend you were a knight in shining armor when you were really the villain of the tale.

I pressed my lips to the crown of her head, grateful for the gift that was her on Christmas morning, before I rumbled, "Little one, time to wake up." I stroked a hand over her hair, gently slipping my fingers along her scalp, scraping there, knowing the sensation would make her shiver.

She pressed her face into my throat, muttering, "Go to sleep."

I grinned up at the ceiling. "It's Christmas."

"Sleep."

"Christmas."

"Sleeeep." She pushed deeper into me, so that her breath brushed my skin with every exhale. "Too early. We didn't fall asleep until late."

That was very, very true.

Not even my dick twitched with morning wood. She'd drained my balls twice in less than an hour. I hadn't done that in years, probably because the Oxy had been more exciting than any of the women I'd fucked since I'd met her.

"I have a gift downstairs for you."

"Thank you," she said sleepily.

I laughed. "Don't you want to open it?"

"No."

Snorting, I murmured, "I can give it to one of the others."

She pshawed. "They know not to take another woman's gift." Her hand came up and flopped against my belly as she patted me. "Nice try. Sleep is better."

"We wake up, open our gifts, have pancakes—" At least, we usually did. "—then we go back to bed."

That had her growing still. "You lying to me about the sleep part?"

"Nope." I chuckled. Trust her to think that was the part I was lying about.

She grunted, then pretty much flung herself off the bed, grousing, "Okay, hurry up. I stopped waking up at this time of the night when I left TVGM."

Though I was just as tired, I got up, and grabbed my bathrobe from the back of the bathroom door and pulled on some boxer briefs. She dragged on some sweats and a sloppy tee, did this thing with her hair that was like a knot that pulled it out of her face, then held out her arms when I offered her the robe she'd brought with her.

Once covered, she yawned, then trudged out of the room, then braked to a sudden halt. Her eyes were wide as she made a move to turn back to my side, and we walked, slowly, to the stairs.

I hated that she saw my pain.

I fucking loathed it.

Even as I appreciated her sticking by my side.

Even as I loved her for not thinking I was weak.

"Aidan?"

"Yes, little one."

"Next year, my Christmas gift can be us going to the doctor's and sorting out your knee."

I grimaced.

She scowled.

I grunted.

She sniffed.

"You going to wag your finger at me?"

"Maybe. Will it work?"

"Depends where you wag it."

Her cheeks burned up at that. "Shut up."

I grinned. "Make me."

She harrumphed, then tightened her fingers around my hand as we moved sedately into the family room, neither of us mentioning my knee even though I was pretty sure we both knew I'd do as she asked.

I was facing all kinds of shit this week. Memories, the past, lies and hard truths. Why not my irrational fear of hospitals too? Why not the fact that I struggled to read so when they plunked ten tons of shit in front of me, crap that I needed to understand, my brain—though it needed to focus—just wouldn't process it.

I had Savannah now, though, didn't I?

She'd help. If I admitted the truth to her.

"About time," Conor called out as we entered the living room where the large eight-foot-tall tree stood proud beside the TV and where he, as self-appointed gift adjudicator, was also standing, ready to hand out gifts.

The tree was decked with hundreds of ornaments, some new, a lot old and ones I remembered from childhood, and was a mishmash of colors. There was no theme, none other than 'O'Donnelly.' The string lights were on, and they were the only source of illumination in here apart from a few candles that made the place smell of mulled wine.

On the sofa, all around, there was my family. My brothers and new sisters, their kids, a sister-in-law, a family friend, even my folks who were looking worse for wear. We were exhausted, with only Conor not yawning and, for once, not looking strung out.

When I took a seat that was meant for me, I tugged Savannah onto my lap, loving that she was careful with my leg, and loving, even more, that she snuggled sleepily into me.

Conor passed out gifts, handing them out according to the tags. Most of us only had one apiece, whereas the kids had several. Shay and Victoria in particular had a few larger boxes which they opened, snuggled up together, as they conferred over their gifts, while Jake had lots of little ones I knew would be toys, but he was fast asleep on Aoife's chest, his mouth still curled around her breast from feeding, and even Conor had the wherewithal not to wake him up again.

When Finn opened his box, he frowned. "You gave me the wrong box, Kid. This is Jake's."

"I did not," Conor retorted, his tone insulted. "Look at the tag."

Finn squinted. "Don't know how you can see anything. Can't we turn on a fucking light?"

"Not my fault you need glasses," Conor sniped.

Aoife laughed. "Stop arguing you two." To Finn, she murmured, "It's for you."

I watched Finn frown, then his eyes widened as they looked at one another. Neither speaking. Neither saying a word while somehow communicating a whole lot.

"Would someone explain what's going on?" Inessa grumbled. "We're not all mind readers. Did Finn get Jake's gift or not?"

"Not," Conor inserted, his tone confident.

"Really, baby?" Finn breathed, and if I wasn't mistaken, he sounded pretty choked up which had me frowning at him too.

Aoife smiled, and nodded.

"Congratulations," Savannah murmured drowsily.

"Congratulations?" I asked.

She yawned. "She's obviously pregnant."

As the family bombarded Finn and Aoife with questions, which Aoife laughed at and smiled through and Finn, looking at her like she'd just conquered the moon, held her as close to him as possible, it settled something inside me to know how happy she made him. To see, with my own eyes, how right they were for one another.

"Mind reader," I whispered in Savannah's ear.

She hummed. "I'll take that title. But she's drinking nothing but peppermint or ginger tea." She made a gagging noise. "Plus, last night, I heard her puking in the safe room."

"Observation is everything," I intoned with a smile. "Open your gift."

Amid the cacophony of the family celebrating, something I was glad for because Ma and Da looked a little less like walking skeletons, even if Da's head was bruised and bandaged in patches, she tugged on the wrapping paper, revealing a jewelry box that was flat and square in shape.

She arched a brow at the sight of the Harry Winston logo, then popped it open. Inside, there was a bracelet with a single charm on it. Her smile peeped up at me.

"For the woman whose Dad can buy her anything she wants, who has her own fortune to buy her own jewelry, why not get something that we can load with our own memories."

Eyes sparkling, she murmured, "I love it." Her nose crinkled as she told me in an assured tone, "You won't like my gift."

"No? You sure? I mean, all I want for Christmas is for you to do as you're fucking told—"

She snorted. "Not going to happen."

I mean, I already knew that. I had a lifetime ahead of me, a lifetime's worth of her pain-in-the-ass self driving me crazy, but Christ, I needed that.

Even through the grimmest of gray skies, with thunder in the distance, and rain falling, a sliver of sunlight could peek through.

That was my Savannah.

Anyway, I already knew she'd disobeyed me. Having seen what Brennan had to collect from Conor's apartment, it didn't take a genius to work out what she'd bought me as a gift.

Amused by her honesty, however, I picked up the smaller of the two boxes. When I opened it, I found a handle that I knew would screw onto a cane. L-shaped, if the tongue of the L was pointing down, it was adorned by a skull with a crown on his head. The crown was tipped with two fleur-de-lys and two crosses, each one decorated with emeralds.

"For the future King of the Five Points," she teased, pecking my cheek with a kiss. "You know you like me disobedient anyway."

I did. But not where her safety was concerned. That was something she'd learn with time—I just hoped it wasn't a lesson that'd resonate too late. If I had my way, she'd learn it ASAP, because I never wanted her to be broken. Not like Ma.

This life wasn't a game. More exposure to it would teach her that. Right?

I had to fucking pray that was so.

Pressing a kiss to her lips, I muttered, "Thank you."

"How much do you hate it?"

"On what scale?"

"As good as my blowjob was last night to how it first felt when you got your dick inside me."

I cackled. "So, I've got a selection point between awesome and epic?"

"Exactly."

I shook my head. "I love it. Thank you."

She grinned at me. "I have to watch out for you. Not sure the Five Points is ready for a Queen to rule without its King."

I wasn't sure if truer words had ever been spoken.

As the rest of the O'Donnellys stopped teasing Finn and Aoife, then opened their gifts, revealing anything from expensive jewelry to a weird clay pot that had Aela sobbing with thanks and kissing Declan with a little too much gusto for Shay's liking, I realized this was the new shape of our family.

Inessa had only joined the ranks in May, followed by Aela and Shay, and Camille and Victoria shortly after. With Savannah here now, the family had never been bigger, but truthfully, I looked forward to it growing.

The future was here, in this room, and with some of the shadows of the past behind us, it had never looked brighter.

As I promised Savannah, we retreated to bed after we ate pancakes that Ma and Aoife whipped up together. None of us were up before one, which was when all the women congregated in the kitchen once more.

There was a rule of thumb in the household that no business was discussed on Christmas Day, but Da broke it an hour before dinner by calling all his boys into his office.

Of course, the term 'all his boys' had a different connotation now.

Finn had always been a trusted member of the family. Da had given him access to the firm's money at a young age once he'd proved himself in the Five Points, much as I'd done—I guessed I knew why he'd believed in him so much now. I couldn't resent that, was, if anything, glad for Finn.

You blamed the father for his sins, not the son.

At least, in my opinion.

Da was sitting behind his desk when we all walked in, where he explained what was going to happen over the next few days. This wasn't a discussion; this was a prepared speech with a detailed plan of action for tomorrow for which he fully expected our support. Seeing as there wasn't much we had to do, none of us said anything, just nodded when he was done.

Shortly after, we were called in to dinner, where we ate like kings thanks to the women slaving away in the kitchen.

Two fifteen-pound turkeys, perfectly roasted, were on platters at either end of the table with bowls of stuffing and three different kinds of veggies.

There were two types of casseroles, green bean and sweet potato, two industrial-sized vats of mashed potatoes and cranberry sauce, and after, there was the traditional Christmas pudding served with frozen custard for Conor and ice cream for everyone else.

There was also a Yule log, but unlike every other year, it wasn't cake covered in icing, but an ice cream cake coated in frosting.

As we ate, it made me wonder about what Savannah had said—did we appreciate these quiet times more because of the low times we had? Was that the case?

After the siege, and then what Ma, Da, Finn and I had gone through, with the fear and the adrenaline, I had to wonder if it really was true because none of us bickered.

Not even Conor.

We ate every bite, reveling in the feast, enjoying each other and the day itself for what it was.

It was, in a word, unusual.

The strange calm continued with a basketball game that the guys watched in the family room, and Savannah joined us too.

At first, I thought it was cute she wanted to stick with me, but then she and Da started bonding over the fucking Knicks, and I had to question how this woman was so perfect for the O'Donnellys. She slotted right in, and I was beyond grateful for the many quirks that had her fitting into the family with such ease.

By the time the game was over, we all started preparing for bed, but Savannah tugged on my hand and asked, "Aidan? I want to FaceTime my folks. Do you want to meet them?"

I arched a brow. "I thought you'd talked to them already."

"I did. But I told them about you, and they want to meet you."

My nose crinkled. "Over FaceTime?"

"Well, they're curious."

"Do they know who I am?"

"Relatively speaking. They know you're an O'Donnelly, but they don't know you're in the Irish Mob.

"I mean, it wasn't the first thing I told them," she scoffed. "Plus, they're not native New Yorkers. It's not like that side of you is known outside of certain circles in Hell's Kitchen."

I wanted to meet them, but not over a fucking screen. Scraping a hand over my jaw, I murmured, "What time is it there?"

"Three in the afternoon. It's six hours behind us." She pouted. "You really don't want to meet them?"

"Well, I do, but I wanted to ask your dad for your hand in marriage."

She grinned at me. "How traditional are you?"

"What about my family makes that come as a surprise?" I asked wryly, amused that she was amused.

"True" Her lips twisted. "But I don't need you to ask for my hand." She shoved it at me, and the engagement ring charm danced from the bracelet dangling off the wrist that wasn't wearing a support bandage. "See, you can have it now."

I squinted at her. "You know that's not how that works, right?"

"I do, but I'm being facetious." She teased, "Would you like Mom and me to leave the room while you ask him?"

"No. It's not that big a deal—"

"Isn't it? If that's stopping you from wanting to meet them on FaceTime?"

I heaved a sigh. "You're not going to drop this, huh?"

"It's Christmas, Aidan! Don't be the Grinch."

"I thought I'd been remarkably cheerful today actually."

"Why? Are you normally a grouch?"

I winced. "Sometimes. It's the first Christmas in years I've been lucid and didn't need to pop pills."

She tipped her head to the side. "I meant it when I said I expect you to get your knee sorted out within the next twelve months. You can't manage the pain with meds, so you're going to have to do something else.

"Even if they can just check the knee replacement, maybe there's something wrong with it. I know they misalign. Maybe it's a quick and simple fix. Either way, you have to try because the addiction will be ten times harder to control when you're in constant pain."

I pursed my lips. "I have to tell you something."

"What?" She frowned when I grimaced. "Is it bad?"

"Well, no. Not really. Maybe not anymore. When I was a kid, it was weird."

"What is it?"

"I have dyslexia."

"And?"

I heaved another sigh. "I guess a lifetime of this is going to get wearing."

"What? Me knowing your secrets before you do?" She laughed. "You take a long time to read things, Aidan.

"Plus, the first time we met, you said to me that you read the reports on me, but then later on, you mentioned that you listened to them." She hitched a shoulder. "That's more common now, but five years ago, less so. I could be wrong, but it just stood out to me at the time, so I made sure to watch out for signs. You mouth letters and whenever you're reading, it's like you're doing math."

Embarrassment filtered through me. "I didn't realize it was so obvious—"

Her hand came to my shoulder. "Aidan, haven't you figured it out yet? I was obsessed with you." She chuckled, and I knew she'd had one too many glasses of wine because that chuckle was a little slurred. It also eased my mortification. "I watched you all the time. No one else would be that fascinated by you. When you were reading, it gave me the chance to watch you without you knowing." Her eyes twinkled. "I was such a stalker. If anything, your mom should have clipped me by the ear, not you."

I snorted, then reached around her, palmed the back of her neck and hauled her into me so I could give her a kiss. God, this woman. She took my shame and made it into a thing. *Our* thing. "Such a fucking pair. Me watching you, you watching me," I said, shaking my head.

"Would have saved a lot of time if we'd watched each other simultaneously."

Laughing, I nodded. "You're not wrong."

"Of course not." Her grin peeped out. "Is that what the problem was, do you think? You didn't read what the doctors were doing or something?"

I shrugged. "Maybe." I wondered if she knew how hard that was to choke out. "On the other hand, it could be that I did something wrong. I had physio and everything and tried to do what she said, but, I don't know... Maybe this time, it'll be better if you're around."

"Well, naturally it will," she chirped. "I'm going to make everything better."

Snickering, I asked, "How much have you been drinking?"

"Waaaay too much. Now, are you going to meet my folks?"

FORTY-FIVE

CONOR

ACOOOOIG: **Thank you**

Lodestar: **You're welcome. Did you like it?**

aCooooig: **I love it.**

Lodestar: **I figured. You mentioned the cat before and then, the other night, Eoghan did as well. I don't know, I figured you needed a dog to level shit out.**

aCooooig: **How does that level shit out?**

Lodestar: **Well, it's like yin and yang. Don't you think you're either a dog or a pussy person?**

aCooooig: **Lol! Well, I'm definitely a pussy person, but I appreciate your yin.**

Lodestar: **My dog is yang. Haha. I want to see a picture.**

aCooooig: ***Two mins.***

aCooooig upldd pctr to cht

Lodestar: **Oh, my God, they go so perfectly together! It's fate!**

aCooooig: **They do actually. Where did you get it from?**

Lodestar: **That would be revealing my source. How am I going to surprise you next year if you know where I get the good shit from? **

aCooooig: **This is very true.**

aCooooig: **Although... does that mean we'll still be talking next year?**

Lodestar: **Well, yeah? Duh. You're the only person who can beat me from time to time.**

aCooooig: **We both know it's more than time to time. :P**

Lodestar: **Don't be a jerk.**

aCooooig: **Being truthful doesn't make me a jerk.**

Lodestar: **It does! You're mean! After I got you the perfect Christmas gift too. Men. Sheesh.**

aCooooig: **Haha. It is pretty perfect. Exactly what I didn't know I wanted.**

Lodestar: **Of course, it is.**

aCooooig: **I'm glad you want to talk to me.**

aCooooig: **Until next year at least.**

Lodestar: **Well, don't piss me off and that won't change.**

aCooooig: **It's funny because it's true.**

Lodestar: **Damn straight.**

aCooooig: **Your gift is underway.**

Lodestar: **I didn't expect one.**

aCooooig: **Bullshit. You did. And you were right to. But... it's an odd gift.**

Lodestar: **Oh! I love odd.**

aCooooig: **You believe me? That it's underway?**

Lodestar: **Why wouldn't I? You wouldn't tell me it was otherwise, would you?**

aCooooig: **No. I wouldn't. But I didn't know if you knew that.**

Lodestar: **So, when do you think I'll get it?**

aCooooig: **When I finish making it.**

Lodestar: **You're making me something?**

aCooooig: **Yes.**

Lodestar: **Like... woodwork?**

aCooooig: **Do I look like the kind of guy who crafts in his spare time?**

Lodestar: **True. But I mean, even cuties can get jiggy with it with Elmer's glue.**

aCooooig: **Yeah, well, let's not forget I'm an Irish mobster too. Allegedly.**

Lodestar: **Allegedly. Shit, yeah, I forgot.**

Lodestar: **Oddly enough, that makes you hotter. Allegedly.**

aCooooig: **Good to know.**

Lodestar: **Isn't it though? :P You going to give me a clue?**

aCooooig: **Nope. But the second it's complete, I'll send it to you. I was hoping to have it done in time, but... well, you weren't ready for it so even though it was in my head, and I could foresee what I wanted, I didn't really bother.**

aCooooig: **Also, nice to know you think I'm cute. O.o**

Lodestar: **Allegedly.**

Lodestar: **Anyway, you have a mirror. Not telling you anything you don't see every day.**

aCooooig: **You'd be surprised. Reflections aren't always an accurate depiction.**

Lodestar: **Actually... I know what you mean. You're right. I don't know why I said that. Sorry.**

aCooooig: **You don't have to apologize.**

Lodestar: **Don't I? You ever say shit and don't mean it? It just flows out of your mouth?**

aCooooig: **Like diarrhea?**

Lodestar: **Lol. Yes.**

aCooooig: **I know what you mean. I do it with my brothers. Sometimes, I prod them just to get a reaction. I don't really know why.**

Lodestar: **To test them?**

aCooooig: **Maybe.**

Lodestar: **You sure you don't know why?**

aCooooig: **It's just something I've always done.**

Lodestar: **I've had a lot of expensive therapists in my time. They all said that I tried to get reactions out of people to test them.**

aCooooig: **Why?**

Lodestar: **To push their limits. To make sure that they were loyal. That they'd remain true to me no matter what I said or did.**

aCooooig: **That because of your mom? Her murder?**

Lodestar: **I guess. I do it even more now. I think it's what victims do.**

aCooooig: **Hate that word.**

Lodestar: **Really? Survivor is more fitting tbh.**

aCooooig: **Now I'm humming the theme tune to Survivor. Thanks.**

Lodestar: **Lol. You're welcome.**

aCooooig: **I promise, Star, when I have your gift, I'll send it to you.**

Lodestar: **I'm looking forward to receiving it.**

aCooooig: **:D**

aCooooig: **You never did tell me how you knew exactly when to call me during that mini-siege.**

Lodestar: **Mini? Deal with sieges every week, do you?**

aCooooig: **Allegedly.**

Lodestar: **That goes hand in hand with where I bought the dog statue.**

aCooooig: **You didn't see it, but I just rolled my eyes.**

Lodestar: **The nerve!**

aCooooig: **What have you hacked and do I need to patch it?**

Lodestar: **Nope. Not on your system. *smirks* You can't control satellites, Conor.**

aCooooig: **You hacked into a satellite?**

Lodestar: **You haven't? Comes in handy.**

aCooooig: **Jesus. How aren't you in jail?**

Lodestar: **Because I'm very, very, very good.**

aCooooig: **No one's that good.**

Lodestar: **True. I know people in high places. Allegedly.**

aCooooig: **God? He up there with the satellite?**

Lodestar: **Lol. You're funny.**

aCooooig: **I try. How am I supposed to sleep knowing you're watching us on a satellite?**

aCooooig: **How am I supposed to resist the urge to go and make snow angels butt naked?**

Lodestar: **Has snow fallen?**

aCooooig: **Has here.**

Lodestar: **I wouldn't be averse to seeing that. O.o**

aCooooig: **Consider it done. Merry Christmas, Star.**

Lodestar: **Merry Christmas, Conor. <3**

FORTY-SIX

AIDAN

"YOU'RE sure you want her? I mean, I love her, but I kind of have to. She's very nosy. This Sparrows' thing is just the tip of the iceberg."

"Dad! OMG. Mom, tell him!"

I laughed, despite myself, despite the weird feeling I had that Dagger Daniels was actually trying to avoid giving me her hand, and I reached over, hauled Savannah under my arm and murmured, "I already know you're nosy, remember?"

Lorelei Daniels, ironically enough, was Irish. Da'd have semi-Irish grandbabies through us if we were so blessed. She was also unimpressed by her husband's fame, and when she smirked at Dagger, I got chills down my spine because I knew, point blank, I was looking at my future.

Mother and daughter weren't very alike, their hair color was different, their eyes too, and Savannah had a more heart-shaped face in comparison to Lorelei's angular one, but that smirk? Savannah channeled that something fierce. It was clear to see that Dagger was owned—I knew that'd be me down the line as well.

Sometimes, you could be a Hall of Fame rockstar. Sometimes,

you could be the King of the Five Points. But the right woman still made you own up to being a jackass when you were being a jackass.

"You just want to think she's still a virgin. I don't understand where you get off being all repressed."

"Yeah, Dad. You've had more groupies than I've had hot dinners."

"Which is a lot!" Aspen called out in the background.

Savannah squinted at her. "Are you calling me fat? Just you wait, you little shit, I'm going to bust your ass when we're in front of a hoop."

She didn't just like watching basketball, she played it too?

Now wasn't the time to get a boner, but, if fate was going to be unkind, well... might as well take advantage of it.

"You're perfect," I rumbled and below the desk where the computer was perched, I grabbed her hand and pressed it to my cock.

"Leave your sister alone, Aspen," Dagger hollered, peering over his shoulder at her. The movement revealed a room which was more befitting of a house in Boston at Christmas than Hawaii, with a massive pine tree and red wreaths and swags of scarlet draped over a bannister.

"And we don't fat shame in this family." Lorelei shook her head, and shot her daughter a scowling glance. "What's come over you, Aspen?"

"It's that bitch Manda," Paris chimed in.

"Is Aspen the one you said got hooked on speed?" I whispered in Savannah's ear, trying to keep up.

"She has an eating disorder now," Savannah confirmed, a hint of sorrow in her eyes. "Who's Manda, Paris?"

"That supermodel." Paris made a gagging sound. Unlike her sister, who was Miss All American, Paris clearly took most of the rocker genes from her dad. "She totally posts about how great it is on her website to starve herself."

"Leave her alone!"

Lorelei shot me an embarrassed glance. "Girls! Would you stop showing your sister up, please? Aidan's just asked your father for Savannah's hand in marriage!"

Paris cackled, "Does Camden know?"

"Do I know, what?"

"How could he know? He's been at the gym," Lorelei chided.

She tipped her head to the side so that Camden could dip down and press a kiss to her cheek. As he did so, I caught a glimpse of a face I'd seen on way too many billboards over the years.

Lorelei grabbed his chin as he swooped out of the camera, and asked, "Did you get into a fight?"

Dagger frowned up at his son, and ground out, "You went out without security?"

"Jesus, Dad, I went to the fucking gym."

"And got beaten by your PT?" Savannah queried, scooting closer to the screen so she could see more.

One of the main reasons I knew Savannah was even okay with being here was because she'd argued with her brother, but now he turned and revealed a black eye, apparently that memory had flown away with the wind.

"It's okay. I'm okay," Camden muttered. "And no, my PT didn't beat me up."

"Then who did?" Savannah hounded, her brow furrowed. "Did he hit you with brass knuckles?"

I kind of loved how she shot me a look that asked for confirmation.

I also loved how un-normal violence clearly was for the Daniels. Talk about a luxury that wasn't available in my world.

Trying not to smile because, genuinely, it wasn't funny, I leaned in and said, "Yeah, they're bruises from brass knuckles."

"You'd better call the cops, Lorelei," Dagger intoned with a snarl. "How many fucking times do I have to tell you kids? You take your goddamn guards to the shitter with you!"

"Dad!" Aspen gasped.

"That's gross," Paris mumbled.

"What's grosser is coming back on Christmas Day with a fucking shiner. What if you'd been overpowered? Then, what?"

Camden cast a glance at me, then at his sister. "I wasn't. I don't want to call the cops. I'm not going to press charges."

"The hell you aren't!" Dagger roared.

"What happened?" Savannah repeated doggedly, her scowl mutinous.

"Nothing. Who's the guy?"

"Aidan O'Donnelly," I introduced myself.

"Your sister's fiancé," Dagger clarified at the same time. "As well as the reason why she's not here..." He glowered at Savannah. "I assume."

My lips twitched. "Does that mean I've got your approval, sir?"

"Don't call me 'sir' and you might."

"That's not true," Savannah argued. "I didn't come because of that asswipe behind you."

Dagger frowned, but before he could say anything, Camden growled, "You're getting married? When did this happen? Who is this guy?"

"I've known him for five years—"

"You were dating for five years without telling us?" Camden screeched, making me see how he'd won so many goddamn Grammys because his voice just slipped through the octaves like a knife through the gut.

"If you'd listen," Savannah sniped, "and didn't interrupt all the goddamn time, I'd have had the chance to finish. I met him five years ago, and we reconnected recently."

"What broke you up?" Camden demanded, his tone suspicious, his gaze fervently holding mine.

"My job," I explained. "I had to move away." Figuratively speaking.

His eyes narrowed. "If he didn't prioritize you before, Savannah, what makes you think he will now?"

"When did you turn into this big of a dipshit?" She huffed. "This is exactly the reason why I'm not in Hawaii right this second, you judgmental pain in my ass! You can't stand that I don't listen to you and that I flow to my own beat. Well, screw you—"

"Savannah!" Lorelei gasped.

Voice dark, Dagger intoned, "What did you say to piss your sister off enough that Savvie didn't want to come celebrate the holidays with us?"

I processed the nickname, thought about how apt it was—Savannah *was* savvy about a lot of things—then tuned back in when Camden muttered, "You didn't tell them?"

"No. I didn't want to cause another argument," my woman said with a sniff. I tucked her deeper into my hold. "Anyway, it made sense to stay here, what with the exposés."

"I'm so proud of you, honey," Lorelei told her with a beaming smile that hit me straight in the fucking heart.

I was proud of her too, but I was even gladder that Lorelei was, and Dagger as well if his nodding indicated anything.

The only time Da had told me he was proud of me was the other night when he'd learned I killed McKenna. Thirty years of fucking grunt work for his ass, and that was the first time he'd told me that.

Squeezing Savannah, I hugged her tighter to me, grateful she had a better relationship with her parents than I did.

"Thanks, Mom," Savannah told her, voice redolent with a warmth I basked in.

"We only found out you were releasing those articles on the 21st," Dagger said with a scowl. "You told Camden first? Is that what you argued about?"

She scoffed, "No. I didn't tell Jackass anything about the exposés, not after he said that I sacrificed my career on TVGM for nothing."

"You went live on breakfast TV assaulting a guy, Savannah!" Camden ground out. "Why do you always have to do shit the hard way?"

"Because he was raping women on set! Routinely! He had one woman so fucking terrified to go to the head office for meetings because he cornered her—" Her nostrils flared. "Anyway, he dropped the charges."

Yeah, I'd seen to that.

You couldn't press charges when you were in the Hudson.

"Oh, sweetheart," Lorelei murmured. "Did you give her my number? You know I do pro bono stuff for rape victims."

"I did, but if she hasn't called, then she doesn't want to deal with it yet. He deserved worse than what he got from me."

Well, was there worse than having your dick cut off before you were shoved in concrete boots alive and kicking before drowning in the river while blinded?

I didn't think so, but she didn't need to know that.

Tucking her tighter into me, I murmured, "I dealt with the legal side of things for Savannah. You don't have to worry. And TVGM is going through a massive sweep with workshops and such to eradicate a casting-couch environment. I think that's probably why she didn't call—the studio is providing therapy for victims free of charge."

Lorelei's eyes widened. "How do you know all this?"

"I recently became the majority shareholder of the company."

Savannah gasped and twisted to look at me. "You're kidding?"

I smiled at her. "No. It was supposed to be a gift, getting you your job back and then I realized you don't like early mornings."

"She's such a bitch first thing," Aspen confirmed, peering at me now from between her parents, more curiosity in her gaze as I'd done something interesting.

"You know, what? You're supposed to be upselling me here!" Savannah grumbled. "All of you can kiss my as—"

"Savannah!" Lorelei chided.

"Well, you don't have to, Mom. But Dad, Camden, Aspen and Paris totally can kiss it." She huffed. "I can't believe I actually wanted you to meet them," she told me.

I smiled at her and then at my new family. "I prefer for things to start with a bang." After I pressed a kiss to her forehead, I murmured, "You know that."

My smile deepened when she squirmed against me, and Dagger's expression turned pensive as our eyes clashed and held.

Though no one had asked him a question while Lorelei bitched at Camden for details on whatever had happened at the gym, and Aspen and Paris verbally sparred with Savannah, he nodded at me.

We both knew what that meant.

FORTY-SEVEN

SAVANNAH

THE 26TH OF DECEMBER

"HOW FUCKING DARE YOU? YOU MONSTER!"

Attention pricked, I twisted around and found a woman, with a very pissed off baby in her arms, screaming at an older version of herself.

When I thought about Aidan, who was the spitting image of his dad, then Shay and Declan who were close to twins with just a massive age gap, I wondered what it was about the Irish Mob that had them looking alike so much.

Something in the water?

Nah, I knew there were several pipelines that fed Manhattan its water source, but they didn't specifically drop in Hell's Kitchen. Even if that was a neat fix.

Jen would say it was chemtrails, but that was because she'd seen a documentary on YouTube, and had been obsessed ever since.

"Keep your voice down," the older woman, probably her mother or aunt, spat, taking a deep sip of wine after.

"Mom, if you'd just leave me alone, I would."

I frowned at the sight, then stalked over to them both. I had no idea what they were arguing about, but the baby looked like he was going to explode with outrage.

"Is everything okay?" I asked quietly, aware that people were looking without looking.

In my world, we'd have drawn all the stares. Everyone would be watching. Here, I guessed there was worse shit at sea than a mother and daughter raging at each other.

"No! Everything isn't okay," the younger one snapped, not looking at me. Then, she cast me a glance and blanched. Literally blanched. "I'm so sorry," she whispered, her eyes wide.

The about-face was enough to have me blinking. "It's okay. I didn't mean to intrude."

"Look what you've done now, Mary Catherine. For God's sake, you've never been able to comport yourself with decency, but ever since you took up with that biker—"

I frowned. "I beg your pardon, but who are you?"

The woman shot me a smarmy smile. "I'm sorry if we caused a stir. Ever since she gave birth, my daughter's been prone to hysteria." She snapped out her hand and grabbed Mary Catherine's arm. I saw how badly she pinned her fingers around the soft flesh, because the woman's knuckles bled white. "We'll get out of your hair."

While Aidan had said jack about me to the people gathered at his house today, somehow the crowd had picked up on the fact that I was Aidan Jr's.

Whether that was by Morse code or intuition, but I'd been getting wide berths from the men, and women kept shooting me either simpering looks or catty ones.

Mary Catherine was the first to show outright fear.

Apparently, I had power here.

Oh, boy, the Five Points were not ready for that.

As I measured the older woman with a glance, one that had her coming up wanting, I tipped my chin to the side. "No. I don't think you will." I smiled at Mary Catherine then eyed the squalling baby who was wearing a suit. I didn't even know you could buy that kind of shit for such young infants, but he had a little vest on, bright blue, with black pants. I assumed it was a onesie, but hell, he looked dapper if pissed off. "Would you like to come with me? We can sort out your son. He probably needs his diaper changed or something. I can show you where to clean him up."

"Thank you," Mary Catherine rasped, tearing away from her mother's clasp.

"I'll come with you," the woman retorted.

"No. It's okay. I'm sure the speeches will start soon. I'll show her the way." While I smiled at her, I received a quickly hidden glare for my pains, but I ignored her and took Mary Catherine away from the large room filled with people who'd been willing to listen to her get raked over the coals without defending her.

Apparently, the Five Points weren't feminists. Who'd a thunk it?

We were in, what could only be called, a wintergarten. A massive sunroom with more plants and foliage than an English garden, that was attached to the side of the property, something I hadn't even known the house had until Aoife asked me to help carry things in there from the kitchen.

Inside, there were over eighty men with their wives and kids, each drinking Aidan Sr.'s alcohol while the women primped and gossiped like curious peahens as they tried to figure out why they were here and what Aidan's upcoming speech was about—because not all of them were dumbasses, the odds were high it was about the cathedral and the church's 'arson attacks.'

Aidan hadn't told me specifics, but then, we'd been busy. Last night, after my call with the family, we'd gone to bed, then he'd woken me up with an orgasm that made me wonder why I hadn't gotten that kind of wake-up call on Christmas morning.

After, I'd passed out, and when I woke up, it was because Aoife was knocking on my door, telling me I had thirty minutes to get ready.

Charming.

Determining next Christmas would be spent with his face

between my legs and not being hauled out of bed before the dawn birds started singing, and that Aidan really needed to start getting better at communicating—it took way longer than thirty minutes for something this good to look *this good*—I guided Mary Catherine away from the crowd and into the house itself.

"I hope you don't mind me getting involved," I said sheepishly. "I can't keep my nose out of other people's business."

"Are you kidding?" Mary Catherine sent me a tired look. "You spared me more humiliation than usual."

I frowned. "I'm so sorry to hear that." Beside the wintergarten, there was a suite of rooms that was a bedroom/bathroom/living room combo. Though tastefully appointed, it was pretty standard stuff. Like going to a hotel or something.

As I stepped into the living room though, I asked, "Do you need anything? Is he sick?"

"Sick of being dragged around more than anything." Mary Catherine shot me a tired smile. "Mostly, he just needs to eat. Can I take a seat?"

"Sure, please do." I wafted a hand at a small club chair and she heaved a sigh as she plunked her butt down. "I'll leave you—"

"No!" Her eyes flared wide. "Please, don't."

"Are you sure you don't want privacy?" I asked uncomfortably.

"She'll see you and—" Mary Catherine swallowed.

"And?"

"She'll come in and it will start again."

"Do you want me to grab your husband?"

"He's not here."

"Oh! He's not?"

"There are only Lieutenants here and above." She bit her lip. "Digger isn't even a Five Pointer. That's why Mom was giving me shit."

"Because she doesn't approve of him?"

A shaky laugh escaped her. "That's the understatement of the year. He's a biker." Her chin tipped up like she was expecting criticism as she declared, "He's a Satan's Sinner. He had to go on a run four days ago, and ever since, she's been crazier than usual."

I frowned. "A Sinner?" I thought back to Cruz and the other guys who'd helped free the compound of dead bodies. "I almost met some of them a little while ago."

Mary Catherine blinked. "You did?" Her hand moved to the back of her son's head as she started fidgeting around, unfastening buttons and popping a boob out. The kid, clearly scenting gold, dug right in. "How did you meet them? Who did you meet? Did you meet Sin?"

I blinked. "I don't know. I only heard one name. Cruz."

She shot me a bright smile. "I know Cruz. He has brilliant tattoos. Have you seen them? He's, like, covered in black ink with bare skin peeping through."

"Negative ink. I've heard of that."

"His makes him look like a skeleton."

Walking death. How fitting for a dude who could boil down corpses and make them into batter.

Yuck.

"Who's Sin?"

"My brother." Her smile twisted a little. "I wish he were here. I need him to save my butt while Digger's away."

"Why? What's going on?"

She gnawed on her bottom lip. "Mom's trying to make out that I'm an unfit mother."

Rearing back in surprise, brows lifting, I asked, "Say, what?"

"Crazy, right? She just came out with this bullshit when Digger went on a run, and then she somehow got Aidan Sr. involved and she's—" Tears pricked her eyes. "This has been going on since Maddox was born, and I didn't even know it. I'm not a bad mom. I'm just tired. That's all."

"Your baby has a big head and you popped that out of a hole smaller than a golf ball. Damn straight you're tired." I scowled as I sank into the armchair opposite her.

"I'm sorry. I shouldn't be telling you stuff like this." She sniffled and scrubbed at her cheeks.

"Why are you then?" I asked softly.

"I don't know. I didn't expect anyone to be nice to me. Everyone treats me like I'm trash now that I'm a Sinner."

My spine straightened. "Even the O'Donnellys?"

She blinked. "Oh, no. They're like cousins four times removed though. It's different."

Four-times-removed cousins? Was that even a thing? "It had better frickin' be." I grunted. "Do they know?"

"I mean, I don't know. Aidan Sr. doesn't usually get involved in stuff like this, but, maybe he thinks I'm an unfit mom too. I can't stop crying and—"

"Isn't that normal?"

"They're making me feel like it isn't." She reached up and cupped the back of the baby's head. "I can't believe this is happening. I only came back because Mom said she had complications when she gave birth to me and Sin, and that it could be hereditary.

"My sister-in-law just miscarried, so I was super nervous anyway, and I wanted the best healthcare." Her hand trembled. "What an idiot I was."

"You're being too hard on yourself," I argued. "It's not every day a mother would try to make out you're unfit just because you're hormonal." I grunted. "When's your... Digger, when is he coming back?"

"Supposed to be next week, but this is the Mob. He thinks because the Sinners are a one-percenter MC, they're on par, but they're not. The political connections the Five Points have are insane."

I blinked. "You can't seriously think that they're going to take your kid away from you?"

She started sobbing which, I guessed, was all the answer I needed.

I stared at her a second, trying to compute what my best next move would be. I could go and find Aidan Sr. and ask him what the fuck he was doing, which could, potentially, piss me off enough that I'd smack the shit out of him. I'd already gotten off his 'to die' list once, so did I really want to make it back on there? But there was no way I could let this lie.

"Wait, how about you just go home?"

"They won't let me. Mom's everywhere I go."

For a second, I pondered her, wondering if there really was something wrong with Mary Catherine that would have her parents, and Aidan Sr., so concerned for the baby's sake, but as I watched the boy nurse, as I watched her with him, maybe it was facile, however I just couldn't see that she wanted to do him any harm.

She looked healthy, blanched from crying and fatigue, but there were no signs of addiction or anything like that—and I'd be the one to know having been around them all my life—and the baby, Maddox, was cuddling into her, comfortable and cozy in his mommy's arms. By comparison to his temperament in the solarium, with his grandmother, he was relaxed and quiet. He wouldn't be like that if she was an unfit mom, surely?

Well aware that I needed to get back to the room because the speeches were going to start soon, speeches that had everyone nervous which, of course, meant they were going to be interesting to listen to, I also accepted that I needed more information.

I pulled out my phone and contacted Star. Thanking God when she answered immediately, I asked, "You know someone called Sin?"

"I know two someones called that, actually."

I froze. "You do? How do you know all these people with cool names?"

She snorted. "C-I-N. You met her already. It's Dead To Me."

I had a name. Holy fuck. I had a name!

"And S-I-N, the unimaginative kind, is a biker. Why?"

"I have someone here called Mary Catherine—"

"Yeah, I know her. She's sweet. How's the kid doing? She gave birth like, what, five weeks ago or something."

"I'm watching him nurse. He's alive and well."

"Alive and well? What are you? On TVGM?"

I snickered. "We have a problem."

"Problems are my jam."

"Mary Catherine—"

"We call her MaryCat."

"—well, MaryCat, then, has an issue with her mom. Apparently they're trying to take the kid away from her."

"Huh? Why?"

"They're saying she's hormonal or something."

MaryCat stared at me. "Is that Lodestar?"

I nodded.

"Can I talk with her?"

"Sure. You're going on speaker, Star. I don't want you to think I'm being rude. God forbid."

She sniffed. "Hey MaryCat, what's going on?"

Which was how an ex-TV news anchor and a hacker smuggled a woman and her kid out of a Five Points' Mob post-Christmas get-together.

Never let it be said that I didn't know how to cause trouble.

When I'd sneaked MaryCat and her kid, Maddox, off the compound, with Star helping to open the gates where a car was waiting for her—I had no idea why or how, but that was on Star—after I waved her off, satisfied with having fulfilled my one good deed for the day, I retreated to the wintergarten and made it back just in time to see both Aidans climbing onto a raised dais that had appeared in my absence.

Eying it, and eying how Aidan was standing, I twisted my head to the side to see why he looked so straight.

That was when I saw the cane.

I smiled at the sight. I didn't see him use it yesterday, so I guessed it was going to be a habit I'd have to knock into his skull, but that was okay. We were going to have to build a lot of habits together.

Things had been crazy since the twenty-first. Over the next

weeks, months, and years, that was when the pill addiction would rear its ugly head, so my way to fix it was to take away the reason for its existence in the first place. If, of course, that was even possible. I hoped it was, but we had time, plenty of it, to get him back on track. For us to share a less than orthodox, but nonetheless happy future together.

"The Christmas period is a special time, brothers," Aidan Sr. rumbled, breaking into my musings about his son. Not just about the cane, either, but about how fine he looked in that navy suit.

Dayuuuum.

"For the children, it's when miracles happen, but for adults, miracles can happen too, and miracles are what we need right now.

"We're at war. There's no evading it, no getting away from it. While my daughter-in-law-to-be is helping bring the biggest names to the table in her exposés—" Oh, shit. Aidan had told his dad that he proposed? "—they still messed with our holy sanctuaries.

"These bastards think we're the ones with no principles, but we're the ones who uphold our religion, who uphold our faith above everything else. They went to the pinnacle of Catholicism and burned it down. They went to our parish, and destroyed St. Patrick's.

"If they hadn't declared war on us with countless untold small acts of aggression, this is merely confirmation that these enemies need eradicating."

Because I'd come to think of Aidan Sr. as a kind of deranged monster who liked to crucify people in his spare time, it was weird to see him speak lucidly about this situation. Even weirder to realize that he was a good orator who sold his lies as if they were gospel truth. It shouldn't have come as a surprise though. Men with this kind of power often could weave a spell over a crowd.

And this crowd, well, it could be considered bespelled.

They were shuffling, wriggling, talking, and chattering. Whispering among themselves and taking deep gulps of their drinks. Even the kids were listening. The elder ones no longer messed around on their phones, and the younger ones stopped playing their games.

As silence reverberated around the room with all the power of a wrecking ball about to dive into the glass walls of the solarium, Aidan let the tension ratchet up, and up, and up, and up.

Even though their leader looked like he'd gone up against a WWE wrestler and lost, they were still clearly terrified of him.

Impressed, I peered around, curious what the pressure was doing to people.

Some guys looked angry, others looked nervous.

Was the anger at the arson attacks? At the war? Were the nerves because these Captains and Lieutenants had something to hide?

"It's come to my attention," Aidan Sr. rumbled, "that we have rats in our midst. People who've been speaking with the Sparrows, maybe even dealing with them for decades." Gasps surged around the room like a tidal wave. "We've come to learn their MO.

"They approach a man about a crime they purportedly committed. That man is in fact innocent of that offense, but they will fit him up for the job if he doesn't comply with their wishes.

"When faced with a choice like that, well, it's easy to see why someone could fall into temptation. If Adam and Eve could do it," he declared, "how can simple creatures like us resist?

"But when I spoke of miracles, I was speaking of the offer I'm about to give you.

"On Christmas Day 1914, in the trenches, my grandda told me of a game of soccer he played with the Germans. For those ninety minutes, there was peace in No Man's Land. Peace in the midst of war. I'm going to offer a ceasefire to the men in this room right now. An armistice, as it were.

"Over the next few hours, you'll each come into my office and speak with me. You will have a moment to confess.

"If you had dealings with the Sparrows, and you admit to it in my office, there will be no retaliation. Nobody apart from myself and Aidan Jr. will know you betrayed the Points." His eyes narrowed. "If, however, you do not speak out, and we learn another way that you're a Sparrow, you'll wish you hadn't been born, because I'll be sending you back to your Maker in more pieces than a jigsaw puzzle."

Some kids, quite naturally, started crying. Their gulps and snotty sobs could be heard, as could shushes from their mothers.

"I say this here, in front of your families, in front of children who are too young to understand, because *you* will understand the generosity of this miracle I'm offering you.

"Each of you is married and has children. Each of you knows what it is to be a family man. You acted against the Five Points. Ordinarily, that would be a death sentence. But I'm telling you, here and now, confess or you won't be the only ones who die the day I find out the truth."

I saw my Aidan's hand tighten around the cane, and I knew he didn't approve of what was happening here, but there was no evading the truth—the crowd was shook.

"I will not stand for rats in my midst. We are at war, we need our people around us to keep the families within the Points safe. If I can't trust you to look after my family, then you don't deserve to be trusted with yours.

"Now, take the gift I'm giving you, don't be fucking stupid, don't question my generosity, and use your goddamn brains." His jaw worked as he cast a look around the room that seemed to dance from each man, imprinting a warning that couldn't be denied.

Even I felt it when he stared at me, and we both knew I wasn't guilty of any of the crimes he was speaking about. A shudder ran down my spine, the warning making me well aware of the many screws that Aidan Sr. had loose.

I straightened up though, and stared right back at him. I wasn't afraid. Not of this.

Of course, he hadn't found out that I'd helped Mary Catherine escape the Five Points yet.

But that was a problem for later, maybe even tomorrow.

At least, I hoped it was.

FORTY-EIGHT

AIDAN

"YOU'RE A TROUBLEMAKER."

She smirked at me on the ride back to my estate. "If you expect me to feel bad, then you're in for a disappointment."

"I don't expect you to feel bad about what you did, but how you did it, sure. Why didn't you come to me?" I grumbled, unsure if she knew how much fucking trouble she'd actually caused.

"Because I'm a grown-ass woman with a voice and a head on my shoulders that can get things done?" She huffed. "What was I supposed to do when someone was being railed at in public by her mother, then starts crying when I break them apart and says that her mom is trying to steal her kid?"

"Bring the situation to me?"

"Why? She said your father was in on it."

"He was," I agreed. "*I wasn't.* Anyway, I don't think he'd take the same stance now."

"'Think?' That'd really reassure MaryCat when her kid was being ripped from her arms, wouldn't it?"

"It's not like Maddox would have been taken into custody. He'd have stayed with her mom."

"Is that supposed to make it better? She said her mom was only doing it because she didn't like her choice of partner." I pulled a face which had her declaring, "Aha! That's why your father doesn't approve, but you can bet your ass that if my dad knew what you were and who, he'd disapprove as well.

"Maybe if we had a kid, they'd have the right to steal it away from me because they think I'm insane for having a child with a mobster, hmm?"

"Don't even use that as a hypothetical," I growled, hands tightening on the wheel, my head snapping to the side as I glared at her. "Don't, Savannah."

Her eyes flared wide but she grunted. "It's the same thing."

"Anyone or anything tries to break us or our family apart, I will annihilate them." My jaw tensed. "Do you hear me?"

"I hear you, Mr. Neanderthal. Jeez, and you're the one saying I'm being irrational." She heaved a sigh. "If you feel that way about me, imagine how MaryCat's man feels about her? He went away on business, and will come back to his family torn apart all because he's a biker?"

I didn't like that she could draw similarities between us.

With Inessa, Aela, and Camille, they'd all been raised in the life. They all knew how it worked. Aoife didn't, now Savannah. But Aoife was alone in the world, an orphan. She'd made the O'Donnellys her family, and last night, I'd seen that Savannah would embrace my side, but she was quite happy with her own too.

Aoife was also happy in her sphere. She was independent enough to want her own business and worked hard to achieve her goals, but she had the heart of a homemaker too. Savannah wasn't like her. At all.

Aoife, in the same situation today, would undoubtedly have found Finn. As would my other brothers' wives. Savannah went to her hacker friend first, then confessed second when MaryCat's mom had kicked up a stink when they couldn't find her.

She'd put me in a bad position, and didn't even care about it.

I gritted my teeth at the thought, and knew that unless I explained rationally, she'd do it again and again—that couldn't happen. Not without making me look weak.

"Okay, I know what you're saying. You're also right—"

"I am?" she sputtered. "If you think that, then why on earth are we arguing?"

"Savannah, you've studied the mafia enough to know there's a certain order to the way we do things, for God's sake. You have to know that going behind my back wasn't going to look good for me. I understand there'll be a learning curve, but you can't just go off the cuff anymore. You have to bring these things to me. I'd have resolved the situation without you involving outsiders."

"Star isn't an outsider," Savannah pointed out. "She was integral the other night."

"She isn't bound to help us. She chooses to. There's a difference." When she didn't argue, I knew she agreed with me, just didn't want to say it out loud. "I've been meaning to talk with Da about MaryCat since I found out about what they were doing. I'm not sure why he didn't involve Ma, but he chose not to.

"Anyway, her mom's a bitch, and I know she's been biding her time to find ways to take the baby from MaryCat—"

"Why would your father even consider something so horrible as tearing MaryCat away from her child?"

"He wouldn't. Not unless her mother had proof, because Da isn't exactly into family law," I mocked. "I doubt he'd have backed it otherwise."

"What kind of proof could she have had?"

"She was diagnosed with postpartum depression, but that's it as far as I know, and it doesn't matter now, does it? All we know is MaryCat's in the wind, God knows where because, trust me, Da called Rex, the Sinners' Prez, to see if she'd turned up there and she hadn't. You let a mother loose who might, just might, have issues—"

"Don't you dare try to make me be the bad guy here. She was

raking MaryCat over the coals in public, and no one was doing a damn thing. If you think I can just sit by—"

With a growl, I pulled the car over to the side of the road. We were five minutes away from my estate, but this was too important a subject to waste any second on.

After I pulled over, I twisted in my seat and snapped, "You don't sit by. You come to me. You're not on your own anymore, Savannah. Do you hear me? You're not a rogue reporter trying to find stories. You're my woman. My fiancée. Eventually, you'll be my goddamn wife.

"We're going to be a team. We work together to find the best outcome for situations like this. You're supposed to come to me and we figure it out together. You get me?"

"Would you have listened though?"

I blinked. "Didn't I listen about Uncle Paddy?"

Her mouth tightened. "Men don't listen to these things," she argued. "They just blame the mom. She has postpartum depression, that means this is the exact opposite of what she should be dealing with. If I get that if we have a kid—"

"When," I rumbled, watching as her cheeks flushed.

"—will you have someone take my kid away just because my body can't cope with all the hormones flushing through it? Wouldn't you treat me with kindness and love, and protect me while reassuring me that we're safe?"

"Of course I would," I said with a sigh, reaching over to grab her hand and squeeze it with my own. "But sometimes, you have to think of the baby too."

"A baby should be with its mom."

"I agree. Unless she's a danger to it."

"I refuse to believe that MaryCat was a danger to herself or to that child. She was more of a danger to her mom, and I can't blame her. I wanted to hit her over the head with a wine bottle too."

I grunted. "She's a piece of work, that's for sure. But, look. This isn't the point. You can't go behind my back on shit like this. If you do, you undermine me, Savannah. You can't do that. I need to present a strong front otherwise, when I'm the head of the Points, people will think they can worm their way into any weakness I have and find a way to take me down." I glowered at her. "You're one of those weaknesses. I can't have that.

"You need to make sure you come to me, and we will fix things in private. You might not always like my decision, and I'm pretty fucking sure I won't always like yours, but we will find a stalemate that doesn't make us want to strangle each other.

"You're from a different world, and it's going to take time to settle into this one. But this wasn't the way to achieve anything. Now MaryCat's out there, unsafe, unprotected—"

"If you think Star let her loose without anyone watching over her, you're nuts."

My mouth tightened. "I hope you're right."

She blew out a breath. "Did anyone come forward as a Sparrow?"

"You know I can't talk about that."

Her gaze was measured upon mine. "If I concede to some things that you ask, and if I listen where I only want to block my ears, you can do me the decency of compromising too."

"Not where your safety is concerned."

"Nothing about this affects my safety—"

Frustrated, I snapped, "Savannah, my mother put a blowtorch to the Archbishop's dick until he was squealing like a pig." She blanched, but her shoulders straightened. "That was my ma. What do you think my enemies would do if they got to you? What do you think they'd do to get information out of you? It's best if you don't know—"

Her hand reached out and she grabbed my lapels. "Aidan, haven't you learned anything? You tell me to sit back, I stand up. You tell me to hide, I leap into the fray. It's how I'm built.

"Maybe it's crazy to you but I could have died two nights ago, and I would do it all again because being stuck in that safe room would annihilate me. I can't deal with that. It's not how I'm wired.

"Nothing about your world scares me. Makes me nervous, yeah, I'm human. But scared? Not so much.

"Sure, it's freaky learning that your mother-in-law broiled another dude's dick, and do I want to know what happened to it? Of course I do. I have many questions. Did you throw it in the trash? Put it in the corpse soup Cruz made? But the point is, if you keep me in the dark, the only thing you're going to encourage is me sneaking around and finding out in my own way.

"You can't keep me from the truth because the truth is the only thing that keeps my monsters at bay," I yelled, tightening my grip and hauling him forward. "You can't expect a kid to see someone being killed and then think they'll just erase that from their memories.

"My sister was kidnapped, we know she was raped, and I know she had an abortion because she got pregnant—Aidan, I live in a messed up world too. I have coping mechanisms for a reason. The way I cope is to know exactly what's going on and when.

"So, I won't go looking for things to be curious about. I won't seek shit out. But when your father invites everyone to a fucking party and tells people that he's going to enable an amnesty for Sparrows in his midst, you bet your ass I need to know how many fuckers you've had hiding in your ranks."

FORTY-NINE

SAVANNAH

I WAS BREATHING hard by the time I was done, which was when he pushed a button. That button worked just as he grabbed me by the waist and hauled me onto his lap.

At first, I had no idea what he was going to do, then his mouth was on mine, tearing into me, our tongues not just thrusting together, but tangling, encouraging me to fight back. His hands were everywhere, where mine just went to his hair, and I was happy with that because we were both eating each other alive.

Tearing, ripping, shredding into one another, fighting fire with fire, blasting each other with our annoyances and grievances.

His hands cupped my ass, molding the cheeks, before he pulled back and snapped, "Why do you always have to wear fucking pants?"

I smirked at him, then hauled my ass over to the passenger's seat. It was awkward, and I was very grateful for the stretch of private road, but I shucked out of my pants, well aware that we could have just driven to the estate, but neither of us wanted that.

Naked from the hips down, apart from that goddamn bandage he still insisted I wore on my upper thigh, which irritated more than it helped, I scuttled over to him, and rested my ass on his lap.

When his mouth reached for mine again, his fingers delved between my legs at the same time as I reached for his fly and unfastened the zipper.

With his cock in my hands, my pussy already molten hot, I pressed him against my slit and welcomed him home.

I tore my mouth from his as I gasped the second he started filling me, and that was when he pressed a kiss to my throat, his tongue sliding along the sinewy arches before he reached my ear and whispered, "Twenty-four."

I blinked at him, dazed, groaning as gravity pushed me onto him.

Then, I remembered what he was talking about, and I retorted, "No fair."

"Nobody ever said that I'd be fair," he countered, and his hands started to encourage me to ride him.

I did.

But not at the pace he insisted upon. I took it faster, slamming onto him because I knew pleasure was within my grasp. One hand went to the back of his neck, and I pressed our mouths together before I slipped my fingers down and started rubbing my clit.

A couple minutes later, I screamed out my pleasure, and my hoarse cries entwined with his roar of satisfaction.

It was hard, it was fast, and it was mean.

Much like this world I was diving into.

There were laws I'd never understand, some I'd come to learn, but he was right. It wasn't the orgasm that let me see the woods for the trees, either.

We'd only survive if we were a team. If we were united against the world. And we couldn't do that if I undermined him and went behind his back.

With that in mind, I murmured, "I'm not like your ma."

Panting, his nose crinkled. "Do we have to talk about her right now?"

I grinned at his squeamishness. "I'm not the little wife, the woman who'll be happy to make Christmas dinner for the family when a perfectly good caterer can be hired to do the job.

"I'm not going to sit back and let this world tear me to shreds. I'm a fighter, Aidan. You know that. That's why you're here, sitting in the wet spot. You wouldn't be doing that if you didn't want me to be me." I bowed my head, pressed a kiss to his lips, a softer one, then murmured, "I love you. Thank you for telling me the truth."

He grunted, his head rocking back against the rest, as he stared up at me. "I love you too."

And if that wasn't the verbal equivalent of a signature on a new contract, I didn't know what was.

FIFTY

MAXIM

THREE DAYS BEFORE NEW YEAR'S EVE

WHEN WE SET off from my new Brighton Beach compound, satisfaction filled me as I stared out onto the world with a view from between the driver and passenger seat.

Now, I sat in the backseat.

Now, someone drove me.

Five minutes into the journey toward the Irish-owned warehouse, I got a notification on my phone.

Arson attacks attributed to the New World Sparrows on one of New York City's most beloved landmarks.

When I clicked into it, I read some of the article.

Today, as the city still reels in horror from the brutal attack against an intrinsic part of our culture, the country waits for more news of this ever-pervasive group of people who have wormed their way into our republic.

With the world watching, Savannah Daniels will be live today on Channel Four, detailing how she discovered the traitors who have riddled our society like a cancerous tumor.

As I was reading, another news notification pinged.

Chief Justice of the Supreme Court arrested for ties to the New

World Sparrows. Dramatic footage shows the moment the keystone of our justice system was arrested under The Patriot Act.

I arched a brow in surprise at both news' items. I knew the Irish were working hard to take down the Sparrows, wasting precious resources on something that wasn't their business, but that the Chief Justice was a Sparrow came as a surprise.

Yet another notification had my phone buzzing.

A stunning reel of names exposed by Savannah Daniels, reveals the extent of the NWS' infiltration into our democracy. The Speaker of the House, Andrew Litten, Generals Ozarc and Lindenstein from the Joint Chiefs of Staff, as well as the Head of Homeland Security, Secretary Robert Pansen, were all arrested under The Patriot Act.

Amused, I barked out a laugh.

"America says it is so democratic," I mocked, calling out to Kirill, my new Obschak. "And yet, it's keystones are all fucking Sparrows." I cackled my glee at the aftershocks these revelations would have on the nation, and then, before I could celebrate too much, my phone rang.

The second I saw the name on the Caller ID, I hit the privacy button so Kirill and Tima, my Sovietnik, my security man, wouldn't be able to hear me, and hit the 'connect' button.

"Victoria, I'm glad you received my gift."

There was silence on the other end of the line.

A silence loaded down with the sound of her breathing.

"All is well, *katyonok*?" I asked eventually. Her silence didn't perturb me, but I would be reaching my destination soon and I didn't want to rush her.

A small sigh escaped her. "I shouldn't be calling you."

"The phone is for emergencies, Victoria."

"Emergencies?"

"In case you ever need someone to help you out of a dangerous situation," I told her quietly, wondering if she understood how precarious her current predicament was.

She pondered that for a second, then asked, "Why do you keep sending me gifts?"

I supposed I had my answer.

"Did you like them?"

I heard an audible swallow. "The head scared me."

"Unavoidable, *katyonok*." Her security was assured and so was my position. At least, momentarily. "I wished you to know that you're safe."

"Couldn't you have just called me or something?"

"You will see that my actions speak louder than my words."

"Oh." She cleared her throat. "The icon is beautiful. I'm not sure how you got the doorman to give it to me, but I'm thankful you did. I'll treasure it."

I'd scoured the city for one that would be easily exchangeable in a reputable art dealership.

"I'm glad you like it."

"Why did you get me that though?"

"Freedom and safety. I wish you to associate those two things with me. You can sell that icon anywhere in the city and have sixty thousand, minimum, in your account.

"The burner cell, well, as I told you, if you're ever in danger, you can call me and I will always answer. *Always*.

"As for Boris, he was going to force you to be his wife. I couldn't allow that, could I?"

My candor had her growing quiet. I wasn't surprised. Girls like her were kept in the dark, but in my mind, a young woman in this world should be out in the light.

That was the only place she'd ever be safe.

"*Katyonok*, all is well?"

She gulped. "Yes. I-I, why are you talking to me now? Is it because Papa's dead? You didn't speak to me before."

"No. Because I didn't have a death wish," I said wryly. "You think he'd have allowed a lowly *boyevik* to speak with one of his princesses?"

She released a soft breath. "Oh."

"Yes. Oh." I smiled. "It is a pleasure talking with you, Victoria. We must do it often. You should call me."

"Do you really mean you'll always answer?"

I hummed. "Yes." I knew she wouldn't call me often, but giving her the option meant that, if she was ever in a position where she needed help, she'd think of me. "No matter where you find yourself, Victoria," I intoned, intending on ramming this lesson home, "whether you believe it will anger your sisters or your new brothers-in-law, I will always answer and I will always come to you if you need me."

"If they find out, they won't be happy."

"The Irish understand my loyalty to you," I told her, trying to be diplomatic.

The O'Donnellys were well aware that I intended on making her my bride when she was of age. Even Camille knew that. Hadn't we made a deal, her and I? My silence and aid for her sister's hand in marriage?

She swallowed. "They do?"

"They do," I repeated. "Now, I must go, *katyonok*. I have business to attend to."

"Merry Christmas, Maxim," Victoria whispered.

"*Schastlivogo Rozhdestva*," I replied, waiting for her to cut the call, not me.

When she did, I smiled to myself and tucked my cell back into my pocket.

The Sparrows didn't interest me at the moment. I'd have to talk about them when I arrived in Hell's Kitchen and discuss that with the head of the Irish Mob, and the new Don of the *Famiglia*. For now, I pondered where I saw myself in three years' time.

That was when I could claim my prize.

When this lowly peasant, born to a whore, raised on the Muscovite streets, reared in fire and bound by blood, could take a Bratva Princess as his own.

FIFTY-ONE

SAVANNAH

"WE'RE JOINED this evening by Savannah Daniels, daughter of Dagger Daniels, and the writer of the exposés that have taken the country by storm. Welcome, Savannah, and thank you for being here."

I shot Jason Newell a tight smile. "I'm not sure why you have to bring my father into it, Jason," I baited him. "As far as I'm aware, his music didn't help me write the exposés."

His smile froze. "No, I suppose you're right."

"There's no supposing about it."

He cleared his throat, but I saw his brain whirring as, A, the producer probably yelled in his ear, while B, he tried hard not to glower at me for being difficult.

Deciding not to make his life easier, I waited for him to speak, and when dead air hit, I had to hide a smile.

This felt good.

Women were too often without a voice, and that was revealed in my exposés. Countless voices forever silenced, countless women sold and traded like commodities, countless bodies crossing borders to become the pleasure slaves of men with too much money and power in their hands.

If it made me militant, then so be it. Especially when I knew Newell had a rep as bad as Wintersen's.

"So, Savannah," Newell eventually gritted out, "the exposés you've written have been utterly fascinating."

"Thank you," I demurred.

"How long have you been working on them?"

"Quite a while."

His jaw tensed. "How did you discover the New World Sparrows?"

"Through research and some sources that shall remain nameless." He relaxed when he saw I was willing to speak freely. "It's quite interesting how the current political climate enabled this group to metastasize inside the country's government, on both a federal and state level.

"I admit, the first time I came across them, I thought it was a conspiracy. Then, I met some of the real victims of the New World Sparrows."

Newell tipped his head to the side, his interest clear. "Real victims? You've never mentioned the specifics in your articles about how you came across this information."

"No. For a reason." I'd been waiting until I was invited onto a TV news station. "I've spoken with the women who were prostituted by the NWS for their own members' pleasure, as perks of the job, if you will. Never mind to make the group richer and more powerful as members began cropping up in both low-level government positions and at the top of the ladder too."

"You've spoken with these women? What did they say?" he prompted eagerly.

I blinked. Wasn't he listening? I'd literally just answered that. .

When I didn't reply, he cleared his throat again. "Over the holiday period, you released key names that are integral to the running of this country—"

"—and the NWS."

He grimaced at my interruption. "Yes. Is there a reason you decided to do so now?"

"Should I have waited until after Christmas?" I asked dryly. "Should I have let these monsters have one last Christmas with their families?"

"No, that's not what I'm saying."

"Isn't it?"

His eyes narrowed at me, but I ignored his agitation.

If he'd started any other way than by introducing me as my father's daughter, I wouldn't have been this difficult. But I was more than just Dagger Daniels' kid. I was Savannah Daniels, and through the NWS, my name would come to mean a whole helluva lot more in the annals of this nation's history than as the spawn of a rockstar.

"From the twenty-first of December through to the twenty-third, I endured three separate attempts on my life. That's the reason I decided to continue publishing my exposés over the Christmas period. If they didn't think I should see another holiday, why should I care about them?"

Newell straightened up at something that was fresh news. "They tried to kill you?"

"They did."

"There have been no police reports filed—"

"No. My private security handled it." I shrugged, lying with ease. "Even with the identities of the Sparrows slowly being released, there are still so many who are flying under the radar, and there's no way of knowing who was truly behind the attacks against me.

"These crimes were perpetrated by nameless, faceless men who wished to see me dead. Unfortunately for them, I'm not so easy to kill."

"How many more exposés will you be publishing?"

"I can't put a number on something I don't know."

"You don't have an exact amount?"

"No. Aren't you listening to me?"

His nostrils flared. "Why don't you just give them to the police?"

"Because the police can't be trusted." I tipped my head to the side. "Haven't you realized that yet, Jason?"

His mouth tightened. "The current NWS members, such as the Chief Justice and the Head of Homeland Security, have been arrested under The Patriot Act. Don't you believe that the FBI will use those same laws to gather all the information you have?"

"What information? I'll never reveal my sources and it's not as if I have a USB drive for them to take. I'm protected by the First Amendment, Jason. The U.S. Supreme Court's 1968 decision in Pickering v. Board of Education proves that.

"Anyway, they can raid my apartment, take my computer, try to hack their way into my emails, all under The Patriot Act, but there's one thing they'll never take away." I smiled at him. "My voice."

His eyes narrowed. "That's all well and good, but—"

"But nothing. I will not be silenced, Jason, because behind me, there are hundreds of thousands, maybe even millions of women, who were victimized and traded like their bodies were fruit at a market.

"I will not be silenced, because that means *they* are once again voiceless. I won't allow that to happen." The camera panned in on me, and to the city, the country, and the rest of the world, I declared, "*We* will not be silenced."

SAVANNAH

NEW YEAR'S EVE

AS THE CLOCK chimed throughout the room, as the city skyline lit up with fireworks, and the ball dropped in Times Square, I cheered along with the rest of my family as we celebrated the new year.

Bouncing on my heels, I laughed as Aidan swept me over his arm and swooped me down into a dramatic kiss worthy of the first New Year's of the rest of our lives together.

Squeezing me as we stood up, I pressed my hands to his cheeks and looked up into his eyes as we simultaneously murmured, "I love you."

A grin made my face feel as if it were splitting in two, and his smile felt just as powerful and pervasive. It sank into me, settling into my bones, filling me up in a way that went beyond sexual, that was more than lust. It was love. Real, honest to God, love.

We had a way to go still. He was bossy and cocksure. Arrogant because of his position, prone to being a possessive pain in my patootie—especially when I basically told the FBI on live TV to come at me, bruh—and traditional to the point of being amusing, we were bound to knock heads, especially as I was nosy, disobedient, and with a voice that wouldn't quit. We had things like his addiction to maneuver, the Sparrows, his parents' clear mental breakdowns thanks to what they'd learned about their son, never mind the basics of his being a Five Pointer, but I knew we'd do it.

We were born to fight this war together.

I felt that in my very bones.

As his brothers came around us, clapping Aidan on the back and vice versa, I slipped away, wanting to wish Jen a Happy New Year.

When I found her standing by one of the massive picture windows in Finn's apartment, I saw Aoife hugging her then slipping away to the party, and I was glad. I was starting to like Aoife, but I wanted to speak with Jen. I knew she was concerned about the upcoming court case that was heading her way, and I had a solution.

A dramatic one.

She wouldn't like it.

I knew she wouldn't.

But I had to give her the option.

Of course, that meant potentially breaking our friendship with irreparable consequences, but maybe it was time to come clean.

Huh, perhaps being around so many of these Catholics was making me feel all that Catholic guilt in buckets?

Trying not to let my confidence buckle, knowing she needed this because she'd only accept so much help from me, I slipped over to her and rested my head on her shoulder.

As always, she wore enough clothing to constitute a child's dress, whereas I, on the other hand, was in a tailored suit. I'd been smart about it though—I wore cream pants to hide any potential hanky panky that might occur, after having learned the hard way that black only made bodily fluids stand out in stark relief—and a black shirt, but my jacket was gold silk embroidered with lilies. My heels, stilettos that were going to be digging into Aidan's butt at some point this evening, were shiny black patent crimes against mankind.

Aidan had called them Boner-Makers.

Of course, that meant I was wearing them all the time now.

Today was also the first day I didn't need that goddamn bandage on my leg. My bruises and cuts were close to clearing up, and the only marks and soreness left on my body were consensually caused thanks to way too much sex.

Yeah, this was me, living my best life.

She slipped an arm around my waist as we peered out onto the skyline ahead. "Happy New Year, sweetheart."

"Back at you, hon." I sighed. "You look pensive. I thought you'd be drunk by now."

"Did you taste the cranberry vodka?"

I smirked. "Do bears shit in the woods?"

"I don't know where they got that crack from, but it was delishusss."

"It has maple syrup in it."

"I should have been born Canadian," Jen muttered. "They put it in everything."

"But then we might not have met," I complained.

"True." She huffed. "I wouldn't know Aoife either. But I wouldn't owe like a gazillion million to my douche ex."

"It isn't that much."

"Right now it isn't," she grumbled. "What about court fees and stuff?" She heaved a sigh. "Sorry, I shouldn't be talking about this tonight. You should go and party with Aidan. Girl, you look gorgeous together. Him all broody and—"

I snorted. "You mean brooding."

"Do I?" Jen cackled. "You're about to get pumped sooo full of O'Donnelly jizz you're going to be pregnant until you're fifty."

My nose crinkled. "Ew."

"Shut up, bish. You know you want it."

Laughing, I grumbled, "Maybe one."

"Ha. We'll see."

Turning my head on her shoulder, I muttered, "Jen?"

"Yes, babe."

"I need to tell you something."

She arched a brow. "So, tell me?"

"It's hard."

"You told me about that time you nearly orgasmed when you had a Pap smear."

"Shut up," I hissed, peering around to make sure no one had overheard that.

She grinned. "See? You can share that with me but not this?"

"Well, it's different."

"How?"

"It's bad."

"Bad, how?"

"It's about how we met."

Her brows rose. "Through work?"

"Yeah, but..." I sucked in a breath then admitted on a rush, "I knew you worked there. That's why I went to that particular accountant. I'd always stuck to my dad's before, but I wanted to find a way to meet you."

Jen tensed. "What? Me? Why? I'm nobody."

I bit my lip, sensing the confusion was going to turn to hurt soon. "It started off a certain way, but like, we have so much in common, Jen. We're both loudmouth bitches who don't like being told what to do and have really expensive shoe habits. You're my BFF for real."

Jen shook her head. "I don't understand. Why would you switch accountants to meet with me?"

I gulped. "I was researching a story on Padraig O'Donnelly."

"Aidan Sr.'s brother?"

"Yes."

"Why?"

"I wanted to get close to Aidan Sr. I wanted to write his biography."

Her eyes bugged. "You wanted to do, what? Jesus, girl, do you want to die young?"

"Well, I wouldn't put it like that," I grouched.

"I don't believe you. You're crazy!"

"I know. That's how I met Aidan."

"Shit! You're just telling me now?"

"It didn't turn out well, did it? He ghosted me and I sulked for a while. Then, I happened upon this coffee shop. All these women get together and they talk about stuff.

"Gossiping, basically, about the Five Points. About five months before we met, I heard one of them talk about Paddy and how he was a ladies' man..."

"They all are. They're O'Donnellys," Jen said wryly. "I'm just not sure what I have to do with this."

I reached for her hand. "Can't you figure it out, sweetheart?" I bit my lip again. "You don't have to worry about money. Not anymore."

"What are you talking about? Why don't I?"

"You're Padraig O'Donnelly's illegitimate daughter, Jen, and I have the DNA test results to prove it."

AIDAN

SEVEN MONTHS LATER

THE SECOND THE elevator doors closed behind me, I grabbed Savannah around the waist, hauled her over my shoulder, then strode down the hallway to my bed.

Her squeal made me laugh, as did the way she bit my ass through my pants.

"You're going to have to work harder than that to get me to put you down," I teased, laughing even more when she tried to shove my pants down. "Gravity is on my side."

"Don't be a jerk!" she groused, but she was chuckling too.

I heard her happiness, knew she felt it as much as I did.

I was free.

Four months ago, I'd had knee replacement surgery to fix the clusterfuck of the botched job the previous surgeon had done.

Sixteen weeks of physio later, the pain was manageable, like the brush of a butterfly's wings to my skin rather than the tsunami to my senses of before, and I could walk properly again.

The doctor said if I overdid it, I might need a cane from time to time, but as long as I stayed away from marathons and long hikes, that I should be okay.

Without the physiological need for Oxy, it made my addiction more bearable, though there were days I knew I was a bastard because it clawed at me tooth and nail, but it was a struggle Savannah understood.

One that had her barking at me to come and do yoga with her, or that had us angry fucking our way through the drowning sensation that was the need for chemical substances.

Today had been my final physio session and I was celebrating in more ways than one.

"I can't believe you're holding me to this."

I grinned. "You can't believe it? Seriously?"

She huffed. "I didn't realize you wanted to pop my ass cherry so bad."

"Bullshit. That's why you leveraged it with knee surgery."

She blew a raspberry I didn't see.

Cackling, I walked straight down the hallway through our new penthouse.

We drifted between the city and upstate now Da was pulling back and leaving some tasks to me. He'd gone from being hands on to being hands off in a ridiculously short space of time, and right now, Brennan and I as well as the rest of my bros, had so much on our plates that I simply didn't have the hours in the day to commute upstate. Not if I ever wanted to see my wife.

Which I did.

A lot.

"This is quite painful," she told me, her tone pleasant.

"Well, I'm almost there," I said dryly.

"Your shoulder's bony."

"Forgive me."

"I will when you give me an orgasm."

"Oh, baby, you're going to get more than one," I purred, which made her squirm. I slapped her ass. "Don't do that, or I'll drop you."

"Then don't get me horny."

"I breathe and I make you horny, little one."

She squirmed again, so I spanked her ass again.

When we made it to the bedroom, a space that was navy on black, pretty masculine apart from the softer touches she'd added to the room with blankets and cushions and shit, I tossed her onto the bed and immediately grabbed her belt buckle.

For all her talk, she was as eager for this as me. We'd promised each other this months ago, and both of us were ready.

As we stripped down, taking this logically, we didn't stop until we were both naked. I made her keep her stilettos on, of course, and then I did what I hadn't been able to do in years.

The missionary position.

Goddammit, it felt good.

So fucking good just to lie on top of her, all those curves melting into my hardness, her legs spread, my cock against her pussy, as I put pressure on my knee without wanting to howl.

I was tentative at first, but when I didn't experience any pain, I breathed out and finally pressed my lips to hers. Slowly, I seduced her, which was in direct contrast to the way I'd hauled her over my shoulder out in the hall, but God, her patience with me deserved nothing less.

Her arms wound around my neck and she wriggled beneath me, which made her pussy collide with my dick, her juices soaking me as she anointed me with her slick heat.

I growled against her mouth, then whispered, "You fucking set me on fire, you filthy witch."

She cackled against my lips, then murmured, "It's the arsonist in you. It digs my heat."

I grinned as I rocked my hips, making sure that I always caught her clit on the way back. She soon stopped laughing, soon stopped doing anything other than grinding into me, those fucking heels of hers digging into me so hard that the pain was electric.

Ironic, yes.

I knew that.

Still, everything about what I had with her was topsy-turvy and, in my life, I'd never been fucking happier.

With a snarl, I pulled away, tunneling down the bed so that I could snack on her clit. She squealed, her legs coming around my head in a way that was sure to suffocate me soon—but what a fucking way to go.

"Oh, God, it feels differently like this!" she squeaked.

Yeah, we had a lot of firsts coming to us. Firsts that were normal for regular people who didn't have such a misaligned joint that they could have sued their surgeon.

Me?

I'd be getting my own back for my descent into hell thanks to him in a different way. I'd be taking my da's suggestion, that was for goddamn sure...

As I sucked on her clit, I thrust two fingers inside her, making sure she was as wet as I wanted. Then, I pulled away, grabbed her legs and pinned them to her front.

"Hug your calves," I rumbled, loving how she snapped to it.

Those heels were like weapons, the 'knives' glinting at me from her new position which squished her pussy lips between her thighs and opened up her asshole to me when I grabbed her hips and angled her so that I'd have better access to it.

"No pain?" she rasped.

Her concern soothed me like nothing else could. "No pain," I confirmed.

I sighed as I twisted around to grab the lube I'd bought for this very occasion, and she watched me with eager eyes as I slicked the liquid around my erect cock.

She moaned at the sight, and I gave her more of a show, whacking off to the point where I was close to coming because I wanted to see creamy ropes of cum landing against that plump pussy of hers, but I wanted in her ass more.

Groaning under my breath, I reached beneath my dick, rubbed my balls together and twisted slightly to ease the ache.

"What is it about you that makes my cock forget I was inside you six hours ago?"

Her laughter was choked. "What is it about you that makes my pussy forget you were inside me six hours ago?"

"At least this madness is mutual," I agreed as I let my slick fingers dip down to her asshole.

We'd prepared her for this moment, because I wanted no pain that first time I took her, but sweet fuck, when her butt clenched down around them, I knew when I got my length inside her, it'd be like flying through St. Peter's gates.

I spread them, scissoring wider so she wouldn't be overwhelmed when I stuffed her full of dick, while I carried on playing with her clit. I didn't stop doing this until she was writhing against the bed, and I knew I was going to get it again—I fucking loved when she squirted.

Setting the tip of my erection to her rosette, I murmured, "Don't fight me, little one."

She groaned, and I watched the concentration in her eyes as she struggled to do as I asked.

A keening moan escaped her as she endeavored to take each inch, and when I was all the way in, she croaked, "When did you get so big?"

"Stop stroking my ego."

Her ass clenched around me. "That's how I'll stroke it. I'm being serious." She panted then disobeyed by letting her legs spread wide. Her heels dug into the duvet, as she kept her knees high and I had to admit, the visual was even better.

Her lips were splayed apart, her slit wet and hungry, visibly clenching for me. For more.

The sight had me wishing I was double jointed because I wanted to suck on those lips so fucking bad, but I didn't. Instead, I slid my pointer and middle finger back in there, twisted them around and hooked up against the front wall of her cunt.

A shaky breath escaped her, and her eyes, deep inside, spaced out. I saw it happen. Saw the second I found that delicious little place that made her come for me, and I began to tease it.

Each thrust of my hips bumped my fingers and that rocked harder into her G-spot.

Every thrust had her whining and wriggling on the bed.

Every thrust had her releasing a shaky breath.

Every thrust took her higher, made her freer, liberated her so that I knew she was close to flying.

I just wanted to fly with her.

Patience wasn't my strongest virtue, but for her, it'd always be my best. I took her to the precipice, then I twisted my thumb to her clit and started to rub it with the edge.

When she went off, it was like a fire alarm sounded in the room—she screamed. Loud. It hurt my fucking ears, but my dick rejoiced as she clamped down around me so hard that I didn't just see stars, but a goddamn light display as a universe was born and died behind my eyes.

Then I felt it.

The pressure reached fever pitch, and she broke.

Slick wetness flooded the space where our bodies met, and she cried out, her back arching, tits shaking, her hands coming up to cover her face as she sobbed out her pleasure.

When she was like this, broken, ruined by ecstasy, she was never more beautiful to me than here and now.

Then, because I couldn't help myself, I did as I wanted earlier.

I pulled out of her ass, grabbed a hold of my dick, and jacked off. The creamy ropes of cum anointed that glossy flesh, and she moaned, dropping her hand at the sound of my grunts, as we both watched the show.

When I was done, when I was broken and then fixed, she smiled at me, and that was a beacon. Of light, hope, need, and love.

One that, I knew, would guide me into the future, one that would always be my way back to her.

My home.

My Savannah.

Aidan said it himself...
Filthy lies and filthier secrets.
Wellllllll...
FILTHY SECRET is the next novel in the Filthy Feckers' series!
Can you guess which brother it is? ;)
You can read it here: www.books2read.com/FilthySecret
I'm also pleased to announce that **THE DON** has his own novel!
You might hate the Italians now, but wait until a Sicilian is in charge... you ain't seen nothing yet.
This enigmatic Valentini is my new obsession.
Seriously, ladies, get ready to swoon.
Hope you're excited for this next adventure!
You can enjoy the first 'The Valentini Family' duet here:
www.books2read.com/ValentiniOne
www.books2read.com/ValentiniTwo

AFTERWORD

I know some of those chapters were hard-hitting.

I know that you might have stopped and had to restart a couple times.

I know that you hurt for these men.

I do too.

Secrets... so toxic.

Just remember, if you're a survivor, that secret shelters them too.

They deserve no shelter.

They deserve the spotlight right in their goddamn face.

You might not have two Aidans who'll kill for you, but your voice is heard.

Savannah said it all...

WE WILL NOT BE SILENCED.

Every choice you make, however, is yours to make.

I support you.

I hear you regardless of whether you let the words slip from your lips, and I wish you peace.

Much love to you,

Serena

xoxo

Ps. Filthy Secret is coming October 2021! You can preorder it here: www.books2read.com/FilthySecret

Pps. Don't forget, this is the reading order for the crossover universe. <3

FILTHY
NYX
LINK
FILTHY RICH
SIN
STEEL
FILTHY DARK
CRUZ
MAVERICK

FILTHY SEX
HAWK
FILTHY HOT
STORM
THE DON (Coming Soon)
THE LADY (Coming Soon)
FILTHY SECRET (Coming Soon)

FREE BOOK!

Don't forget to grab your free e-Book!
Secrets & Lies is now free!

Meg's love life was missing a spark until she discovered her need to be dominated. When her fiancé shared the same kink, she thought all her birthdays had come at once, and then she came to learn their relationship was one big fat lie.

Gabe has loved Meg for years, watching her from afar, and always wishing he'd been the one to date her first and not his brother. When he has the chance to have Meg in his bed—even better, tied to it—it's an opportunity he can't refuse.

With disastrous consequences.

Can Gabe make Meg realize she's the one woman he's always wanted? But once secrets and lies have wormed their way into a relationship, is it impossible to establish the firm base of trust needed between lovers, and more importantly, between sub and Sir...?

This story features orgasm control in a BDSM setting.
Secrets & Lies is now free!

CONNECT WITH SERENA

For the latest updates, be sure to check out my website!
Or join my newsletter here: www.serenaakeroyd.com/Newsletter
But if you'd like to hang out with me and get to know me better, then I'd love to see you in my Diva reader's group where you can find out all the gossip on new releases as and when they happen. You can join here: www.facebook.com/groups/SerenaAkeroydsDivas. Or you can always PM or email me. I love to hear from you guys:
serenaakeroyd@gmail.com.

ABOUT THE AUTHOR

I'm a romance novelaholic and I won't touch a book unless I know there's a happy ending. This addiction is what made me craft stories that suit my voracious need for raunchy romance. I love twists and unexpected turns, and my novels all contain sexy guys, dark humor, and hot AF love scenes.

I write MF, menage, and reverse harem (also known as why choose romance,) in both contemporary and paranormal. Some of my stories are darker than others, but I can promise you one thing, you will always get the happy ending your heart needs!

Made in United States
North Haven, CT
29 December 2023